# PEOPLE, LAW AND JUSTICE

## A CASEBOOK OF PUBLIC-INTEREST LITIGATION

## VOLUME I

# PEOPLE, LAW AND JUSTICE

## A CASEBOOK OF PUBLIC-INTEREST LITIGATION

## VOLUME I

Sangeeta Ahuja

with contributions by S. Muralidhar

and preface by S.P. Sathe

*Orient Longman*

ORIENT LONGMAN LIMITED

*Registered Office*
3-6- 272 Himayatnagar, Hyderabad 500 029 (A.P.), India

*Other Offices*
Bangalore, Bhubaneshwar, Calcutta, Chennai, Cochin, Guwahati,
Hyderabad, Jaipur, Lucknow, Mumbai, New Delhi, Patna


First Published 1997

ISBN 81 250 1188 9

*Typeset by*
Scribe Consultants
New Delhi 110 029

*Printed in India at*
Baba Barkha Nath Printers
New Delhi 110 015

*Published by*
Orient Longman Limited
1/24 Asaf Ali Road
New Delhi 110 002

# Contents

## VOLUME 1

## VOLUME 2

# List of Cases

## Case Chapter 1

*Aeltemesh Rein* v. *Union of India*
(1988) 4 SCC 54

*Anil Yadav and others* v. *State of Bihar*
1982 (1) SCALE 43 [278]
(1981) 1 SCC 622

*B. R. Kapoor and others* v. *Union of India and others*
AIR 1990 SC 752

*Chinnamma Sivadas* v. *State (Delhi Admn.)*
1992 (3) SCALE 31 [85]

*E. Sharma* v. *State of Assam and others*
AIR 1992 Guwa 58

*Free Legal Aid Committee, Jamshedpur* v. *Mahatama Gandhi Memorial Medical College Hospital, Sakchi, Jamshedpur*
1987 (1) SCALE 327 [1321]

*Gurdev Singh and others etc.* v. *State of Himachal Pradesh and others*
AIR 1992 HP 76

*Hussainara Khatoon and others* v. *Home Secretary, State of Bihar*
(1980) 1 SCC 81
(1980) 1 SCC 93
(1980) 1 SCC 98

(1980) 1 SCC 108
(1980) 1 SCC 115

*In the matter of: Prison Reforms Enhancement of Wages of Prisoners etc.*
AIR 1983 Ker 261

*In Re the Petitions of Nawal Thakur, a convict kept in the Kulu Jaiil*
(1984) 3 SCC 572

*In Re: A Prisoner*
1993 (2) KLT 10

*Kadra Pehadiya and others* v. *State of Bihar*
AIR 1981 SC 939

*Karamjeet Singh* v. *Union of India*
JT 1992 (5) SC 598

*Khatri and others* v. *State of Bihar and others*
(1981) 1 SCC 623
(1981) 1 SCC 627
(1981) 1 SCC 635
(1981) 2 SCC 493
(1983) 2 SCC 266

*Kishore Singh Ravinder Dev etc.* v. *State of Rajasthan*
AIR 1981 SC 625

*Mathew Areeparamtil and others* v. *State of Bihar and others*
AIR 1984 SC 1854 / 1984 (2) SCALE 85 [402]

*Niamathulla* v. *State of Kerala*
1992 (2) KLT 699

*Poola Bhaskara Vijayakumar* v. *State of Andhra Pradesh and another*
AIR 1988 AP 295

*Prem Shankar Shukla* v. *Delhi Administration*
(1980) 3 SCC 526

*Pt. Parmanand Katara* v. *Union of India and others*
AIR 1989 SC 2039

*R. M. Tewari* v. *Home Secretary, State of U P & Ors*
1991 (1) SCALE 71 [249]

*Rakesh Kaushik* v. *B. L. Vig, Superintendent, Central Jail, New Delhi and another*
AIR 1981 SC 1767

*Rakesh Chandra Narain* v. *State of Bihar*
1986 (Supp) SCC 576
AIR 1989 SC 348
1993 (4) SCALE 103 [509]

*Rudul Sah* v. *State of Bihar*
AIR 1983 SC 1086

*Sant Bir* v. *State of Bihar*
1982 (1) SCALE 144 [668]

*Sheela Barse* v. *State of Maharashtra* (access to prisons)
(1983) 2 SCC 96
(1987) 4 SCC 373

*Sheela Barse* v. *Union of India and another* (non-criminal lunatics)
(1993) 4 SCC 204

*Siddha Raj Dhadda* v. *State of Rajasthan*
AIR 1990 Raj 34

*Simranjit Singh Mann* v. *Union of India and another*
1992 (2) SCALE 102 [506]

*Sunil Batra (II)* v. *Delhi Administration*
(1980) 3 SCC 488

*Upendra Baxi* v. *State of U. P. & Ors* (Agra Protective Home)
1982 (1) SCALE 84 [502]
(1983) 2 SCC 308
(1986) 4 SCC 106 / AIR 1987 SC 191

*Veena Sethi* v. *State of Bihar and others*
(1982) 2 SCC 583

*Vikram Deo Singh Tomar* v. *State of Bihar*
AIR 1988 SC 1782

## Case Chapter 2

*Chaitanya Kalbagh and another etc.* v. *State of U.P. and others*
AIR 1989 SC 1452

*Delhi Judicial Service Association* v. *State of Gujarat and another*
1989 (2) SCALE 140 [748]

*Delhi Judicial Service Association* v. *State of Gujarat and another (for Clarification)*
1989 (2) SCALE 174 [877]

*Delhi Judicial Service Association, Tis Hazari Court, Delhi* v. *A.K. Srivastava and others*
AIR 1991 SC 2176

*Hindustani Andolan and others* v. *State of Punjab and others*
AIR 1984 SC 582

*In the Matter of Complaint received from Delhi Judicial Service Association Tis Hazari Court, Delhi*
1989 (2) SCALE 119 [654]

*In the matter of: Judical Enquiry into Gang-Rape Demanded, and, Concerted Demand for Judicial Probe*
(1988) 1 GauLR 489

*Nathulal Jain, Advocate and others* v. *State of Rajasthan and others*
AIR 1993 Raj 149

*Niloy Dutta* v. *District Magistrate, Sibsagar District*
(1991) 2 GauLR 217

*P.M. Antony* v. *Distt. Collector and others*
1986 (2) SCALE 290 [1254]

*P.V. Kapoor and another* v. *Union of India and another*
1991 (3) Delhi Lawyers 391 (DB)

*People's Union for Democratic Rights* v. *State of Bihar and others* (Arwal firing)
AIR 1987 SC 355

*Peoples Union of Democratic Rights through its Secretary and another* v. *Police Commissioner, Delhi Police Headquarters and another* (police atrocities)
1989 (1) SCALE 114 [599]

*Peoples Union for Democratic Rights and another* v. *Ministry of Home Affairs* (riots)
AIR 1985 Del 268

*Punjab and Haryana High Court Bar Association Chandigarh through its Secretary* v. *State of Punjab and others*
1993 (4) SCALE 147 [636]

## Case Chapter 3

*Naga People's Movement for Human Rights (NPMHR)* v. *Union of India and others*
AIR 1990 Gau 1

*Niloy Dutta* v. *District Magistrate, Sibsagar District*
(1991) 2 GauLR 217

*People's Union for Human Rights (represented by Ramesh Kumar Jain and others)* v. *Union of India and others*
AIR 1992 Gau 23

*Sebastian M. Hongray* v. *Union of India*
AIR 1984 SC 571/1984 (1) SCALE 106 [629]
AIR 1984 SC 1026

## Case Chapter 4

*All India Democratic Women's Association and Janwadi Samiti* v. *Union of India and others*
AIR 1989 SC 1280

*Bholanath Tripathi* v. *State of UP*
1990 (Supp) SCC 151

*Gaurav Jain* v. *Union of India and others*
AIR 1990 SC 292
1991 (1) SCALE 201 [963]

*Gudalure M.J. Cherian and others* v. *Union of India and others*
1991 (2) SCALE 241 [1305]

*In the matter of: Judicial Enquiry into Gang-Rape Demanded, and, Concerted Demand for Judicial Probe*
(1988) 1 Guwa LR 489

*Joint Women's Programme* v. *State of Rajasthan*
AIR 1987 SC 2060

*Kasturi Lal Sharma* v. *State of UP*
1990 (Supp) SCC 748

*Brij Bala* v. *State of HP and others*
(1984) 2 SLR 408

*Madhu Kishwar and others* v. *State of Bihar and others*
1991 (2) SCALE 148 [794]

## Case Chapter 5

*Sheela Barse* v. *Secretary, Children's Legal Aid Society and others* (children's home)
(1987) 3 SCC 50 / AIR 1987 SC 756

*Sheela Barse and another* v. *Union of India and others* (children in jails)
1986 (2) SCALE 1 [1]
AIR 1986 SC 1773 / (1986) 3 SCC 596 and 632
(1987) 1 SCC 76
AIR 1988 SC 2211 / (1988) 4 SCC 226

*Supreme Court Legal Aid Committee* v. *Union of India and others*
1989 (2) SCALE 73 [400]
(1989) 2 SCC 325 / AIR 1989 SC 1278

## Case Chapter 6

*Fertilizer Corporation Kamagar Union (Regd.) Sindri and others* v. *Union of India and others*
AIR 1981 SC 344

*Hira Lal and another* v. *Zilla Parishad, Kanpur and others*
1982 (1) SCALE 123 [545]

*Labourers Working on Salal Hydro Project* v. *State of Jammu and Kashmir and others*
(1983) 2 SCC 181
(1984) 3 SCC 538

*M.K. Sharma and others* v. *Bharat Electronics Ltd. [BEL] and others*
(1987) 3 SCC 231

*Nagendra Dutt Jagudi* v. *State of UP*
1987 (2) SCALE 306 [1301]

*People's Union for Democratic Rights and others* v. *Union of India and others* (Asian games)
1982 (1) SCALE 158 [817]
AIR 1982 SC 1473 / 1982 (1) SCALE 159 [818]

*Ram Kumar Misra* v. *State of Bihar and others*
AIR 1984 SC 537

*Rohit Vasavada and another* v. *General Manager, IFFCO, Kalol*

*and others*
1983(2) GLR XXIV(2) 1529

*Sand Carrier's Owners' Union and others* v. *Board of Trustees for the Port of Calcutta and others*
AIR 1990 Cal 176

*Sanjit Roy* v. *State of Rajasthan*
AIR 1983 SC 328

*Social Work Research Centre Etc.* v. *State of Rajasthan*
1986 (2) SCALE 232 [905]

*Special Works and Research Centre through Sanjit Roy and others* v. *State of Rajasthan*
1986 (Supp) SCC 561

*Workers of M/s Rohtas Industries Ltd.* v. *M/s Rohtas Industries Ltd.*
(1987) 2 SCC 588
1987 (Supp) SCC 462
AIR 1990 SC 481

## Case Chapter 7

*Balram and others* v. *State of MP etc.*
1989 (2) SCALE 125 [667]

*Bandhua Mukti Morcha* v. *State of Tamil Nadu*
1986 (Supp) SCC 541

*Bandhua Mukti Morcha* v. *Union of India and others* (Haryana Mines I)
AIR 1984 SC 802 / (1984) 4 SCC 161
1991 (1) SCALE 79 [295]
AIR 1992 SC 38

*Bandhua Mukti Morcha, through Chairman, Swami Agnivesh* v. *State of Haryana and others* (Haryana Mines II)
1983 (1) SCALE 121 [543]

*Chattisgarh Krishak Mazdoor Sangh* v. *State of MP and others*
1984 (3) SCALE 93 [603]

*Hav P.V. Sivaswamy* v. *State of Tamil Nadu*
1983 (2) SCALE 45 [240]

*Kameshwar Prasad Sharma* v. *State of Bihar*

1983 (2) SCALE 160 [897]
1983 (2) SCALE 161 [897]
1993 (2) SCALE 31 [127]

*Mukesh Advani* v. *State of MP*
AIR 1985 SC 1363

*Neeraja Chaudhary* v. *State of MP*
AIR 1984 SC 1099 / 1984 (1) SCALE 148 [874]

*P. Sivaswamy* v. *State of Andhra Pradesh*
(1988) 4 SCC 466

*Rajinder K. Sail* v. *State of MP*
1988 (1) SCALE 176

*T. Chakkalackal* v. *State of Bihar*
JT 1992 (1) SC 106

*Upendra and others* v. *State of MP and another*
1986 (Supp) SCC 558

## Case Chapter 8

*Bangalore Medical Trust* v. *S. Muddappa and others*
AIR 1991 SC 1902

*Bhaghubhai H. Devani* v. *Porbander Municipality and others*
AIR 1984 Guj 134

*Bombay Hawkers' Union and others* v. *Bombay Municipal Corporation and others*
AIR 1985 SC 1206 / (1985 ) 3 SCC 528

*Citizens Action Committee, Nagpur* v. *Civil Surgeon, Mayo (General) Hospital, Nagpur and others*
AIR 1986 Bom 136

*D.D. Vyas and others* v. *Ghaziabad Development Authority, Ghaziabad and another*
AIR 1993 All 57

*Desh Raj Khurana and others* v. *Delhi Administration*
1987 (1) SCALE 321 [1313]

*Footpath Dukandar New Lajpat Rai Market Patri Union (Regd.)*

*and others* v. *M C D and others*
1986 (2) SCALE 169 [711]

*Foreshore Cooperative Housing Society Limited, Bombay* v. *Nivara Hakk Suraksha Samiti Bombay and others*
1991 (1) SCALE 33 [109]

*Forward Construction Co. and others* v. *Prahbat Mandal (Regd.), Andheri and others*
AIR 1986 SC 391 / (1986) 1 SCC 100

*Janki Nathubhai Chhara and another* v. *Sardarnagar Municipality, Sardar and another*
AIR 1986 Guj 49

*K. Chandru* v. *State of Tamil Nadu and others*
1985 (2) SCALE 3 [31]

*L.K. Koolwal* v. *State of Rajasthan and others*
AIR 1988 Raj 2

*M.B. Sadashivaiah and others* v. *City Improvement Trust Board, Mysore and others*
1988 (3) KLJ 91

*M.C. Mehta* v. *State of Orissa and others* (Cuttack municipality)
AIR 1992 Ori 225

*Madras Citizens Progressive Councel* v. *The Secretary to Govt. of Tamil Nadu and other*
AIR 1991 Mad 390

*Mangalore Municipal Market Welfare Society and another* v. *The Corporation of the City of Mangalore and others*
AIR 1993 Kant 220

*Municipal Council, Ratlam* v. *Vardhichand and others*
AIR 1980 SC 1622

*Olga Tellis and others* v. *Bombay Municipal Corporation and others*
AIR 1986 SC 180

*Pramod Kumar* v. *NDMC and others*
1987 (1) SCALE 305 [1300]

*Professor A. Lakshmisagar and others* v. *State of Karnataka and others*
AIR 1993 Kant 121

*Rajatha Enterprises* v. *S.K. Sharma and others*
(1989) 1 SCR 457

*Ram Prasad Yadav (Deceased) and Bombay Mineral and Allied Industries Employees' Union and Bombay Coal and Coke Workers' Union* v. *Chairman, Bombay Port Trust and others*
(1989) 2 SCC 378

*Ram Sahai Varma* v. *State of MP and another*
AIR 1989 MP 334

*S.S. Sobti* v. *Union of India and others*
AIR 1982 Del 51

*Sachidanand Pandey and another* v. *State of West Bengal and others*
AIR 1987 SC 1109

*Scheduled Caste and Weaker Section Welfare Association (Regd.) and another* v. *State of Karnataka and others*
(1991) 2 SCC 604

*Self Employed Women's Association and others* v. *Municipal Corporation of Ahmedabad and others*
1986 (2) SCALE 291 [1254]

*T. Damodhar Rao and others* v. *Special Officer, Municipal Corporation of Hyderabad, and others*
AIR 1987 AP 171

*T.N. Rugmani and another* v. *C. Achutha Menon and others*
AIR 1991 SC 983

*V. Lakshmipathy and others* v. *State of Karnataka and others*
AIR 1992 Kant 57

## Case Chapter 9

*Andhra Pradesh Adimajati Seva Sangham and others* v. *Guntur Municipal Council and others*
AIR 1987 AP 193

*B. Sakarama Somayaji* v. *Assistant Commissioner, Kundapura, D.K. and others*
AIR 1992 Kant 364

*B.V. Narayana Reddy and others* v. *State of Karnataka and others*
AIR 1985 Kant 99

*Banwasi Sewa Ashram* v. *State of Uttar Pradesh*
(1986) 4 SCC 753 / AIR 1987 SC 374
1991 (2) SCALE 38 [261]
AIR 1992 SC 920
1993 (1) SCALE 103 [613]

*Bombay Environmental Action Group and another* v. *State of Maharashtra and others*
AIR 1991 Bom 301

*Chhetriya Pardushan Mukti Sangarsh Samiti* v. *State of U.P. and others*
AIR 1990 SC 2060

*Consumer Education & Research Centre and others* v. *State of Gujarat and others*
1981 GLR (XXII) 712

*Dahanu Taluka Environment Protection Group and another* v. *Bombay Suburban Electricity Supply Company and others*
(1991) 2 SCC 539

*Environment Protection Council* v. *Union of India and others*
1986 (2) SCALE 231 [904]

*Environmental and Ecological Protection Samithy* v. *Executive Engineer*
1991 (2) KLT 493

*Executive Engineer* v. *Environmental & E.P. Samithi*
1993 (1) KLT 800

*F.K. Hussain* v. *Union of India*
AIR 1990 Ker 321

*Geetha Timbers, Chalakudy* v. *State of Kerala and others*
1990 (1) KLT 402 (F.B.) / AIR 1991 Ker 350

*Goa Foundation and another* v. *Konkan Railway Corporation and others*
AIR 1992 Bom 471

*Gramin Sewa Sanstha* v. *State of MP and others*
1986 (Supp) SCC 578

*K.K. Vasant* v. *State of Karnataka and another*
AIR 1992 Kant 256

*Karjan Jalasay Yojana Assargrasth Sahkar Ane Sangarsh Samiti* v.

*State of Gujarat and others*
1986 (Supp) SCC 350

*Kerala Leprosy Patients Organization Committee* v. *State of Kerala and others*
AIR 1992 Ker 344

*Kinkri Devi and another* v. *State of Himachal Pradesh and others*
AIR 1988 HP 4

*Kota Shivaram Karanth and others* v. *State of Karnataka and others*
1987 (1) SCALE 185 [691]
JT 1992 (3) SC 167

*Krishna Nagar Gram Panchayat Tadepaeli* v. *State of AP and another*
1983 (2) SCALE 125 [735]

*Kutti Padmarao, Gen Sec* v. *State of AP*
1986 (Supp) SCC 573

*M.C. Mehta* v. *Union of India* (pollution of the River Ganges)
(1987) 4 SCC 463
1988 (1) SCALE 99 [441]
(1988) 1 SCC 471
1991 Supp (1) SCC 181
1991 (2) SCALE 87 [478]
1993 Supp (1) SCC 434
1992 (1) SCALE 42 [196]

*M.C. Mehta* v. *Union of India* (information on the environment)
AIR 1992 SC 382

*M.C. Mehta* v. *Union of India and others* (Shriram gas leak)
1985 (2) SCALE 151 [1280]
1986 (1) SCALE 23 [153]
(1986) 2 SCC 176
(1986) 2 SCC 325
(1987) 1 SCC 395

*M.C. Mehta* v. *Union of India and others* (air pollution of Delhi — vehicles and industries)
(1991) 2 SCC 137
1991 (1) SCALE 104 [427] / (1991) 2 SCC 353

*M.C. Mehta* v. *Union of India and others* (air pollution of Delhi — stone crushing)

1992 Supp (2) SCC 85
1992 Supp (2) SCC 86
(1992) 3 SCC 256

*Mathew Lukose* v. *Kerala State Pollution Control Board*
1990 (2) KLT 686

*Mukthi Sangarsh Movement* v. *State of Maharashtra and others*
1990 (Supp) SCC 37

*Murali Purushothaman* v. *Union of India*
1993 (1) KLT 595

*Niyamavedi* v. *State of Kerala and others*
AIR 1993 Ker 262

*People United for Better Living in Calcutta — Public and another* v. *State of West Bengal and others*
AIR 1993 Cal 215

*Professor Sergio Carvalho* v. *The Staff of Goa and three others*
1989 (1) GLT (276)
1989 (1) GLT (266)

*Rabin Mukherjee and others* v. *State of West Bengal and others*
AIR 1985 Cal 222

*Rajiv Singh alias Lallan Singh* v. *State of Bihar and others*
AIR 1992 Pat 86

*Rural Litigation and Entitlement (R L & E) Kendra, Dehradun and others* v. *State of Uttar Pradesh and others*
1985 (2) SCALE 25 [119]
AIR 1985 SC 652
1987 (2) SCALE 164 [790]
(1987) 1 SCR 637 / 1985 (2) SCALE 113 [906]
AIR 1987 SC 359
AIR 1988 SC 2187
AIR 1989 SC 594
(1990) 3 SCR 72
AIR 1991 SC 2216

*S. Ravinder Singh Kaleka and others* v. *Union of India and others*
AIR 1984 P & H 235

*Satyavani and another* v. *A P Pollution Control Board and others*
AIR 1993 AP 257

*P. Bawa Chaudhary* v. *State of MP and others*
1989 (2) SCALE 200 [1012]

*Social Reformation and Development Club by its Secretary Shri Leishangthem Kumar Meetai* v. *State of Manipur, through the Secretary (Revenue) Government of Manipur, Imphal & Others*
(1992) 1 GauLR 163

*Social Work and Research Centre, Banswara and another* v. *State of Rajasthan and others*
AIR 1987 Raj 26

*State of Himachal Pradesh and others* v. *Umed Ram Sharma and others*
AIR 1986 SC 847

*Subhash Kumar* v. *State of Bihar and others*
AIR 1991 SC 420 / (1991) 1 SCC 598

*Sudip Mazumdar* v. *State of Madhya Pradesh*
1994 (2) SCALE 25 [329]

*Tarun Bharat Sangh, Alwar* v. *Union of India and others*
AIR 1992 SC 514
1994 (2) SCALE 68 [516]

*Tehri Bandh Virodhi Sangarsh Samiti and others* v. *State of UP and others*
(1990) 2 Supp SCR 606

*V. Lakshmipathy and others* v. *State of Karnataka and others*
AIR 1992 Kant 57

*V. Subramanian* v. *Union of India and another*
1990 (Supp) SCC 775

## Case Chapter 10

*Akhil Bharatiya Grahak Panchayat (Bombay Branch) and others* v. *State of Maharashtra and others* (bus fares)
AIR 1985 Bom 14

*Akhil Bharatiya Grahak Panchayat* v. *Andhra Pradesh State Electricity Board and another* (electricity tariff)
AIR 1983 AP 283

## Case Chapter 11

*Kedar Nath Singh Gautam* v. *Secretary, Board of High School & Intermediate Education UP at Allahabad and another*
AIR 1991 All 381

*Krishna Kant Jaiswal* v. *Vice Chancellor, Banaras Hindu University, Varanasi and others*
AIR 1984 All 350

*Manubhai Pragaji Vashi* v. *State of Maharashtra and others*
AIR 1989 Bom 296

*Naginder Singh* v. *Punjab University, Chandigarh and others*
AIR 1990 P & H 157

*Nandjee Singh* v. *P.G. Medical Students' Association and others*
(1993) 3 SCC 400

*Pratap Kishore Misra* v. *State of Orissa and others*
AIR 1988 Ori 273

*Shivajirao Nilangekar Patil* v. *Dr Mahesh Madhav Gosavi*
(1987) 1 SCC 227

*State of Himachal Pradesh* v. *Parent of a Student of Medical College, Simla and Others*
(1985) 3 SCC 169 / AIR 1985 SC 910

## Case Chapter 12

*A.C. Datt* v. *Rajiv Gandhi and others*
AIR 1990 All 38

*A.G. Prayagi* v. *State of MP and others*
AIR 1987 MP 25

*Anand Mohan* v. *Union of India and others*
AIR 1987 All 351

*B. Purushotham Reddy* v. *Nallapureddy Srinivasulu Reddy*
AIR 1988 AP 178

*B.M. Gangadhariah* v. *H.D. Devegowda*
AIR 1989 Kant 294

*Bimal Prasad Das* v. *Bijayananda Patnaik and others*
AIR 1992 Ori 10

*Dhronamraju Satyanarayana* v. *N.T. Rama Rao and others*
AIR 1988 AP 62

*Dhronamraju Satyanarayana* v. *N.T. Rama Rao and others*
AIR 1988 AP 144

*Duyal Chandra Bhuyan and others* v. *Secretary to the Government of Assam, Panchayat and C.D. Department and others*
AIR 1986 Gau 56

*I.K. Jagirdar* v. *State of Karnataka and others*
AIR 1992 Kant 175

*J. Kapathianga* v. *State of Mizoram and another*
(1991) 1 GauLR 226

*K.C. Chandy* v. *R. Balakrishna Pillai*
1985 KLT 762

*Kailash Meghwal and others* v. *State of Rajasthan and others*
AIR 1983 Raj 182

*Kallara Sukumaran* v. *Union of India and others* (speech made by Minister in Kerala)
AIR 1987 Ker 212

*Kallara Sukumaran* v. *Raghuchandra Bal* (spirit smuggling)
1993 (1) KLT 699

*Kashinath G. Jalmi and another* v. *Speaker and others*
AIR 1993 SC 1873

*Madurai Adheena Peedathipathi, Madurai* v. *State of Tamil Nadu*
AIR 1984 Mad 241

*Maharishi Avadhesh* v. *State of UP*
AIR 1991 All 52

*P. Nalla Thampy Terah* v. *Union of India and others* (election law)
1985 (Supp) SCC 189

*P.N. Dubey* v. *Union of India and others*
AIR 1989 MP 225

*Panna Lal Agyan and others* v. *Hon'ble Speaker, Sri Balram Jakgad, and others*
AIR 1988 All 167

*Rajendran* v. *Vakkom Puroshothaman* (politics)
1985 KLT 40

*Sunil Kumar Mondal and others* v. *Union of India and others*
AIR 1989 Cal 197

*V.R.V. Sree Rama Rao* v. *Telugu Desam, a Political Party, and others*
AIR 1984 AP 353

*V.R. Sreerama Rao* v. *Telugudesam, a political party, and another*
AIR 1983 AP 96

*Vidadala Harindhababu and etc.* v. *N.T. Rama Rao, Chief Minister of the State of Andhra Pradesh, Hyderabad and others*
AIR 1990 AP 20

## Case Chapter 13

*A.S. Mittal and others* v. *State of UP and others*
AIR 1989 SC 1570

*Acchan Rizvi* v. *State of Uttar Pradesh and others*
1992 (2) SCALE 85 [457]
1992 (2) SCALE 150 [706]
1992 (3) SCALE 65 [246]
1993 (1) SCALE 9 [28]
1993 (1) SCALE 46 [174]

*Akhil Bharatiya Soshit Karamchari (ABSK) Sangh (Railway)* v. *Union of India and others*
(1981) 1 SCC 246

*B. Rarmlamma* v. *State of Andhra Pradesh*
1993 (1) SCALE 27 [90]

*B. Krishan Bhat* v. *Union of India*
(1990) 3 SCC 65

*Babubhai Jashbhai Patel and others* v. *Union of India, New Delhi and others*
AIR 1983 Guj 1

*Brijithamma* v. *State of Kerala*
1990 (1) KLT 399

*Central Bureau of Investigation and another* v. *Harinder Singh Chowdhary and another*
1990 (2) SCALE 244 [1172]

*Chandanmal Chopra and another* v. *State of West Bengal*
AIR 1986 Cal 104

*"Common Cause" a Registered Society and others* v. *Union of India* (commutation of pensions)
AIR 1987 SC 210

*Common Cause Registered Society* v. *Union of India and others* (property tax)
(1987) 4 SCC 44

*D.C. Wadhwa and others* v. *State of Bihar*
AIR 1987 SC 579 / (1987) 1 SCC 378

*D.S. Nakara and others* v. *Union of India*
AIR 1983 SC 130

*George Mampilly and another* v. *State of Kerala and another*
AIR 1985 Ker 24

*Indra Sawhney and others etc.* v. *Union of India and others etc. etc.*
JT 1992 (6) SC 273

*Jagat Singh* v. *Delhi Administration and others*
1989 (2) SCALE 1498 [767]

*Jagram* v. *Gwalior Town and Country Development Authority Gwalior and others*
AIR 1987 MP 11

*Janata Dal* v. *H.S. Chowdhary*
1991 (2) SCALE 71 [400] / (1991) 3 SCC 756
(1992) 4 SCC 305 / 1992 (2) SCALE 67 [338]

*Jaram Singh* v. *State of HP and others*
AIR 1988 HP 13

*Katheeja Bai* v. *Superintending Engineer and others*
(1984) 3 SCC 518

*Kishen Patnayak and another* v. *State of Orissa*
AIR 1989 SC 677 / 1989 (1) SCALE 4 [32]

*Kochupennu Lakshmi* v. *The Chairman, Kerala State Road Transport Corporation, Trivandrum*
AIR 1984 Ker 97

*Lucy R. D'Souza and etc. etc.* v. *State of Goa and others*
AIR 1990 Bom 355

*Mohd. Aslam Alias Bhure* v. *State of UP and another*
1993 (2) SCALE 196 [994]

*N. Parthasarathy* v. *Controller of Capital Issues and another*
(1991) 3 SCC 153

*N. Kunhiraman* v. *State of Kerala and others*
AIR 1992 Ker 265

*Narendra Kumar Maheshwari* v. *Union of India*
1990 (Supp) SCC 440

*National Federation of Blind* v. *Union Public Service Commission and others*
(1993) 2 SCC 411

*Odyssey Communication Pvt. Ltd.* v. *Lokvidyayan Sanghatana and others*
(1988) 3 SCC 410

*P. Jagajeevan Ram and etc.* v. *Government of India and others*
AIR 1989 Mad 149

*P.N. Narasimha Murthy* v. *Regional Transport Officer and Licensing Authority for grant of Driving School Licence and another*
1990 (1) KLJ 143

*P.K. Martiyani* v. *Regional Provident Fund Commissioner, Ahmedabad and another*
1983(2) GLR XXIV(2) 927

*Poonamal and others* v. *Union of India and others*
1985 (3) SCC 345

*Quilon District Private Bus Operators Association, Kollam-1* v. *State Transport Appellate Tribunal, Ernakulam and others*
AIR 1992 Ker 267

*R.R. Delava* v. *Indian Overseas Bank and others*
AIR 1991 Mad 61

*R.K. Garg* v. *Union of India and others*
(1981) 4 SCC 675

*R. Palaksha* v. *State of Karnataka and others*
1990 (1) KLJ 251

*Rakesh Dhar Tripathi* v. *Union of India and others*
AIR 1988 All 47

*Ram Pyari* v. *Union of India and others*
AIR 1988 Raj 124

*Ramesh s/o Chotalal Dalal* v. *Union of India and others*
(1988) 1 SCC 668

*Rudraiah Raju K. and others* v. *State of Karnataka and others*
1986 (1) KLJ 164

*S. Rangarajan* v. *P. Jagjivan Ram and others*
(1989) 2 SCC 574

*Shiv Rao Shanta Rao Wangla and others* v. *Union of India and others*
(1988) 1 SCC 452

*Shivarao Shantaram Wagle and others(II)* v. *Union of India and others*
(1988) 2 SCC 115

*Surendra Kumar Lanka and others* v. *Union of India and others*
1992 (1) SCALE 47 [212]

*T. Vasudeva Pai* v. *Union of India*
1990 (1) KLJ 403

*Thressia* v. *K.S.E.B.*
AIR 1988 Ker 206

*V.M. Tarkunde and another* v. *Union of India and others*
1989 (2) SCALE 188 [937]

*Vincent Panikurlangara* v. *Union of India*
AIR 1987 SC 990

*Vineet Kumar and another* v. *The Board of Control for Cricket in India*
1989 (2) SCALE 145 [764]

*Vishwabharathi House Building Co-operative Society Limited and another* v. *Bangalore Development Authority, Bangalore and another*
AIR 1991 Kant 133

## Case Chapter 14

*Aeltemesh Rein* v. *Union of India*
(1988) 4 SCC 54

*All India Judges' Association* v. *Union of India*

(1992) 1 SCC 119
(1993) 4 SCC 288

*All Kerala Poor Aid Legal Association* v. *Chief Justice*
1990 (1) KLT 1

*Arun Kumar* v. *Union of India*
AIR 1982 Raj 66

*B. Purushotham Reddy* v. *Nallapureddy Srinivasulu Reddy*
AIR 1988 AP 178

*Capt. Virendra Kumar, Adv* v. *Shiv Raj Patil, Speaker, Lok Sabha* (impeachment of Justice V. Ramaswami)
1993 (3) SCALE 61 [303]

*Captain Virendra Kumar* v. *Union of India* (allegations against the Court)
1993 (3) SCALE 97 [492]

*Centre of Legal Research and another* v. *State of Kerala*
AIR 1986 SC 2195

*Charan Lal Sahu* v. *Union of India and another*
(1988) 3 SCC 255

*Dalip Singh Gill* v. *Union of India and others*
AIR 1993 P & H 263

*Free Legal Aid Committee, Jamshedpur* v. *State of Bihar*
1990 (1) SCALE 45 [145]

*Hon'ble Chief Justice, High Court Madhya Pradesh, Jabalpur and others* v. *Mohan Kumar and others*
1993 (4) SCALE 154 [656]
1994 (1) SCALE 18 [82]

*K. Ashok Reddy* v. *Government of India and others*
(1994) 2 SCC 303

*K.P. Verma* v. *State of Bihar and others*
AIR 1989 Pat 276

*Krishna Swami* v. *Union of India and others*
1992 (2) SCALE 66 [311]

*Krishnaswami* v. *Union of India and others*
1992 (1) SCALE 87 [484]

*Kumar Padma Prasad* v. *Union of India and others*
AIR 1992 SC 1213

*Lily Thomas, Advocate* v. *Speaker, Lok Sabha and others*
1993 (3) SCALE 105 [543]

*M.L. Sachdev* v. *Union of India and another*
1990 (2) SCALE 196 [926]

*M.L. Puri* v. *The Punjab and Haryana High Court, Chandigarh and others*
AIR 1993 P & H 287

*M.C. Mehta* v. *Union of India and others* (Industrial Tribunals)
1986 (Supp) SCC 562

*P.N. Duda* v. *P. Shiv Shanker*
(1988) 3 SCC 167

*R.J. Mehta* v. *His Lordship the Chief Justice, Venkat Srinivas Deshpande and others*
AIR 1982 Bom 125

*R.K. Jain* v. *Union of India*
1993 (2) SCALE 168 [843]

*Rajendran* v. *Ayyappan* (Advocate General)
1985 KLT 307

*Ranjan Dwivedi* v. *Union of India*
1983 (1) SCALE 111 [487]

*S.P. Sampath Kumar* v. *Union of India and others*
AIR 1987 SC 386

*S.P. Gupta, V.M. Tarkunde, J.L. Kalra and others* v. *President of India and others etc [amended to Union of India and others]*
1981 (Supp) SCC 87 / AIR 1982 SC 146

*Sarojini Ramaswami* v. *Union of India and others*
1992 (2) SCALE 65 [257]

*Satish Chandra Misra* v. *State of UP and others*
AIR 1990 All 119

*Sub-Committee for Judicial Accountability* v. *Union of India and others*
1991 (2) SCALE 160 [844]

*Subhash Sharma and others* v. *Union of India*
1991 Supp (1) SCC 574

*Subir Chowdhury* v. *Union of India and others*
AIR 1984 Cal 7

# Preface

Public interest litigation (PIL) has been one of the most important innovations in the Indian judicial process of the last two decades. It emerged in response to a need to make judicial process more accessible to the disadvantaged sections of society and to ensure adequate judicial protection of their human rights. PIL is essentially an integral part of the poverty jurisprudence of the Supreme Court of India, which has taken shape since the late seventies. It became articulate during the post-emergency period. During the Emergency, the Supreme Court reached the nadir of its public law image when in *A.D.M. Jabalpur* v. *Shrikant Shukla*,[1] it totally abandoned its responsibility towards the protection of individual liberty. Such self-abdication by the apex Court was really not surprising to those who had witnessed the positivist stance it displayed in its decisions since *A. K. Gopalalan* v. *Madras*.[2] The Shukla decision manifested the farthest extent to which such legal positivism could be stretched.

The Emergency laid bare the lawlessness of the State as well as judicial helplessness. The post-emergency Court had to make a great effort to re-establish its institutional credibility as a bulwark against State repression and as the protector of people's rights. It did this in two ways: first by reinterpreting the constitutional provisions more

[1]*A. D. M. Jabalpur* v. *Shrikant Shukla*, AIR 1976 SC 1207. See generally, H. M. Seerval, *Emergency, Future Safeguards and Habeas Corpus Case: A Criticism* (Tripathi, 1978).

[2]*A. K. Gopalan* v. *Madras*, AIR 1950 SC 27.

liberally and thus expanding the scope and content of various fundamental rights [*Maneka Gandhi* v. *India*[3]] and then, by restating various rules of procedure such as standing, prematurity and laches, with a view to facilitating the common man's access to the Court. [*P.U.D.R.* v. *India*[4]] A new paradigm of public law litigation, which includes public interest litigation emerged out of such judicial activism. This paradigm contained a new conceptualization of the judicial role in public law litigation and new rules of interpretation as well as procedures to facilitate access. If the courts were accessible only to the rich, how could they inspire confidence among the large number of half starved, naked and illiterate "people of India"? Professor Upendra Baxi rightly observed that the Supreme Court of India for the first time became a court for Indians.[5] This writer tends to agree with Baxi that the proper nomenclature for what is called PIL should have been Social Action Litigation (SAL). Such a description helps to clarify its conceptual distinction from public law litigation on the one hand and class litigation on the other. I will endeavour here to put forward such a conceptual distinction.

All over the common law system, the sphere of judicial control of legislative and administrative action has been gradually expanding. The courts in England, of the fifties and sixties, abjured the judicial restraint that had been a characteristic of the Second World War period. The welfare state doubtless created greater opportunities for the abuse of power by the Executive. The courts were therefore more willing to scrutinize closely the exercise of discretionary powers by the Executive. Planned development involved making decisions regarding the distribution of resources and such decisions were bound to evoke collective opposition. Class actions or collective actions were therefore bound to proliferate.

Even the traditional paradigm of judicial process, deeply steeped in the adversary setting, contained provisions for accommodating collective actions.[6] In public law litigation, the frequency of collective or class petitions against the State increased. Public law litigation is

[3]*Maneka Gandhi* v. *India*, AIR 1978 SC 597.

[4]*P. U. D. R.* v. *India*, AIR 1982 SC 1473.

[5]Upendra Baxi, "Taking Suffering Seriously: Social Action Litigation in the Supreme Court of India" In Dhavan, Sudarshan and Salman Khurshid (ed.) *Judges and the Judicial Power*, p. 289 (Sweet and Maxwell-Tripathi 1985).

[6]Order 1, Rule 8, The Code of Civil Procedure, 1908.

essentially concerned with conflict resolution rather than dispute resolution. The traditional paradigm of the judicial process was designed for private law adjudication which emphasized dispute resolution. Private law adjudication in common law countries followed a strict adversary model that had prescribed parameters about who can activize the judicial process, the reasons for which it can be activized, when it can be activized, and the limits within which the court could render its decision. A court would not decide on questions other than those it needed to give relief to the litigant. The focal point of litigation was the rights and liabilities of the parties and it culminated in giving relief to the wronged party. In public law litigation, the interests involved tend to transcend far beyond the litigating parties. The questions involved therein often pertained to the proper exercise of power by the State or its functionaries and the scope of individual liberty. The private law paradigm of the judicial process therefore always needed to be modified in its application to public law litigation. The Supreme Court of India's rejection of a petition under Article 32 of the Constitution on the grounds of delay[7] or *res judicata*[8] or error of law within jurisdiction[9] were criticized in juristic writings.[10] There were always more liberal rules of *locus standi* in respect of the writs of *habeas corpus* and *quo warranto*, because of the larger public interest involved.[11] In respect of the other fundamental rights, the Supreme Court of India has been flexible as far as the *locus standi* of the petitioners was concerned.[12] In a recent case,[13] the Supreme Court held that it would be most reluctant to uphold the plea of delay where usurpation of a public office was alleged.

[7]*Tilokchand Motichand* v. *H. B. Munshi*, AIR 1970 SC 898 (1970) 1 SCC 859.

[8]*Daryao* v. *U.P.*, AIR 1961 SC 1457.

[9]*Ujjam Bai* v. *U.P.*, AIR 1962 SC 1621.

[10]See Upendra Baxi "Laches and the Right to Constitutional Remedies: *Quis Custodiet Costodes?*" in Alice Jacob (ed.) *Constitutional Developments Since Independence*, p. 559 (ILI, 1975): Alice Jacob "Laches: Denial of Judicial Relief under Article 32 and 226" 16 *JILI* 352 (1974).

[11]See S. P. Sathe, *Administrative Law*, p. 393 (5th ed. Reprinted with Supplement, 1994).

[12]S. P. Sathe, "Standing to Assert Fundamental Rights of Third Parties: An Analysis of Judicial Policy", 14 *Journal of the Indian Law Institute* 352 (1976).

[13]*Dr. Kashinath C. Jalmi* v. *The Speaker* (1993) 2 SCC 703. See Sathe, *Administrative Law, Supplement 1994*, p. 12.

Traditionally, the courts would not act except in cases or controversies.[14] This provision of the United States Constitution was a mere replication of the common law prescription of judicial function. The courts in the United States for a long time did not take up a matter for adjudication which had not become mature. The anti-contraceptive legislation of the state of Connecticut was not allowed to be challenged in court on the grounds of its alleged unconstitutionality for a number of years because the law had in fact not been enforced.[15] However, exceptions to this rule were made in the United States as well as India.[16] The rules of *locus standi* and prematurity were justified on the ground that a court could act most efficiently in concrete situations and that it should not answer hypothetical or abstract questions. This was why the United States Constitution did not provide for an advisory jurisdiction of the Supreme Court.

In legal theory, a distinction is made between *ratio decidendi* and *obiter dictum*. The former means a binding rule which emerges out of the decision of the court in a given dispute. Since the law-making function of the courts was conceded rather reluctantly by analytical jurists, the *ratio decidendi* was supposed to be most narrowly conceived. Its scope was limited to the precise rule on which the decision was based and without which it could not have been reached. *Obiter dicta* consisted of the reflections and expressions of the judges and had merely a persuasive function. This distinction between *ratio* and *obiter* was based on the traditional concept of judicial function which was confined to dispute resolution. With the growth of the public law functions of the courts, particularly where they had to review the acts of the Executive as well as the legislature, many axioms of the private law paradigm came under question.

Under the public law dispensation the courts are not mere dispute-settling institutions but have to play a political role in securing human rights entitlements guaranteed by the Constitution. The courts must act to resolve conflicts such as those between liberty and authority, equality and social justice, federal government and the state governments, due process of law and the need to suppress criminality, and development and environment. The courts were called upon to

[14]Art. III of the Constitution of the United States.

[15]*Poe* v. *Ullman*, 367 U.S. 467 (1961).

[16]S. P. Sathe, "Avoidance of Premature Constitutional Questions by the Supreme Court", *Year Book of Legal Studies 1975*, p. 23–47.

articulate the rights of the underdog such as prison inmates, bonded labour, unorganized labour, women in protective homes, children, etc. No public law litigation could really be concerned only with the litigating parties. It often involved larger issues which transcended the litigating parties and extended to the public at large. Every public law litigation is concerned with the exercise of State power, limitations thereupon, or the rights of the people. In that sense, every public law litigation involves public interest. Can we then say that every PLL is a PIL? The expression "Public Interest Litigation" (PIL) has not been used here in its etymological sense but rather in the conceptual sense which has been articulated through experience.

In my view, every public law litigation (PLL), is not a public interest litigation (PIL) in the sense the term is used in this discourse. Although every public interest litigation (PIL) is a public law litigation (PLL), the reverse is not true. At present PIL is mainly the litigation which comes within the writ jurisdiction of the Supreme Court and the High Courts. That, however, is not the only sense in which PIL is understood. Can PIL not originate in a trial court? The origins of *Ratlam Municipality* v. *Vardhichand*,[17] the first case on environmental law, can be traced to a trial court. Was the prosecution of Antulay, the Chief Minister of Maharashtra, under the Prevention of Corruption Act not a PIL?[18] However, these cases have not been included by the author in this casebook because they dealt more with facts, did not contain any substantial legal discourse and operated at the trial court level, the author's focus being on the writ jurisdiction of the High Courts and the Supreme Court. Both *Ratlam* as well as *Antulay* involved questions of non-exercise or abuse of public power, neither was a mere dispute between the contesting parties and neither could be described as a class action. The petitioners were not seeking any benefit to themselves or redressal of their own grievances. In *Ratlam*, the petitioner wanted the municipality to provide drainage and other amenities of public hygiene to ensure good quality of life to the people of that town and in *Antulay*, the prosecutor was mainly interested in establishing deterrents against corruption and misappropriation of power. Many years later, a similar use of PIL was invoked to unearth another scandal called Bofors.[19] All

[17]AIR 1980 SC 1622.

[18]See Upendra Baxi, Liberty and Corruption-The Antulay Case and Beyond. (Eastern 1989).

[19]See Rajiv Dhavan, "Law As Struggle: Public Interest Law in India", 36 *Journal of the Indian Law Institute*, p. 302, 311 (footnote 50) (1994).

such litigation is PIL. However, cases in which a government servant objects to a seniority list or a class of government servants object to the discriminatory pension rules as in *D. S. Nakara*[20] or all those petitions in which administrative actions are challenged as being *mala fide* or against the rules of natural justice or *ultra vires* are PLLs but not PILs. PIL is a species of PLL. Every PLL has a legislative/constituent element. For example, the law that the basic structure of the Constitution cannot be destroyed or tampered with by Parliament even by a constitutional amendment was laid down in *Keshavanand Bharati* v. *Kerala*.[21] The fact that PIL is essentially a PLL may also give birth to a new law. While PLL involves law-making regarding the content and meaning of the Constitution, PIL often involves law-making pertaining to the entitlements of the underdog and the processual innovations necessary to secure them. [*Olga Tellis*][22]

PILs are usually made in espousal of the rights of a class of people who may be disadvantaged or the interests of a motley group so diffused as to elude a neat or specific description such as the people in general or the inhabitants of a locality. In that sense it is a class action. It is a class or collective action in that the grievances of the actual litigants may be shared by many similarly placed persons. But all such persons do not necessarily come to the court as parties. A petition may be made by a single person such as Sunil Batra[23] against the torture of prison inmates or a social activist on behalf of four pahadia boys who had languished in jail as undertrial prisoners for more than ten years.[24] Since each of them raised questions of human rights such as the treatment of prison inmates or the indefinite detention of undertrial prisoners, the Court made historic precedents in laying down the rights of the disadvantage people which till then had remained inarticulate. PIL therefore obliterates the distinction between *ratio decidendi* and *obiter dicta* and the Court becomes an important instrument of public advocacy of human rights or due process or public accountability. In fact, the *obiter dicta* of the Supreme Court are considered as binding by the High Courts.[25] To that extent Indian decisional law has already

[20] *D. S. Nakara* v. *India*, AIR 1983 SC 130.

[21] AIR 1973 SC 1461.

[22] *Olga Tellis* v. *Bombay Municipal Corporation*, AIR 1986 SC 180.

[23] *Sunil Batra* v. *Delhi Administration*, AIR 1978 SC 1675.

[24] *Kadra Pahadiya* v. *Bihar*, AIR 1981 SC 939.

[25] *Deepchand* v. *Raghurai*, AIR 1977 All. 370.

shown its independence from the traditional common law theory of *stare decisis*. The Supreme Court of India's *obiter* that it could overrule its own decision[26] came almost a decade before the House of Lords policy statement in England that it would not be bound by its own decision.[27] Further, the Supreme Court of India actually overruled itself in *Golaknath* v. *Punjab*[28] in 1967 and invoked the doctrine of prospective overruling. All such innovations in the jurisprudence of the Court came in the exercise of its public law function of judicial review.[29]

PIL needs to be distinguished from class actions or collective actions. PILs are class actions in that the grievances alleged therein are of a class of people or a society or the entire nation. They seek protection for the people suffering as bonded labour[30], prison inmates[31], or undertrial prisoners.[32] An environmentalist group challenging mining in the Doon valley[33] is an instance of a collective or class action. But M. C. Mehta raising the question of the pollution of the Ganges[34] or Sheela Barse raising the issue of children's rights[35] are cases initiated by individuals and though the collective interest exists in a diffused form, the collectivity of the petitioners is not present to make it a class action or a collective action. PILs for obtaining the rulings of the Court regarding the appointment of judges and their transfers were motivated by a concern for the independence of the judiciary, in which the entire legal profession had a stake.[36] Similarly, the litigation undertaken by an organization called Common Cause to obtain orders from the Supreme

[26] *The Bengal Immunity Co.* v. *Bihar*, AIR 1955 SC 661. Also see *Sajjan Singh* v. *Rajasthan*, AIR 1965 SC 845, 855.

[27] *Policy Statement*; (1966) 3 All. E.R. 77.

[28] AIR 1967 SC 1643.

[29] See Sathe, *Fundamental Rights and Amendment of the Indian Constitution*, p. 34 (University of Bombay, 1968).

[30] *Bandhu Mukti Morcha* v. *Bihar*, AIR 1984 SC 802.

[31] *Charles Sobrai* v. *Supdt. Central Jail*, AIR 1978 SC 1574.

[32] *Hussainara Khatoon* v. *Bihar*, AIR 1979 SC 1360.

[33] *Tarun Bharat Singh* v. *India*, (1993) Supp. 1 SCC 4.

[34] *M. C. Mehta* v. *India*, (1987) 4 SCC 463.

[35] *Sheela Barse* v. *Secretary, Children Aid Society* (1987) 3 SCC 50; 1987 SCC (Cri.) 458.

[36] *S. P. Gupta* v. *India*, AIR 1982 SC 149: (1987) Supp. SCC 87: *Supreme Court Advocates on Record Association* v. *India*, (1993) 4 SCC 441: AIR 1994 SC 268.

Court mandating the State Governments to set up district forums which they were obliged to do under the Consumer Protection Act, 1986[37] was on behalf of a crowd of consumers. We can then say that though PIL usually involves the interests of a large number of people, all of them are not collective or class actions in the manner that terms is used in law. There are collective actions or class actions which cannot be called PIL such as an industrial dispute under the Industrial Disputes Act[38] or a grievance raised by a consumer association or a collective body of consumers before a forum established under the Consumer Protection Act.[39] These are class actions but not PILs.

How do we distinguish a PIL from a collective action since both involve wider public interests? Why do we say an industrial dispute is not a PIL? Are people not interested in the resolution of such a dispute? They are and yet we do not classify it as PIL. The shareholders of a company demanding its closure or suing it for arrears is not a PIL, but the workers asking for fair returns on the disposal of old machinery of a public sector corporation[40] or seeking to be heard in the winding-up proceedings of a company[41] are PILs, because in each of them the petitioners were required to obtain recognition of their *locus standi* in contrast to their position under the traditional rules of judicial process. The litigation challenging the statute under which the Government of India took upon itself the responsibility of prosecuting and/or suing Union Carbide on behalf of and to the exclusion of all the victims of the gas tragedy[42] as well as the litigation questioning the competence of the Supreme Court to approve a settlement between the Government and Union Carbide[43] were PILs. They were not mere class actions because some well-meaning people had taken up cudgels on behalf of the victims. In all these cases, the petitioners did not possess *locus*

[37] *Common Cause* v. *India*, (1992) 1 SCC 707.

[38] S. 2 (R), The Industrial Disputes Act, 1947.

[39] S. 2 (b), The Consumer Protection Act, 1986.

[40] *Fertilizer Corporation of India* v. *India*, AIR 1981 SC 344: (1981) 1 SCC 568.

[41] *National Textile Workers Union* v. *P. R. Ramkrishnan*, AIR 1983 SC 75. See S. P. Sathe, "Public Participation in Judicial Process With Special Reference to Administrative Law" 26 *Journal of the Indian Law Institute*, p. 1–12 (1984).

[42] *Charanlal Sahu* v. *India*, AIR 1990 SC 1480. See Sathe, *Administrative Law*, p. 427 (5th ed. 1991).

[43] *Union Carbide Corporation* v. *India*, (1991) 4 SCC 584: AIR 1992 SC 248, See Sathe, *Administrative Law*, opp. cited n. 7 Supplement p. 40.

*standi* under the rules of the traditional judicial process but sought it because of their claims that the matter involved a vital public interest.

A class action is an adjudication of a dispute within the four corners of the adversary system, and the only difference between it and other litigation is that many parties can be joined as plaintiffs or respondents and the decision affects all those who have been parties to it. PIL on the other hand tends to be a departure from the strict adversarial model of litigation and the decision involves judicial law-making.

While all PLLs and collective actions are generally governed by the traditional legal technology of the adversarial system, PIL is essentially inquisitorial and has various elements of an ombudsman. The appointment of commissioners by the Court to collect data in support of a petition, where the petitioner lacks the professional expertise to collect such information, is the most valid example of the unorthodox processual character of PIL. The growth of epistolary jurisdiction under which a letter written to a judge or even a newspaper report could trigger the judicial process is another example. Both aim at espousing the interests of the disadvantaged party to the litigation and thus facilitating his access to the justice system. In that sense Chief Justice Bhagawati rightly said that PIL was an arm of the legal aid movement in India.[44] While in PLLs as well as class actions, the petitioner or petitioners, as the case may be, have to satisfy the court that they have or are likely to suffer some injury from the alleged illegality, in PIL, even if the petitioner does not suffer any such injury, his petition will be entertained if he establishes that it would or could cause injury to some third parties who are not in a position to approach the court, or to society in general. The fact that the petitioner has no personal interest or that he has no axe to grind strengthens rather than weakens his claim to be a petitioner.

PIL may therefore be described as satisfying one or more of the following parameters. These are not exclusive but merely descriptive:

- Where the concerns underlying a petition are not individualist but are shared widely by a large number of people (bonded labour, undertrial prisoners, prison inmates).
- Where the affected persons belong to the disadvantaged sections of society (women, children, bonded labour, unorganized labour etc.).

[44]*P.U.D.R.* v. *India*, AIR 1982 SC 1473.

- Where judicial law making is necessary to avoid exploitation (inter-country adoption,[45] the education of the children of the prostitutes.[46]
- Where judicial intervention is necessary for the protection of the sanctity of democratic institutions (independence of the judiciary, existence of grievance redressal forums).
- Where administrative decisions related to development are harmful to the environment and jeopardize people's rights to natural resources such as air or water.[47]

In PIL, the courts combine the function of an ombudsman and a human rights court. Here we do not use the word 'ombudsman' in the sense of a lokpal or lokayukta but rather in its true and original meaning as institutionalized by the Ombudsman in Sweden or the Parliamentary Commissioner in England.

Much of the criticism of PIL arises out of our commitment to the paradigm of judicial process steeped in the adversary system of justice.[48] PIL is doubtless a rebellion against such legal orthodoxy. The success or failure of PIL cannot be measured in terms of how far the evils attacked by it have disappeared. The evils are so deep-rooted that their eradication would take decades if not centuries. What PIL does is to make us conscious of the extremely formal nature of the adversary system of justice and the need to develop alternative models of justicing which are quick, economical and demystified. At the same time, but for PIL, many under-privileged groups of people would have been totally alienated from the system of justice and the rule of law. Through PIL, the Court has articulated the human rights of such a large section of humanity. PIL has doubtless acted as a catalyst in the process of social transformation. It must be seen as one of the strategies of making justice available to common people.

However, two cautions must accompany such an optimistic appraisal of PIL. One is that the judges and lawyers have a great responsibility towards avoiding an over-use of PIL. The legal profession must know

[45] *Laxmikant Pandey* v. *India*, AIR 1987 SC 232.

[46] *Vishaljit* v. *India*, AIR 1990 SC 1412: (1990) 3 SCC 318.

[47] *R.L. & E. Kendra* v. *U.P.*, AIR 1985 SC 632, AIR 1988 SC 187 and a series of cases, see Rajiv Dhavan, opp. cited notc 14, footnote 46 on page 309. This article gives an exhaustive documentation of PIL cases on various issues such as social justice.

[48] S. K. Agrawal, *Public Interest Litigation*, K. M. Munshi Lectures. Indian Law Institute (1985).

where this valuable resource can be used most efficiently. The courts are welcome to relax the requirement of *locus standi*, but must not get involved in non-justiciable issues. A petition challenging the validity of the *Quoran* was filed and it was admitted by the Calcutta High Court.[49] This is an instance of the extravagant use of PIL. This writer has commented on such judicial indiscretion elsewhere.[50] Secondly, PIL can cause disillusionment if it lingers on for an inordinately long period. The delays which afflict normal litigation have also started polluting PIL. The courts must step up their court management skills to eliminate delays and reduce costs. They should be more selective in extending the facility of PIL. This will require socially conscientious and imaginative lawyering as well as justicing. The government and the Parliament in India cannot afford to remain oblivious to the needs and aspirations of the people of India to have an economical, efficient and expeditious system of justice. Reform of the mainstream system of justice is overdue and needs urgent attention. PIL is not an alternative to the existing system but an input which ameliorates some of the evils of the mainstream system thereby alleviating the suffering of the litigating public. However, if the mainstream system continues to degenerate, PIL will also degenerate and get contaminated by the same ailments. There are other alternatives to courts such as tribunals, arbitrators, and lok adalats. Such alternatives must be strengthened so as to reduce the burden on the courts. In addition, reform of the procedures, training and sensitization of judges, and greater meaningfulness of professional legal education, would have to be taken up as additional inputs to truly reinvigorate the legal process.

Sangeeta Ahuja's casebook is most timely, PIL is now a subject that deserves serious study by prospective lawyers as well as social activists. PIL requires a class of lawyers with a good understanding of the theory of interaction between law and society and the skills of anticipatory lawyering. Such a capacity to theorize and use the skills of anticipatory lawyering can develop when one studies a subject through first hand exposure to decided cases and by subjecting them to critical inquiry. A critical mind is the first requisite of imaginative and socially conscientious lawyering and the case method combined with the lecture method can surely catalyse the thinking process so as to spearhead such lawyering. Such a method of study is desirable not only for the elite

[49]*Chandramal Chopra* v. *State*, AIR 1986 Cal. 104.

[50]See Sathe, *Administrative Law*, op. cit. p. 384.

undergoing a course in professional legal education but even for those who are using law in their struggle against social injustice, oppression and denial of human rights. If the legal system is to be rescued from the hegemonic control of legal professionals, it must be demystified and informalized. PIL and its use by social activists will doubtless reduce societal alienation from the regime of law and this book will be greatly useful to all such motivated social activists.

Pune 1996 S.P. SATHE

# Acknowledgements

This book is a cumulative effort by many people over many years. Most of the fieldwork was conducted in three periods, in 1990–91, in early 1992 and intensively from 1992–1994. Judges have been generous with their time, and the staff of the Registries of the Supreme Court and many of the High Courts have been patient with my questions.

The principal interviewees, whose insight and engagement wth PIL provided the base upon which this book has been built, include: Smriti Acharya, Rani Advani, Shakuntala Advani, Swami Agnivesh, Tejinder Singh Ahuja, Justice Janaki Amma, Vidya Bal, Sheela Barse, Indrajit Barua, Pancu Gopal Baruah, Upendra Baxi, Vidyut Bhagwat, Ravi Bhagwat, Justice P.N. Bhagwati, Prem Bhai, Anupam Bhatia, Ela Bhatt, Mahesh Bhatt, Subir Bhaumik, Ajit Kumar Bhuyan, Abha Bora, Celine, Shyam Chainani, K. Chandramouli, K. Chandru, Jyotsana Chatterjee, Chinmai Chaudhary, Poornima Chikarmani, Anubha Das, Horon Das, Parag Kumar Das, Mona Daswani, Justice D.A. Desai, Krishna Devarao, Vasudha Dhagamwar, Rajeev Dhavan, Niloy Dutta, Walter Fernandes, R. Gandhi, R.K. Garg, Gnanapragasam, Neelam Gorhe, Anand Grover, Nandita Haksar, Kalpana Hingorani, Justice V.R. Krishna Iyer, Jeemon Jacob, Harish Jagtiani, Indira Jaising, Kamini Jaiswal, Nalini Jayal, Jayashree, Rani Jethmalani, Ram Jethmalani, Manju Jugran, Yogesh Kamdar, K.G. Kannabiran, Rani Karan, Madhu Kishwar, Smitu Kothari, Miloon Kothari, Sharad Kulkarni, Vijay Kumar, Vatsala Kumari, Sugatha Kumari, Jose Kuriakose, Madhusoodanan, Krishan Mahajan, K. Manoharan, Ruth Manorama, P.T. Mathew, Siby Mathew, Babu Mathew, T.U. Mehta, M.C. Mehta,

Subhash Mendapulkar, N.R. Madhava Menon, Surojit Mitra, Inder Mohan, Mukul Mudgal, Gobinda Mukhoty, Chot Murada, Ravi Nair, K. Nandini, N.D. Pancholi, Sriram Panchu, Gourishayam Panda, Lasmi Kant Pandey, Vincent Panikulangara, P.H. Parekh, Sheela Patel, Mina Patel, Pranab Pathak, Ila Pathak, Vidya Patwardhan, Sujit Patwardhan, Pradip Prabhu, M.K. Prasad, Mahesh Prasad, Raja, Geeta Ramaseshan, G. Ramaswamy, Asha Ramesh, M.A. Rane, Prabhakar Rao, P.P. Rao, Rajendra Ravi, Bunker Roy, Dipali Das Roy, Hrishikesh Roy, Justice Rajinder Sachar, Jaya Sagade, D.N. Saraf, Lotika Sarkar, Mukunda Kant Sarma, R.P. Sarmah, Vijay Sathe, Navroz Seervai, S.R. Sen, Atul Setalvad, Harsh Sethi, Haribhai Shah, Manubhai Shah, Kavita Sharma, Pravin Sheth, H.D. Shourie, M.N. Shroff, Kapil Sibal, Chhatrapati Singh, Kirti Singh, B. Sivarammaya, Suniti Sonowal, D.D. Sood, Soli Sorabjee, A. Subashini, H. Subalekshmy, R. Sudarshan, Lekha Suresh, Syedbhai, Rashid Talib, Rajesh Tandon, Justice V.M. Tarkunde, Henry Tiphagne, Enakshi Ganguly Tukhral, Gautam Uzir, S.S. Vasudevan, Elizabeth Vatsyayan, R. Venkataramani, A.X. Varghese, Jose Verghese, James Vincent.

There are some people I would like to thank individually: Professor S.P. Sathe for his intellectual rigour; Ripin Kalra for his witty illustrations; Madhu Mehra, M.P. Raju and Deepa Rathore for their collaboration. Many others have provided invaluable support throughout my research: Dr. Y.P. Chhibbar, Veronique Dupont, Asish Gupta, Vivek Pandit and Rukmini Sekhar. The hospitality and warmth extended to me has been remarkable, in particular by Dr. and Mrs Chawla who provided me with a home for many months, Vandana Chawla, Mr. R. Indusekhar, Mrs. Indira Ramanathan, Achyut Yagnik and by many members of my extended family.

Usha Ramanathan and S. Muralidhar have inspired my continuing interest in law. They have been lively friends and thorough critics. My research has been enriched by their support and strengthened by Murali's contributions. In writing the appendix on filing a petition, in co-writing the glossary, and in writing the epilogue, he has brought with him insight gained from years of legal practice.

Several librarians have helped me to locate material: in England at the British Library of Political and Economic Science, the British Library, Cambridge University and the School of Oriental and African Studies: in Delhi at the Hindustan Times, the Indian Law Institute and Teen Murti House; and throughout India, including the Indian Law

College in Pune and the National Law School of India University in Bangalore.

This case book emerged out of research at the School of Oriental and African Studies and at the London School of Economics and Political Science. Professor Tom Nossiter, Peter Muchlinski and Dr Werner Menski encouraged me throughout my work. Essential support for the book came from the Ford Foundation in New Delhi, through program officer Maja Daruwala who recognized the need for this documentation, and earlier through the Economic and Social Research Council in Britain.

Closer home, Jan's unqualified encouragement has helped me through endless days of writing and revising. Finally many, many thanks to my parents, Drs R.K. and S.K. Ahuja, and my brother, for their generosity and patience.

SANGEETA AHUJA
October 1995

# List of Abbreviations

| | |
|---|---|
| AP | Andhra Pradesh |
| AIR | All India Reporter |
| All | Allahabad |
| CA | Civil Appeal |
| CWJ | Civil Writ Jurisdiction (equivalent to a civil writ petition) |
| Cal | Calcutta |
| CILAS | Committee for the Implementation of Legal Aid Services |
| Del | Delhi |
| Gau | Gauhati/Guwahati |
| GauLR | Gauhati Law Reporter |
| GLR | Gujarat Law Reporter |
| Guj | Gujarat |
| Guw | Guwahati/Gauhati |
| HC | High Court |
| HCLAC | High Court Legal Aid Committee |
| ILR | Indian Law Reporter |
| J&K | Jammu and Kashmir |
| JT | Judgements Today |
| Ker | Kerala |
| KLJ | Karnataka Law Journal |
| KLT | Kerala Law Times |
| LA | Legal Aid |
| LAAB | Legal Aid and Advice Board |
| LAB | Legal Aid Board |
| MP | Madhya Pradesh |
| OP | Original Petition (equivalent to a writ petition) |
| Ori | Orissa |
| P&H | Punjab and Haryana |
| PIL | Public Interest Litigation |
| SLP | Special Leave Petition |
| SAL | Social Action Litigation |
| SC | Supreme Court |
| SCALE | Supreme Court Almanac |
| SCC | Supreme Court Cases |
| SCLAC | Supreme Court Legal Aid Committee |
| SCR | Supreme Court Reporter |
| SLAAB | State Legal Aid and Advice Board |
| SLR | Service Law Reporter |
| WP | Writ Petition |

## Codes

> Indicates that a judge has given an order
☆ ☆ ☆ Indicates the end of a case

The citation of each of the orders taken from SCALE gives the number of the case in ascending order in the volume, and in square brackets, for ease of reference, the page number.

# Introduction

This casebook of Indian public interest litigation (PIL) presents all the reported[1] and many unreported cases since the inception of PIL in 1979 to April 1994. Hundreds of PIL petitions have been filed throughout the country, covering a broad spectrum of issues. The anticipation with which they were filed, their number and their diversity, signalled the need for this compilation. PIL cases demonstrate the extent to which laws, and their implementation, depend upon the social, economic and political situation. The law is not autonomous. The operation of law and the legal process embody the priorities of those involved in establishing and maintaining a legal system. PIL provided a means through which the terms of legal argument were sought to be changed, by ensuring that the voice of more people was heard on the judicial forum.

Public interest litigation in the late 1970s was first envisaged by its proponents as a way of ensuring that justice was made available to those without the knowledge or resources to approach the courts, and as a forum for the resolution of issues of public importance. Many of the earliest PIL cases detailed the conditions in prisons and instances where fundamental rights had been abused. Individuals or organizations were permitted to approach the Supreme Court and

[1] All the Supreme Court orders and judgements in PIL that have been published in AIR, SCC, SCR or SCALE have been referred to, along with some JT and SLR. All the High Court orders and judgements that have been published in AIR have been referred to, together with some from State law reporters.

High Courts "in the public interest" (*pro bono publico*)[2] on behalf of those unable to do so themselves. To quote a leading judgement in 1982:

> Public interest litigation is brought before the court not for the purpose of enforcing the right of one individual against another as happens in the case of ordinary litigation, but it is intended to promote and vindicate public interest which demands that violations of constitutional or legal rights of large number of people who are poor, ignorant or in a socially or economically backward position should not go unnoticed and unredressed.[3]

Although the Fundamental Rights, applicable to every Indian citizen, could be enforced in the Supreme Court under Article 32 of the Constitution, and all other legal rights could be enforced in the High Courts under Article 226 of the Constitution, the procedures governing the use of these provisions were determined by the rules of each court and by accepted practice.[4] Acknowledging that the application of procedures was limiting access to justice, some judges began to disregard the restrictions that had become established. It was Justice V R Krishna Iyer, during his tenure as a judge of the Supreme Court, who first noticed the possibilities:

> a new class of litigation—public interest litigation—where a section or whole of the community is involved (such as consumers' organizations or NAACP—National Association for [the] Advancement of Coloured People—in America), emerges. In a developing country like ours, this pattern of public oriented litigation better fulfils the rule of law if it is to run close to the rule of life. The Bar Council clearly comes within this category of organizations when a lawyer is involved.[5]

2 A glossary of legal terms have been appended as Appendix E.

3 Justice P N Bhagwati in *People's Union for Democratic Right (PUDR) and others* AIR 1982 SC 1473 at 1476-7. See the chapter on 'Labour'

4 See Appendix A for a listing of the provisions of these articles. This casebook examines all kinds of cases, with the exception of those filed as *habeas corpus* petitions. Only those *habeas corpus* petitions which have been critical to PIL are included, as the recent history and case law on *habeas corpus* would easily fill another casebook.

5 *Bar Council of Maharashtra v M V Dabholkar* AIR 1975 SC 2092 at 2104.

He described how:

> Procedural prescriptions are handmaidens, not mistresses, of justice. Test litigation, representative actions, *pro bono publico* and like broadened forms of legal proceedings are in keeping with the current accent on justice to the common man.[6]

Certain legal developments of the 1970s fostered the growth of PIL. Legal aid was first discussed at a national level,[7] Fundamental Duties were included in the constitution,[8] and a number of enactments, like the Bonded Labour (System) Abolition Act, 1976, were passed aiming to ensure that social justice was realized. During the period of internal emergency declared by Prime Minister Indira Gandhi in 1975, the Supreme Court's function as a forum for political battles became more overt. Judicial appointments became contingent on the support of the ruling party, and the Supreme Court was unable to uphold basic civil liberties such as the right to life.[9]

By 1979, when political circumstances had changed, the Supreme Court found a new focus in prisoners' rights cases and concentrated on the procedural impediments to access to justice,[10] with the support of subsequent constitutional amendments.[11] Implicit was a

6 Justice V R Krishna Iyer in *The Mumbai Kamgar Sabha, Bombay v M/s. Abdulbhai Faizullabhai and others* AIR 1976 SC 1455 at 1458.

7 Section 304 of the Code of Criminal Procedure, 1973, mandated the provision of free legal aid, the Code of Criminal Procedure, 1908 was amended in 1976 to provide free legal services to indigent persons and Article 39A of the Constitution was inserted by the Constitution (Forty-second) Amendment Act, 1976. See 'Processual Justice to the People' Report of the Expert Committee on Legal Aid (Department of Legal Affairs, Ministry of Law, Justice and Company Affairs, Government of India, May 1973) and 'Report on National Juridicare: Equal Justice—Social Justice' (Committee on Juridicare, New Delhi, August 1977). These reports, known, respectively, as the Krishna Iyer Committee Report and the Bhagwati Committee report, were the first national studies of legal aid. Both the reports mentioned PIL.

8 See Appendix A, volume two.

9 See *Additional District Magistrate, Jabalpur v Shivakant Shukla* AIR 1976 SC 1207. When the power to suspend Article 21 of the Constitution under Emergency rule was questioned, the Supreme Court held that the petitioners did not have the standing to approach the court under Article 226 of the Constitution. This ruling denied the petitioners their right to life.

10 See the chapter on 'Prisons and State Institutions'

11 For example the Constitution (Forty-fourth Amendment) Act, 1978.

recognition that few people had the resources or knowledge to approach the courts of their own accord. An advocate was allowed to approach the Supreme Court on behalf of prisoners, and this relaxation of the rules governing *habeas corpus* petitions was soon extended to other petitions, as the courts began to allow anyone acting in the 'public interest' to petition on behalf of the disadvantaged and deprived, or to bring an issue of public importance to the Court.[12] In *Fertilizer Corporation Kamagar Union (Regd.) Sindri and others*[13] the Supreme Court held that procedures had to be relaxed to meet the ends of justice. In *People's Union for Democratic Rights* (*PUDR*) *and others*[14] the Supreme Court liberalized the procedural rule of *locus standi* to allow a petition to be filed on behalf of the workmen on the Asiad Games project. Letters were registered as writ petitions, and attempts were made to foster a more conciliatory form of justice. In *S P Gupta*[15] the Supreme Court enunciated a general need to relax procedures and in *Bandhua Mukti Morcha*[16] the importance of social action groups in furthering the cause of social justice was stressed.[17] By 1981, Justice Bhagwati articulated the basis upon which a PIL could be filed:

> where a legal wrong or a legal injury is caused to a person or to a determinate class of persons by reason of violation of any constitutional or legal right or any burden is imposed in contravention of any constitutional or legal position or without authority of law or any such legal wrong or legal injury or illegal burden is threatened and such person or determinate class of persons is by reason of poverty, helplessness or disability or socially or economically disadvantaged position, unable to approach the court for relief, any member of the

[12] See 'PIL and the Judicial Process' at the end of volume two for a detailed discussion of procedural changes.

[13] See the chapter on 'Labour'.

[14] *ibid*, for the judgement reported in AIR 1982 SC 1473.

[15] See the chapter on 'Judges, Courts, Lawyers' in volume two.

[16] See the chapter on 'Bonded Labour' for the judgement reported in AIR 1984 SC 802.

[17] This has been done in other cases, for example *Neeraja Chaudhary* in the chapter on 'Bonded Labour'.

> public can maintain an application for an appropriate direction, order or writ in the High Court under Article 226 and in case of any breach of fundamental right of such persons or determinate class of persons, in this Court under Article 32 seeking judicial redress for the legal wrong or injury caused to such person or determinate class of persons.[18]

Judges, lawyers, social activists and mediapersons formed an informal nexus, exposing injustice and petitioning the Supreme Court and High Court. It was recognized that something needed to be done, and the courts were perceived as the only alternative, the "last resort", short of extra-legal action. Groups working for civil liberties and activist organizations concerned with the working and living conditions of people with meagre resources had gained strength in opposition to authoritarian tendencies in politics. The characteristics of the Constitution promoted a belief in the law, which had never before been mobilized to secure rights to all citizens.[19]

In tandem with the growth of activist groups concerned with issues relating to the poor, investigative journalism began to expose some of the injustices that were to become the bases for many PILs. As many members of the political opposition had been imprisoned during the 1975–1977 emergency, this contributed to the focus on the penal system, which was to become one of the first major sites of struggle in PIL. Newspapers and journals published articles that were read by lawyers, judges and activists. The conception of PIL was thus dependent upon the synthesis of interest outside the courtroom, as well as within it. Whilst urging the liberalization of procedures, Justice Krishna Iyer described PIL not merely as a last resort for the disadvantaged, but as a legal mechanism to contain growing unrest:

> We have no doubt that in competition between court and streets as dispenser of justice, the rule of law must win the aggrieved

[18] Justice P N Bhagwati in S P Gupta 1981 (Supp) SCC 87 at 210.

[19] For a listing of relevant constitutional provisions, see Appendix A. A list of alternative remedies that could be used in preference to PIL can be found in Appendix B. Critiques of the Constitution do exist, but, for the purpose of this casebook it will be assumed that if constitutional goals had been realised, the aim of ensuring social justice would be nearer.

person for the law court and wean him from the lawless streets.[20]

In spite of the clarity of purpose in the early days of PIL, the diversity of cases that have been described as PIL prevents this legal phenomenon from being described in simple terms. PIL only refers to cases brought under Articles 32 and 226 of the Constitution, or appeals from judgements made under Article 226 of the Constitution in the High Court, to the Supreme Court (under Article 136 of the Constitution). The courts intended it to be a mechanism through which the grievances of those unable to participate in political administrative and legal processes could be addressed. In practice PIL has evolved beyond these parameters. Cases involving broad 'public interest' issues have come within the scope of this litigation. The huge range of issues raised and the lack of parameters defining "public interest" or "public importance" has meant that any usable definition of PIL has to refer back to the cases themselves.[21]

While seeming to differ from ordinary litigation on two fronts, the subject matter of the petition and the manner in which it is brought to court, it is the latter characteristic that is more valuable when attempting a definition. Procedural characteristics that help to identify a PIL are when any or all of the following are relaxed—*locus standi*, the method of filing the petition (for example by allowing letters as writ petitions), the stipulation that the petition must be filed without undue delay (laches), the availability of an alternative forum/remedy which must first be used, the existence of disputed questions of fact, the norm of strict pleadings and the determination of an award of costs.

It is the range of issues that has caused more concern. The term 'Public Interest Litigation' had first been used to describe a legal

[20] *Fertilizer Corporation Kamagar Union (Regd.) Sindri and others* v. *Union of India and others* AIR 1981 SC 344 at 353.

[21] Professor Sathe's preface touches upon this definitional conundrum which I have dwelt with extensively in Ahuja, Sangeeta, "Public Interest Litigation in India: a Socio-Legal Study", (PhD thesis, Department of Government and Department of Law, London School of Economics, 1995). Locating certain cases within or outside the boundaries of PIL is problematic. For example the *National Textile Workers' Union v P R Ramakrishnan* AIR 1983 SC 75, can be described as a PIL, as in Professor Sathe's preface, but has been excluded from this casebook, as it can also be described as a class action.

development in the United States. In his essay "Taking Suffering Seriously", Upendra Baxi expressed his reservations at the description of developments in India as public interest litigation:

> The issues within the sway of PIL in the United States concerned not so much state repression or government lawlessness but rather civic participation in governmental decision-making. Nor did PIL groups there focus pre-eminently on the rural poor. And, typically, PIL sought to represent "interests without groups" such as consumerism or environment.[22]

Preferring to describe this legal phenomenon as Social Action Litigation (SAL), Baxi stressed the distinct social and historical forces that determined the issues for redress in India.[23] PIL as it emerged in India was to be a mechanism for social change, a means through which the problems of the disempowered victims of endemic poverty could be resolved in the legal forum. Thus, the term SAL sought to provide a more apt description of an ideal type of PIL that was promoted by certain judges and social activists when the concept was nascent. By changing the terminology, Baxi sought to avoid the extension of this litigation, originally evolved for the disadvantaged and deprived, into a more general legal tool for all public interest issues.

The categorization which follows and the documented cases provide some justification for Baxi's anxieties. The range of concerns means that PIL has to be defined in procedural terms—a situation which contradicts the initial hope that PIL would primarily be concerned with the poor. Many judgements have been passed with the intention of providing social justice to individuals or groups, but few have been implemented. As the definition of success in a PIL petition in India has had to extend beyond Court orders, increasingly, it is in the cases which have mobilized PIL for general public interest issues that real successes have been achieved. Environment, consumer, governmental accountability and the

22 Baxi, Upendra, 'Taking Suffering Seriously: Social Action Litigation in the Supreme Court of India' in Baxi, Upendra (ed) *Law and Poverty* (N M Tripathi, Bombay, 1988), 387-415 at 389.

23 I shall use the term PIL, in preference to SAL, as it is the term in common usage both within and outside the courtroom.

conduct of examinations are examples of cases that fall within the category of civic participation rather than of issues of direct concern for "the poor". Issues that transcend political ideology, without challenging notions of development and participation, have achieved general success. Moreover, differing conceptions of the polity and of development have polarized the Court and activists. The inherent limitation of PIL is that it is itself part of the system that it seeks to question. Thus while procedures and increased access to justice were a means by which petitions could be filed, the cases themselves are better understood in the context of the following categories:

## PIL for the Marginalized/Excluded

These cases have arisen when an individual or group is pitted against the State, having been excluded from the ambit of civil and political rights, as found in the Fundamental Rights. Those disadvantaged as a direct result of executive action, or more pertinently, inaction, had, for the first time, a recourse to law. Criminal jurisprudence cases horrified the courts and judgements were given directing the State administration to act. Conditions in protective homes, hospitals and other State institutions were exposed, cases attempting to vindicate executive power and gain relief for the victims of custodial rape and those who had not received their legitimate dues (for example widowed women who had not been paid any pension) were filed.

Aside from individual exceptions, this group of cases, which formed the bulk of the petitions in the early days of PIL, have been scantily implemented as they have relied upon the offenders themselves for implementation. The horror of some of the cases has created an increased public awareness of conditions in jails and other institutions, causing some betterment in conditions and more discussion of jail reforms.

There are some striking features in the orders given in these cases. The courts have condemned the apathy of the state, but have not condemned its functionaries, and have rarely made individuals responsible for their actions. The courts have mourned the injustices meted out, for example to prisoners, by the State administration, but have not analysed the laws and procedures which are responsible for the presence of so many prisoners and detainees. Using arguments about the separation of powers the courts have not even been able meaningfully to employ Article 13 of the Constitution. By neglecting to examine the ways in which existing legislations criminalize the most disadvantaged, and the practical difficulties in using legal services, the courts have not explored areas which could have alleviated certain injustices. Hence, enactments that give the army and police wide powers and deny people's basic right of hearing have not been disputed by the courts, or have simply not been heard. In spite of these shortcomings, PIL has given prisoners an opportunity to be heard and has been instrumental in generating attention to punishments and prison conditions.

The chapters on 'Prisons and State Institutions', 'The Army', 'The Police', 'Injustices Specific to Women', and the chapter on 'Children', deal especially with this.

## PIL for the Disadvantaged and Deprived

These cases are for those people who have not secured the equality promised by the constitutional scheme. Challenging structural injustice and prejudice, these cases have a complex background and appertain to many state and private bodies. Bonded labour cases form a major portion of the PILs in this section, as do other labour and wage issues and cases relating to more distinct groups like women, scheduled castes or tribes and children. There is a greater focus on economic and social rights (than on civil and political rights), and therefore on the realization of the Directive Principles of State Policy. In tandem with this is the expansion in the courtroom or, rather, recognition on the judicial forum, of the scope of Fundamental Rights such as Article 21 of the Constitution. The right to life was no longer constructed in a narrow way, now including the right to livelihood and the right to live in a clean environment. However, as with the cases for the marginalized/excluded, implementation has been problematic.

In particular see the chapters on 'Bonded Labour', 'Children', 'Injustices Specific to Women', and the chapter on 'Urban Space'.

## PIL for Development/Resource Rights

The cases that fit into this section bring into the courtroom issues of development, environment, community rights and resource rights. Petitions complaining of environmental pollution have largely been successful in gaining the attention of the Court. Others, raising issues of economic and social policy, have received a mixed reception as at times judges have been welcoming and at other dismissive. Thus, although the suitability of using law has been questioned, it is in this category of cases that the courts' willingness to innovate can be most clearly evaluated—both in procedural and substantive terms. Property relations which had been set beyond the courts' jurisdiction by constitutional amendments are again raised, but with a different emphasis. Instead of individual rights to property, the Court has had to consider, for example, the community rights of tribal people who have been displaced by a development project. In the instances where they have been asked to assess the correctness of a development project itself, courts have been reticent, remaining within the accepted limits of judicial action and at most making a concession, for example on environmental safeguards. The famous case of pavement dwellers in Bombay sets out many of the problems in using the court to reallocate resources.[24]

The law has acted as a catalyst, conferred certain freedoms and provided an ideological framework of organization and action for those petitioning the courts. However, in dealing with the most disadvantaged in rural areas, as in the section on the disadvantaged/deprived, the Court could not provided the necessary structural changes.

The chapters on 'Environment and Resources' in volume two and 'Urban Space' focus on this.

## Where Does PIL End?

Increasingly in recent years, petitions have been filed relating to a myriad often legitimate complaints, as well as those which attempt

[24] See the chapter on 'Urban Space' for *Olga Tellis and others v Bombay Municipal Corporation.*

to appropriate PIL for corporate gain, political advantage or personal interest. The majority of the cases in this section might be described as well-intentioned but inappropriate. Since PIL is widely perceived as an easy way to focus an issue, the courts have been approached for grievances which could, and should, be addressed to other agencies. Nonetheless, many cases relating to a group or class of people, for example land allotments and pensions, would not have been possible without PIL. Procedures do exist in the civil and criminal manuals and in other provisions for the presentation of such petitions, but endemic problems of long pending cases, obstructive procedures, high costs and the lengthy process of appeals when petitioning a lower court, have made PIL into an attractive option. Recourse to PIL is a common practice for many Supreme Court and High Court lawyers. It provides the opportunity to participate in the well-being of society—and to display this participation, to vindicate causes and, for the young lawyer, valuable experience of the Court. That public interest sentiments can be misplaced is seen in the case of an advocate whose first PIL petition asked the court to direct the telephone company to prioritize the allocation of telephones to advocates as well as to medical doctors, because of the importance of the legal profession to the general public.[25] Moreover, personal grievances are often framed in terms of public importance to take advantage of the benefits of using PIL. Undoubtedly the manifold difficulties of dealing with public authorities can be frustrating, but the use of a legal tool intended as a last resort for those to whom the legal system is inaccessible should not be the first refuge for those already able to access to the courts.

Most pernicious has been the arrogation of PIL as another tool in the weaponry of corporate warfare and political manipulation. Numerous petitions have been filed with questionable motives, including one attempting to ban the Koran,[26] another to expel a minister from office (although such a petition has import for judicial review)[27] and to manipulate urban planning regulations.[28] Often hard

25 See *M Balagovindam* in the chapter on 'Consumer Issues' in volume two.

26 See *Chandanmal Chopra* in the chapter on 'Public Policy and Administration' in volume two.

27 For example, see A G Prayagi in the chapter on 'Politics and Elections' in volume two.

28 See the section on 'Land and its Use' and 'Construction' in the chapter on 'Urban Space'

to distinguish from petitions filed in the public interest, especially as lawyers themselves have been petitioning the courts, judicial vigilance has not always interceded.

In particular see the chapters on 'Public Policy and Administration', 'Politics and Elections', 'Education', 'Consumer Issues' and 'Judges, Courts and Lawyers' in volume two.

Although this categorization provides a way of understanding the PIL cases documented, none of the categories are exclusive of all the others, and many cases can only be understood in terms of two or more categories. For example, gender issues cut across all the sections outlined here. Women have suffered appalling conditions in jail, have been displaced from their homes, have been discriminated with regard to labour conditions and have been the subject of petitions seeking judicial review of legislation.

Aside from the actual procedural mechanisms and the issues raised, PIL began, in the courtroom, with much discussion of the role of the judiciary and the need for the benefits of law to accrue to those who have previously not had access to courts. The entire law of standing has been re-evaluated,[29] along with the use of the forum of the Court. In contrast to the adversarial methods employed in other forms of litigation, the courts have stressed the importance of a non-adversarial jurisprudence which would deal with cases relating to the "have-nots". Emphasis has been placed on the need for both parties of the dispute to work together in PIL, because of the particular nature of the issues coming before the Court, and the importance of legal aid. In all types of cases, the Court has appointed commissions of enquiry and has monitored its directions; lawyers too have tried to ensure that cases are kept pending so that the Court will continue to supervise the implementation of its orders. PIL has also been used by both judges and petitioners as a means of generating interest on an issue or to revive a petition. While the judgements of the Supreme Court are binding on the lower courts, the range available ensures that the High Court judge can choose between those that support and those that are critical of PIL. Moreover, the impact of PIL on the lower courts has been limited as Court procedure has not been amended and discussions on procedure have been limited to the Supreme Court and High Courts.[30]

[29] See 'PIL and the Judicial Process' at the end of volume two.

[30] PIL has had an impact on the lower courts, for example in the use of Section 91

It is not just the procedural changes initiated by PIL that have contributed to changes in the judicial process. Activism in the Court has taken on new dimensions through PIL, as judges have begun to enter realms of decision-making previously reserved for the legislative or executive branches of government. Disregarding accepted standards, some judges have acted *suo moto* and awarded compensation. A general reassertion of the integrity of the court and its essential function as an organ of the state can be witnessed in PIL actions. Parameters and functions of judicial review and judicial action have been evaluated and expanded, and the judicial process examined. In *S P Gupta*[31] and the body of cases that follow, the Supreme Court addressed the essential requirements of the judicial/democratic process, inevitably including issues of public policy. Questions of jurisdiction have been considered in cases that have raised the nature of parliamentary sovereignty. The courts have discussed the parameters of constitutional adjudication and decision making, definitions of the state, liability and torts, and the disclosure of documents in court. Political impasses have been brought to the court and while some have been resolved, others have not gained the Court's attention. By ignoring certain PIL matters the Court has left some controversial areas of policy making or executive action untouched.[32]

PIL has also provided a forum for the resolution of other issues important to the judiciary itself. Judicial appointments and transfers have been examined, judges have directed that court vacancies be filled and have determined their own conditions of service, sometimes even deciding the kind of cars they should drive. Allegations of corruption by judges have been heard, as have issues relating to the integrity of the Court in cases of contempt.[33]

The large numbers of documented PIL cases have been divided into two volumes. All the cases are discussed according to issues rather than legal doctrine or a particular time period. As issues were

of the Civil Procedure Code, 1908, as listed in Appendix B in volume two. Procedural changes initiated by PIL have also mobilised legislative changes. Appendix B lists the amendments made to existing enactments, after 1986, to introduce relaxed standing provisions.

31 See the chapter on 'Judges, Courts, Lawyers' in volume two.

32 The chapter on 'Environment and Resources' in volume two provides many such examples.

33 *ibid.* Also see the chapter on 'Public Policy and Administration' in volume two.

the initial mobilizing principle for the use of PIL, they are used as the focal point for the analysis.[34] Most of the cases through which PIL was introduced in the Supreme Court and High Courts are found in this volume. The analysis begins with the petitions filed on 'Prisons and State Institutions', the concern of the first PIL petitions heard. 'The Armed Forces' are then considered, to give an overview of issues raised and the response of the Courts to the agencies of law and order. As 'Injustices Specific to Women' were amongst the issues to gain prominence by the early 1980s, they are discussed next. An analysis of cases relating to 'Children' covers a range of issues, salient to the other chapters, and is followed by an evaluation of the litigation of 'Labour' and 'Bonded Labour'.

Focusing on issues concerning the disadvantaged/deprived and the marginalized/excluded, most of the questions central to the study of Social Action Litigation (SAL), as opposed to PIL, are raised in this volume. The cases display the concerns and the response, in the early 1980s, for social justice and for disadvantaged citizens. Some themes have emerged, and extend into volume two, as the breadth of PIL, already conspicuous, becomes even more striking. These themes include the inability of the Court to respond to many of the petitions with adequate depth, the consistent non-implementation of court orders and the continuing crisis of the legal system.[35]

Before the case chapters, both volumes begin with a guide to reading the cases. The indelible effect of PIL on the judicial process is surveyed in a conclusion, at the end of volume two. The appendices listing extracts from the Constitution of India and a glossary of legal terms which may need further explanation appear at the end of volume two. In addition to case details, there are wider political and sociological issues raised in the PIL process which are not addressed in this casebook. These will be dealt with at length in a forthcoming study of PIL.

[34] Included amongst the cases are numerous documents, including unreported court orders, which are only available in India. These can be found in Ahuja, Sangeeta (1995).

[35] See Baxi, Upendra, *The Crisis of the Indian Legal System*, (Vikas Publishing House Pvt Ltd, New Delhi, 1982).

# Reading the Cases in Volume I

CASE CHAPTERS

1. Prisons and State Institutions
2. The Police
3. The Armed Forces
4. Injustices Specific to Women
5. Children
6. Labour
7. Bonded Labour
8. Urban Space

Each chapter tells its own story as it recounts the judicial response to numerous petitions, through PIL. Each story has many strands, and so the cases on particular issues have been placed together. Conspicuous by its absence is a chapter documenting cases filed for Scheduled Castes, Scheduled Tribes and Other Backward Classes. Recognized as constituting the most disadvantaged groups of people, they are the easiest people to displace and harass. PIL seems to be tailor-made for people who have rarely been able to approach the courts themselves. There is no separate chapter because there is no one story. Lumped together under the official description "Scheduled Caste", "Scheduled Tribe" and "Other Backward

Classes", the people who constitute these groups could not be more diverse. The case chapters are riddled with case relating to tribal peoples.[1] One study of bonded labourers put the percentage from scheduled castes and tribes at 86.6 per cent. The cases relating to slum dwellers, prisoners, and those displaced by development projects, are some examples in which scheduled castes and tribes have a disproportionately high stake.[2]

While the core documents in volume one and volume two of this casebook have been taken from journals reporting Court orders,[3] other sources have been used.[4] Unreported orders and documents have been gathered, and interviews have been conducted.[5] For each documented order, many have remained undocumented, and not all the information given is up-to-date. This casebook does not document petitions in the nature of *habeas corpus*—although some have been included because of the close link between *habeas corpus* petitions and the inception of PIL.

The hundreds of PILs documented in both volumes of this casebook have been presented in a standardized format. The cases in each chapter are documented chronologically, that is in the order in which they were filed. When necessary, Supreme Court cases have been given preference over those from High Courts, and placed in alphabetical order.

[1] I use this terminology not to create the sense that all "tribal" people display identifying characteristics, but because this is the term used in many of the petitions and judgements.

[2] In addition to those documented, many other cases have been filed. For example in the Kerala High Court on behalf of people from the Kuchar community in the Kelakam-Kannur whose person and property had been attacked at the behest of local landlords, after allegations of theft of some areca nuts had been denied. Another case was filed on behalf of people from the Irula community, traditional snake catchers who extract snake venom for a serum. The petition challenged the imposition of a royalty on the income made from the serum.

[3] All the Supreme Court orders and judgements in PIL that have been published in AIR, SCC, SCR or SCALE have been referred to, along with some published in JT and SLR. All the High Court orders and judgements that have been published in AIR have been referred to, together with some from State law reporters. The Supreme Court case law is correct till April 1994.

[4] In particular, two journals have been invaluable: the *PUCL Bulletin and The Lawyers.*

[5] In Delhi, Gujarat, Madhya Pradesh, Rajasthan, Maharashtra, Karnataka, Tamil Nadu, Assam, Meghalaya, Himachal Pradesh and Kerala.

With few exceptions,[6] each documented petition has originated in the Supreme Court, having been filed under Article 32 of the Constitution, or in a High Court, where they were filed under Article 226 of the Constitution. Appeals to the Supreme Court, from orders of the High Court, filed under Article 136 of the Constitution, have also been documented. Where an order has been given by a High Court, its name has been noted at the beginning of the case details, after the petition numbers have been given. For example "W P No 100 of 1990, Karnataka" would have been filed in the Karnataka High Court in 1990. The names of the judge or judges who gave the order or have contributed to a judgement are indicated with the sign ">".

In the chapters which follow, introductory observations will be made about the kind of petitions filed, by whom, and with what results in the courtroom and at ground level. Each chapter is introduced in four sections: 'framing the issue', 'access to justice', 'the courts' response' and 'the contribution of PIL'.[7] The extent of

[6] For example see the chapter on 'Urban Space' for *Municipal Council, Ratlam* v. *Vardhichand and others* and the chapter on 'Injustices Specific to Women' in this volume for *State (Delhi Administration) v Laxaman Kumar.*

[7] With the exception of the chapter on 'Judges, Courts, Lawyers' in volume two.

judicial response to the petitions, the development of legal doctrine and the potential for increasing awareness and support for an issue or cause are indicated. The section on 'framing the issue' introduces the issues raised in the chapter. The lack of cohesion amongst those involved in PIL necessitates a discussion of the reasons for approaching the court and the constituencies in question. Even though the potential for appeal is exhausted while petitioning the Supreme Court in comparison to the layered remedies available for approach to lower courts, many petitioners prefer to directly access the apex judiciary.[8] The judges in the Supreme Court and High Court are more visible, the lawyers more committed, the procedures are less forbidding, and the judgement or order of a higher court is more high profile. Also many organizations and activists prefer not to fight their legal battles close to the site of struggle, as the nexus between those who hold and wield power can have negative effects.[9]

A fuller discussion of the methods adopted by the Court to provide the 'access to justice' discussed in each chapter, can be found in the conclusion. The section on 'the courts' response' sets out the orders given. That the administration plays a vital role in PIL is seen most clearly in the section on 'the contribution of PIL'. In spite of judiciary's efforts to sensitize the administration and legislature to numerous issues raised in PIL petitions, success in real terms has been elusive. The cases themselves form the main part of each chapter and each documented case has been summarized, emphasizing the aspects of the petition and order(s) relevant to PIL.

The chapter on 'Urban Space', and the chapters on 'Environment and Resources' and 'Consumer Issues' in vlume two are interconnected and need to be considered concurrently. The potential dichotomy between PIL and SAL (Social Action Litigation) discussed in the Introduction is encapsulated in the chapter on 'Urban Space'.

[8] For the purposes of this book, PIL refers only to those cases initiated in the Supreme or High Courts under Articles 32 or 226 of the Constitution, with few exceptions, op. cit. note 6. Although it is arguable that the use of the alternative remedies listed in Appendix B is also a form of PIL, a narrow procedural definition has been used for this documentation.

[9] See Appendix B on alternative remedies. Another forum is the National Human Rights Commission set up in 1993. This is not a viable alternative to PIL as its decisions are not binding, as the mandate of the Commission does not cover violations by the armed forces and because the Commission has been constituted of retired members of the judiciary.

CASE CHAPTER 1

# Prisons and State Institutions

## Framing the Issue

The duty of the State to ensure the well-being of those in its care is nowhere more apparent than in relation to prisons and other state institutions. Removed from the rest of society, as a punishment or for protection or care, the inmates of such institutions are dependent upon the State for all aspects of their life. It is because the State has failed to treat such people with dignity that the cases discussed in this chapter have come before the Court. The sections on prisons and prisoners, mental health and detention, hospitals and institutions for women all reveal a common concern.[1]

The first question to be raised when examining how the issues have been framed, is: who has been removed from society and why? The failure of the criminal justice system to quickly dispense justice and the questionable methods by which the mentally unstable have been committed to institutions and jails, have led to a situation where many people have been confined wrongly, without a valid reason and with little attention paid to their needs. The majority of inmates belong to economically and socially disadvantaged sections of the population, to Scheduled Castes and Scheduled Tribes, easily intimidated and harassed by officials. The second consideration is

[1] In the chapter on 'Children', the cases mentioned in the section on prisons highlight many of the issues examined in this chapter.

to examine the conditions of this confinement. Provided with few basic amenities, such as water and clothing, the inmates of State institutions have had to live in appalling conditions. Violent and corrupt, many of these institutions foster the characteristics which initially led to the confinement of an individual.

Investigative journalism was the catalyst in framing these issues. Journalists increasingly began to investigate into the conditions in jails exposing the delays in trials, torture and deprivation. These revelations were supported by a series of judgements given by the Supreme Court, mainly by Justice Krishna Iyer, in which the rights of prisoners had begun to be enunciated and criminology discussed in ways that were new to the Court. As a response to this new climate, petitions were filed by advocates and letters sent to the Court by prisoners and legal aid organizations.[2]

The legal framework governing prisons and other institutions is contained in old manuals and enactments, for example the Prisons Manual and the Jail Manual. The ethos of punishment as a deterrent, the lack of accountability of the administration and the unwillingness to provide prisoners with any facilities have been exacerbated by the overcrowding that had become endemic in jails. Moreover the prison administration, like the criminal justice system, was shown not to be functioning correctly, if at all.

It was only by the enactment of the Mental Health Act, 1987 that the Indian Lunacy Act, 1912 was superseded. Under the latter many "sane" persons were confined. The concept of a lunatic, devoid of human characteristics and to be kept away from others, resulted in the confinement of such sane persons for decades. The separate categories of criminal and non-criminal lunatics had not been based on sound criteria and the elaborate procedure for release was prolonged by a malfunctioning administration.

## Access to Justice

As prisons and prisoners were the subject of the first PIL matters, the Court can be seen taking its first tentative steps in broadening the scope of its jurisdiction and relaxing procedural barriers. Lack

2 See the chapter on 'Children', specifically the sections on prisons and on institutions.

of access to justice had been the major obstacle preventing those confined, illegally or in terrible conditions (or both), from approaching the Court. By invoking Article 39A of the Constitution and discussing the need for legal aid, the Court responded to the horrific situations brought before it. For the first time it was tacitly accepted that the Court had only concerned itself with a small proportion of the population.

The first recorded public interest litigation order in the Supreme Court came in *Hussainara Khatoon*, a *habeas corpus* case filed by an advocate on the basis of a news report. On being apprised of the facts of the case, the SC relaxed the procedural rule that a *habeas corpus* petition can only be filed with a power of attorney or by a close relative. The distinction between a letter-petition and a PIL has never been fully clarified because of the connection between *habeas corpus* petitions and PIL. The courts have always allowed letters to be sent for *habeas corpus* matters, but it is only with the advent of PIL that the letter-petition was admitted for all kinds of reliefs. The letter became the key to gaining access to the Court, and often the Court was urged to, and did, give orders covering a whole class, be they prisoners or undertrials. The first PILs were in the form of letters from convicts which departed from the standard plea in *habeas corpus* letter-petitions.[3] By appointing an advocate as *amicus curiae* and directing that legal aid be made mandatory, the Court welcomed the cases brought before it.

The common practice of filing *habeas corpus* petitions has continued, but with the exception of the initial notable cases which pioneered the way for the establishment of PIL, none have been included. The mass of litigation on *habeas corpus* matters could itself fill a whole book. In the case *In Re the Petitions of Nawal Thakur,* a convict kept in the Kulu Jail, the SC acknowledged its inability to deal with the number of complaints it received, stating that the HC should first be approached. The justiciability of the complaints was not questioned, neither was the *locus standi* of the petitioners — the Supreme Court perhaps was seeking to avoid a failure similar to that of the criminal justice system.

3 An example is the letter sent to the Bombay High Court by a convict complaining of torture and ill-treatment. In 1984 the High Court issued directives regarding the procedure for redressing the grievances of prisoners, including that the Sessions Judge was to nominate lawyers to make visits to the jails.

The *locus standi* of the petitioners in this chapter has rarely been questioned. The marked division between the academics, journalists, advocates or legal aid committees, and the inmates whose rights are in question, has meant that malafides could not be suspected. The justiciability of the issues has been clear in the light of the constitutional provisions. A remarkable difference from the rest of the cases can be seen in the issues raised in the cases filed by *Dr (Miss) E. Sharma* and the *Non Aligned Congress of Youth*, so it is unsurprising that the *locus standi* of the petitioners was questioned, and in the former case, malafides found. The Court also refused to allow third party involvement in death sentence cases (see *Simranjit Singh Mann* and *Karamjeet Singh*) but not on the ground of malafides.

Gaining access to the courts may have become easier, but an examination of the *Sheela Barse* case on non-criminal lunatics shows how access has not necessarily been quickly available. The letter which was sent to the Chief Justice of India on 27/1/89, was received by the SC PIL Cell on 16/2/89, an office note put up to Justice G L Oza on 7/4/89 following which finally on 11/4/89 it was ordered that the letter be treated as a petition. The arbitrary nature of the procedure for admitting a PIL petition is also highlighted, as Justice Oza could have refused to admit the letter as a writ petition had he chosen to take the advice offered by the Registry.

## The Court's Response

In many of these cases, the Court has proceeded without any clear framework for understanding the requirements of the case and the context of the grievance. There are only two recorded instances in which a sitting judge has visited a jail to see the conditions there. In the first, the *Sunil Batra* case[4] which was not a PIL, Justice Krishna Iyer visited Tihar Jail, Delhi and in the case filed by Smriti Acharya, two judges of the Mizoram Bench of the Guwahati HC visited the Aizwal Central Jail. Judges were thus advancing into new territory and learning which responses were more appropriate and

[4] Reported in (1978) 4 SCC 494. In this case the petitioner-prisoner complained of being kept in solitary confinement, while under sentence of death. The Court, in a detailed judgement, discussed jail conditions and the rights of prisoners.

useful in situations with which they had been unfamiliar. Many ad hoc orders were then given, unlike those given in other notable PILs. In *Anil Yadav* and *Khatri*, both on the same incidents of torture, the Court dealt with the cases separately, giving similar orders, but without linking the two.

The Court's activism in this chapter has been self-critical, both admitting and depicting the failure of the criminal justice system. By stating that speedy justice is a fundamental right, the Court acknowledged that the rights of undertrials were violated by delays and procedural difficulties.[5] Moreover the legislative framework in which the Court has had to operate has been criticized, as in *Hussainara Khatoon*. In *Sunil Batra (II)*, the Court noted the need to amend the Prisons Act and to overhaul the Prison Manual. Again in *Kishore Singh Ravinder Dev* the Court stated that the old rules governing prisons were incongruous with the Constitution. However, in *E. Chidambaram*, the Court declined to issue a direction to the State to implement the Mental Health Act, 1987, on the grounds that it was not within the powers of a court. The activism has been limited in other ways, as there is very little evidence of any action taken against prison administrators. In *Sunil Batra (II)*, *Anil Yadav* and *Khatri* the Court did acknowledge the need to punish the officials responsible for the torture, but did not record any such punishment. In the last reported order in the *Khatri* case in 1982, the Court directed that the trial of the police officials must go on speedily. There has been no subsequent reported order indicating that a trial has commenced.

There have been many developments in the law relating to prisons. The conditions of confinement of undertrial prisoners were greatly improved as the Court held that they could not be held in fetters or tortured, and bail procedures were relaxed. In *Hussainara Khatoon* the Court held that Article 21 of the Constitution incorporated the right to a speedy trial and again in this case, as in others, like *Khatri* the right to free legal aid was stressed. In judgements from the High Court the applicability of Article 23 of the Constitution to prison

[5] In addition to the cases in this chapter, many other petitions have been filed e.g. by the People's Union for Democratic Rights in the Supreme Court referring to the conditions under which 35 undertrial foreigners were confined in Tihar Jail, Delhi and by the People's Union for Civil Liberties in the J & K High Court asking for a list of detenues lodged in various jails.

labour was considered. The exploitation of prison labour was first referred to by the Supreme Court in *Sunil Batra (II)*. While in *In the matter of: Prison Reforms, Enhancement of Wages of Prisoners* and in *Gurdev Singh* the HCs of Kerala and Simla held that Article 23 of Constitution was available to prisoners, in *Poola Bhaskara Vijayakumar* the Andhra Pradesh HC held that only Article 21 of the Constitution was applicable.

The right of a prisoner to society and not to be put in solitary confinement unnecessarily was conferred by the Court in *Sunil Batra (II)*. In a detailed judgement, the Court asked district magistrates to monitor the many directions that it made, and suggested that a Central Bureau of Investigation (CBI) enquiry be instituted. Nonetheless, in cases on access to prisons the Court has not clearly conferred this as a right, stating that, as in a case filed by *Sheela Barse*, that permission must be obtained from the prison authorities under the prison regulations.[6]

In *Kadra Pahadiya* the Court ordered that the undertrials in question stand trial even though they were only aged between nine and eleven when arrested. While realizing the unsuitability of putting such persons in prison, the Court has limited its response to condemning the practice; little alternative is provided by the Court. In *Hussainara Khatoon*, the Court noted that women were held in "protective custody" in prisons. The link between the inmates of prisons and other institutions becomes apparent when examining the Court orders. In the *Sheela Barse* case on non-criminal lunatics, we see how many have been lodged in jails.

The plight of those who had been considered to be mentally ill and then declared sane, is seen in *Veena Sethi* and *Sant Bir*, when the Court noted how those represented by the petitions had been detained for years after the release order. The order given in *Veena Sethi* has been repeatedly used in other cases in this chapter. In addition, the procedure for a declaration of sanity was discussed in *Rudul Sah*. The terrible conditions in institutions for the mentally ill were chronicled by the Court in *Rakesh Chandra Narain* and

[6] Petitions have been filed in the Madras High Court challenging the refusal of the Jail Administration in the State of Tamil Nadu to provide facilities to lawyers to meet prisoners and to conduct interviews and challenging the validity of circulars issued by the Inspector-General of Police which stated that lawyers should not be allowed to interview prisoners. The High Court passed orders declaring that lawyers should be given all safeguards in conducting confidential interviews with prisoners.

similarly, with reference to a home for women, in *Upendra Baxi*. In *B.R. Kapoor* and *Rakesh Chandra Narain*, the administration of the institutions in question was taken out of the hands of the local administration as the Court reacted to the lack of response from the Delhi Administration and the State of Bihar, respectively. Moreover, in the *Sheela Barse* case on non-criminal lunatics, the Court expanded the scope of the case by impleading all states.

The petition filed by *Rudul Sah* though not a PIL even in terms of the Court's response, has been included in this chapter because of the importance it has had for PIL in general. Although the issue of compensation for violation of Article 21 of the Constitution was raised in *Anil Yadav* and *Khatri*, it was in *Rudul Sah* that compensation was first awarded for the abuse of a fundamental right. In *Paschim Banga Khet Majdoor Samity* the Court awarded compensation, while acknowledging that its order may have wide-reaching financial implications.

The cases filed by *Upendra Baxi*, *Rakesh Chandra Narain* and *Sheela Barse* on non-criminal lunatics in many ways represent an ideal-type of PIL; from their antecedents and method of gaining access, to the kinds of issues raised in that the petitioners brought issues of the disadvantaged and deprived to the Court. During the process of these cases, the Court has shown remarkable perseverance, given the unresponsiveness of the concerned authorities and the appalling abuses of rights brought to the fore. Commissions have been appointed, enquiries conducted and the cases have been monitored by the judges. This monitoring has been particularly valuable for individual institutions. In cases on mental health, such as *B. R. Kapoor* and *Rakesh Chandra Narain*, the Court suggested that the institutions in question be modelled on NIMHANS, an institution in Bangalore.

The investigation and monitoring taken on by the Court in many of the cases in this chapter have been supplemented by the affirmation of the Court's power to intervene and decide with reference to the issue before it. In *B. R. Kapoor*, four Commissions were appointed by the Court to monitor implementation. In *Siddha Raj Dhadda*, the Rajasthan HC affirmed its duty to investigate in a case, even while it could not order the government to constitute a commission of enquiry. Rules of evidence were discussed in this context, in the *Khatri* case and in *Siddha Raj Dhadda*, when the Court admitted that while newspapers may not be the most reliable form of evidence, they did indicate that things were remiss. In *Parmanand Katara*, the media was mobilized in support of the Court's orders. However, although recognizing the importance of the provision of medical treatment to all, in *Niamathulla*, the Kerala HC held that even a skinflint could afford the Rs 2 needed for a homoeopathic consultation, thus displaying a lack of sensitivity for those to whom Rs 2 is a significant proportion of their income.

## The Contribution of PIL

Violations of rights continue in jails, and a large proportion of the population is still confined in jails and other institutions under State control. The courts have given innovative decisions, which, because of the nature of the legal process, have had little lasting effect. Except in the individual instances of a home or hospital or prison having undergone some reform, the appalling conditions, pendencies in trials and confinement of the mentally ill continue. The catalytic role of the courts' orders has not been fully realized. As one petitioner noted, monitoring a case can only affect the situation in one state institution, and described the aim of the case on the Agra Protective Home, *Upendra Baxi*, as being to find model rules for the whole country:

> We were very fortunate with Agra, there has been real progress. The District Magistrate visits the Home and reports each month. I never have any regrets about the case. I do have fears, that these injustices will continue. It is not enough because it is just one home in one huge country. The rules need to be accepted state-wise, and we will argue for this in the next hearing. First let them accept it for Agra and then we will ask for U.P. and the whole of India. There shouldn't be any difficulty. The U.P. State counsel thinks it should cover the whole of U.P.

However, the case will one day be closed, and the fear remains that the situation in many of the institutions will revert to the days before Court intervention highlighted the ineffective, irresponsible and even callous administration.[7]

[7] At the request of the interviewer, confidentiality has been maintained.

Certain decisions, because of their more generalized nature as in the case of *Pt. Parmanand Katara*, have effected changes in the status of enacted law and procedure. By stating that hospitals cannot refuse to treat medico-legal cases, a new precedent has been set.[8] However, in others the Court stopped short of giving a meaningful order. An example is that the constitutional validity of the Indian Lunacy Act, 1912 was never considered. A critique of the Court's treatment of the petition filed by B. R. Kapoor noted that, in addition to not examining the validity of the 1912 Act in the context of Article 21 of the Constitution, there were many other problems. The Court orders focussed on the institution and not on the inmate, the basic reason for the filing of the petitions (the violation of fundamental rights) was obscured, and at no point in the litigation did the Court consider the rights of the mentally ill.

After the Bhagalpur blindings, brought to the Court by *Khatri and others* v. *State of Bihar and others* and *Anil Yadav and others* v. *State of Bihar and others*, the police officers concerned were arrested but those who disclosed the facts were victimized[9] and the Superintendent of the jail who admitted that the torture had been meted out, was suspended. This resistance of the administration to the problems of the underprivileged, was echoed by the Court, when in *Mathew Areeparmtil* adivasi undertrials, after being detained for many years were warned not to take the law into their own hands but rather to depend on the criminal justice system. In the absence of an effective legal system, can the Court expect law and order to be upheld? Moreover the courts have not discussed the reasons why those in prison resort to crime.

The difficulties of the petitioners cannot be underestimated. When filing the case regarding non-criminal lunatics in Aizwal Central Jail, the petitioner described how the authorities changed all the figures and details regarding the implementation of the 1987 Mental Health Act, in their documents, and threatened her with a defamation suit. One analyst of the cases filed for undertrials in Bihar noted that the official figures available for the number of such prisoners did not reveal the true situation, and that, the cases only

[8] See the chapter on 'Consumer Issues' in volume two for: *Cosmopolitan Hospital and Anr* v. *Vasantha P. Nair* [reported 1992 (3) SCALE 59 [228]].

[9] Dhagamwar, Vasudha, "Trends in Public Interest Litigation: Straws in the Wind" in, *ILS Law College, Diamond Jubilee Volume 1985, 17-25.*

related to a tiny proportion of the affected people. Again, in the cases on the Bhagalpur Blindings, the State was obdurate in its response:

> The Bihar Government adopted an attitude of obstruction if not hostility. Police and jail officials who disclosed the facts were victimized, the press was accused of sensation mongering, and told not to make the police nervous and the people insecure.

Although some exceptions do exist to the squalid and violent institutions described in the petitions, notably NIMHANS and Tihar Jail, they are not the norm. In the introduction to a casebook on prisoners' rights, the cases documented were described as merely of academic interest, or perhaps appealing to "the brooding spirit of law [and] the intelligence of a future day".[10]

## Prisons and Prisoners

### Speedy Trial

***W P No 57 of 1979***

***Hussainara Khatoon and others* v. *Home Secretary, State of Bihar***

A *habeas corpus* petition was filed under Article 32 of the Constitution by an advocate on the basis of news reports in the *Indian Express* on 8-9/2/79 describing how some undertrial prisoners had already been imprisoned for longer than the maximum sentence that could be imposed upon conviction. In some cases investigations and trials had not begun, in others there had been a lapse of several years. The petition stated that this was because of the inability of such persons to arrange for their defence and furnish their bail. The petition invoked Article 21 of the Constitution and referred to provisions of the Cr P C, 1973.

In an order D/-12/2/79 by > Justice P.N. Bhagwati, > Justice R.S.

[10] Gonsalves, Colin; Desai , Mihir and Cox, *Leading Cases on Prisoners' Rights*, (Legal Resource Centre, Bombay) at 2.

Pathak (concurring) and Justice A.D. Koshal
[reported (1980) 1 SCC 81]
Justice Bhagwati held that as a speedy trial is the essence of criminal justice, delay in a trial constitutes a denial of justice. The right to a speedy trial was held to be implicit in the broad sweep and content of Article 21 of the Constitution. The bail system was described as oppressive and discriminatory against the poor, so the Court held that the background of the accused should be examined and the lower courts should not necessarily insist on bail with sureties. All of the prisoners mentioned in newspaper articles were directed to be released on "personal recognisance bond". The Court noted that the respondent-state did not appear for the hearing and mentioned the need for a provision in the Cr P C, 1973 to ensure that trials are conducted expeditiously.

In an order D/-19/2/79 by > Justice P.N. Bhagwati and Justice R.S. Pathak
[reported (1980) 1 SCC 91]
The orders passed on 12/2/79 were reviewed and clarified, and the Court again emphasized the need for an immediate review so that the cases against the undertrials could be withdrawn. The jail authorities and Social Welfare Department were directed to make suitable arrangements for the care of women and children released on personal bond.

In an order D/-26/2/79 by > Justice P.N. Bhagwati and Justice A.P. Sen
[reported (1980) 1 SCC 93]
Referring to section 167 of the Cr P C, 1973, the Court issued directions to the sessions judges, state governments and high courts to ensure compliance with these provisions. The state government was directed to immediately release women held in "protective custody" and put them in welfare centres to be opened by the state.

In an order D/-9/3/79 by Justice P.N. Bhagwati and Justice D.A. Desai
[reported (1980) 1 SCC 98]
The Court reiterated that section 167(2) of the Cr P C, 1973 must be strictly complied with, stating that imprisonment for more than the maximum sentence possible violates Article 21 of the Constitution. It was held that the right to free legal services provided by Articles 14 and 39-A of the Constitution is implicit in Article 21 of the Constitution, as without it the procedure in the courts cannot

be said to be "reasonable, fair and just" as required by section 304 of the Cr P C, 1973. The Court recommended that the Government of India and the state governments introduce a comprehensive Legal Aid programme. It was held that the State is obliged to provide speedy trial under section 309, Cr P C, 1973. The state government was asked to provide particulars as to the number of cases where FIRs had been lodged and those cases pending investigation on 31/12/78, and also for those instances where cases had been pending for more than six months. The State was directed to give reasons for the delay. The Supreme Court Bar Association was requested to assist the Court in the final hearing fixed for 4/4/79.

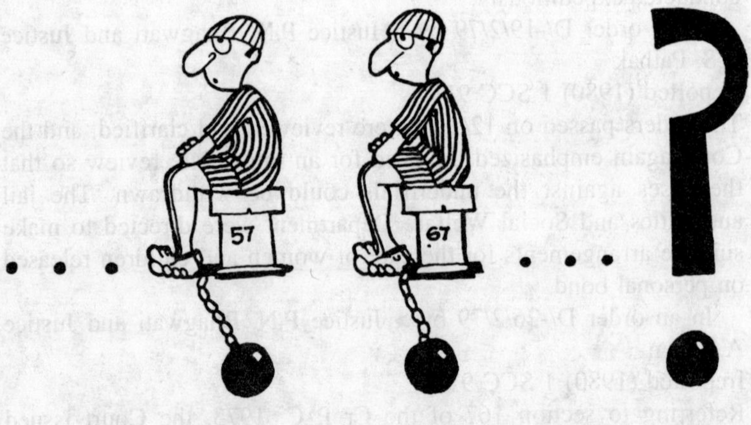


In an order D/-19/4/79 by > Justice P.N. Bhagwati, Justice O. Chinnappa Reddy and Justice A.P. Sen
[reported (1980) 1 SCC 108]
The Court held that all undertrials must be informed of their entitlement to bail and that they must be released if they had been undertrials for longer than the maximum possible sentence. The Court directed that "lunatics and persons of unsound mind must not be kept" in ordinary jails. It was held that each accused person who cannot engage a lawyer on account of poverty, indigence or incommunicado situation, has a constitutional right to free legal

services provided by the State. The Court affirmed the duty of the State to make such a provision and held that if free legal services were not provided to such an accused, the trial itself may run the risk of being vitiated as contravening Article 21 of the Constitution. The Court also considered the extent to which its earlier directions had been complied with and passed further directions. Referring to data supplied in Annexures I and II to the affidavit of B. Srinivasan, Superintendent of Police, CID, Government of Bihar, it was noted that 10,339 major offences and 17,687 minor offences were pending investigation in Bihar as on 31/12/78, of which 5,835 major offences and 7,228 minor offences had been under invesitgation for more than six months.

In an order D/-4/5/79 by Justice P.N. Bhagwati and Justice O. Chinnappa Reddy
[reported (1980) 1 SCC 115]
The Court noted that detailed provision must be made for multiple offenders and that more information from the state governments and the HCs was required. It was held that anyone charged with multiple offences who had been in prison for more than the total maximum period imposable for all the offences, was to be released. The Court stated that where the period in prison was less than the total maximum period possible but more than the maximum if the sentences were to run concurrently, such undertrials were to be released on a personal bond of Rs 50, without surety, and without verification of their financial solvency.

☆ ☆ ☆

***W P No 5943 of 1980***
***Kadra Pehadiya and others* v. *State of Bihar***

A letter was sent to the Court by Vasudha Dhagamwar, researcher and social scientist working in the Santhal Pargana region of the State of Bihar. The letter was registered as a petition under Article 32 of the Constitution. Four boys of 18 to 22 years of age were listed as petitioners. They belonged to the Paharia tribe and were lodged in Pakud sub-jail in the Santhal Parganas and allegedly being kept in leg irons. At the time of their arrest they were no more than 9 to 11 years old, but because of the delays in the Sessions Court, they had not been tried. The letter described the commencement of their trial in 1977 as merely symbolic because it was not concluded.

The petition invoked Article 21 of the Constitution and section 56 of the Prisons Act, 1894.

In an order D/-17/12/80 by > Justice P.N. Bhagwati and Justice A.P. Sen

[reported AIR 1981 SC 939]

Referring to *Sunil Batra (II)* (infra), the Court directed the removal of leg irons from the boys. Legal assistance was to be provided by the State for the continuation of the trial which the Court ordered must be done immediately. The Sessions Judge, Dumka was asked to submit a report to the Court on these cases and on the details of the number of pending cases together with details of the undertrials. The Court noted, at 940:

> These four petitioners who entered the jail as young lads of 12 or 13 have been languishing in jail for over eight years for a crime which perhaps ultimately they may not have committed.

☆ ☆ ☆

***W P (Cri) Nos 371-375 of 1983***

***Mathew Areeparmtil and others v. State of Bihar and others***

A petition was filed under Article 32 of the Constitution on behalf of undertrial adivasi prisoners. Reports and documents were submitted by the petitioners stating that large numbers of people were detained in jails for petty offences, sometimes for seven years or more, without trial.

In an order D/-20/9/84 by S. Murtaza Fazal Ali, Justice A. Varadarajan and Justice Sabyasachi Mukharji

[reported AIR 1984 SC 1854 / 1984 (2) SCALE 85 [402]]

Referring to section 169 of the Cr P C, 1973, the Court directed the release, on personal bond, of those in prison for seven or more years. It was held that section 144 of the Cr P C, 1973 should not be misused and that orders under this section should be passed in the light of principles laid down by the SC in other cases. The Court further stated, at 1855:

> At the same time, we would like to warn Adivasis accused that they should not take the law in their own hands by shooting or using their arrows on Government Officers or other forest officers. If they have any complaint they can move the appropriate authority and get suitable orders from him.

☆ ☆ ☆

***Special Civil Juris No 4 (HC) of 1990, Guwahati (Mizoram Bench)***

A *habeas corpus* petition was filed under Article 226 of the Constitution by Smriti Acharya, a social activist working in Mizoram. The petition complained of conditions in Aizwal Central Jail and the inaction of the judicial administration in Mizoram. It stated that undertrials should have their cases heard expeditiously, that facilities should be provided to the jail authorities, including an adequate number of vehicles, that compensation should be paid to undertrials under Articles 21 and 22 of the Constitution because of the delays and jail conditions, and that a Legal Aid Society be established to give legal aid and advice to the prisoners.

In an order D/-14/7/90 by Justice Y.I. Singh and Justice W.A. Shishak

The Court issued notice for the petitioner to appear in Court on 26/7/90, as neither the petitioner nor any counsel for the petitioner was present in Court in this hearing.

In an order D/-27/7/90 by Justice Y.I. Singh and Justice W.A. Shishak

The Advocate-General for the State of Mizoram was directed to file an affidavit within one week.

In a memo D/-31/7/90, the Court made two directions: that the petitioner appear before the Court on 2/8/90 and that an inspection of the Central Jail was to take place on 19/7/90 by Justice Y.I. Singh and Justice W.A. Shishak.

In the Notes of Inspection of Aizwal Central Jail on 19/7/90 by Justice Y.I. Singh and Justice W.A. Shishak:

The judges noted that the inspection was being conducted to verify the correctness of the allegations in this PIL case filed by a public spirited individual. Directions were made regarding the maintenance of history sheets of convicts, and with reference to certain convicts and undertrials. The judges stated that it was unfortunate that some of the undertrials had been in the jail since 1982, some of them even without remand orders, and held that this was not to be allowed. The judges also noted that some undertrials had been in jail for more than one year, whereas the maximum sentence they could get on conviction would be six months. Accordingly, the Court directed the Magistrate to consider releasing these undertrials on personal bonds. The judges praised the jail administration for maintaining the prison compound properly and stated that they were happy that the prisoners they met had no complaints regarding the amenities in the jail.

The petition was withdrawn at the request of the judges, who assured the petitioner that she could approach the HC again if nothing was done within one month.[11]

A letter was then sent to the SC in 1990 complaining of the conditions in the Central Jail, Aizwal, in which undertrials were lodged. The letter described the overcrowding and terrible sanitary conditions and opposed the proposal by the Government of Mizoram to convert the District jail into a drug de-addiction centre. It was contended that this jail could be used to hold the undertrials. Delays in the hearing of cases were also brought to the attention of the Court. The letter was sent with the plea that it be treated as a petition under Article 32 of the Constitution.

A reply was sent by the Deputy Registrar of the PIL Cell in the SC asking that a proper petition be filed under the Supreme Court Rules, 1966. Ms Acharya then sent another letter to the Court saying that she had no legal training and so could not file a regular petition. No response was received to this letter.

### Fetters, Handcuffs and Solitary Confinement

***W P No 1079 of 1979***
***Prem Shankar Shukla* v. *Delhi Administration***

A telegram was sent to the Court by an undertrial prisoner of Tihar jail stating that in spite of court order and directions in *Sunil Batra (I)*,[12] handcuffs were forced on him and other prisoners. The telegram was registered as a *habeas corpus* petition under Article 32 of the Constitution.

In an order D/-29/4/80 by > Justice V.R. Krishna Iyer, > Justice R.S. Pathak and Justice O. Chinnappa Reddy
[reported (1980) 3 SCC 526]
The Court noted that general advice had been issued by the Delhi Administration to the effect that ordinary Indian undertrials shall be routinely handcuffed during transit between jail and court but the

11 Smriti Acharya, Interview, Pune, 1/4/92.

12 Reported (1978) 4 SCC 494.

better class of prisoner shall be so confined only if reasonably apprehended to be violent or in need of rescue. Discussing the scope of Articles 14, 19 and 21 of the Constitution, the Court held that undertrials should only be handcuffed where there is sufficient cause to do so, and this cause shall be recorded to avoid arbitrariness, at 537-8:

> We lay down as necessarily implicit in Articles 14 and 19 that *when there is no compulsive need to fetter* a person's limbs, it is sadistic, capricious, despotic and demoralizing to humble a man by manacling him. Such arbitrary conduct surely slaps Article 14 on the face.

Noting that in an earlier order the Court held that even a detainee is entitled to minimum freedom under Article 19 of the Constitution, the Court held that no class differentia was permissible. The Court referred to sections 46 and 49 of the Cr P C, 1973, volume III of the Punjab Police Rules, 1934, chapater XXVII, rules 26.22 and 26.21-A of the Prisoners (Attendance in Courts) Act, 1955, and Article 10 of the International Covenant on Civil and Political Rights, 1966, which states that "all persons deprived of their liberty shall be treated with humanity and respect for the inherent dignity of the human person". However in the facts of the case the Court stated, at 544-5:

> In the present case it seems sufficient, in my judgement, that the question whether the petitioner should be handcuffed should be left to be dealt with, in the light of the observations made herein, by the magistrate concerned, before whom the petitioner is brought for trial in the cases instituted against him.

☆ ☆ ☆

***W P No 5287 of 1980***

***Kishore Singh Ravinder Dev etc. v. State of Rajasthan***

A telegram D/-3/10/80 was sent to the Court by a prisoner on behalf of prisoners who had been kept in solitary confinement in fetters for more than eight months.

In an order D/- 4/11/80 by > Justice V.R. Krishna Iyer and Justice

R.S. Pathak
[reported AIR 1981 SC 625]
Referring to section 46 of the Prisons Act, 1894, rules 1(f), 46 and 79 of the Rajasthan Prisons Rules and invoking Articles 14, 19 and 21 of the Constitution, the Court held that solitary confinement could only be justified in extreme cases and that the infliction of physical torture violated Article 21 of the Constitution. It was held that prison authorities must comply with the directions issued by the Court in earlier cases, and held, at 630:

> We find the old rules and circulars and instructions issued under the Prisons Act are read incongruously with the Constitution, especially Article 21 and interpretation put upon it by this Court. We, therefore, direct the State Government of Rajasthan — and, indeed, all other State Governments in the country — to convert the old rulings of this Court bearing on Prison Administration into rules and instructions forthwith so that violation of the prisoners' freedoms can be avoided and *habeas corpus* litigation may not proliferate. After all, human rights are as much cherished by the State as by the citizen.

The Court noted, at 627:

> Counsel's services under our litigative process, are a necessary facility for remedial justice and so we took this step of appointing Shri P. H. Parekh as *amicus curiae*. The whole bar, if it has a larger dedication, is *amicus curiae*, because no case should be dearer to a people-orientated, justice-centred profession, despite its esoteric genes, elitist strands and lucrative slant, than to be a decisive actor in the democracy of judicial remedies so that no man — be he poor man or prisoner, dissenter, delinquent, eccentric or extremist — shall suffer what the law forbids.

As the prisoners in question had already been released, the Court did not issue any specific orders.

☆ ☆ ☆

***W P (Cri) No 163 of 1988***
***Aeltemesh Rein v. Union of India***
A petition was filed under Article 32 of the Constitution by an

advocate stating that the government should apply the SC's judgement in *Prem Shankar Shukla* (above) regarding the handcuffing of the accused arrested under the provisions of criminal law.[13]

In an order D/-4/8/88 by > Justice E.S. Venkataramiah and Justice M.M. Dutt
[reported (1988) 4 SCC 54]
On the question of handcuffing, the Court directed the Union of India to frame rules or guidelines within three months detailing the circumstances in which handcuffing of an accused can be resorted to.

## Torture

***W P No 1009 of 1979***
***Sunil Batra (II) v. Delhi Administration***

A letter was sent to a SC judge by Sunil Batra, a prisoner in Tihar Jail, complaining that a jail warder had pierced a baton into the anus of another prisoner serving a life term in Tihar Jail in order to extract money from him. The letter was registered as a *habeas corpus* petition under Article 32 of the Constitution and the Court issued notices. An *amicus curiae* counsel was appointed who was authorized to visit the prison, meet the prisoner, see the relevant documents and interview witnesses.

In an order D/-20/12/79 by > Justice V.R. Krishna Iyer, > Justice R.S. Pathak (concurring) and Justice O. Chinnappa Reddy
[reported (1980) 3 SCC 488]
The Court described how the *amicus curiae* advocate found that the victim had been placed in a punishment cell by the jail authorities, that the Jail Hospital Register showed that the victim had developed a tear in his anus. As the bleeding from this wound could not be stopped in the jail hospital, the prisoner was moved to Irwin Hospital, Delhi. The prisoner's later narration to the doctor in the hospital corroborated the case. The Court invoked Articles 14, 19 and 21 of the Constitution and discussed provisions of the Prisons

[13] Another plea was included in the petition regarding the implementation of section 30 of the Advocates Act, 1961. This has been documented in the chapter on 'Judges, Courts and Lawyers'.

Act, 1894, the Prisoners Act, 1900, and the Punjab Prison Manual. The protection afforded by Articles 32 and 226 of the Constitution was upheld as the Court allowed a case "in the nature of" *habeas corpus* to be registered as a *habeas corpus* petition. It was held that true and legal niceties are not an impediment to entertaining even an informal communication to the Court as a writ petition. Allowing the petition, the Court issued extensive guidelines:

It was held that as Article 21 of the Constitution calls for fair procedure, there should be no deprivations visited upon a prisoner beyond the sentence of the Court, and that any inflictions on a prisoner, including that of solitary confinement, must be done under guidelines provided in the previous case filed by the same petitioner, *Sunil Batra (I)*[14] and with Articles 14, 19 and 21 of the Constitution in mind. The Court held that the separation of the sexes must be upheld and that sexual excesses and the exploitation of labour, both of which violate Article 19 of the Constitution, must be stopped, especially when extracted from adolescents. It was held that prisoners have a right to society (family etc.) and that this cannot be denied under Article 19 of the Constitution, but is subject to search and other security criteria. While describing the parole system as unsatisfactory and arbitrary, the Court decided not to explore this issue. The District Magistrate, the Sessions Judge, the HC and the SC were asked to nominate lawyers who were to be given facilities for interviews, visits and confidential communication with prisoners, subject to discipline and security considerations. The District Magistrates were directed to visit prisons in their jurisdiction, personally or through surrogates, so that prisoners could relate their legal grievances. These District Magistrates were then to make enquiries, take suitable remedial action and in appropriate cases report to the High Court so that, if necessary, *habeas corpus* action could be initiated. Grievance deposit boxes for prisoners were to be maintained by, or under the orders of, the District Magistrates and Sessions Judges and were to be opened "as frequently as deemed fit". As mandated by section 61 of the Prisoners Act, 1900, a prisoners handbook was directed to be prepared in Hindi and circulated. A wallpaper was to be put up, for the prisoners to write upon to reduce stress. The State was directed to take steps to keep up to the standard minimum rules for the treatment of prisoners as

[14] Reported in (1978) 4 SCC 494.

recommended by the UN, especially those relating to work and wages, treatment with dignity, community contact and correctional strategies. The Court noted the need for an amendment of the Prisons Act, 1894 and a total overhaul of the Prison Manual. The need for a correctional- cum-orientation course for prison staff to teach constitutional values, therapeutic approaches and tension-free management was acknowledged. The Court held that prisoners rights were to be protected by the Court in its writ jurisdiction and contempt power. Free legal aid services were ordered to be made available to prisoner programmes and the District Bar was directed to keep a cell for prisoner relief. Justice Krishna Iyer also suggested the institution of transcendental meditation courses in prisons.

Referring to the victim-prisoner in question, the Court directed the Superintendent of Tihar Jail to ensure that no more corporal punishment or physical violence was meted out to him. On the facts of the case, the Court held that it could not decide upon guilt as a criminal case was pending. However, the Court did state that it resented the attempts by the Investigating Officer to hush up the crimes committed by the jail warder and destroy primary incriminating evidence. It was suggested that a CBI enquiry be instituted and the Court criticized the hearsay affidavit filed by the Under-Secretary (Home), Delhi Administration, which shows the "affiants indifferent and omnibus approval to every official's conduct".

☆ ☆ ☆

***W P Nos 393 and 549 of 1980***
***Rakesh Kaushik* v. *B.L. Vig, Superintendent, Central Jail, New Delhi and another***

A prisoner sentenced for life wrote to Justice Krishna Iyer in September 1979 complaining of torture. The complaint was registered as a petition under Article 32 of the Constitution as a "quasi *habeas corpus* petition". The prisoner alleged that a complaint had been lodged with the Vigilance Department of the Delhi State.

In an order D/-30/4/80 by > Justice V.R. Krishna Iyer, Justice O. Chinnappa Reddy and Justice A.P. Sen
[reported AIR 1981 SC 1767]
The Court held, at 1767:

> Prison torture is not beyond the reach of this Court in its constitutional jurisdiction and so we appointed Shri Subodh Markandeya as *amicus curiae* and directed the Superintendent of the Jail to make available for him facilities to meet the prisoner Kaushik and to present, after a brief fact-finding enquiry, the facts necessary for taking further action, if any. Shri Markandeya has, with a gush of gusto, executed his work of assisting this Court and made a report, and we record our appreciation therefor. What makes law a force is a lawyer with a cause.

The District and Sessions Judge was directed to hold an open enquiry within three months on the jail premises and issue directives to the jail authorities.

☆ ☆ ☆

***W P No 5352 of 1980***

***Anil Yadav and others v. State of Bihar and others***

A petition was filed under Article 32 of the Constitution by an undertrial prisoner in Bhagalpur Central Jail, on behalf of himself and others who had been blinded while in custody. The petition invoked Articles 19 and 21 of the Constitution.

In an order D/-1/12/80 by Chief Justice Y.V. Chandrachud and Justice O. Chinnappa Reddy
[reported (1981) 1 SCC 622]
The full text of the Court's order stated:

> The report of the doctor which we had called for by our Order dated October 10, 1980 shows that eight out of the ten petitioners before us lost their eyesight totally or partially. The report submitted by Dr. K.S. Roy in each individual case shows that
>
> (i) most of the petitioners are suffering from the collapse of one or both of the eyeballs;
> (ii) the sight of one or both of their eyes is lost;
> (iii) there is perforation of the eyeballs by burn with corrosive substance; and that
> (iv) their eyes have been punctured by some sharp and pointed weapon.

The remaining two petitioners have been released and therefore no report could be sent regarding them.

The report of the doctor will shock the conscience of mankind. There has been the most flagrant violation of the safeguards provided by Articles 19 and 21 of the Constitution. There is nothing that the Court can do to restore the physical damage which seems irreparable. But the offenders must at all events be brought to book at least in the hope that such brutal atrocities do not happen again.

With that end in view, we direct that the Superintendent of the Bhagalpur Central Jail will file an affidavit in this Court within two weeks from today stating:

(a) the names of convicts and undertrial prisoners in the jail whose eyes have been damaged or impaired before or after their lodgement in the jail.

(b) the names of policemen, police officers and members of the jail staff who were in charge of those prisoners at the relevant time;

(c) the names of the doctors who were in charge of the jail dispensary or hospital at the relevant time; and

(d) the names of the doctors who have examined, from time to time, the petitioners or prisoners whose eyes have been damaged or impaired after their lodgement in jail.

We direct the Registrar of the Supreme Court and one other officer to visit the Bhagalpur Central Jail during this week and obtain first-hand the version of the petitioners or prisoners similarly situated as regards the impairment or blinding of their eyes. The two officers of the Court shall be granted every facility to meet the prisoners, to talk to them beyond the hearing of any jail officer or police officer and to record the statements of the prisoners. We direct the Jail Superintendent to ensure full compliance with these directions.

Issue notice to the State of Bihar asking it to show cause on the petition as also as to why the petitioners should not be released on their personal recognisance.

In an order D/-23/3/82 by Chief Justice Y.V. Chandrachud, Justice A. Varadarajan and Justice A.N. Sen
[reported 1982 (1) SCALE 43 [278]]
A miscellaneous petition had been filed on behalf of the petitioners

after the Superintendent of the Bhagalpur Central Jail was suspended, challenging the suspension order on the grounds that the State Government acted *malafide* and with a view to prevent him from filing an affidavit as directed by the Court. Dismissing the miscellaneous petition, the Court noted that the Superintendent had filed an affidavit after he was suspended. However, it was held that the petitioner was at liberty to challenge the order of suspension, but that the legality of the order could not be considered at this time as the Court was only asked to deal with the contention that the order of suspension was passed for that purpose. The Court noted, at 281:

> We would not normally have entertained a petition of this nature in the normal circumstances, because an order of suspension cannot be challenged in this manner in an incidental proceeding. We, however, decided to hear the miscellaneous petitions filed by the petitioner for quashing the order of suspension, since he alleged which, at first blush, seemed plausible, that he was suspended in order to defeat the order passed by this Court on December 1, 1980.

The Court also directed, at 283:

> It is desirable and proper that the State Government ought not to visit the petitioner with any penalty or punishment for approaching this Court or for having attempted to lay before this Court, what according to the petitioner, was the truth of the matter in regard to the bizarre blindings of the undertrial prisoners.

☆ ☆ ☆

***W P No 5670 etc. of 1980***
***Khatri and others v. State of Bihar and others***

Two petitions were filed under Article 32 of the Constitution on behalf of seventeen undertrial prisoners who had been blinded while in police custody in Bhagalpur Central Jail.

In an order D/-3/12/80 by > Justice P.N. Bhagwati and Justice E.S. Venkataramiah
[reported (1981) 1 SCC 623]
The Court discussed the scope of Articles 19 and 21 of the Constitution and directed the State to ensure treatment of those

undertrials who had been bailed out but not covered by an earlier order D/-1/12/80. The prisoners were directed to be treated in the Rajendra Prasad Ophthalmic Institute, New Delhi (attached to the All India Institute of Medical Sciences) at the cost of the State of Bihar. The State of Bihar was asked to give details of the arrested persons, how long they were in police custody before they were put in jail and whether any legal representation was provided to them. The State of Bihar was directed to give each blinded prisoner Rs 500 for the expenses of their journey to Delhi and Rs 300 per month as maintenance during treatment at the Institute.

In an order D/-19/12/80 by > Justice P.N. Bhagwati and Justice A.P. Sen
[reported (1981) 1 SCC 627]
In this order the Court decided to deal with the broad contentions, leaving the arguments with regard to each specific blinded prisoner to be dealt with at a later stage. Mrs Hingorani, the counsel for the blinded prisoners stated that it was not safe for those who had finished treatment to go back to Bhagalpur, so the Court ordered that they be kept in a home run by the Blind Relief Association of Delhi. The State of Bihar was directed to pay the expenses of those blinded so they could remain in Delhi temporarily. The question of the availability of compensation under Article 21 of the Constitution was also raised and the Court decided to hear arguments on this issue, to be heard at a later date. The Court noted that the records of the Judicial Magistrate showed that no legal representation had been made available to prisoners, so the right to free legal aid as a constitutional obligation was reiterated. Discussing the scope of Articles 21 and 38 of the Constitution, it was held that the right to free legal aid cannot be constrained by the plea of financial constraints by the Administration. The State of Bihar and all other states were directed to ensure that this is provided. Referring to the report received by the Court, the Registrar noted that some prisoners stated that they had never been produced before a Judicial Magistrate, and that therefore they had not been produced within 24 hours as mandated by Article 22 of the Constitution. Thus the Court noted that either the prisoners had not been brought before a Judicial Magistrate, who signed the necessary papers without seeing the accused, or that the Judicial Magistrate did not enquire about injuries inflicted. It was held that any arrested person must appear before a Magistrate within 24 hours of arrest, and an enquiry was ordered to

be held into the procedure adopted when the prisoners in question were arrested.

Eleven petitions had been sent to the District and Sessions Court by the prisoners on 30/7/80 complaining of torture and stating that they could not afford an advocate. The District and Sessions Judge in a letter D/-5/8/80 to the Superintendent of the Bhagalpur Central Jail stated that there was no provision in the Cr P C under which legal assistance could be provided, and stated that the letters had been forwarded to the Chief Judicial Magistrate for necessary action. The Chief Judicial Magistrate held that he could not do anything. The Superintendent of the Jail then sent the petitions to the Inspector-General, Prisons, Patna stating that the matter should be brought to the notice of the State Government. The Inspector-General then forwarded the petitions to the Home Department. Reflecting on these events the Court said that it failed to understand why no action had been taken, at 634:

> We should like the State Government to inform us clearly and precisely as to what steps they took after July 30, 1980 to bring the guilty to book and to stop recurrence of such atrocities. We want to have this information because we should like to satisfy ourselves whether the blindings which took place in October 1980 could have been prevented by the State Government taking appropriate steps on receipt of information in regard to the complaint of the blind prisoners from the I G Prisons. We would direct the State Government to furnish us full and detailed particulars in this behalf before the next hearing of the writ petition.

The trial of the petitioners was stayed during the pendency of the petitions.

In an order D/-14/1/81 by > Justice P.N. Bhagwati and Justice A.P. Sen
[reported (1981) 1 SCC 635]
The Court clarified that by its earlier order only the trial had been stayed and not the investigation into the blinding of the prisoners. The Court held that the investigation by the police was to continue and charge-sheets, if any, were to be filed within three months. The respondent-state was directed to take responsibility for the lodging, board and vocational training of those prisoners staying at the institute, and was ordered to provide them with warm clothing. The

State was directed to get the prisoners examined to ascertain the method and manner in which the prisoners were blinded, so that the Court could then decide if the fundamental right under Article 21 of the Constitution had been violated because the blindings were effected by the police.

In an order D/-10/3/81 by Justice P.N. Bhagwati and Justice Baharul Islam
[reported (1981) 2 SCC 493]

The Court noted that under section 3 of the Police Act, 1861 the State Government had directed a senior police officer (DIG) to investigate the blindings of prisoners. The Court then called for copies of the reports as well as correspondence, notings, etc. made by the investigating officer. The State objected on the grounds that the documents were protected under sections 162 and 172 of the Cr P C, 1973. This objection was rejected as the Court held that section 162 had been enacted for the benefit of the accused, and that the bar in section 172 is limited. It was held that the bar can have no application where a case diary is sought to be produced for use as evidence in a civil proceeding or in a proceeding under Article 32 or 226 of the Constitution, and when the case diary is not being called for by an accused to whose offence the diary relates. Referring to section 35 of the Evidence Act, 1872, the Court held that the reports submitted are relevant and should be produced. It was noted that the inquiry instituted by the Court was not to find the guilt of the officers but to see if Article 21 of the Constitution was violated and if compensation was to be paid. It was stressed that this was a civil proceeding, separate from the criminal proceeding. The Court hoped that the CBI enquiry already instituted would be conducted quickly.

In an order D/-25/11/82 by Justice P.N. Bhagwati, Justice R.S. Pathak and Justice A.N. Sen
[reported 1983 (2) SCC 266]
The Court noted that the vocational training of certain prisoners was complete, and that they were using grants from the State Government. In an order D/-31/8/82 the Court had asked the CBI to provide charts showing the progress of cases pending against the police officials. The chart showed that several cases had been delayed so the Court stated that it would wait for the trials to be completed in accordance with law before considering the question of compensation:

> when Mrs Hingorani, learned counsel appearing on behalf of the petitioners, applied to the Court for disclosure of the report of the investigation carried out by the CBI we rejected her request since we felt that disclosure of the CBI report might prejudice the fair trial of the accused.

and held that:

> The trial must go on fairly and speedily in accordance with law.

The cases continue, as seen in a magazine article in 1993:

> Four victims of the infamous Bhagalpur blindings in 1980 travelled all the way to Delhi recently seeking redressal. In an appeal to the Supreme Court, they pleaded that the goverment allowance of Rs 500 per month wasn't enough to see them through. But their lawyer, Kapila Hingorani, had bad news for them. She said the case will not be heard until 1995. Consequently even these most resolute of justice seekers are beginning to lose hope. Even after receiving training from the National Institute for the Visually Handicapped, these men have been unable to find a job.[15]

## Labour/Exploitation

***O P Nos 6566 and 7472 of 1982-S, Kerala***

***In the matter of: Prison Reforms Enhancement of Wages of Prisoners etc.***

Some letters were sent to the Court by prisoners in various jails while others, deposited in the grievance deposit boxes maintained in the jails, had been forwarded by the HC to the Government. These letters asked that the wages of prisoners be enhanced. In this case the HC responded to a request of 19 prisoners, which had been forwarded to the government with a request from the registry that they be dealt with expeditiously. They were not, so petitions were registered under Article 226 of the Constitution referring to the Kerala Prison Rules, 1958, the IPC, 1860, the Travancore-Cochin Prisons Act, 1950, the Prisons Act, 1894 as well as Articles 23(1), 39 and 43 of the Constitution.

[15] "Justice is Blind", *Sunday*, 19-25/9/93.

In an order D/-13/4/83 by > the Acting Chief Justice P. Subramonian Poti and Justice T. Chandrasekhara Menon [reported AIR 1983 Ker 261]

The Court had appointed a committee to look into these matters, to which the Government had responded by nominally revising the minimum rate of wages to 50 paise and the maximum to Rs 1.60. Another committee was then appointed by the Court, which, in its report, asked the government to adopt a reasonable wage structure. Noting that there had been many delays in the disposal of the petition, the Court decided to hear the matter fully, notwithstanding the objections of the state government, and ordered that its decision be postponed.

The different purposes of imprisonment were discussed by the Court. The advantages of giving fair wages to prisoners were listed as the imperative of imparting just and fair treatment, increasing the possibility of rehabilitation on release, ensuring that the dependants of prisoners get some of the wages, recognition of humanhood and self respect, the elimination of vengeance, the encouragement to dedication to the work done, and the elimination of exploitation by the State. The Court referred to the Universal Declaration of Human Rights, 1948, the International Covenant on Civil and Political Rights, 1966 and discussed earlier orders, especially of the SC, pertinent to the present case. The Court then held, at 272:

> If on a proper understanding of Article 23 (1) of the Constitution there is no justification to read that Article as excluding the case of a prisoner who is asked to do work on payment of illusory wages we see no compelling reason to do so. The consequence is that to deny a prisoner reasonable wages in return for his work will be to violate the mandate in Article 23 (1) of the Constitution. Consequently the State could be directed not to deny such reasonable wages to the prisoners from whom the State takes work in its prisons.

It was decided that Rs 8 per day was a reasonable wage, subject to alteration after the government conducted study, research and assessment. The Court hoped that the government would look into the matter forthwith and decide on a reasonable wage structure which the Court could not do definitively.

☆ ☆ ☆

***W P No 1822 of 1985, Andhra Pradesh***
***Poola Bhaskara Vijayakumar* v. *State of Andhra Pradesh and another***

A petition was filed under Article 226 of the Constitution by a student of Criminology who as part of his third year of a B.L. degree course had visited the Visakapatnam Central Jail on 16/2/85. In this petition he described the conditions in which the prisoners live and work and the way in which they were exploited and subjected to forced labour. As this violated Article 23 of the Constitution, the petition asked the Court for directions compelling the authorities to pay the prisoners adequate wages.

In an order D/-24/4/87 by Justice P.A. Choudary [reported AIR 1988 AP 295]

The humane heart and public spirit of the petitioner was commended by the Court which agreed to entertain the petition despite objection filed by the Advocate General as to its maintainability. The Court held that Article 23 of the Constitution was not violated as forced labour in this article connotes employment of labour productively and not as a punishment. It was held that if extracting prison work were to be held violative of Article 23 of the Constitution, a major part of prison punishment would immediately collapse. Stating that this provision was not intended to be a fundamental right directly available against the State, Article 23 of the Constitution was described as more of a prohibition directed against the social practices of one member of the society against another rather than a prohibition against the state. However, the Court held that prisoners should be paid for their labour by the State because of the scope of Article 21 of the Constitution and that these rights and duties could only be taken away by legislation. The petition was allowed as it was held that the wages paid were inadequate. The State Government was ordered to constitute a committee to consider the various aspects of the issue and fix a scale of wages payable to the prisoners which would be fair and considerate to them and not unfair to the rest of society.

☆ ☆ ☆

***Cri W P Nos 6 and 49 of 1985, Simla***
***Gurdev Singh and others* v. *State of Himachal Pradesh and others***

Letters sent to the Court by prisoners were registered as petitions under Article 226 of the Constitution. The prisoners claimed that they were not being paid the minimum wages for their work, that there were many irregularities in the prison and that jail conditions were deplorable.

In an order D/-14/3/91 by > Justice Bhawani Singh and Justice Devinder Gupta
[reported AIR 1992 HP 76]
The Court had appointed an *amicus curiae* for the petitioners, who invoked the Prisons Act, 1894, the IPC, 1860, the Minimum Wages Act, 1948, together with Articles 21, 23 and 43 of the Constitution. The Court held that the State Government should undertake comprehensive jail reforms within a year by appointing a high powered committee comprising men from the jail administration, social workersand criminologists to advise the State Government in this field. The Court itself appointed a committee to look into the averments in the letters as well as to look into the possibilities of starting open air institutions with agriculture, provision of adequate work and different jail/correctional institutions for young prisoners, special treatment of hardened criminals, opèning more open air jails including one for women, education and vocational training for prisoners, liberal remissions and regular paroles, greater opportunities to meet friends and near relatives away from policeman's gaze, proper attention for health and entertainment facilities, procurement of work and living wages, better diet facilities, comprehensive management of wage funds and the provision for after-release guidance and help. The Court stated that a prisoner who has committed an offence is not to be condemned outright, and that crime is a kind of disease which has to be cured like other diseases by various methods so that the criminal is usefully cultivated for the society. It was held:

> Renumeration, which is not less than the minimum wages, has to be paid to anyone who has been asked to provide labour or service by the State. The payment has to be equivalent to the services rendered, otherwise it would be *forced labour* within the meaning of Article 23 of the Constitution. There is no difference between a prisoner serving a sentence inside prison walls and a free man in society. Although on account of incarceration, a prisoner may lose enjoyment of some of the rights, but there is no total extinction by reason of the jail sentence. Section 53 of the Indian Penal Code may provide for assignment of work in cases of rigorous imprisonment,

> however it does not say that the labour provided by such a prisoner has to be free. Again, it does not envisage subjecting the prisoner(s) to obnoxious, harsh, uncalled for duties which are *ex facie* condemnable.

Referring to allotment of work to prisoners sentenced to rigorous imprisonment under the Prisons Act, the Court stated that subjecting prisoners, sentenced to rigorous imprisonment, to hard work and providing work to others is not at all bad, but stressed the need to keep in view their will, physical strength and the uppermost obligation to make payment for the work done by them. The Court held that there could be no distinction between the work inside the prison and outside it, and that similarly, there could be no distinction between open and closed prisons. The petitions were allowed and the Court directed that prisoners be paid minimum wages.

## Conditions

A letter was sent to the Chief Justice of the HC of Karnataka in 1988 by undertrial prisoners lodged in the Central and some district prisons in Karnataka complaining that when they were taken to courts, prisoners were not given enough money for food. On 3/6/88 the letter was registered as a writ petition under Article 226 of the Constitution and the government was ordered to take notice and file its objections. As there was no response from the State Government, the Court ordered that in such matters of public interest litigation involving personal liberty, the State should not be callous and indifferent. A Committee was then appointed to investigate the complaint and submit a report within four weeks.[16]

☆☆☆

A letter was sent to the Deputy Registrar of the Patna HC at Ranchi in 1988 by Mr A.K. Chakraborty, General Secretary of the Public Interest Litigation & Legal Aid Service Society, Ranchi. Mr Chakraborty had been sent to jail on a three-month sentence for

16 "News: Karnataka: Conditions of Prisoners", *PUCL Bulletin*, Vol 8, No. 9, September 1988, 31.

contempt of court on April 1, 1988 and was there for eleven days before being bailed out. The letter asked for the appointment of a committee to go into the deplorable conditions in the Ranchi Central Jail where he had been held. The letter stated that while the jail capacity was for 325 prisoners, it contained over 1100 prisoners. It was contended that there were only 12 wards for all the inmates, seventy unflushed lavatories with no provision for flushing, that prisoners were forced to survive on a very poor diet and that no medication was provided for patients with leprosy and TB. The letter told the Court that literate prisoners were being paid Rs 100 per month to teach other prisoners, an amount much less than the minimum wage and that prisoners employed as sweepers were also not being paid minimum wages. Female prisoners were allegedly being kept within the main jail. The letter noted that some lawyers would regularly visit the Jail office to collect clients, through the jail officials, in the name of a "Free Legal Service". Apparently these lawyers were cheating the relatives of the accused persons in the name of fighting their cases in the law courts for bail.[17]

☆ ☆ ☆

***Crl M C No 179 of 1989, Kerala***
***In Re: A Prisoner***

A letter was sent to the Court by a prisoner in Thiruvananthapuram Central Jail and registered as a petition under Article 226 of the Constitution. The letter detailed the inhuman conditions in this and other prisons which apparently have a trigger effect on crime and vice.

The Court ordered a team of advocates to visit various prisons and rehabilitation centres and report to the Court.

A report was submitted by advocate James Vincent on 25/3/93. The report noted that urgent orders were required to be made with regard to the establishments listed in the report, including: directions for the provision of an adequate water supply, pest control, fixing of sewers and leaking roofs, and supply of mats and sheets to the prisoners. Suggestions and recommendations were made in the report with regard to the workforce, victim compensation, women prisoners, education and recreation, rehabilitation, police

[17] Chakraborty, A.K., "Conditions in Ranchi Central Jail", *PUCL Bulletin*, Vol. 8, No. 8, August 1988, 6-8.

harassment, water shortage, medical care, parole, sheets and mats, food, shaving, lights and fans, mosquito and bug control, overcrowding, classification and segregation, repairs and maintenance, sewage handling, trees and the environment, audit, sentencing, prisoners' appeals and law officers, prison administration and staff, complaints against lawyers, cruelty and assault and with regard to dangerous criminals. It was also suggested that a public defender organization be established.

In an order D/-31/5/93 by Justice Sankaran Nair
[reported 1993 (2) KLT 10]
The Court discussed the past cases on the issue and the need for it to act. Directions were made relating to the prisons, conditions, pay, appointments of prison staff and the establishment of a fund for victim care. The State was asked to consider shorter prison terms where possible. The directions were not time bound. Allowing the petition the Court directed that expenses of Rs 4,000 be given to James Vincent, the advocate, who had appeared for the prisoner.

☆ ☆ ☆

A petition was filed under Article 226 of the Constitution in 1991 in the J & K High Court by the PUCL, Srinagar, asking that a team of doctors and lawyers be allowed to go around the various jails to survey the conditions of the detenues.

In an order D/-3/10/91
The Court ordered the Additional Chief Secretary (Home) to make available a list of injured and ailing detenues to the petitioners and to allow a doctors' team to examine them and to recommend necessary treatment. It was held that this arrangement should take care of the mutual convenience of parties and meet the interests of justice.[18]

**Forum**

***In Re the Petitions of Nawal Thakur, a convict kept in the Kulu Jail***

In an order by Vacation Judge E.S. Venkataramiah
[reported (1984) 3 SCC 572]

[18] Imroze, Parvez, "Srinagar PUCL", *PUCL Bulletin*, Vol. 11, No. 12 December 1991, 16-17 at 17.

The full text of the Court order stated, at 572-573:

> This Court has been receiving a large number of letters, telegrams etc. from persons residing in different parts of the country seeking relief regarding many matters. It may not be possible for this Court to take action on every one of them. Many times the parties may not be able to come to this Court from distant places to prosecute the cases. In some cases the High Courts having jurisdiction may be able to deal with the matters more effectively as courts of the first instance than this Court. Hence, I feel that it is desirable that in all such cases where it is not possible for this Court itself to take action and it is felt that the High Court can deal with them effectively, this Court should forward the letter, telegram, etc. to the High Court having jurisdiction over the matters with a request to the High Court to take needful action on them as if they had been sent to the High Court at first instance and to give adequate relief to the concerned parties. In all such cases, the High Court to which the document is sent, may, if it is found necessary, call upon the person who has sent it to appear before it, ascertain necessary further facts from him and proceed to dispose of the matter in accordance with the law.
>
> This Court shall assign a number to each of such documents sent to the High Court and retain a true copy or a photostat copy of the document on its file for reference.
>
> In accordance with the above procedure, the two accompanying petitions of Nawal Thakur, a convict who is kept in the Kulu Jail are forwarded to the High Court of Himachal Pradesh, Simla for disposal in accordance with the law.

## Access to Prisons

***W P (Cri) Nos 1053-1054 of 1982***

***Sheela Barse* v. *State of Maharashtra***

A letter was sent to the Court by a journalist and social activist, which was registered as a petition under Article 32 of the Constitution. The letter complained of the custodial violence inflicted upon women while they are confined in the police lock-up in the city of Bombay. The petitioner had interviewed fifteen women prisoners between 11-17/5/82, of whom five had been assaulted by the police and two were assaulted and tortured. The petition invoked Articles 14, 21 and 39A of the Constitution together with section 41 of the Cr P C, 1973.

In an order D/-15/2/83 by > Justice P.N. Bhagwati, Justice R.S. Pathak and Justice A.N. Sen
[reported (1983) 2 SCC 96]
The Court directed that Dr (Miss) A.R. Desai, Director of the College of Social Work, Nirmala Niketan visit the Bombay Central Jail to interview women prisoners and submit a report to the Court, stating at 99:

> We are not concerned here directly with the conditions prevailing in the Bombay Central Jail or other jails in the State of Maharashtra because the primary question which is raised in the letter of the petitioner relates to the safety and security of women prisoners in police lock-up and their protection against torture and ill treatment. But even so we would strongly recommend to the Inspector-General of Prisons, Maharashtra that he may have a look at this report … and consider what further steps are necessary to be taken in order to improve conditions in the Bombay Central Jail and other jails in the State of Maharashtra and to make life for the women prisoners more easily bearable by them. There is only one matter about which we would like to give directions in this writ petition and that is in regard to the need to provide legal assistance not only to women prisoners but to all prisoners lodged in jails in the State of Maharashtra.

The Court issued directions and guidelines to the State of Maharashtra regarding the persons in lockups and directed the Maharashtra SLAAB to instruct the District LACs to nominate lawyers practising in the District Court to visit jail(s) once a fortnight to ensure implementation of the Court's orders.

An application was filed by the petitioner who had been unable to interview prisoners. She had been granted permission orally but then refused on the grounds that she was not attached to any respectable newspaper. The application also challenged certain prison regulations.

In an order D/-18/9/87 by > Justice Ranganath Misra and Justice

M.M. Dutt
[reported (1987) 4 SCC 373]
Referring to its earlier orders in other petitions, the Court noted, at 381:

> We have already pointed out that the citizen does not have any right either under Article 19(1)(a) or 21 to enter into the jails for collection of information but in order that the guarantee of the Fundamental Right under Article 21 may be available to the citizens detained in jails, it becomes necessary to permit the citizens access to information as also interviews with prisoners. Interviews become necessary as otherwise correct information may not be collected but such access has got to be controlled and regulated.

It was held, at 382:

> The petitioner is free to make an application to the prescribed authority for the requisite permission and as and when such application is made, keeping the guidelines above, such request may be dealt with. There will be no order for costs.

## Sentencing, Detention, Parole

***W P (Cri) No 755 of 1990***
***R.M. Tewari* v. *Home Secretary, State of U.P. and others***
A petition was filed under Article 32 of the Constitution demanding premature release of life convicts who had been sentenced prior to 18/12/78 when section 433A was introduced into the Cr P C, 1973 and for the premature release of those who were convicted after 18/12/78. Section 433A states that life convicts shall not be released unless fourteen years of imprisonment has been completed.

In an order D/-14/2/91 by Justice A.M. Ahmadi, Justice V. Ramaswami and Justice M. Fathima Beevi
[reported 1991 (1) SCALE 71 [249]]
Noting that the petition was in the nature of a PIL, the Court held that those prisoners listed in the annexures to the petition, who have served ten actual years or fourteen years with remissions, shall be considered for premature release within six months. It was also held that those convicted after 18/12/78 would be considered for release according to the provisions of the U.P. Prisoner Release on

Probation Act, 1938 and the Jail Manual within nine months of this order. However, those considered and rejected after 1/1/89 were to wait for the stipulated time before their sentences were reviewed and the Court held that those whose cases were considered prior to 31/12/88 should be govered by this direction.

Disposing of the petition, the Court stated, at 250:

> If the State Government fails to comply with this direction it will be open to the petitioner to seek appropriate orders from this Court as and when required.

☆ ☆ ☆

***W P (Cri) No 536 of 1992***

***Simranjit Singh Mann* v. *Union of India and another***

A petition was filed under Article 32 of the Constitution by the President of the Akali Dal(M), an acknowledged political leader vitally interested in upholding the rule of law and ensuring that it is applied with fairness, equity and good conscience to all. The petition challenged the death penalty sentence for the murder of General Vaidya and the sentence of ten years rigorous imprisonment for injury to his wife Bhanumati, contending that the affirmation of the death sentence by the Court was technically illegal and that the trial violated Articles 14, 21 and 22 of the Constitution. The petition referred to sections 120B, 212, 302, 307, 465, 468 and 471 of the IPC, sections 3 and 4 of the Terrorist and Disruptive Activities (Prevention) Act, 1985, and section 10 of the Passports Act, 1967.

In an order D/-16/9/92 by > Justice A.M. Ahmadi and Justice K. Ramaswamy
[reported 1992 (2) SCALE 102 [506]]
The Court postulated a preliminary question for consideration, at 507:

> Does a petitioner—third party who is a total stranger to the prosecution culminating in the conviction of the accused—have any *locus standi* to challenge the conviction and the sentence awarded to the convicts in a petition brought under Article 32 of the Constitution?

The Court first put this question aside, at 508:

> Before we proceed to deal with this petition we must refer to the fact that this very petitioner had addressed a letter dated 1st February, 1990 to the Hon'ble Chief Justice of India requesting that he may be heard on the propriety, validity and constitutionality of the trial as well as the sentence imposed on the two convicts which was awaiting confirmation by this Court. Mr R.S. Sodhi, the present counsel for the petitioner, was appointed *amicus curiae* at State expense to argue and assist the Court. However, at the hearing of the State's appeal as well as the death reference, no submission was made by Mr Sodhi on the petitioner's application dated 1st February, 1990. If that had been done, the need for this petition could have been obviated.

On these grounds, the Court denied standing to the petitioner, at 508-509:

> The two convicts could, if so minded, have raised the contention in the earlier proceedings but a third party, a total stranger to the trial commenced against the two convicts, cannot be permitted to question the correctness of the conviction recorded against them. If that were permitted, any and every person could challenge convictions recorded day in and day out by the courts even if the persons convicted do not desire to do so and are inclined to acquiesce in the decision. ... Unless an aggrieved party is under some disability recognized by law, it would be unsafe and hazardous to allow any third party to question the decision against him.

☆ ☆ ☆

***W P (Cri) No 585 of 1992***
***Karamjeet Singh* v. *Union of India***

A petition was filed under Article 32 of the Constitution by a friend of convicts Sukhdev Singh and Harjinder Singh (Sukha and Jinda) who had been sentenced to death. The petitioner claimed standing on the ground that the three had participated together in a *kar sewa* (offering of labour in worship) for restoration of the Harminder Sahib in the Golden Temple, Amritsar. The petition referred to the Cr P C, 1973 and the IPC, 1860.

In an order D/-8/10/92 by Justice A.M. Ahmadi and Justice

K. Ramaswamy
[reported JT 1992 (5) SC 598]
The Court noted that the convicts had given oral and written instructions that none or their relations should file mercy petitions for them, so the petition filed on behalf of the convicts was strongly opposed by the Additional Solicitor General on behalf of the respondent. The question of *locus standi* was raised, and the Court stated, at 599:

> neither the provisions of the Code of Criminal Procedure, 1973 nor any other statute permitted a third party stranger to question the correctness of the conviction and the sentence imposed by the Court after a regular trial.

The claim advanced that the two convicts were under a legal disability due to their intense obsession that the person who was responsible for desecrating the Harminder Sahib cannot be allowed to and has no right to live, being guilty of such a high act of sacrilege against divinity, was not allowed by the Court. The Court said that any legal disability must be legally recognized under Cr P C, 1973. As the petitioner did not have standing the petition was summarily rejected.[19]

A magazine article discussed this order:

> On 9 October at 4 a.m., Sukinder Singh alias Sukha and Harjinder Singh alias Jinda were hanged to death at Pune Central Jail for the murder of the former Chief of Army Staff, General Arun Kumar Vaidya. On 30 January 1986, General Vaidya was shot dead by Sukha and Jinda. They were arrested on 7 September 1986 and their trial concluded in September 1989. Sukha and Jinda were sentenced to death. On 8 October 1992, Justices A.M. Ahmadi and K. Ramaswamy of the Supreme Court dismissed three petitions seeking stay of the execution on the ground that the petitioners had no *locus standi* following which Sukha and Jinda were hanged.
>
> While the murder of General Vaidya was undoubtedly a cowardly act that should have been punished, a fundamental question raised by the Court's judgement remains. The

[19] The sentence of the Court was passed in the case *State of Maharashtra* (1992) 3 SCC 700.

> Supreme Court has still not decided the question of the constitutional validity of TADA, nor is it making any effort to do so, although Sukha and Jinda were arrested and initially charged under TADA. Tomorrow, if TADA is struck down, how can the earlier wrong be corrected?[20]

And another article noted:

> Members of the Sikh Panthic groups also forwarded a petition to M.H. Kania, the Chief Justice of India. They contended that the death sentence had been confirmed although the Court had not determined the constitutional validity of TADA, under which the two were initially charged and held. Despite their efforts, Sukha and Jinda were hanged.[21]

☆ ☆ ☆

***Cri Misc Case No 1475 of 1992, Kerala***
***V.J. Jayakumar Abraham* v. *State of Kerala and others***

A petition was filed under Article 226 of the Constitution by advocate James Vincent in the name of one of his junior colleagues. The petition challenged the legality of a provision in the Kerala Prison Rules, 1958 that permitted the government to grant parole to prisoners indiscriminately. It was contended that officers had been receiving bribes from, and then granting parole to, wealthy citizens or those with political influence. The petition referred to many newspaper reports giving examples of this abuse of the prison rules.

In an order issued by Justice Shankaran Nair in 1993 the rule was struck down.

## Mental Health and Detention

***W P (Cri) No 1378 of 1982***
***Rudul Sah* v. *State of Bihar***

A *habeas corpus* petition was filed under Article 32 of the Constitution by a man who had been illegally detained in prison for

20 "Newsfile: Hanged", *The Lawyers*, Vol. 7, No. 11, November 1992, 29.

21 "Crime and Punishment", *The Lawyers*, Vol. 7, No. 12, December 1992, 26.

fourteen years after his acquittal in the competent trial court. The petition claimed that he should be awarded compensation because of this violation of Article 21 of the Constitution, in addition to rehabilitation, and reimbursement of expenses that he may incur for medical treatment.

In an order D/-1/8/83 by > Chief Justice Y.V. Chandrachud, Justice A.N. Sen and Justice Ranganath Misra
[reported AIR 1983 SC 1086]
Referring to its past order, the Court stated, at 1087:

> If past experience is any guide, no useful purpose is likely to be served by adjourning the petition in the hope that the State authorities will place before us satisfactory material to explain the continued detention of the petitioner in jail after his acquittal.

It was contended by the respondents that the petitioner was insane at the time of the acquittal order, which is why he was detained further. The Court noted that the criteria upon which he was defined as insane had not been given, that no medical opinion had been produced and that if he was insane then his trial would have been invalid, at 1088:

> We are inclined to believe that the story of the petitioner's insanity is an afterthought and is exaggerated out of proportion. ... the Jailor has been made a scapegoat to own up vicariously the dereliction of duty on the part of the higher officers who ought to have known better. ... The Bhagalpur blindings should have opened the eyes of the Prison Administration. ... We hope (and pray) that the higher officials of the State will find time to devote their personal attention to the breakdown of the Prison Administration in the State and rectify the grave injustice which is being perpetrated on helpless persons. The High Court of Patna should itself examine this matter and call for statistical data from the Home Department of the Government of Bihar on the question of unlawful detention in the State jails.

It was held that the HC could then release those who had been unlawfully detained. Discussing the claim for compensation, the Court noted, at 1089:

> We have no doubt that if the petitioner files a suit for damages for his illegal detention a decree for damages would have to be passed in that suit ... In these circumstances, the refusal of this Court to pass an order of compensation in favour of the petitioner will be doing mere lip-service to his fundamental right to liberty which the State Government has so grossly violated. ... The right to compensation is some palliative for the unlawful acts of instrumentalities which act in the name of public interest and which present for their protection the powers of the State as a shield.

The Court ordered the State of Bihar to pay Rs 30,000 as an interim payment, on the basis that this would prevent Article 21 of the Constitution and other fundamental rights from being rendered meaningless. This sum was awarded in addition to the Rs 5,000 already paid by the state as exemplary costs. The Court stated that its award would not prevent the petitioner from bringing a suit for damages against the state and erring officials.

☆ ☆ ☆

***W P (Cri) No 73 of 1982***
***Veena Sethi v. State of Bihar and others***

A letter sent to Justice Bhagwati by the Free Legal Aid Committee, Hazaribagh, Bihar on the basis of an article in the *Indian Express* on 17/12/81, was registered as a petition under Article 32 of the Constitution. The letter contended that mentally ill patients, many of whom had been declared sane, had been in jail for 20 to 30 years.

In an order D/-11/5/82 by Justice P.N. Bhagwati and Justice D.A. Desai
[reported (1982) 2 SCC 583]
In a detailed order, the Court examined each case, with "horror and amazement". When it found that the allegations were true for many of the prisoners, it stated, at 590:

> One day the cry and despair of large numbers of people like Bhondua Kurmi will shake the very foundations of the society and imperil the entire democratic structure of our polity and if that happens, we shall only have ourselves to blame.

The Court gave specific directions with regard to the patients, ordering that some be released from jail and given travelling expenses and maintenance for one week. Those of unsound mind were to be put in special institutions, and the Court noted, at 585:

> We would like to take this opportunity of impressing upon the State Government that in a large State like the State of Bihar, there must be an adequate number of institutions for looking after the mentally sick and the practice of sending persons [who are] lunatics or persons of unsound mind to the jail for safe custody is not at all a healthy or desirable practice, because jail is hardly a place for treating those who are mentally sick.

The Superintendent of the Hazaribagh Central Jail was directed to have the prisoners examined by a psychiatric specialist every six months and to submit a report of the examination to the District Judge, Hazaribagh, who was to order the release of those declared sane. The Court also directed that the case under section 309 of the IPC, 1860 against one prisoner who had attempted to commit suicide be quashed, as he had been imprisoned for 37 years, having been sentenced for only three. No orders were given in the cases of those prisoners whose sentences were yet to expire. The question of the right to compensation under Article 21 of the Constitution raised in the Court was to be considered at the following hearing of the petition.

☆ ☆ ☆

***W P (Cri) No 1052 of 1982***
***Sant Bir* v. *State of Bihar***

A petition was filed under Article 32 of the Constitution by the Free Legal Aid Committee, Hazaribagh, Bihar on behalf of a prisoner in a jail in Bihar who had been sentenced to life imprisonment on 28/2/49, defined as mentally unstable. In 1966 he was found to be normal, but no action was taken for his release for sixteen years. The petition invoked Article 21 of the Constitution and referred to section 302 of the IPC, 1860.

In an order D/-24/8/82 by > Justice P.N. Bhagwati and Justice A.N. Sen
[reported 1982 (1) SCALE 144 [668]]
The Court directed that the prisoner in question be released and sent

home with money for the journey and maintenance for one week. The Court noted that legal aid could not reach everyone despite rendering yeoman service in the field of legal services for the poor. The State Government was therefore directed to file a statement before the Court containing the names and particulars of all those who have been detained as criminal lunatics inspite of having been categorized as fit for discharge, as well as an annual census of undertrial prisoners. The Court decided that it would consider the question of compensation under Article 21 of the Constitution at the next hearing of the petition.

☆ ☆ ☆

***W P (Cri) Nos 1777-78 of 1983***
***B.R. Kapoor and others v. Union of India and others***

A petition was filed under Article 32 of the Constitution by a member of the PUCL together with a member of the Union Welfare for Human Rights, regarding the mismanagement of the Hospital for Mental Diseases at Shahdara (Delhi). An inmate of the hospital had given birth on 22/10/81 in the hospital itself and another inmate had committed suicide on 10/8/83. The PUCL had then sent a team to the hospital, which found that fundamental rights were being violated. It was then that this petition was filed.

In an order D/-28/9/84 by Justice D.A. Desai and Justice Ranganath Misra

In an earlier order, D/-27/2/84, the Court had appointed an Enquiry Committee consisting of four psychiatrists, to ascertain the prevailing ecological atmosphere in the home and to submit a detailed report to the Court. In the present order, directions were made in this regard.

In an order D/-29/4/87 by Chief Justice, P.N. Bhagwati and Justice Ranganath Misra

The Court directed that the three-volume enquiry report submitted by a committee of experts constituted by the Court should be examined urgently by the Delhi Administration and that recommendations should be made to rectify the defects in the management of the hospital. The Court asked for a report on the CBI enquiry into specific inmates.

In an order D/-9/5/89 by Justice Ranganath Misra and Justice M.N. Venkatachaliah
[reported AIR 1990 SC 752]

The Court noted that the 35 suggestions of ways in which the running of the Home could be improved, submitted by the committee of experts, had not been acted upon by the Delhi Administration. Accordingly, the Union of India was ordered to take over the running of the hospital because of the delay by the Delhi Administration. As suggested by the committee, the Hospital was to be modelled on the institution run by NIMHANS at Bangalore.

☆ ☆ ☆

***W P No 1537 of 1984, Bombay***
***S.P. Sathe v. State of Maharashtra***

A petition was filed under Article 226 of the Constitution on 3/4/84 by a law professor in Pune on behalf of the undertrial victims of torture by the Yervada Central Jail Authorities, Pune. Information had been received from advocate Ajay Adhiya that undertrial prisoners were being subjected to electric shocks as treatment for being of unsound mind. The advocate had made enquiries but was unable to gain access to the jail. An earlier request made by the Legal Aid Centre of ILS Law College in Pune for permission to visit the jail and meet the prisoners had been turned down by the jail authorities, sô a petition was filed asking for the Court to enquire into the matter. The petition invoked sections 14, 37, 38 and 59 of the Prisons Act, 1894, and asked that a commission be appointed to inspect the hospital for evidence and submit a report.

In an order D/-5/4/84 by Justice Dharmadhikari and Justice Kamath

The Court issued notice on the petition. As the respondents denied the allegations of torture, the Court advised the petitioner to ask the District LAC to ascertain if the allegations were true.

The HC disposed of the petition by giving certain final directions at the admissions stage. It was held that reports were to be made whenever a prisoner was to be given electric shocks by a prison psychiatrist. The Court clarified that its directions were tentative and did not preclude the appropriate authority from framing the necessary statutory rules to deal with the contingencies discussed. No commission was appointed by the Court.

The petitioner later expressed his hope that the goverment and the Indian Medical Council would make rules to deal with such circumstances and noted:

> Since the above decision was reported in the press, we have been getting letters from prisoners complaining about harassment and illegal behaviour by the jail authorities. The Law College Legal Aid Centre has its own limitations and we might not be able to attend to many of them, but should our legal aid committee not examine them?[22]

☆ ☆ ☆

***W P (C) No 339 of 1986***
***Rakesh Chandra Narain v. State of Bihar***

A letter was sent to the Chief Justice of the Supreme Court by two people living in Patna. The letter detailed the substandard conditions in the Mansik Arogyashala, a mental hospital at Kanke, near Ranchi, Bihar. The letter invoked Article 21 of the Constitution and was based on newspaper reports which had exposed the appalling conditions in the hospital. It therefore asked the Court to direct an improvement in these conditions. The letter was registered as a petition under Article 32 of the Constitution.

In an order D/-11/8/86

The Court noted that the report of the Chief Judicial Magistrate, asked for by the Court, showed that the home and its inmates were in a terrible condition. Accordingly the Court observed:

> The report makes a painful reading and shows how badly this institution is managed and in what inhuman conditions the patients are made to live and work. It is surprising that the State of Bihar has allowed this situation to degenerate into the present condition. It is necessary that immediate steps be taken to improve the functioning of this institution in all respects. We would therefore direct the Chief Secretary and Health Secretary to the Government of Bihar to file an affidavit or affidavits putting forth a definite scheme for improving the working of the institution and for remedying the drawbacks and deficiencies pointed out in the report, including the neglect

22 Sathe, S.P., "Electric Shocks to Prisoners", *EPW* Vol. 19, No. 35, 15/9/84, 1612-1613 at 1613.

> of patients by the Medical Superintendent attached to the institution. This matter must have urgent priority since it concerns the well-being of the mentally handicapped. We would therefore direct that the affidavit be filed within three weeks from today setting out a time-bound programme for improving the functioning of the institution. We would like to observe that the Chief Judicial Magistrate has done an excellent job of the task assigned to him and we express our sense of appreciation for the work done by him. These observations may be sent to the High Court of Patna and the Chief Judicial Magistrate.

In an order D/-20/10/86 by Justice V. Balakrishna Eradi and Justice G.L. Oza
[reported 1986 (Supp) SCC 576]
The Court directed that conditions be improved and ordered that the provisions provided to the patients be bettered, together with an increase in the patients' diet allocation, a supply of an adequate quantity of pure drinking water, restoration of sanitary conditions in lavatories and bathrooms, provision of mattresses, blankets and cots, and removal of the ceiling limit on the cost of medications. The State Government was ordered to take steps to appoint a qualified psychiatrist and Medical Superintendent for the hospital. The Chief Judicial Magistrate was directed to visit the hospital every three weeks to monitor the implementation of the orders and submit quarterly reports to the Court. The counsel for the State of Bihar complained that the States of Orissa and West Bengal were not paying their share of the costs for running the hospital, which had inmates from all three States. Accordingly the SC ordered that these payments be made.

In an order D/-27/9/88 by > Justice Ranganath Misra and Justice M.N. Venkatachaliah
[reported AIR 1989 SC 348]
The Court referred to a number of earlier orders and the suggestion that Mansik Arogyashala should be developed along the lines of NIMHANS, Bangalore. On 14/3/88, the Court had directed the Chief Secretary to file a report. This report had been belatedly received and the Court noted that a detailed scheme had been established regarding sanitary conditions, electricity and medical care, at 354:

> We do not find that the report of the Chief Secretary covers all aspects. … From his report, however, it is clear that in spite of several orders made by this Court and assurances held out by the State Government of Bihar, the defects were not remedied. Awareness of the governmental authorities of the sordid situation prevailing in the hospital, as admitted in the scheme furnished to this Court, the non-compliance in an effective way with the directions made from time to time by this Court and the general lethargy shown in rising from slumber leaves a clear impression in our mind that the institution cannot be run as a mental hospital of that magnitude unless there be a change in the administrative setup, the method of control is altered and a totally new service with a patient oriented thrust given to the institution.

Describing the scheme as half-hearted, only attending to certain obvious deficiencies and shortfalls, the Court noted that it did not touch on a scheme for reorientation, except to say that NIMHANS has been contacted, at 354-5:

> There does not seem to be the slightest interest on the part of the persons handling the matter to improve the environment. In these circumstances, it becomes difficult for the Court with any sense of confidence to leave the management to the Health Department of the State of Bihar if the institution is to be run as a good and useful hospital.
>
> We are cognisant of the position that it is difficult for the Court to monitor the management of a hospital — particularly when it is located a thousand kilometres away; but since there have been some improvements with the Court's intervention, to get out of the picture at this stage would only mean that the situation will again deteriorate as soon as the Court's attention is withdrawn.

A Committee of Management was appointed with full powers to look after all aspects of the institution, with a sitting Judge of the Patna HC, Ranchi Bench, to be nominated by the Chief Justice of the Patna HC, as its chairman and nine other officer-members. The Court stated, at 355:

> We hope and expect that the concerned governments and

authorities would accord the necessary consent/permission to the nominated officers to act on the Committee.

The Committee was instructed to meet once every month in the first six months and then quarterly if the improvements were satisfactory. The Commissioner of the Ranchi Division, a committee member, was directed to submit a report to the Registry of the Court each month. The Committee was also instructed to deal with the finances of the home, for example the claim that the State of West Bengal is in arrears, and directions were made about the provision of funds by the Bihar Government. The Court held, at 365:

> We are of the view that if the hospital is transformed into a better one, just as the hospital run by NIMHANS at Bangalore, the quality of the hospital would improve and the patients would have the benefit of modern scientific treatment. The Committee shall, therefore, take expeditious steps to explore the possibility of transforming the Mental Hospital at Ranchi into the pattern obtaining in the Hospital run by NIMHANS at Bangalore by taking such steps as are necessary and furnish a report to this Court by the end of February, 1989 when this question will have to be considered by this Court after hearing the concerned State Governments and the parties.

Referring to allegations that cured women patients had not been released, the Court noted the need for a rehabilitation centre and asked the Committee to take steps for its establishment.

In an order D/-4/10/93 by Chief Justice M.N. Venkatachaliah, Justice S. Mohan and Justice A.S. Anand
[reported 1993 (4) SCALE 103 [509]]
The Court noted that the report D/-23/8/93 by Justice Satyeshwar Roy, Chairman of Ranchi Manshik Arogyashala made sad reading. The report stated, at 510:

> From about March of this year all development work in the hospital has stopped as the Union is not allowing any work to be done. By spending rupees fifty lakhs, a water supply system has been constructed; due to non-availability of electricity, it could not be made operational. For supply of electricity, an electric sub-station within the hospital campus is to be constructed. This work was taken up by the Bihar State Electricity Board (BSEB), but work has stopped because of

> inaction due to alleged lack of funds on the part of the BSEB...
>
> The Deputy Commissioner, Ranchi, who is a member of the Committee, does not take any interest. The Divisional Commissioner, who is also a member of the Committee, could not solve the dispute within the Union. The Committee cannot take any action against the employees or against any erring officer of any agency e.g. BSEB, PHED, PWD etc. No action can be taken against an erring officer of the District administration, if he does not comply with the decision of the committee. I, as Chairman of the Committee, am a helpless spectator. The Union is annoyed with me as I did not agree to release any money from the development fund for meeting its demand so far [as] quarters are concerned or any other demand which has financial implication.

In an earlier order the Court had requested Justice Roy to continue as chairman of the committee after his retirement. Noting the burden of the post, the Court recorded its appreciation of the services rendered, asked him to continue as a member of the committee, and directed the Chief Justice of the Patna HC to take over as chairman for three months to set the current situation right. Thereafter the Chief Justice was directed to appoint another sitting Judge as chairman. The report of the committee was to be sent to the Court by end-November 1993.

☆ ☆ ☆

### *C W P No 1733 of 1986*

### *E. Chidamabaram* v. *State of Bihar*

A letter was sent to the Chief Justice of India on 19/7/86 enclosing a news clipping which reported that, over a period of five years, the eyes of about 800 inmates of Ranchi Mental Home had been gouged out by employees of the home and sold. The letter was treated as a petition under Article 32 of the Constitution and was heard with the case of *Rakesh Chandra Narain* (supra).

In an order D/-21/4/92 by Justice A.M. Ahmadi and Justice K. Jayachandra Reddy

In an earlier order D/-9/10/90 the Court had appointed a team of eye specialists to visit the Home and make a report to the Court on the allegations. The State of Bihar was directed to pay Rs 10,000 for the expenses of the specialists. The report, submitted on 15/11/91, found:

> no pattern suggestive of removal of eyes from the dead bodies or from the living inmates for the purposes of corneal grafting.

Examining individual allegations, the Committee concluded that Shri Subodh Singh had injured his eyes in a scuffle with another inmate Shri Hirendra Prasad, both of whom were described as excitable, schizophrenic inmates of the Home. The Report did make some recommendations about the running of the home. Mr Venkataramani, the counsel appointed to assist this Court, asked the Court for directions about the running of the home and for a show cause notice to be issued to the Union of India as to why the 1987 Mental Health Act has not yet been brought into force, as the reliefs prayed for had reference to section 81 of this Act.

Dismissing the petition, the Court held that it failed on the facts of the case and because the running of the home had been dealt with in *Rakesh Chandra Narain* (supra). The Court refused to direct the Union of India to show cause why the provisions of the Mental Health Act had not been brought into force, holding that such a direction is not within the jurisdiction of the Court. Another plea was made by the advocate for the petitioners that action be taken against the employees of the home for their negligence in not taking care to avoid a scuffle of this type. The Court held that the scope of the writ petition does not warrant such a direction and that action of this nature could only be taken by the State authorities.

☆ ☆ ☆

***O P No 7588 of 1986, Kerala***

***People's Council for Social Justice and others* v. *State of Kerala***

A petition was filed under Article 226 of the Constitution by an organization in Ernakulam regarding conditions in mental hospitals in Trivandrum, Trichur and Calicut.

The HC appointed a commission which submitted "The Report of Enquiry into the working of Mental Hospitals in Kerala" by V Krishnamoorthy, former Health Secretary, Government of Kerala. A number of improvements were ordered, and the hospitals in question were ordered to be restructured and upgraded. These improvements were not carried out as the State pleaded financial problems. A contempt petition was then filed for implementation.

☆ ☆ ☆

***W P (Cri) No 237 of 1989***
***Sheela Barse* v. *Union of India and another***

A letter was sent to the Court by a journalist and social activist based on an article she had written entitled "Jailing the mentally ill". In this she described the situation of many children and adults who were committed to jail in Calcutta as lunatics. She contended that most were not mentally ill at all, that some were normal, some were under stress or in a period of mental disturbance and very few were actually retarded. The letter described how when produced before a Judicial or Executive Magistrate in West Bengal, an instant assessment is made of the mental health of the inmates and they are committed to jail under the pretext that they are interned for treatment and classified as "Non-criminal lunatics" (NCL). She noted that at the time of committal, the next date of hearing is not fixed, nor the time limit of detention. The lack of health facilities in the jail were described, together with the apathy of the State Government. The letter referred to the Mental Health Act, 1987, the Mental Health Authority Rules, 1990 and the Indian Lunacy Act, 1912, and stated that by invoking section 13 of the 1912 Act, which has been repealed, the magistrates are arrogating to themselves a power which they do not have. The letter was registered as a writ petition under Article 32 of the Constitution.

The letter was sent to the Chief Justice of India on 27/1/89. It was received by the SC PIL·Cell on 16/2/89.

An office note D/-7/4/89 from the Joint Registrar of the Supreme Court was put up before Justice G. L. Oza, the judge appointed to scrutinize letter petitions, for directions as to whether the letter should be registered as a writ petition. The office note stated that Sheela Barse had approached the Acting Chief Justice and two other judges of the Calcutta High Court but they were unwilling to take *suo moto* notice. She then drafted a letter petition and handed it over to the Socio-Legal Aid Research and Training Centre, Calcutta but the Director of the Institute did not pursue the matter. As a last resort she wrote to the SC for help for the mentally ill and sane women locked up in the Presidency Jail, Calcutta. The office note asked for directions from

Justice Oza as to how the letter should be treated: whether it should be forwarded to the Supreme Court Legal Aid Committee for filing a proper petition; whether the papers should be forwarded to the Registrar of the Calcutta High Court; whether the petitioner may be asked to file a proper petition in accordance with the Rules if so advised, in view of her past conduct in W P No 1541 of 1985, a PIL matter.[23] The note suggested that the matter be sent to the Calcutta High Court.

The note was seen by Justice G. L. Oza on 11/4/89 and he directed that the matter be listed in the SC. Accordingly, the letter was registered as a writ petition under Article 32 of the Constitution.

In an order D/-13/3/90 by Justice M.N. Venkatachaliah, Justice N. D. Ojha and Justice J. S. Verma

The Court issued notice to the State of West Bengal asking it to file an affidavit replying to the contents of the petition, the written submission and the following questions put by the Court: details of jails/institutions where mentally ill were being kept; details of inmates; details of procedure and practice adopted for the admission/release of inmates; details of care/treatment facilities provided; details of medical examinations; details of staff and their qualifications; details of procedure for follow-up action if any; details of any social workers or organizations or other agencies associated with this exercise. The Court also asked what had been done in respect of the guidelines issued in *Veena Sethi* (supra) for the care of the mentally ill, and requested the Union of India to file an affidavit on the implementation of the Mental Health Act, 1987.

In an order D/-16/8/90 by Justice M. N. Venkatachaliah and Justice M. M. Punchhi

The Court stated that it did not appreciate the delay in the filing of an affidavit by the State of West Bengal and gave two weeks more for it to be filed. The matter was to be called on 30/5/90.

A counter-affidavit was filed by the State of West Bengal on 5/10/90. During the case the Union of India did not file a counter-affidavit.

An application for directions D/-9/5/92 was filed by advocate S. Muralidhar on behalf of the SCLAC. The application referred to newspaper reports in the *Times of India* and *The Hindu* D/-25/12/91 about nineteen NCL prisoners who died in the Dum Dum Central

23 See the chapter on 'Children' for Sheela Barse.

Jail in Calcutta "because of total collapse of medical treatment in the Jail". A news report in the *Times of India* on 26/3/92 was also referred to, which detailed the writ petition filed in the Bombay High Court by Mr Aldrick Wilfred D'Souza who inspite of being certified fit for discharge in April 1980 from Thane Mental Hospital, Maharashtra, by a Board of Visitors, was still being detained there. Also included in the application was another news report from *India Today* on 15/5/92 by Ramesh Vinayak entitled "Undertrials: Trapped in Limbo" on the appalling conditions in which the inmates of the government-run Dr Vidya Sagar Mental Hospital in Amritsar were forced to live. The application used these examples to demonstrate that the problem of violation of basic human rights of the criminal and non-criminal lunatics in jails and hospitals exists in more than one state in India. The State of Punjab was impleaded as a party to the petition.

In an order D/-13/5/92 by Justice M.N. Venkatachaliah and Justice R. C. Patnaik

The matter was directed to be listed in the second week of June.

In an order D/-16/6/92 by Justice M. N. Venkatachaliah (Vacation Judge)

The Court acknowledged receipt of the counter-affidavit of the State of West Bengal 25/5/90, and noted:

> That affidavit is conspicuous by the lack of relevant and full particulars required to be furnished.

The Court also recorded the fact that in the last two hearings the State of West Bengal had failed to appear. Two commissioners were appointed by the Court: Dr R. Srinivasa Murthy, Professor and Head, Department of Psychiatry, National Institute of Mental Health and Neuro Sciences (NIMHANS), Bangalore and Ms Amita Dhanda of the Indian Law Institute. The Commissioners were directed to submit a detailed report on: the number of institutions/jails in West Bengal; the number of mentally ill inmates at these places together with their classification and period of stay; the procedure and practice for release and the authorities concerned; care/treatment facilities; a district-wise study of mental health facilities (from Primary Health Centres to Private Hospitals); procedure and practice of medical examination at the time of admission and thereafter; pattern of staff, with qualifications and suitability for nature of work; follow up action (if any); care and rehabilitation facilities; social workers or organizations or other outside agency involved with this exercise; the steps taken to implement guidelines ordered by the Court in *Veena Sethi* (supra). The Commissioners were asked to provide complete information on the death of the 19 prisoners in the Dum Dum Jail, and to draft guidelines on: the procedure of commitment to institutions, and the minimum care and treatment facilities that should be available. The Commissioners were to indicate the most appropriate monitoring mechanism. The State of West Bengal was directed to facilitate compliance with this order and to deposit Rs 20,000 in the SC Registry for expenses of the commission.

In an order D/-15/7/92 by Justice M. N. Venkatachaliah and Justice N. P. Singh
The State of West Bengal was again directed to deposit the money in the Registry and the Commissioners were asked to submit an interim report to the Court. The Union of India was asked to file its affidavit, as was the State of Punjab — the latter with special reference to the conditions within Dr Vidya Sagar Mental Hospital, Amritsar.

In an order D/-5/2/93 by Justice M. N. Venkatachaliah and Justice G. N. Ray
The Court stated:

> The Commissioners have submitted the report. We place on record our appreciation of the work done by the Commissioners. The report will be of much assistance to the Court in the matter. The State of West Bengal is directed to pay the balance of Rs 11,286 to the Commissioners towards expenditure.

In an order D/-5/5/93 by the Chief Justice M. N. Venkatachaliah and Justice S. Mohan
The Court noted that the arguments had been heard but reserved orders.

In an order D/-17/8/93 by Chief Justice M.N. Venkatachaliah and > Justice S. Mohan
[reported (1993) 4 SCC 204]
The Court noted that in its counter-affidavit, the State of West Bengal stated that the jails in the state only receive prisoners on the authority of a warrant or other document issued under seal by a competent court. The affidavit claimed that facilities are provided to

these inmates. In a counter-affidavit from the Union of India it was clarified that the 1987 Act had been notified on 22/5/87 and the 1990 rules notified on 29/12/90, and that the 1912 Act had indeed been overridden. The Court referred to the report of the commission which stated that there was a delay in specialist help reaching the patient, a lack of specialized human resources, a of supervision and care, the absence of a health team, and variety of treatment facilities necessary for health care, and of an excessive deprivation of liberty. The Commissioners, Dr Murthy and Ms Dhanda, suggested improvement schemes for mental hospitals and the composition of their managing bodies. On the basis of this report the Court issued certain directions. These directions were a reproduction of the draft order that had been framed by the *amicus curiae*, S. Muralidhar, as requested by the Court:

1) It is declared that admission of non-criminal mentally ill persons to jails is illegal and unconstitutional.

2) It is directed that admissions of mentally ill persons to jails in West Bengal on any ground whatsoever be stopped forthwith and that the State of West Bengal issue instructions to this effect immediately.

3) It is directed that the function of getting mentally ill persons examined and sent to places of safe custody hitherto performed by the Executive Magistrate shall hereafter be performed only by Judicial Magistrates.

4) The Judicial Magistrates will, upon a mentally ill person being produced, have him or her examined by a Mental Health Professional/Psychiatrist and if advised by such MHP/Psychiatrist send the mentally ill person to the nearest place of treatment and care.

5) The Judicial Magistrate will send reports every quarter to the High Court, stating the number of cases of persons sought to be screened and sent to places of safe custody and action taken by the Judicial Magistrate thereon.

6) The Government of West Bengal is hereby directed to:

(i) take immediate action and issue instructions for implementation of the directions given herein above.

(ii) order inquiry into the death of 19 persons in the Dum Dum Central Jail in December, 1991 and take action to rectify the factors that resulted in such a calamity. A copy of the enquiry report and details of the steps taken thereon should be placed before the court within a period of two months from today.

(iii) take simultaneous immediate steps for:

(a) immediate upgradation of mental hospitals.

(b) setting up psychiatric services in all teaching and district hospitals. This will include filling the posts of psychiatrists in these places.

(c) integrating mental health care with the primary health care system.

(iv) regulate the admission-to-discharge procedure, from the mental hospitals in West Bengal, of mentally ill persons by issuing a fresh set of instructions in accordance with the recommendations made in the report of the Commissioners...

(v) send a quarterly report to this Court through the Health Secretary on the steps taken to implement each of the directions given in this order. This will be in the form of an affidavit.

Any difficulty encountered in the implementation of the order will be forthwith brought to the notice of this Court.

7) The High Court of Judicature at Calcutta is requested to appoint a committee consisting of a mental health professional/psychiatrist, a social worker and a law person to evaluate the state of the existing mentally ill in jails. The Committee will in a report make detailed recommendations to:

(i) discharge such of those persons found fit and ensure their return to their homes and/or their rehabilitation.

(ii) move such of those persons requiring continued treatment and care out of the jails, to the nearest places of treatment and care.

The report will be submitted within two months of its appointment by the Committee to the High Court with a copy to this Court. The High Court is requested to monitor, in such a manner as it deems fit, the implementation of the recommendations of the Committee. This Court will be kept informed of the steps taken in this regard.

The Court went on to expand the scope of the case, at 213:

Though the report of the Commission relates only to the State of West Bengal in order that these recommendations are properly implemented in other States as well, it is hereby directed:

1) Notice shall be sent to the Chief Secretary of every State together with —

(a) a copy of the order dated June 16, 1992 passed by this Court,

(b) a copy of the report submitted by the Commissioners (Volume I).

2) The Chief Secretary is hereby directed to indicate to the Standing Counsel of the State in the Supreme Court:

(a) the facts and figures in respect of every item mentioned in the order dated June 16, 1992 of this Court.

(b) the response of the State Government to the recommendations and plan of action suggested in the report of the Commissioners. and

(c) the willingness of the State Government in taking action in line with the recommendations made by the Commissioners in their report.

3) The Chief Secretary shall respond to this notice wihin a period of three months and this time-limit will be adhered to strictly.

In addition to the service of notice to the Chief Secretary, notice will also be served upon the Standing Counsel of the State to ensure strict compliance with this order.

## Hospitals

***W P (Cri) No 58 of 1982***

***Free Legal Aid Committee, Jamshedpur* v. *Mahatama Gandhi Memorial Medical College Hospital, Sakchi, Jamshedpur***

A petition was filed under Article 32 of the Constitution complaining of conditions in this medical college hospital in Bihar.

In an order D/-4/5/87 by Justice O. Chinnappa Reddy and Justice K. Jagannatha Shetty

[reported 1987 (1) SCALE 327 [1321]]

The Court noted that in an earlier order D/-12/1/87, the District Judge, Jamshedpur, submitted a report which described the deplorable conditions in the hospital. Detailing these conditions and the lack of facilities and staff, the Court held, at 1322:

> Having regard to the sad state of affairs in the hospital, we think that it is absolutely necessary that we should issue some directions if the dignity of the individual mentioned in the preamble to the Constitution, the right to life guaranteed by Article 21 of the Constitution, the duty of the State under Article 41 to make effective provision for securing public assistance in cases of sickness and disablement and the further primary duty of the State under Article 47 to raise the level of nutrition, the standard of living of the people and improvement of public health are to have any meaning.

The State of Bihar was directed to submit a report within three months specifying the modalities of a comprehensive scheme for improvement of the hospital and services rendered to the patients of the hospital.

☆ ☆ ☆

***Cri W P No 270 of 1988***

***Pt. Parmanand Katara v. Union of India and others***

A petition was filed under Article 32 of the Constitution by a human rights activist, referring to a report written by him that appeared in the *Hindustan Times* entitled "Law helps the injured to die". A man died after an accident having been refused treatment from a hospital which was not permitted to treat medico-legal cases. Invoking Article 21 of the Constitution, the petition contended that instant treatment should be available for the injured and that in the event that it is not, compensation should be paid.

In an order D/-28/8/89 by > Justice Ranganath Misra and > Justice G.L. Oza

[reported AIR 1989 SC 2039]

Referring to section 33(m) of the Medical Council Act, 1956, and clauses 10 and 13 of the Code of Medical Ethics, the Court held that it is the duty of doctors to treat the injured. It was also held that everyone should receive treatment in such cases and that zonal regulations could not be an excuse for refusal of treatment. The Court directed that its order be published in all Court journals and be given publicity in the national media, including Doordarshan and

All India Radio. Copies of the order were to be sent to all HCs, medical colleges and State Governments.

☆ ☆ ☆

***C W P No 1938 of 1988, Rajasthan***
***Siddha Raj Dhadda* v. *State of Rajasthan***

A petition was filed under Article 226 of the Constitution by a freedom fighter with a long association with the Sarvodaya Movement and claiming to believe in the philosophy of Mahatma Gandhi. The petition referred to newspaper items which had revealed the malfunctioning of the SMS Hospital Jaipur and other government hospitals in Rajasthan. The Court was asked to appoint a commission to inquire into deaths and other incidents in these hospitals, and to find out who was to be held responsible. The petition invoked Article 27 of the Constitution.

In an order D/-2/6/89 by > Justice M.B. Sharma and Justice I.S. Israni
[reported AIR 1990 Raj 34]
The HC referred to an earlier decision of the SC (*Manmohan Kalia v. Shri Yash and others* AIR 1984 SC 1161) in which the SC had held that newspaper clippings may not be a reliable source of evidence. Accordingly, the HC stated, at 39:

> what appears in the newspaper clippings filed on behalf of the petitioner as also on behalf of the State, may or may not be correct, may even be exaggerated, but we are satisfied that all is not well, and the health of SMS Hospital and other hospitals is not sound and even the State Government has appointed inquiry committees to go into the incident of P.N. Pareekh, death of Kamle Nawalkha as well as the alleged malpractice in the purchase of medicines and other equipments in the hospitals.

Referring to the request for the appointment of a commission and to section 3 of the Commissions of Inquiry Act, 1952, the Court stated that it is discretionary upon the appropriate government to set up a commission under the Act and it can only be mandatory to set up a commission if a resolution is passed by the Lok Sabha, or by the legislature of a state. Accordingly, it was held that the Court cannot issue a direction to the State Government. However, it was held that Court did have the power to appoint a commission to make inquiries, collect data and submit a report to the Court, which should then be made available to both the parties. The Court stated:

> Once a matter of public importance like the one in the instant case namely, relating to conditions in the govenment run hospitals where crores of rupees of public funds are involved and to the treatment made available to the poor and downtrodden weaker sections of society who by and large come to the hospital, comes before the Court it becomes the duty of the Court to appoint the commissioner/commissioners to go into the matter and submit their report with remedial measures which are required. The Court cannot then be a silent spectator and should, rather must, intervene. The mere fact that the Government agrees to the appointment of a committee or has made an administrative order in that direction will not make the petition filed before the Court infructuous.

A commission was appointed with two doctors and an advocate.

☆ ☆ ☆

***C R No 735 of 1989, Guwahati***

***E. Sharma* v. *State of Assam and others***

A petition was filed under Article 226 of the Constitution asking for the seizure of all books of accounts of the Assam Branch of the Red Cross Society and a direction from the Court that the Society open for new membership and call an annual general meeting. The petition alleged mismanagement of the Red Cross Society Hospital and asked the Court to appoint a committee to enquire into all the accounts of the Hospital for the last few years.

In an order D/-27/8/91 by Justice S. Haque and > Justice J.M. Srivastava

[reported AIR 1992 Gau 58]

The Court noted that the petitioner was a former doctor of the Red Cross who resigned on 12/5/89 and filed a petition on 23/5/89. The respondents alleged that the petition was filed without any real motive, to which the Court responded, at 63:

> We are inclined to think that it cannot be said that the petitioner has no motive to file this petition, for it could be

> just to embarrass the respondents. It is true that the institution in question is a public institution but just because the petition has been filed in this regard the petition does not necessarily become a public interest petition, particularly, when there is a background of some differences between the petitioner and the respondents and the petitioner filed the petition soon after she left service. We are inclined to think that it is really not a public interest petition.

The Court held, at 63:

> It is true that existence of alternative remedy does not prevent the Court from exercising its jurisdiction under Article 226 of the Constitution of India, but we think that in the disputed facts of the case and with the existence of alternative remedy we should refrain from exercising jurisdiction under Article 226 of the Constitution of India.

The petition was dismissed.

☆ ☆ ☆

***O P No 3857 of 1990, Kerala***
***Social Action and Legal Aid Society* v. *State of Kerala and others***

A petition was filed under Article 226 of the Constitution by an organization of lawyers in Ernakulam based on a newspaper article in the *Indian Express* on 18/4/90. The article reported the death of thirty babies of septicemia in the Newborn Nursery at the Institute of Maternal and Child Health in Kozhikode. So the petition asked for immediate steps to bring down the death rate. A committee of inquiry had been constituted, which the petition claimed was not properly constituted. The Court was asked to broaden its terms of reference or to constitute a fresh committee of inquiry into the causes and numbers of deaths in the Institute. Interim relief of Rs 10,000 was asked to be given to the parents of each of the dead babies and the petitioner requested the HC to give these parents liberty to approach civil courts for higher amounts of compensation. It was contended that there were irregularities in the placing of orders for purchases of equipment and other items, and that records had been tampered with. Accordingly the petition asked that the

Court direct that all relevant records be preserved and that a committee be constituted to look into these allegations.

The petition was admitted and is pending.

☆ ☆ ☆

### *W P (Civil) No 796 of 1992*
### *Paschim Banga Khet Majoor Samity and another v. State of West Bengal and another*

A petition was filed under Article 32 of the Constitution by a union of agricultural workers. The second petitioner, Hakim Seikh, a member of the petitioners union, fell off a train on 8/7/92 and was rushed to the Primary Health Care Centre at Mathurapur with serious head injuries and a brain heamorrhage. He was redirected to a Government-run hospital and was refused admission and treatment in a total of five government-run hospitals on grounds that no bed was vacant. Two private hospitals refused him admission — one on the ground that this was a medico-legal case and the other stating that a deposit of money was a prerequisite to treatment. Finally, in the morning of 9/7/92, after the intervention of a voluntary organization, he was admitted to a private hospital on the payment of an advance of Rs 10,000. He was discharged on 22/7/92 after Rs 17,000 had been spent. Invoking Articles 14 and 21 of the Constitution, the petition contended that the life of the injured was threatened by delayed medical treatment and asked that the State of West Bengal be held liable for this delay. The petitioners stated that they could not approach the District Consumer Forum because of a judgement (annexed to the petition) given by the Consumer Disputes Redressal Commission, New Delhi in 1989, excluding doctors in government hospitals from the purview of the Consumer Protection Act, 1986. The petition challenged the legality of this judgement as earlier judgements of the SC, like *Parmanand Katara* (above), held that the State is under an obligation to provide care under Article 21 of the Constitution. The petition wanted the actions by the government-run hospitals to be declared illegal and unconstitutional, compensation to be given and the decision of the Consumer Disputes Redressal Commission to be set aside.

In an order D/-18/11/92 by Justice M.N. Venkatachaliah and Justice S.C. Agrawal

The Court permitted the Medical Council of India to be impleaded in the petition as the third respondent.

In an order D/-22/4/94 by Chief Justice M.N. Venkatachaliah, Justice R.M. Sahai and Justice S. Mohan

Observing that notice had been issued to the State of West Bengal on 30/11/92, the SC stated:

> We regret to have to observe that the State of West Bengal has been dragging its feet in this case and has not been cooperating. It has not even filed its counter-affidavit though a number of adjournments were granted. On the last occasion, the learned counsel for the State of West Bengal appeared and made an earnest request for an adjournment assuring that the State, if satisfied on the facts of this case, would even consider accepting the claim. But today, when the matter is called, none appears for the State of West Bengal. This is indeed a very unsatisfactory state of affairs.
>
> We have now no option except to ask the State of West Bengal to pay to the second petitioner, by way of interim compensation, a sum of Rs 15,000 within three weeks from today.
>
> We also direct the Health Secretary, State of West Bengal to be present in Court on the next date of hearing as it appears that the arrangements for the conduct of the case on behalf of the State of West Bengal are insufficient and that any pronouncement on the wider issues without an opportunity to the State would have serious financial implications arising out of similar claims.

☆ ☆ ☆

***O P No 8020 of 1992, Kerala***
***Niamathulla* v. *State of Kerala***

A petition was filed under Article 226 of the Constitution challenging the government decision that homoeopathic hospitals were to charge each outpatient Rs 2. The petition contended that under Article 47 of the Constitution the Government should not try to make a profit from poor citizens, and that under Article 265 of the Constitution, the charge was illegal and unconstitutional.

In an order D/-30/9/92 by Justice Thomas
[reported 1992 (2) KLT 699]
The Court found no substance in the grievance, stating that the amount charged was piffling even for a skinflint. The petition was dismissed.

☆ ☆ ☆

A petition was filed under Article 226 of the Constitution in 1993 in the Delhi HC by the Non Aligned Congress of Youth through its Chairman Bhim Singh, who was also a member of the National Integration Council and President of the Panthers Party. The seventh respondent to the petition, S.N.S. Pharma Pvt Ltd., had been running a diagnostic clinic for CT scanning at the Sir Ganga Ram Hospital in agreement with the hospital authorities. The petition asked the Court to direct the hospital authorities and S.N.S. Pharma Pvt Ltd. to continue to provide services to the poor and needy and to prevent the removal of the CT scanning machines.

W1In an order in May 1993 by Justice B.N. Kripal and Justice A.B. Saharya
The Court noted that the advocates for the hospital had stated that the petition had been filed at the instigation of the seventh respondent, and that too when the agreement between the hospital and the seventh respondent had been terminated. The judges stated:

> we have, therefore, no reason to doubt that the writ petition has been filed at the instance of respondent No 7.

and directed S.N.S. Pharma Pvt Ltd. to vacate the hospital premises within 48 hours. The petition was dismissed and Rs 10,000 was ordered to be paid by the petitioner.[24]

☆ ☆ ☆

***O P No 10933 of 1993, Kerala***
***C.V. Sathyan* v. *State of Kerala & others***
A petition was filed under Article 226 of the Constitution regarding the health hazard in Hotel Silver because seven inspection chambers of the nearby Alma Hospital had been fitted in the ground floor of the hotel. The petition stated:

[24] "Frivolous litigation costs petitioner Rs 10,000", *The Times of India*, 28/5/93.

> The inspection chambers are envisaged to clear the clogging of the human excreta and other waste emanating from the latrine. The inspection chambers can be opened for clearing the pipes. Since these inspection chambers are under the ground floor of the hotel, the ground floor itself has to be demolished and the opening of the inspection chambers therein will create a health problem to the public at large.

The petition, filed by a resident of the area, asked for the records in the case, the cancellation of any existing licence issued for the running of the hotel and for a direction that the hall be demolished.

## Institutions for Women

***W P No 1900 of 1981***
***Upendra Baxi* v. *State of Uttar Pradesh and another***

A letter was sent to the Court by two law teachers, Dr Upendra Baxi and Professor Lotika Sarkar, on behalf of the inmates of a protective home in Agra. A copy of this letter was sent to the Chief Justice of India and Justice Bhagwati, and was registered as a writ petition under Article 32 of the Constitution. The petitioners detailed the dehumanized conditions in a protective home for women and girls in Agra. The petition invoked the Suppression of Immoral Traffic in Women and Girls Act, 1956, the U. P. Suppression of Immoral Traffic in Women and Girls Rules, 1961 and Article 21 of the Constitution.

In an order D/-31/7/81 by Justice P.N. Bhagwati and Justice O. Chinnappa Reddy
[reported (1983) 2 SCC 308]
The affidavit of the Superintendent of the Home, Miss Srivastava, stated that the petition had been filed "as a last resort to compel the government to leave the present accommodation". The Court responded to this with surprise, at 309:

> The suggestion of a collusion between the landlord of the building on the one hand and Dr Upendra Baxi and Mrs Lotika Sarkar on the other, is most reprehensible and we unhesitatingly condemn it in the strongest terms.

and noted that the petition was a PIL. The Court also noted that inmates of the Home had been discharged, at 311:

> now, most of these inmates had been in the Home for over two years, some of them being in the Home since 1972, 1974 and 1976 and it is difficult to understant how suddenly at or about the time of making of our order dated April 16, 1981, these 19 inmates took it into their heads to apply for being discharged and were in fact discharged. We cannot help entertaining an uneasy feeling that these 19 inmates came to be discharged from the Home merely in order to avoid an enquiry by this Court.

The Court raised many questions about the Home, its functioning and its inmates. Discrepancies were found, for example between the counter-affidavit and the doctor's report, as the latter described some of the residents of the Home as mentally ill or diseased. The Court ordered the administrators of the Protective Home to carry out their statutory duty and issued directions sending some inmates for treatment. The Court dealt with other administrative matters, for example rehabilitation of the residents, which was already supposed to have been carried out by the State.

In an order D/-13/4/82 by Justice P.N. Bhagwati and Justice R.S. Pathak
[reported 1982 (1) SCALE 84 [502]]
The Court stated, at 503:

> We are happy to note that the State Government has responded to the various directions given by us and taken steps with a view to improving the conditions of living of inmates of the Agra Protective Home so as to ensure them a life of basic human dignity

and issued more directions regarding conditions in the Home and the rehabilitation of those released.

In an order D/-23/7/86 by > Chief Justice P.N. Bhagwati, Justice V. Khalid and Justice G.L. Oza
[reported (1986) 4 SCC 106 / AIR 1987 SC 191]
The Court reviewed its earlier orders of 14/9/81, 1/3/82, 2/3/82, 17/9/82, 19/10/82 and 3/12/82.

In an earlier order D/-1/3/82, the Court observed that the State of

U.P. wished to discuss possible improvements for the Home with the petitioners and Dr Sodhi, at 117:

> We are very happy that a correct approach to the problem has been adopted by both sides to this litigation. It must be remembered that this is not a litigation of an adversarial character undertaken for the purpose of holding the State Government or its officers responsible for making reparation but it is a public interest litigation which involves a collaborative and cooperative effort on the part of the State Government and its officers, the lawyers appearing in the case and the Bench for the purpose of making human rights meaningful for the weaker sections of the community. It marks a step forward in the direction of reaching socio-economic justice to the deprived and vulnerable sections of humanity in this country.

In an earlier order D/-3/2/83 the Court noted that specific directions in its order of 19/10/82 had not been carried out. Directions were issued in this regard and, at 123:

> Since considerable difficulty is being experienced in releasing the girls who are sent there, in view of the order made by us that none of the inmates of the Agra Protective Homes should be released without our permission, we would direct that hereafter whenever the period for which a girl is sent to the Agra Protective Home comes to an end, the Superintendent of the Agra Protective Home will immediately report the matter to the District Judge, Agra …[to decide]… whether such girls should be released or not.

Before release, the Court stated that suitable provision should be made for such girls so that they are "not taken to prostitution".

In these earlier orders, the Court had asked for reports to be submitted, and monitored the development of the case.

In the instant case the Court discussed the plans for the improvement of the Home. The State Government was ordered to evolve a scheme for the rehabilitation of girls. The Court' stressed the non-adversarial character of PIL.

☆ ☆ ☆

***W P (C) No 1426 of 1987***
***Vikram Deo Singh Tomar v. State of Bihar***

A letter was sent to the SC by members of the Yuva Adhivakta Kalyan Samiti, Sasaram, District Rohtas, Bihar alleging, among other things, that the female inmates of the Care Home in Patna were compelled to live in inhuman conditions in dilapidated, old buildings. The letter contended that these women were ill-treated, ill-fed and not given any medical attention.

In an order D/-2/8/88 by > Chief Justice R.S. Pathak, Justice L.M. Sharma and Justice N.D. Ojha
[reported AIR 1988 SC 1782]
Referring to Articles 21 and 39 of the Constitution, the Court stated, at 1783:

> India is a welfare State governed by a Constitution which holds pride of place in the hearts of its citizens. It lays special emphasis on the protection and welfare of the weaker sections of society and seeks to improve their economic and social status on the basis of the constitutional guarantees spelled out in its provisions. It shows a particular regard for women and children ... We live in an age when this Court has demonstrated, while interpreting Article 21 of the Constitution, that every person is entitled to a quality of life consistent with his human personality. The right to live with human dignity is the fundamental right of every human citizen.

The Welfare Department of the State Government was directed to make alternative arrangements for the accommodation of inmates, while the Care Home was put in proper order. Renovation, repairs and refurbishment of the Home was ordered, and the Court held, at 1784-5:

> With these directions, we dispose of this writ petition. We make it clear, however, that in the event of no, or insufficient, compliance being made with this order, we will have no hesitation in reopening the case for such further steps as may be considered necessary for enforcing this order.

☆ ☆ ☆

***W P (Cri) No 2526 of 1991***
***Chinnamma Sivadas v. State (Delhi Admn.)***

A petition was filed under Article 32 of the Constitution regarding the conditions in Nari Niketan, a women's home in Delhi.

In an order D/-23/10/92 by Justice Kuldip Singh, Justice P. B. Sawant and Justice N. M. Kasliwal
[reported 1992 (3) SCALE 31 [85]]
The Court noted that a group of persons (T. C. Sharma, Sivadas, Arun Sharma, B.K. Prasad, and a female student of law) visited Nari Niketan to find out if the women were being looked after properly and if the management was following the various suggestions which have been placed on record by counsel for petitioner. After examining the report submitted to the Court by Mrs Kanchan Kataria, Superintendent of Nari Niketan, the Court decided that the Home was functioning properly. The petitioners had claimed that some mentally ill patients were resident in the Home, so the administrators of Nari Niketan said that these women would be examined. The Court concluded, at 85:

> We place on record the appreciation for the petitioner who has done good job by bringing to our notice the functioning of Nari Niketan by way of this public interest litigation. We give liberty to the petitioner to approach this Court as and when it is necessary in the interest of the inmates of Nari Niketan.

## CASE CHAPTER 2

# The Police

### Framing the Issue

The cases in this chapter have been divided into sections on: the maintenance of law and order (*morchas* and rallies, riots, police protection, general); the Nadiad incident; custodial violence; firings and encounter deaths; negligence; investigations and corruption. With the exception of complaints that the police and administration have been inefficient in their duty to maintain law and order,[1] most of the cases document instances of abuse or misuse of police power.

Members of the police force are considered to hold civil posts, within the meaning of Article 311 of the Constitution. The police force is governed by Central Police Regulations, 1943 and local

[1] There have been other cases on this — see the chapter on 'Bonded Labour' for *Kameshwar Prasad Sharma, 'Slave President', Bandhua Mukti Morcha, Bihar* v. *State of Bihar* [reported in 1983 (2) SCALE 160 [897] and 1983 (2) SCALE 161 [897]] in which the Court directed that police protection be provided to the petitioner and the villagers. Contrast with the case of *Pradeep Prabhu* v. *State of Maharashtra* in the chapter on 'Environment and Resources' in volume two filed because of police harassment of tribal cultivators, the case of *Self Employed Women's Association and others* v. *Municipal Corporation of Ahmedabad and others* in the chapter on 'Urban Space', filed because of police harassment of vendors and the case filed after a woman activist was injured during a demonstration after a police lathicharge — *Janwadi Mahila Samiti and another* v. *Union of India* [Cr] W.P No. 221 of 1988] in the chapter on 'Injustices Specific to Women'.

regulations, framed under the Police Act, 1861, which prescribe the internal procedures to be followed and disciplinary measures adopted. Also applicable are the rules made under section 241 of the Government of India Act, 1935 in so far as they are consistent with the Constitution. In most instances, police powers are determined by the Code of Criminal Procedure, 1973.

The petitioners in the PIL cases filed against the police largely comprise advocates and organizations concerned with civil liberties. While accepting the need for a police force, cases have been filed out of concern for the misconduct of those acting to uphold state power, both in negative and positive terms.[2] The inaction and tacit complicity of the police during riots has been challenged,[3] along with the acts committed in the line of duty

2 See the chapter on 'Injustices Specific to Women' for petitions filed complaining of rapes by the police — Rameezabee: *P. Rathinam* v. *Union of India and another* [reported in 1987 (2) SCALE 317 [1464] and 1993 (2) SCALE 126 [631]]: *In the matter of: Judicial Enquiry into Gang-Rape Demanded, and, Concerted Demand for Judicial Probe* [reported in (1988) 1 GauLR 4891]. In the case of *Niloy Dutta* v. *District Magistrate, Sibsagar District* [reported in (1991) 2 GauLR 217] in which the Court issued guidelines on the interrogation of women by the army and police.

3 A petition was filed in the SC in 1992 by the People's Union for Civil Liberties regarding the Seelampur riots in Delhi.

such as firings, "encounters",[4] custodial violence[5] and corruption. In the absence of any other forum that provides relief for the victims of the abuse of police power, the writ jurisdiction of the courts and the fundamental rights in the Constitution have been invoked.

In the petitions on law and order the court has been asked to arbitrate between fundamental rights when a conflict is perceived. The case filed by Rupinder Singh Sodhi argues that the freedom of movement is paramount, while that of the *Hindustani Andolan* highlights the limitations of the freedom of expression. Other petitions, like that filed by the *Supreme Court Bar Clerks Association*, also ask the Court to limit these rights. The difference in the perception of the petitioners display both inefficiency of the administration in managing public spaces and the restrictions it places on dissent.

The petition known by the name of *Chaitanya Kalbagh* demonstrates how recourse was taken to the law to solve a predominantly political problem, police resistance to dissent. In spite of being discouraged from filing a petition on encounter deaths, the petition was filed, as it was felt there was nothing to be lost by approaching the courts.

The media has been a catalyst, bringing many of the cases to Court. It was after a reading of the situation of the Sikhs in Coimbatore after the riots in 1984 that an advocate made an enquiry into the matter and a case was filed. Similarly, the petition filed after the Mandal riots by advocate P.V. Kapoor was motivated by an issue of the video magazine *Newstrack*. The media attention which focussed on the Nadiad incident, together with a sense of indignation, initiated what was to become one of the seminal PIL cases relating to the police. News reports detailing incidents of custodial violence formed a major part of the petition filed by D.K. Basu.

[4] During so-called encounters with terrorists or seccessionist groups, the police have killed people all over the country. In the petitions, these killings have been challenged as unnecessary and described as extra-judicial.

[5] See the chapter on 'Prisons and State Institutions' for cases on custodial violence, specifically *Sheela Barse* v. *State of Maharashtra* [reported in (1983) 2 SCC 96 and (1987) 4 SCC 373]

## Access to Justice

Media attention on the issues brought to the Court has enabled easier access to justice. The national focus on the Nadiad incident, in which a magistrate was publicly humiliated by the police, was echoed by the attention paid to the case in the courtroom. Similarly, the publicity afforded to the devastating effects of riots, police firings and custodial violence has given the petitions a legitimacy that they might otherwise have lacked. Even the *Supreme Court Legal Aid Committee* petitioned the Court in response to a newspaper article and in "*Re Death of Sawinder Singh Grover*" the Court responded to a news report by registering a case *suo moto*.

In some instances the Court has responded to letters as writ petitions, like those sent by the *Rajasthan Kisan Sangathana* and by the *All India Democratic Women's Association*. However, in the latter instance, it is uncertain whether, because of the limitations of the PIL guidelines, the petition would have been admitted without the timely intervention of the SCLAC. In *People's Union for Democratic Rights and another*, the petitioners were given standing in general but were denied the *locus standi* to ask the Court to direct the government to institute an inquiry under the Commissions of Inquiry Act, 1952. Unwilling to be seen usurping the powers of the legislature, the Supreme Court in response to the Nadiad incident, noted that the enquiry had been for the Court and not under the 1952 Act. In *Punjab and Haryana High Court Bar Association*, and in *P.M. Antony*, the Chandigarh HC and the SC considered the justiciability of the petitions filed, before rejecting them.

## The Court's Response

Inconsistent in its response to the petitions filed on riots, in *Rajendran* the Kerala High Court directed that an alternative remedy be used, in *R. Gandhi* the Madras HC ordered compensation to be paid, and in *Nathulal Jain* the Rajasthan HC refused to allow the petition filed by an advocate, holding that the law of tort was not applicable, and referred to the Bhopal case as justification. The lack of consistency extends throughout the chapter as seen in *Jain's* case and that filed by *Pratul Kumar Sinha*. In the former the Rajasthan

HC dismissed the reference to the [Indian] Railways Act, 1989 [1890] but in the latter, the Calcutta HC invoked the same Act to support its direction that a solatium fund be established. Moreover, there is little correlation in the courts' response to the petitions filed on behalf of the Sikhs after the riots which followed Prime Minister Indira Gandhi's assassination. While reinforcing the flexible nature of PIL, stating that there could be no precedents in PIL, in *People's Union for Democratic Rights and another*, the Delhi HC also reinforced the marginal status of this form of litigation.

Protecting its own officers and asserting support for its own institution, the SC's response to the Nadiad incident was both detailed and exhaustive. Unlike any other case of police excesses, the Court ordered punishment of the police officers concerned and issued guidelines for the arrest of any judicial officer. Contempt powers were assumed on behalf of the lower judiciary as the Court upheld the rule of law by the courts in the face of an encroaching "Police Raj", and the extensive nature of these powers were reinforced.

After filing a petition on custodial deaths in the Calcutta HC, advocate D.K. Basu became a judge of the Calcutta HC. In a lengthy judgement in *Pratul Kumar Sinha*, he dealt with questions already raised by him in *D.K. Basu* and accepted that there is widespread abuse of power by the police. Again, the tendency of the courts to pay specific attention to questions concerning the judiciary is seen when Justice Basu dwelt on the issue of the security of the HC. Enquiries into incidents of custodial violence have also been ordered in the case filed by *Saheli*, the *People's Union for Democratic Rights* and by the *Rajasthan Kisan Sangathana*, and compensation awarded, but there is little evidence of any action taken against members of the police force.

In a number of cases the Court has ordered that a CBI enquiry be conducted. For example in both the cases filed by the *Hailakandi Bar Association* and by the *All India Democratic Women's Association*, the Court has expressed its dissatisfaction with the way in which enquiries have been conducted by the respondent-state and the police. In both cases fresh enquiries were ordered. Conversely, in the petition filed by *Chaitanya Kalbagh* the petitioners were directed to approach the state governments which, as respondents to the petition, would be unlikely to provide any relief.

Although there is little evidence showing that the police has been punished for the crimes it committed, the Court has awarded compensation in many of the cases in this chapter. Dispensing its largesse in the cases filed by *R. Gandhi*, *Rajasthan Kisan Sangathana*, *People's Union for Democratic Rights* (on custodial violence), *R.S. Sodhi* and the *Supreme Court Legal Aid Committee* the courts have been arbitrary in their response. After its order in *R. Gandhi*, the Court made efforts to ensure that the compensation awarded was actually paid. In other cases the SC stated that compensation would not be payable and, in the petition filed by advocate *P.V. Kapoor*, the Delhi HC discussed PIL in detail before directing the Delhi police to pay compensation because of the way the injured persons were treated after the firing, and not for the firing itself. Once awarded, as in the *R.S. Sodhi* case, the SC stayed disbursal of the compensation pending an investigation to determine the recipients.

The importance of relevant information can be seen in the petition filed by the *Social Action and Legal Aid Society*. The investigations by the police have been questioned in the petition filed by the *Association for Protection of Public Rights and Interest through its Secretary*. The SC resorted to trusting and putting faith in the integrity of the CBI inspite of the corruption identified in the police and administration. Similary in *Punjab and Haryana High Court Bar Association* the SC ordered a CBI enquiry because of the alleged inefficency of the police.

## The Contribution of PIL

Some instances of abuse of police powers have been acknowledged by the courts and compensation awarded to the victims. However there are many examples of cases where the Court has refused to recognize police transgressions. There has been an unwillingness by the courts to make police officers into adversaries. Cases have remained pending and the courts have not monitored the proceedings taken against police officials. The nexus between the police and the judiciary, as parts of the same state structure can be seen in the cases of *P.V. Kapoor* and *Chaitanya Kalbagh* where the powers of the police have been upheld, directly and tacitly. It is only in the lengthy judgement given by Justice D.K. Basu in *Pratul Kumar Sinha*, which was subsequently stayed, that efforts were made to include voluntary or social action groups in ensuring safety in custody, and lawyers were described as the saviours of the victims of custodial violence.

Compensation awards have been arbitrary and even when awarded in some of the cases, they have not been disbursed making the orders of the Court meaningless. It was only when the judiciary itself was threatened by the police, that police officials were punished by the SC. Nonetheless, there have been no amendments in the laws governing police behaviour and no limitations prescribed for the exercise of police power.

## Maintenance of Law and Order

### *Morchas* and Rallies

***W Ps Nos 8816 and 8817 of 1982***

***Rupinder Singh Sodhi and another* v. *Union of India and others***

Petitions were filed under Article 32 of the Constitution by advocates and Members of Parliament from the Akali Party asking for the removal of all obstructions on the highways so as to allow unhindered and unintercepted use of highways, railways and airways by them without making any discrimination on the grounds of religion. A declaration had been made by the Akali leaders that a *morcha* would be taken to Delhi on 19/11/82, the date of the inauguration of the Asiad games. Accordingly, the border States of Haryana and Uttar Pradesh took steps to intercept the movement of the Akalis across the border to Delhi in order to prevent the *morcha* and the anticipated disruption to the Asiad in 1982. The petitions referred to the arrest of the Sikhs on the Punjab border because of the Akali party movement, and invoked Article 21 of the Constitution to claim the right to use the highways and not to be discriminated against.

In an order D/-18/11/82 by Justice Y.V. Chandrachud and Justice A.N. Sen
[reported AIR 1983 SC 65]
The Court held, at 66:

> we agree that no one is entitled to barricade a highway so as to prevent members of the public from using it while they are

> on their normal business in the pursuit of normal avocations of life. But the police, whose duty it is to enforce law and order in the wake of threatened mass agitations which are reasonably likely to lead to breach of public peace, are entitled in the discharge of that duty to impose reasonable restrictions on the physical movement of members of the public in order to [ensure] the protection of public property and the avoidance of needless inconvenience to other citizens in their lawful pursuits. But all such restraints on personal liberty, if at all, have to be commensurate with the object which furnishes their justification. They must be minimal and cannot exceed the constraints of the particular situation, either in nature or in duration. Above all, they cannot be used as engines of oppression, persecution, harassment or the like. The sanctity of person and of privacy has to be maintained at all costs, and that cannot ever be violated under the guise of maintenance of law and order.

The petitions were dismissed.

☆ ☆ ☆

***O P Nos 779, 1162, 2271, 6782 and 9578 of 1984, Kerala***
***Sankaranarayanan and others* v. *State of Kerala***

Five letters were sent to the Chief Justice of the Kerala High Court by citizens claiming that their civil rights were being curtailed by the assemblies and demonstrations held on public roads. The letters were registered as writ petitions under Article 226 of the Constitution and invoked Article 19(1)(b) of the Constitution.

In an order D/-24/7/85 by Chief Justice K. Bhaskaran and >
Justice Sivaraman Nair
[reported AIR 1986 Ker 82]

The Court held that the right guaranteed to the citizens to assemble peaceably and without arms does not authorize anyone to insist that he has a fundamental right to conduct a procession or demonstration on populous urban roads without any control or regulation. It was stated that there is nothing in the Constitution to show that the right to take any procession, as such, has been guaranteed by the Constitution as a fundamental right, as the right to assemble peacefully and without arms is subject to restrictions imposed in the interest of public order. The Court held that even fundamental rights are not absolute, and noted, at 86:

> We should, however, add that it is not the absence of the required number of statutes on the relevant subjects that is the real cause of the complaint of the petitioners. There seems to be a growing impression that effective strength of organization can be demonstrated only by holding the public to ransom for long periods of time ... The law enforcement agencies are understandably inactive, their anxiety being not to involve themselves in controversies, which may have political overtones. Instead of acting as law enforcement agencies, they take the role of spectators. Unless there is a change in attitude on the part of the enforcement agencies, any law, however laudable its object may be, is likely only to compound the problem.

While stressing the importance of enforcement of existing statutory provisions, the Court advised the government to promulgate a special enactment, aside from the provisions of sections 133 and 144 of the Cr P C, 1973, to impose effective regulations on the use of public places by public processions.

☆ ☆ ☆

***W P (C) No 336 of 1991***
***Supreme Court Bar Clerks Association (Regd)* v. *Delhi Administration and others***

A petition was filed under Article 32 of the Constitution asking the Court for appropriate directions to the authorities regarding public meetings, rallies and processions in Delhi, particularly those in the vicinity of the Boat Club, situated in central Delhi. The petition stated that people were unable to appear in examinations or reach work on time and that money was lost on fuel because of the continuous disturbances. A rally organized by the Bahujan Samaj Party was cited as an example of the disruption in the vicinity of the Boat Club. Annexed to the petition were various newspaper articles detailing the disturbances. The petition invoked Article 21 of the Constitution stating that the right to life includes quality of life, and asked for a direction to the respondents to review the holding of mass rallies and processions.

In an order D/-19/11/91 by Chief Justice Ranganath Misra and Justice Kuldip Singh
[reported 1991 (2) SCALE 194 [1042]]
The full text of the Court's order stated, at 1042-3:

> This public interest litigation is in relation to the user of the Boat Club and exercise of appropriate regulatory control on its use. We had heard counsel for the parties and reserved orders on 23rd August, 1991. On looking into the papers and the statements and counter-statements in the respective affidavits, we are of the view that the matter should be further heard before any final view on it can be taken. We accordingly direct that the matter be listed again for further hearing before a Bench where Kuldip Singh, J. is a member.

## Riots

***O P No 294 of 1983, Kerala***
***Rajendran* v. *V. Vayalar Ravi and others***

A petition was filed under Article 226 of the Constitution by a journalist asking for an investigation into the incident of rioting, which took place in Alleppey on 29/12/82, while the Muslims were observing Miladi. The police had apparently received a direction not to act, and the petition contended that because of this one man was burned to death, and the airport became unserviceable. The petition claimed that provisions of the IPC, 1860 were infringed, both by the rioters and by the administration which had failed to prevent the riots.

In an order D/-19/1/83 by Justice M.P. Menon
[reported 1983 KLT 100]
The Court noted the petitioner's tendency to approach the HC[6] at 101:

> The petitioner, seemingly a public-spirited journalist has been coming to this Court frequently; this is his fourth approach within a month or so, to my knowledge. The first was for contempt of court against the Chief Minister of Kerala. The

6 Other petitions filed by Rajendran are detailed in the chapters on 'Politics and Elections' and on 'Judges, Courts and Lawyers' in volume two.

second was a so for contempt, against the Home Minister and the Irrigation Minister. The third was for directing the President of India to impose President's rule in the State. Undaunted by the results, he has now come to see whether the Home Minister, the Chief Minister and the Director General of Police (respondents 1 to 3) could be prosecuted at the instance of this Court, for certain offences said to have been committed by them.

While assuming the application to be bona fide, the Court observed that applications under Article 226 of the Constitution have certain limits. It was held that a writ of *mandamus* can only be issued if the applicant belongs to a group with a certain special interest in the matter. The Court noted that a writ cannot undo what has been done and that as the remedy under Article 226 of the Constitution is discretionary, the application was dismissed on the grounds of *locus standi* and suggested that an alternative remedy was available under section 202 of the Cr P C, 1973.

***Crl R P No 428 of 1983, Kerala***
***T.A. Rajendran v. State of Kerala***

Referring to the same riots, a revision petition was filed against the order of the Judicial Magistrate, Trivandrum. A complaint had been filed before the magistrate regarding the rioting and arson which led to the death of a Muslim boy on Miladi in 1982. The magistrate had held the complaint to be defective under section 197 of the Cr P C, 1973 which stipulates that the necessary sanction for the prosecution of public servants was not obtained from the Government.

In an order D/-1/12/83 by Justice U.L. Bhat
[reported 1984 KLT 113]
The Court held that since sanction was not obtained, the order of the magistrate cannot be interfered with. The petition was dismissed.

☆ ☆ ☆

A petition was filed under Article 32 of the Constitution by Madhu Kishwar, Ruth Vanita and Rakesh Bharadwaj, all lecturers in Delhi University, against the State and various officers of the State. It stated that after the assassination of Prime Minister Indira Gandhi, from 31/10/84 to 3/11/84 many Indian citizens belonging to the Sikh community were killed, hurt, molested, raped and prevented from moving freely. Their houses were burnt down and ransacked, their possessions were looted and destroyed, their places of worship desecrated, and some were forced to cut their hair. The most severe riots were in Delhi. Details of the events were given in the petition:

> It is noteworthy that members of the municipal corporation of Delhi and Congress(I) members of the Lok Sabha from Delhi were seen actively abetting and instigating murder, looting and arson. There is evidence that they organized gangs of their supporters to incite crowds to looting and murder, that they made payments to gang leaders to gather and transport large numbers of hoodlums and weapons into the colonies where Sikhs live, especially to those where Sikhs were more vulnerable by reason of their poverty or lack of communication.

The petitioners gathered extensive information from interviews, as personal witnesses and by gathering reports before filing the petition which stated that these crimes violated Articles 13(1), 14, 15(1), 19(1), 21 and 25(1) of the Constitution. The offer by the government of a lump sum of Rs 10,000 as compensation for life lost was described as a "crude and absurd response". The petition asked that an independent inquiry be constituted, that the Court direct the interim suspension from office of those leading the cover up operations, that the enquiry should result in the enunciation of basic principles that should govern the trials of violators of constitutional rights, that pending the Court's decision all assets of those organizations and individuals under inquiry should be frozen, and that the Court frame guidelines for the payment of punitive fines, reparation and compensation from the frozen assets of the extra-governmental organizations and individuals who are convicted. The petition stated:

> We realize that in other circumstances the regular law enforcment machinery of the State would have the responsibility to implement the enquiry within the normal framework of the laws, legislative and administrative

[7] "Organised Riots Against the Sikhs: A Violation of Fundamental Rights. A Petition To The Supreme Court" *Manushi* No. 25, Vol. 5 No. 1, Nov-Dec 1984, 33-37.

> machinery of the State. However, since key functionaries of that very State and its machinery are co-conspirators in the violation of the constitutional rights of the citizens and have also carried out massive attempts at the cover-up of their own culpability, we have no option but to approach this, the highest court in the land.[7]

The petition was dismissed in limine.

☆ ☆ ☆

***C W P No 2697 of 1984, Delhi***
***Peoples Union for Democratic Rights and another* v. *Ministry of Home Affairs***

A petition was filed under Article 226 of the Constitution through the Secretary of the People's Union for Democratic Rights (PUDR) and the People's Union for Civil Liberties on behalf of the survivors of some of the victims of rioting that followed the assassination of Prime Minister Indira Gandhi. The petition referred specifically to the riots which took place from 31/10/84 to 10/11/84 in the Kalyan Puri and Sultanpuri areas of Delhi and asked for the appointment of a commission of enquiry and a direction to the CBI that it conduct an investigation into the role of police. The petition also asked the Court to direct the executive magistrates to keep the peace, to hold an identity parade of the people named by the survivors so that evidence would not be lost, and to ensure that those identified be restricted from going into those areas for six months so that an atmosphere of security and trust could be created. The petition invoked Articles 14, 21 and 22 of the Constitution, Cr P C, 1973 and section 3 of the Commissions of Inquiry Act, 1952.

In an order D/-11/3/85 by > Justice Yogeshwar Dayal and > Justice B.N. Kirpal (concurring)
[reported AIR 1985 Del 268]

Justice Dayal pointed out that there could be no precedents in PIL, as each case is based on its own peculiarities, and that the procedure adopted by the Supreme Court or any other court in any such litigation is not necessarily binding on others. Referring to the Supreme Court's orders in *Bandhua Mukti Morcha* and *S.P. Gupta*, Justice Dayal stated, at 278-9:

> The Courts should not have an attitude that they alone are

> protectors of fundamental rights of citizens and a democratically elected government has no such feeling or inclination. Initial attitude of the courts vis-a-vis the executive organ of a state should not be of suspicion in this behalf. Of course, if the Court after inquiry and due scrutiny finds the state not performing its duty it can and should step in to protect and enforce fundamental rights to the extent it can give relief. The attitude ought to be of trust and not always of confrontation. ... the condition which must be fulfilled before PIL is entertained by a superior Court is that the courts should be in a position to give effective and complete relief. If no effective or complete relief can be granted, the Court should not entertain PIL.

Justice Kirpal expressed similar sentiments, at 290:

> whenever the conscience of the Court is shocked, on account of action or inaction on the part of the State, the Court will exercise its jurisdiction under Article 226 of the Constitution.

The petitions were dismissed on a number of grounds: that none of the rights mentioned had been infringed; that the police was already investigating into the causes and culprits of the riots under the Cr P C, 1973 and that the Court's interference would only cause confusion and imply that the investigation by the authorities was not being conducted correctly; that the Court cannot interfere in any decision by the Government to appoint a commission, as this would be, essentially, a political decision; that it is not just the Court which is the protector of fundamental rights; and that the Court cannot direct executive magistrates to keep the peace under the Cr P C, 1973 as no fundamental right was attracted to this request. After noting that the petitioners had not approached the appropriate authority for the appointment of a commission under the Commissions of Inquiry Act, 1952, the Court held that they had no *locus standi* to make this demand.

☆ ☆ ☆

***W P No 11994 of 1984, Madras***

***R. Gandhi and others v. Union of India and another***

A petition was filed under Article 226 of the Constitution by two secretaries of the Indian Association of Lawyers (Tamil Nadu Chapter) and two students of the Bachelor of Law class, claiming an interest in the welfare of the community especially as they participate in the Free Legal Aid and Advice Centre. The petition asked the Court to provide relief for the trials and tribulations undergone by the minority Sikh community in Coimbatore in Tamil Nadu after the assassination of Prime Minister Indira Gandhi on 31 October, 1984. The petition detailed the injuries to people and damage done to property and places of worship, invoking sections 435 and 436 of the IPC, 1860, together with Articles 14, 19(1)(g), 21 and 300A of the Constitution.

The petition had been filed because, soon after the riots, advocate Geetha Ramaseshan had responded to a general appeal printed in a newspaper by members of the Sikh community asking for help. She visited Coimbatore some 10 to 15 days after the assassination and was angered by the silence after the properties of people were destroyed over for three or four days. As there were only about 30 to 40 Sikh families in the area, she noted that it would have been possible to contain the riots, but the State machinery was inactive. It was as a result of her visit, and a report presented to the Bar Association, that the petition was filed.

In an order D/-31/10/88 by Justice S.A. Kader
[reported AIR 1989 Mad 205]
The Court acknowledged the report submitted by Ms Geetha Ramaseshan to her Lawyers Association after her visit to the riot-torn areas where she had conducted an on-the-spot inquiry. The Court stated that the judicial inquiry requested in the petition was unnecessary because the Collector of Coimbatore had inquired into the matter and submitted a detailed report. The Collector had recommended that a compensation of Rs 33,19,033 be paid to the victims of the riots, and this amount was ordered to be paid within eight weeks. The petition was allowed with no order for costs. The Court recorded its appreciation of Geetha Ramaseshan for her public spirit.

***W A No 314 of 1989, Madras***
***State of Tamil Nadu* v. *R. Gandhi and others***

An appeal was filed in the Madras HC challenging the order for compensation.

During the pendency of the appeal a Government Order was passed, No 2256 D/-14/12/89, detailing the amount of compensation to be given. The order stated that only 19 out of the alleged 34 cases were eligible for compensation, and that the compensation payable to many of these 19 people was to be reduced. It was decided that the total amount due was Rs 4,42,944.

The petitioners filed an objection to this Government Order stating that the rationale used did not meet the ends of justice, that the reduction of the amount of compensation in individual cases was without reason, that the exclusion of others was not explained and that damage to Gurudwaras was not accounted for.

In an order D/-15/10/90 by > Chief Justice A.S. Anand and Justice D. Raju

The Court held that the issues arising out of the objection to the Government Order could only be taken up when the writ appeal itself was taken up for hearing, stating, at 4:

> However, keeping in view the fact that the riots took place in 1984 and for the last almost six years the riot victims have not received any compensation, we are of the opinion that it would be in the interests of justice if at least compensation is paid to the 19 cases of riot victims identified in the G O … the payment of this amount shall be without prejudice to the rights of the parties in the main writ appeal. In the event the appellant fails in the writ appeal, the amount paid by it to the 19 riot victims as detailed in the annexure to the G O … shall be adjusted against the total payment of compensation to be made.

As this was only interim relief, the Court granted six weeks time for its implementation, stating that it is open to the state of Tamil Nadu to claim reimbursement from the Government of India.

☆ ☆ ☆

**_S B C W P No 5426 of 1990, connected with S B C W P No 5541 of 1989 and S B C W P No 1981 of 1991, Rajasthan_**

**_Nathulal Jain, Advocate and others v. State of Rajasthan and others_**

A petition was filed under Article 226 of the Constitution by an advocate from Jaipur in connection with the communal riots that had taken place on 24/10/90 during a *bandh* (general strike) sponsored by a national party. In the violence in different parts of Jaipur, 19 people died, 150 were seriously injured, 200 shops were looted or totally burnt and 300 residential houses were partially burnt. The petition referred to newspaper reports on the arson, blaming it to the failure of the local administration. It was contended that the deployment of force was inadequate and that the administration failed to make any arrangements to prevent the eruption of the anticipated riots. A news item in the Jaipur edition of *Times of India*, on 25/10/90 reported that the District Collector announced that an *ex-gratia* payment of Rs 5,000 would be paid to the families of each of the deceased and Rs 1,000 would be paid to each of the injured. These amounts were later increased by the State Government. The petition claimed that no compensation had been paid and that as under the Railways Act, 1989, the State was obliged to pay two lakh rupees to every citizen who lost his life during an accident, irrespective of whether or not there was any neglect on the part of the railways, the government should fix the rate of compensation for the riot victims on this criteria. The petitioner also mentioned the compensation announced by the State Government in the case of a riot in Chittorgarh district. The Court was asked to direct the State Government to pay a minimum of Rs 2,00,000 in respect of all those persons who lost their lives during the course of the riots and to direct the State Government to pay Rs 30,000 to those who were injured, the amount stipulated under section 82A of the Railway Accidents Rules, 1990.

In an order D/-31/8/92 by Chief Justice K.C. Agrawal
[reported AIR 1993 Raj 149]
The respondents stated that compensation was not liable to be paid because all possible arrangements had been made to prevent the communal riots, and that the petition was not maintainable as the claim, if any, should be made by each individual separately. The State contended that there could be no tortious liability for acts of government servants while discharging their sovereign duties. Discussing the reference to section 82A of the Rules, the Court stated, at 155:

> The analogy ... is mis-placed and mis-conceived. In the present case for damages I am not called upon to decide that controversy. It was not a case on contract or tort, like a case for damages under the Railways Act.

and denied standing to the petitioner, stating that as a principle of common law, damage must have been done to the person claiming compensation, at 152:

> Liability in tort may be predicated upon an injury sustained as

a result of an unlawful or legal act, whether the injury is to the property or to the person. In the instant case neither was the injury suffered to the property of the petitioner nor was it to his person, hence, a tort action cannot be maintained by the petitioner.

The limitations of the availability of a writ petition were enunciated, at 153:

> the mandamus can be issued or employed to compel the performance of a clear statutory duty, when the administrative agency has unlawfully refused to undertake the duty at the request of a person intended by Parliament to benefit from it.
>
> Mandamus can be used only in relation to a duty which as a public duty, is specifically enforceable.

Referring to the many legal arguments framed by the petitioner, the Court concluded, at 156-7:

> The prayers made by the petitioner in this writ petition in itself show that the petitioner is not specific as to whom the compensation has to be paid whether in case of death or injury permanent or otherwise….
>
> The petitioner cannot claim any compensation from the government qua the parties from whom he holds no brief and right to realize on their behalf. The parties may wriggle out and may at any time say that the petitioner was no one to espouse their case. It is by now very commonly known that even in a compromise made by the government in the Bhopal Gas Tragedy case the compromise was challenged though later it was upheld by the Hon'ble Supreme Court but still some part of the compromise relating to the criminal offence committed by Union Carbide was taken out of the performance of the compromise.

The petition was dismissed.

## Police Protection

***W P (Cri) No 2989 of 1983***
***Hindustani Andolan and others* v. *State of Punjab and others***

A petition was filed under Article 32 of the Constitution by two public spirited organizations through their convenor and secretary respectively. The petition invoked section 47 of the Cr P C, 1973 and asked whether the Government and police were unauthorized to enter a place of worship even when there is a criminal suspected to be sheltering there.

In an order D/-24/11/83 by Chief Justice Y.V. Chandrachud, Justice Amarendra Nath Sen and Justice M.P. Thakkar
[reported AIR 1984 SC 582]
The Court held, at 582-3:

> It is impossible and undesirable for any Court to issue a general writ of mandamus to the effect that whenever a criminal is suspected to have taken shelter in a place of worship, the police must enter that place, regardless of the overall situation of law and order. Speaking generally, courts cannot enforce law and order by issuing general direction without reference to specific instances. The Government has to assess, in the context of the prevailing conditions, the impact of the steps taken to enforce law and order. And, it is the executive which has to take a policy decision as regards the steps to be taken in a given situation, after taking into account the demands of the prevailing situation. We do not commend or suggest that the police should be silent spectators to wanton destruction of life but we cannot, as men of some little experience of law and life, commend that the police must enter places of worship forcibly. While enforcing law and order, the executive cannot be oblivious of the possibility that while solving one problem of law and order, others more acute than the one sought to be resolved may arise. That is always a valid and relevant consideration.

The petition was therefore dismissed.

## General

***S L P (Civil) No 15312 of 1986***
***P.M. Antony v. Distt. Collector and others***
An appeal was filed under Article 136 of the Constitution, asking the Court to lift the ban imposed on a play by the Collector of

Ernakulum. The petition was described as a PIL in the headnotes of the reported order.

In an order D/-17/12/86 by Justice Ranganath Misra and Justice M.M. Dutt
[reported 1986 (2) SCALE 290 [1254]]
The Court held that as this was a problem of law and order, it would not be proper for the Court to intervene. The petitioners were directed to approach the Collector who was to dispose of the matter within one month.

### The Nadiad Incident

***In the Matter of Complaint received from Delhi Judicial Service Association Tis Hazari Court, Delhi***

A telegram was sent to the SC regarding an incident in Nadiad. On 25/9/89 the Chief Judicial Magistrate (CJM) of Nadiad, District Kheda in Gujarat, N.M. Patel, was arrested by S.R. Sharma, an Inspector of Police and five others on the charge of having consumed liquor in breach of the prohibition law enforced in the state of Gujarat. He was assaulted, handcuffed, tied with a thick rope and sent through the streets to the hospital for a medical examination. Photographs of the CJM, taken at the behest of the Inspector, were published in newspapers all over the country. It was felt that the dignity of the courts had been undermined and that the police had usurped the rule of law in the state of Gujarat. A number of Bar Associations passed resolutions condemning the action of the police and went on strike. The lower judiciary in Gujarat also went on strike, causing the courts to stop functioning. Following the receipt of the telegram which was registered as a petition under Article 32 of the Constitution, a number of other petitions were filed. These petitions asked the Court to take action against the police officers involved. The petitions stated that the action of the police officers amounted to criminal contempt as it lowered the authority of the CJM and interfered in the administration of justice. The petitions invoked provisions of the Cr P C, 1973.

In an order D/-29/9/89 by Chief Justice E.S. Venkataramiah, Justice K.N. Singh and Justice S. Natarajan
[reported 1989 (2) SCALE 119 [654]]
The Court held, at 654:

> Since this is a matter which requires immediate attention of this Court in order to safeguard the independence of judiciary, we entertain this case as a public interest litigation.

and notices were directed to be issued by telex.

In an order D/-4/10/89 by Chief Justice E.S. Venkataramiah, Justice K.N. Singh and Justice S. Natarajan
[reported 1989 (2) SCALE 140 [748]]
The Court ordered the transfer of the relevant police officers out of Kheda District and passed strictures against the Police Inspector. Justice R.M. Sahai, the seniormost puisne Judge of the Allahabad HC, was appointed as commissioner to inquire into the matter. The Court directed that services and security were to be made available to him, and a fund of Rs 20,000 was to be instituted by the Government for the inquiry expenses. The Court ordered that a copy of its order be published in the local newspapers. Notice of contempt was issued to the police because of the insult to a judicial officer.

In an order D/-24/10/89 by Chief Justice E.S. Venkataramiah, Justice K.N. Singh and Justice N.M. Kasliwal
[reported 1989 (2) SCALE 174 [877]]
The Court ordered that criminal cases be lodged against the police officers concerned. They were directed to appear before a magistrate and permitted to apply for bail. If they failed to appear then they were directed to be arrested.

***Delhi Judicial Service Association, Tis Hazari Court, Delhi* v. *State of Gujarat and others***

In an order D/-11/9/91 by > Justice K.N. Singh, Justice Kuldip Singh and Justice N.M. Kasliwal
[reported AIR 1991 SC 2176]
The Court noted that as there had been a conflict between the parties on the facts of the incident, Justice R.M. Sahai had been appointed to inquire into the matter and submit a report. It was held that the inquiry was made on behalf of the Court, and not under the Commissions of Enquiry Act, 1952. The inquiry found that the conduct of the police and other administrative officers was not aboveboard. The respondents challenged the authority of the inquiry, but this was upheld by the Court. The respondents also claimed that the findings of the commission could not be taken into account for this contempt action as this would violate Article 20(3) of the

Constitution, because of the criminal proceedings which were also pending. The Court responded by stating that the contempt proceedings are *sui generis*, i.e., they stand alone, at 2191:

> The power to take proceedings for Contempt of Court is an inherent power of a Court of record, the Criminal Procedure Code does not apply to such proceedings. Since the contempt proceedings are not in the nature of criminal proceedings for an offence, the pendency of contempt proceedings cannot be regarded as criminal proceedings merely because it may end in imposing punishment on the contemner. A contemner is not in the position of an accused, it is open to the Court to cross-examine the contemner and even if the contemner is found to be guilty of contempt, the Court may accept an apology and discharge the notice of contempt, whereas tendering of an apology is no defence to the trial of a criminal offence. This peculiar feature distinguishes contempt proceedings from criminal proceedings.

Thus as the condemners were not in the position of persons accused of an offence merely because of the notice of contempt, it was held that Article 20(3) of the Constitution was not violated.

Referring to Article 129 of the Constitution, the respondents then contended that the SC had no jurisdiction to indict the police officers even if they were found guilty, as they could not be held in contempt in the Supreme Court for the contempt of an inferior court lower to the HC. The Court responded, at 2204:

> The subordinate and inferior courts do not have adequate power under the law to protect themselves, therefore, it is necessary that this Court should protect them. Under the constitutional scheme this Court has a special role, in the administration of justice and the powers conferred on it under Articles 32, 136, 141, 142 form part of the basic structure of the Constitution. The amplitude and power of this Court under these Articles of the Constitution cannot be curtailed by law made by Central or State Legislature. If the contention raised on behalf of the contemners is accepted, the courts all over India will have no protection from this Court. No doubt the High Courts have power to persist for the contempt of subordinate courts but that does not affect or abridge the

> inherent power of this Court under Article 129. The Supreme Court and the High Court both exercise concurrent jurisdiction under the constitutional scheme in matters relating to fundamental rights under Articles 32 and 226 of the Constitution, therefore this Court's jurisdiction and power to take action for contempt of subordinate courts would not be inconsistent to any constitutional scheme.

However, the Court did state, at 2204:

> We would like to strike a note of caution that this Court will sparingly exercise its inherent power in taking cognizance of the contempt of subordinate courts, as ordinarily matters relating to subordinate courts must be dealt with by the High Courts. The instant case is of an exceptional nature, as the incident created a situation where functioning of subordinate courts all over the country was adversely affected, and the administration of justice was paralysed, therefore, this Court took cognizance of the matter.

After discussing the scope of Articles 32, 124, 129, 131, 132, 133, 134 and 134A of the Constitution, the Court delineated the limits of its jurisdiction under Article 136 of the Constitution, at 2192:

> The Court's appellate power under Article 136 is plenary, it may entertain any appeal by granting special leave against any order made by any Magistrate, Tribunal or any other subordinate court. The width and amplitude of the power is not affected by the practice and procedure followed by this Court in insisting that before invoking the jurisdiction of this Court under Article 136 of the Constitution, the aggrieved party must exhaust remedy available under the law before the appellate authority or the High Court. Self-imposed restrictions by this Court do not divest it of its wide powers to entertain any appeal against any order or judgement passed by any Court or Tribunal in the country without exhausting alternative remedy before the appellate authority or the High Court.

Having dealt with the constitutional issues before it, the Court went on to deal with the incident in question. The findings of the commission, that there was no justification for the extraordinary and unusual behaviour of the police inspector and other police officers, were accepted. The justification of the officers, that the CJM was intoxicated and violent, was not accepted by the Court. It was held that the inspector acted in total disregard of the SC's direction in *Prem Shankar Shukla*[8] that no prisoner be handcuffed or fettered routinely or merely for the convenience of custody or escort. It was held, at 2207:

> If the CJM is led into a trap by unscrupulous police officers and if he is assaulted, handcuffed and roped, the public is bound to lose faith in courts, which would be destructive of basic structure of an ordered society. If this is permitted, Rule of Law shall be supplanted by Police Raj. Viewed in this perspective the incident is not a case of physical assault on an individual judicial officer, instead it is an onslaught on the institution of the judiciary itself. The incident is a clear interference with the administration of justice, lowering its judicial authority. Its effect was not confined to one District or State, it had a tendency to affect the entire judiciary in the country. The incident highlights a dangerous trend that if the police is annoyed with the orders of a presiding officer of a Court, he could be arrested on flimsy manufactured charges, to humiliate him publicly as has been done in the instant case. The conduct of the police officers in assaulting the CJM brought the authority and administration into disrespect, affecting public confidence in the institution of justice.

The Court held that the allegations against the CJM were false and directed that the FIRs lodged against him be quashed. The Court directed that the six police officers guilty of contempt be punished as follows:

S.R. Sharma, the then Inspector of Police, Nadiad — simple imprisonment for 6 months and Rs 2,000 fine

K.H. Sadia, the then Sub-Inspector of Police, Nadiad — simple imprisonment for 5 months and Rs 2,000 fine

Head Constable — simple imprisonment for two months and Rs 500 fine. In the case of default in payment of fine, 15 days imprisonment

[8] See chapter on 'Prisons and State Institutions'.

Constable — same as Head Constable

M.B. Savant, Mamlatdar — simple imprisonment for 2 months and Rs 1,000 fine. In the case of default in payment of fine, one month's imprisonment

D.K. Dhagal, Deputy Superintendent of Police — simple imprisonment for one month and Rs.1,000 fine. In the case of default in payment of fine, 15 days imprisonment.

The Court also stated that the punishments awarded did not absolve these officers of misconduct, and the State Government was directed to conduct disciplinary proceedings against them.

To avoid such an incident in the future, the Court laid down guidelines to be followed by the State and the High Courts in the event of the arrest/detention of a judicial officer of the subordinate judiciary:

The arrest can only be made after intimation to the District Judge or the HC, but if immediate arrest is required then this must be done after fulfilling all technical and formal procedures. Such an arrest must be immediately communicated to the District and Sessions Judge of the concerned district and the Chief Justice of the HC. The arrested officer shall not be taken to the police station without a police order or directions of the District and Sessions Judge, if available. The officer shall be provided with facilities for communication with his family members, legal advisers and judicial officers, including the District and Sessions Judge. No statement is to be taken, nor any panchnama drawn up nor any medical tests conducted of such an arrested officer, except in the presence of the legal advisor of the officer or another judicial officer of equal or higher rank. In ordinary circumstances, no judicial officer should be handcuffed. In the case of violent resistance, if the officer is handcuffed, the burden of proof to show that such handcuffing was necessary will be on the police. If found to be unjustified, the police officers concerned would be guilty of misconduct and liable to pay compensation, the amount of which would be decided by the HC. No judicial officer was to visit a police station on his own except in connection with official and judicial duties and functions.

The Court noted that the guidelines prescribed minimum standards and were not exhaustive. Concluding the case, the Court thanked the members of the bar and judiciary for ending their strike, preventing inconvenience to the public and allowing the administration of justice to continue. The petitions were disposed of.

## Custodial Violence

***W P (Crl) No 539 of 1986***
***D.K. Basu v. State of West Bengal***

A letter D/-26/8/86 was sent by D.K. Basu, Executive Chairman of Legal Aid Services, West Bengal, to Chief Justice P.N. Bhagwati regarding newspaper reports published in the *Telegraph* on 20-21-22/7/86 entitled "Death in Police Custody", in the *Indian Express* on 17/8/86 entitled "Police hushing up lock-up murder" and in the *Statesman* on 5/8/86 entitled "Man Dies in Lock-up". The letter noted that in all of these reported instances of custodial violence, no inquiry had been conducted and no compensation had been paid to the relatives of the deceased. The case law on compensation was discussed in the letter which stated that custodial violence was not just restricted to West Bengal but occurred all over India. The letter asked the Court to call for reports from all over India, suggested that a solatium fund be established to give compensation and that procedural safeguards be directed. The letter was registered as a writ petition under Article 32 of the Constitution.

In a counter-affidavit from the Deputy Commissioner of Police on behalf of the state of West Bengal, the veracity of the newpaper reports was not accepted.

In a counter-affidavit from the DIG, Police, on behalf of the state of West Bengal, it was stated:

> I submit that the police are not hushing up any death in lock-up and the matters do not come under Public Interest Litigation and as such the application should be dismissed.

In an order D/-14/8/87 by Justice O. Chinnappa Reddy and Justice K. Jagannatha Shetty

The Court issued notice to all the state governments to find out whether they desired to say anything in the matter and directed that notice be issued to the Law Commission.

No notice was served on the Law Commission. It was only after reading a newspaper report in the *Indian Express* on 15/12/87, that a member of the commission learnt of the case. The Law Commission then made a statement to the Court on 20/1/88, in which it was pointed out:

> though the Hon'ble Court on August 14, 1987 directed that notice be issued to the Law Commission of India also with a request that suitable suggestion may be made in the matter, no notice however has been served on the Law Commission till date.

Submissions were then made to the Court in which the Commission referred to a study it had conducted on the question of injuries in police custody. This had been taken up by the Commission *suo moto* after a Supreme Court judgement[9] and the 113th Report of the Law Commission on "Injuries in Police Custody" had been released on 29/7/85. This report dealt with the burden of proof and the Evidence Act. The Commission pointed out that the duty lay on the law enforcement agency to ensure that a detainee does not suffer violence and therefore stressed the importance of the procedure for arrest and inquiry.

***W P (Crl) No 592 of 1987***
***Ashok K. Johri v. State of U.P.***

A letter D/-29/7/87 was sent to the chief justice of India by Dr Johri regarding the death of a man in police custody. This letter was registered as a petition under Article 32 of the Constitution and tagged with D.K. Basu's petition.

In an order D/-22/10/90 by Justice B.C. Ray and Justice K. Ramaswamy

The Court directed that the matter be listed on 27/11/90 for final disposal.

Meanwhile some states volunarily filed submissions and preliminary written submissions were put before the Court by Dr Abhishek Singhvi, who had been appointed *amicus curiae*, suggesting general guidelines to be followed by police in matters relating to custody.

[9] State of *U.P.* v. *Ram Sagar Yadav* reported in AIR 1985 SC 4161.

Advocate D.K. Basu was appointed as a judge of the Calcutta HC in 1987 and gave a judgement in the case *P.K. Sinha* v. *State of West Bengal* (below). In written submissions in 1992, Mr V.R. Reddy, the Additional Solicitor General of India, referred to this judgement. Mr Reddy made suggestions in this context, relating to the treatment of detainees and the procedure for detention. The need for proper training and orientation of police officers was stressed.

The petition is pending.

☆ ☆ ☆

***O P No 7742 of 1986-H, Kerala***
***Social Action and Legal Aid Society v. State of Kerala and others***

A petition was filed under Article 226 of the Constitution by an organization in Ernakulam. Justice V.R. Krishna Iyer on a visit to the Poojapura Police Station on 5/10/86 had found a naked man, covering himself with a gunny bag, who complained of having been tortured and kept in the lock up for over a week. Horrified by what he saw the retired SC judge wrote a letter to the State and Union Home ministers and gave a copy to advocate James Vincent, President of the Social Action and Legal Aid Society. It was then that the petition was filed, referring to the practice in Kerala police stations where, as soon as the accused, both men and women, are brought to the police station, they were stripped to their undergarments so that they could not commit suicide. Many allegations were made about the treatment of those in custody — stating that there were incidents of torture and rape. The petition stated:

> In many police stations suspected persons are arrested and kept in police lock-ups, without producing them before a Magistrate within 24 hours of arrest, and such suspects are not provided with the basic amenities of life and are not allowed to maintain the dignity of an individual.

Annexed to the petition were newspaper articles and affidavits of undertrial prisoners.

A counter-affidavit from the first respondent, the State of Kerala, D/-27/1/87 stated that Justice Krishna Iyer's report:

> appears to contain a dramatised and exaggerated version of what actually transpired.

as the accused was actually wearing an underwear which may not have been visible in the darkness of the lock-up, and that the complaint of ill-treatment was baseless.

An application was filed by the petitioners asking for the appointment of an expert committee to investigate conditions in the police stations and lock-ups.

In an order D/-20/10/86 by Justice Varghese Kalliath
The Court held, at 2:

> I feel that it is not possible for me to pass an interim order allowing this prayer. True, custodial violence of undertrial prisoners whilst confined in the police lock-up is at the core of the complaint unfolded in the main petition. I am bound to remember fully that the Supreme Court has repeatedly said that custodial violence of undertrial prisoners is a grave and serious matter primarily concerning personal liberty and the Court is bound to act positively and effectively to redress any such violence to personal liberty, since it involves an imperative mandated by Articles 14 and 21 of the Constitution. But I should avoid an overactivist role at all levels since I should be always conscious that of the 'different types of despotism, judicial despotism is not only inexcusable, but also most irrational'.

The Court did ask for a statement from the respondents on the conditions in police stations and lock-ups.

An application was then filed in 1986 by the petitioners asking for a copy of the circular mentioned in the counter-affidavit. The circular, No 3 of 1985 of the Police Headquarters, Trivandrum, to all superintendents of police and commissioners of Police, was headed "Preventive measures — prevention of suicide of persons in Police Custody". The full text of the circular later obtained by the petitioners stated:

> Instances have come to the notice where some persons in police custody have committed suicide by hanging, using mundus/lungies when they were allowed to use water closets unescorted. It is imperative that persons in custody are searched

carefully, and no garments of length should be allowed on their persons which are likely to be used as a means of suicide.

Another application was filed in 1987 by the petitioners asking for additional evidence.

The petition was again heard by a single judge in 1987 and referred to a Division Bench in 1989, after which it has remained pending.

☆ ☆ ☆

***C W P No 123 of 1987, Rajasthan***
***Rajasthan Kisan Sangathan v. State of Rajasthan and others***

A letter D/-24/12/86 was sent to the Chief Justice of the Rajasthan HC by Mrs Srilata Swaminathan, district president of the Rajasthan Kisan Sangathan, District Banswara. The letter complained of the terror created by the police in Banswara District against the Adivasi Harijans in Hamlet Daba Pada, Village Kundal, under the police station of Danpur. Statements and signed representations of those affected were enclosed with the letter, copies of which were sent to the Chief Justice of India, the chairman of the Commission for Scheduled Castes and Scheduled Tribes and the Union Law Minister. The letter detailed some incidents of violence by the police. Apparently Ram Chandra, a resident of Village Kundal, escaped from the Banswara Jail with twenty other detenues. In their search the police went to the village and took away several persons including two tribal women Smt. Takudi and Smt. Saman. They were taken into custody and kept in illegal detention from 19/11/86 to 22/11/86, and again from 30/11/86 to 3/12/86. The two women were tortured, sexually molested and brutally beaten. It was alleged that the policemen put red chilly powder in their vaginas and that once released from custody the condition of Smt. Takudi was so bad that she had to be hospitalized. The letter also stated that the police had wantonly damaged and broken the huts of ten families on 16/11/86, and the crops of the whole village were damaged. The letter, which invoked Article 21 of the Constitution and asked the Court to order an investigation, was registered as a petition under Article 226 of the Constitution.

In an order D/-22/5/87 by > Justice S.N. Bhargava and Justice G.K. Sharma
[reported AIR 1989 Raj 10]

The Court noted its duty under PIL to give relief to needy persons, but referring to *Sachidanand Pandey*, the Court noted its limitations, at 16:

> On the other hand, we do not want to encourage such sort of litigation, otherwise the traditional litigation will suffer and the courts of law instead of dispensing justice will have to take upon themselves administrative and executive functions and it is high time that some clear guidelines are laid down to outline the correct parameters of entertaining such petitions.

The Court upheld the right of a person to be treated with dignity even during a lawful detention, and the right to monetary compensation in the absence of such basic treatment. Stating its inability to come to any conclusion from the material placed before it, the Court ordered that a proper enquiry be conducted by the Commissioner of District Banswara. If, after a thorough enquiry, it was found that the police had committed atrocities or any act of torture, the Commissioner was asked to decide how much compensation, if at all, should be paid to the persons affected. It was stated that the Commissioner should not be affected by the observations of the Court with reference to the alleged offences. The petition was disposed of with no order for costs.

☆ ☆ ☆

***W P (Cri) Nos 250-53 of 1988***

***SAHELI, a Women's Resources Centre through Ms Nalini Bhanot and others v. Commissioner of Police, Delhi and others***

A petition was filed under Article 32 of the Constitution by a women's organization regarding the death of a nine year old child after being beaten and assaulted by a police officer. The petition was filed on behalf of two women, one of whom, Kamlesh Kumari, was the child's mother. Both the women rented a room in the ground floor of the same house and were being threatened with eviction. Kamlesh Kumari's children were kept in the local police station by police officers until she vacated the room while she was harassed by her landlord and imprisoned. On being released from Tihar Jail she found that her son, Naresh, had been beaten while in custody and was admitted into hospital on 18/11/87. No medico-legal case was registered until 23/11/87. On 26/11/87 he died.

In an order D/-14/12/89 by > Justice B.C. Ray and Justice S. Ratnavel Pandian
[reported AIR 1990 SC 513]
After going into the details about the offence, the Court held at 515:

> It is now apparent from the report dated 5/12/87 of the Inspector of the Crime Branch, Delhi as well as the counter-affidavit of the Deputy Commissioner of Police, Delhi on behalf of the Commissioner of Police, Delhi and also from the fact that the prosecution has been launched in connection with the death of Naresh, son of Kamlesh Kumari, showing that Naresh was done to death on account of the beating and assault by the agency of the sovereign power acting in violation and excess of the power vested in such agency. The mother of the child, Kamlesh Kumari, in our considered opinion is so entitled to get compensation for the death of her son from the respondent No. 2, Delhi Administration.

Referring to the Court's order in a case where compensation was awarded — *Peoples Union for Democratic Rights* v. *Police Commissioner* (infra) — the Court held that the state government would be liable to pay compensation. Accordingly, Rs 75,000 was ordered to be paid to Kamlesh Kumari.

☆ ☆ ☆

***W P (Cri) Nos 401-402 of 1988***

***People's Union for Democratic Rights through its Secretary and another* v. *Police Commissioner, Delhi Police Headquarters and another***

A petition was filed under Article 32 of the Constitution regarding police atrocities in Delhi. The petition contended that the police collected some poor people and took them to the police station so that they could be made to work. Instead of paying them for their work, the police beat the people they had rounded up. The petition stated that one man, Ram Swaroop, died and his body was disposed of.

In an order D/-13/1/89 by Justice G.L. Oza and Justice K.N. Saikia
[reported 1989 (1) SCALE 114 [599]].
The Court noted, at 599:

> we record our appreciation that Mr. A.S. Khan, Deputy Commissioner of Police in his affidavit has frankly accepted the atrocity committed by the police officers and it also appears that some action has been taken and that the Station House Officer has been arrested. The matter is being investigated for criminal prosecution. It is unfortunate that the police to whom the citizen can approach for protection and help acted in such a manner.

The family of Ram Swaroop was to be given Rs 50,000 as compensation. This amount was to be invested in the Life Insurance Corporation of India so that his destitute family would get some money each month. The second petitioner, Patasi, who was stripped of her clothes was to be given Rs 500 as compensation and the eight others taken to the police station were ordered to be paid for their work at the rate of Rs 25 and, at 599:

> It is directed that after investigation and inquiry of officers who are found guilty, the amount paid as compensation or part thereof may be recovered from these persons out of salaries after giving them opportunity to show cause.
>
> This order will not prevent any lawful action for compensation. But in case some compensation is ordered by a competent court, this will be given credit to.

☆ ☆ ☆

***W P (Cri) Nos 277-80 of 1989***

***Sunil Gupta and others* v. *State of Madhya Pradesh and others***

A petition was filed under Article 32 of the Constitution by social workers and members of "Kisan Adivasi Sangathan", Kesala, working against the exploitation of local farmers and tribals in District Hoshangabad. A peaceful *dharna* had been staged on 27 and 28/7/88 demanding the appointment of teachers, as there was only one teacher responsible for a large area. The police initiated criminal proceedings against the first three petitioners and an Adivasi widow aged about 65. They were taken from the prison to the Court and back in handcuffs, without a court order permitting such treatment. The petitioners stated that this violated Articles 14 and 21 of the Constitution and Regulation 465(1) of the M.P. Police Regulations.

In an order D/-2/5/90 by > Justice S. Ratnavel Pandian and

Justice K. Jayachandra Reddy
[reported (1990) 3 SCC 119]
The Court held that this was violative of Article 21 of the Constitution, and directed that action be taken against the erring officials by the state government.

☆ ☆ ☆

***C O No 374 (W) of 1989, Calcutta***
***In re: Marttanda Pratap Chakraborty and others ... Intervenors Pratul Kumar Sinha v. State of West Bengal***

A letter was sent to the HC by advocate P.K. Sinha stating that minimum wages should be paid to convicts in jails and referring to other rights and privileges of such convicts. The Association for the Protection of Democratic Rights intervened asking for the protection of rights and privileges of undertrial prisoners. Then on 11/10/91 M.P. Chakraborty intervened to raise the issue of custodial violence and referred to newspaper reports of custodial violence in his application.

In a judgement D/-2/6/92 by Justice D.K. Basu
The Court described the three phases of the case and decided, at 2:

> I propose to deal with the third phase of PIL — the issue concerning custodial violence during pre-trial detention stage, more particularly, detention in the police custody and consequential atrocities inflicted upon the detainee, culminating in death, rape and physical injury of grievous nature — major or minor, as the case may be.

Responding to Chakraborty's intervention, the Court had directed the state of West Bengal to submit a report on the details of lock-up deaths in general and of the individual case mentioned. The Court detailed the other interventions that had been filed by the Association for the Protection of Democratic Rights stating that there were approximately 108 cases of death in police custody in West Bengal between 1977 and 1991, of which details of 91 incidents had been considered in the report by the state of West Bengal and by the PUCL which submitted its own reports. The Court stated that it would not deal specifically with the averments in these three interventions in the third phase of the litigation, but would pass general guidelines. Another intervention, filed by advocate Tamal Kanti Mukherjee detailing an incident of custodial violence on 20/3/92 when Vidyasagar Rai was arrested and sustained injuries, was examined by the Court. Because the security of the HC was at issue, as Vidyasagar Rai was living in the High Court compound with his father who was an employee of the High Court, and because the facts of the case were disputed, the Court had asked for a report and ordered that Rai be produced before the Court. The Court held that the importance of this incident went beyond that of an individual, as it concerned the security of the HC premises and the protection of case papers and documents, and noted, at 17:

> it has been alleged that the concerned officer had apprehended Vidyasagar Rai from the High Court premises by causing illegal trespass inside the High Court campus without permission from necessary authorities and prior to intimation to the High Court Registry.

As no material had been made available on the details of the arrest, the Court stated in the present judgement that a separate order would be passed later, as, at 17:

> I have reason to believe that some separate agency is required to be appointed for investigation and then only, it would be crystal clear before the High Court administration whether a police officer, attached to the Bhawanipore Police Station, without obtaining any permission from the Registry of the High Court, could go inside the High Court premises....

The CBI was directed to conduct an inquiry into this case.

In the main body of this judgement, the Court gave details of the affidavits and reports requested by it on the numbers of lock-up deaths and their details. The Court detailed the genesis and development of PIL and of legal aid and discussed the leading cases on compensation given by the SC and the HCs. The applicable provisions of the Constitution were discussed, as were issues of criminal law, at 68:

> The Code of Criminal Procedure, 1973 has provided sufficient protection to a citizen who has been taken into custody either for interrogation or otherwise by an authority of *quo warranto* of arrest. The provisions are not being complied with effectively and thus those provisions have become obsolete in so far as enforcement is concerned.

The Court held, at 79:

> If there is any controversy in the factum of custody violence leading to lock-up deaths, rape, torture and illegal detention, the controversy arises only because the factum of such atrocities has been reported by some social action groups or has been ventilated in the newspapers and periodicals. If reports of State instituted inquiry commissions and judicial decisions only are considered then the modus operandi of such custodial violence will be crystal clear where it would be evident that not only police officers attached to the police station but also the connivance of members of the medical profession have some contribution to such vices.

Two suggestions for preventing the recurrence of custodial violence were put forward by the court: that each arrested person should be medically examined and a report sent to the Court at the time of arrest and that the police officers who will take part in the interrogation should *prima facie* be responsible for the death of any person in police custody. The Court noted that PIL was criticized by some who think that, at 121:

> in entertaining Public Interest Litigation and securing access to justice for upholding basic human rights which are frequently denied to the vulnerable section of the society, the judiciary is placing itself above the law and is transgressing its limit. This criticism against the emergence of the concept is not *bona fide* because law cannot remain static. Judiciary has to adopt modalities and strategies to meet the requirement of the society and challenges of the decade.

A number of orders were passed by the Court as listed below:

The state government was directed to start a crusade against custodial violence.

Measures to check and monitor custodial violence were to be taken. The police officer concerned was to provide a custody memo, verified by the suspect, with details at the time of arrest. The detainee was to be informed of his/her rights and the reasons for detention. It was held that in the event of custodial violence or death, the victim, next of kin or family would be entitled to lodge a complaint.

Female suspects were directed to be interrogated only in the presence of female police officers, no female suspects were to be taken to, or detained in, police stations, outposts or lock-ups after sunset and were only to go for interrogation on the production of a written call memo. The Court stated that a telephone call or messenger would not suffice, and ordered, at 130:

> I would direct that in the city of Calcutta a reasonable number of police lock-ups should be set up in reasonably good localities where only female suspects should be kept and they should be guarded by female constables and officers.

A special lock-up for women was to be established in every district town, staffed by an infrastructure of female officers.

The Sessions Judge, Calcutta, was ordered to make surprise visits to police lock-ups and bring any lapses to the notice of the Commissioner of Police.

The Court directed that in the case of female non-criminal lunatics, stray girls, females who were deserted or otherwise, the police was to inform the LAC so that legal aid under Article 39A of the Constitution can be provided. Round-the-clock machinery was ordered to be set up to provide this assistance by Bar Council of West Bengal, and voluntary action groups. A panel of lawyers with a telephone at home was to be established, so that the police officer can inform the advocate of any detention within two hours.

After considering the government reports, the Court held, at 132:

> I am convinced that in most of the cases, enquiries, in respect of lock-up deaths in different districts as also in the city of Calcutta, were held in a perfunctory manner and in many cases statutory requirements were not complied with. Even in those cases where magisterial enquiry was held no reports were submitted indicating genuineness and *bona fide* of such enquiry. I am convinced ... [they] ... had discharged their functions in a casual manner.

A special court was to be set up within six months for the sessions trial of those involved in custodial deaths to date. This Court was directed to look into all allegations of violence including rapes or abuses on the female person. The Court held that the proceedings of the Court would vitiate any criminal trial.

Appropriate steps were to be taken against the perpetrators of the crimes.

A number of inquiries were to be conducted, the money for which was to be made available by the respondents. A "Standing Enquiry Court" was to be set up and the Court went into the details of legal assistance and open information.

Compensation was to be paid to the victims and their families from a solatium fund, to be set up along the lines as those set up by the state government for motor accident cases, under the Fatal Accidents Act, 1855, in Chapter VII of the Indian Railways Act, 1890, and in Chapter II of the Workmen's Compensation Act, 1923.

Compensation from this fund should be given without formal application and the Court held that the State Government could recover the money from the police officers of the concerned police station on a pro-rata basis.

The Court directed, therefore, that steps be taken in a phased manner to check and prevent abuses in police custody by the establishment of exclusive police stations for women staffed by women police officers, by the initiation of an awareness campaign by the Government which would include dissemination of pamphlets, establishment of a training course for police personnel highlighting the protection of human rights and laws, and provision of institutional support through different agencies and social action groups.

A copy of the judgement was directed to be supplied to the petitioners free of charge. Concluding the judgement, the Court noted, at 140:

> Separate orders will be passed in respect of the other two phases of PIL action in respect of "undertrial prisoners" and "jail convicts" in due course.

The registry was directed to submit a compliance report within two weeks. The Court held that while inquiry, supervisory and compensatory powers were to be given to police officials, the only saviours for the victims of custodial violence were the lawyers.

A stay order was passed against this judgement by a Division Bench of the Calcutta HC.

☆ ☆ ☆

***Cri Orig Juris***
***"Re Death of Sawinder Singh Grover"***

The SC took *suo moto* notice of an article in the *Hindustan Times* on 4/3/92 about the death of a south Delhi businessman in custody. He had apparently been tortured and had died under suspicious circumstances while being questioned by the Enforcement Directorate.

In an order D/-5/3/92 by Justice S. Ratnavel Pandian, Justice T.K. Thommen, and Justice Kuldip Singh

The Union of India was directed to file an affidavit in the Court before 13/3/92, and the Commissioner of Police was asked to appear on that date.

In an order D/-13/3/92 by Justice Kuldip Singh and Justice B.P. Jeevan Reddy

On perusing the affidavit filed, the Court decided that the death of Sawinder Singh needed further investigation. The District and Sessions Judge, Delhi was directed to nominate a Senior Additional

District and Sessions Judge, Delhi to investigate and enquire into the circumstances leading to the death of Sawinder Singh while allegedly in the custody of the Enforcement Directorate. The investigation was to be completed within four weeks.

In an order D/-21/10/92 by Justice Kuldip Singh and Justice N.M. Kasliwal

[reported 1992 (3) SCALE 15 [34]]

The Court directed that interim compensation of Rs 2 lakhs be paid by the Union of India and the Directorate of Enforcement to the widow of the deceased Sawinder Singh, within three months from the order. The Court directed that the CBI conduct an inquiry and prosecute the relevant officials.

☆ ☆ ☆

***W P (Crl) No 209 of 1993***
***Secretary, Hailakandi Bar Association v. State of Assam***

A resolution D/-23/3/93 passed by the association was sent to the Chief Justice of India, the Chief Justice of the Guwahati HC and to others. Nurul Haque had been arrested by the police on 9/3/93 and kept in custody. He was produced in court in a healthy condition, and the police were permitted to keep him in their custody for seventy-two hours for interrogation. The resolution noted that Nurul Haque's detention had been extended without his having been physically produced before the Court. He was brutally assaulted and died on 13/3/93. His wife filed a complaint before the Chief Judicial Magistrate on 14/3/93, against some police officials, claiming that her husband had been murdered. Attempts by the police to bury the body were unsuccessful because of protests by the wife and members of the public. The Bar Association then passed a resolution which stated, at 2:

> Considering the gravity of the matter this association unanimously condemn the atrocities alleged to have been committed by some particular police officials and personnel and urge the Government and other authorites to initiate immediate action as may be found appropriate for a judicial enquiry into the matter to bring the culprits to book for maintaining the dignity of the rule of law and protection of

> human rights in general and paying adequate compensation to the unfortunate and helpless mother and wife of the deceased.

The resolution was registered as a writ petition under Article 32 of the Constitution.

In an order D/-20/8/93 by Justice A.M. Ahmadi and Justice N.P. Singh

The Court held that as this was a case of a serious nature, relating to a custodial death, the Director General of Police in the state of Assam was ordered to inquire into the matter and submit a detailed report to the Court within four weeks.

In an order D/-24/9/93 by Justice A.M. Ahmadi and Justice N. Venkatachala

The Court acknowledged receipt of the report, which, inspite of specific orders, had not been conducted by the Director General of Police. The report concluded:

> Nurul Haque neither died in police lock-up nor in police custody. He died while in judicial custody as UTP (undertrial prisoner). He was not tortured during the period of police custody,

and claimed that he was beaten by some members of the public. The Court stated that the report needed close scrutiny and asked for certain contentions to be explained. The SCLAC was asked to nominate an advocate to assist the Court.

In an order D/-29/10/93 by Justice A.M. Ahmadi and Justice R.M. Sahai

The Court stated that the report forwarded by the Director General of Police left much unexplained. It alleged that the deceased died of natural causes and that efforts were made to treat him. However, the Court noted that the postmortem report showed that Haque had external injuries which were denied in the police report. The Superintendent of Police, Hailakandi was directed to file an affidavit explaining these circumstances.

In an order D/-24/1/94 by Justice A.M. Ahmadi and Justice N. Venkatachala

The Court noted that:

> When the Court calls for the report of the Director General of Police, the Court places confidence in the objectivity of a person holding such a high office and when such an officer

> mechanically forwards the report of his subordinate with a forwarding letter he betrays a casual approach shaking the court's confidence in him and dilutes the probative value of the report.

and pointed out:

> The story that the members of the public beat him raises doubts because in that case the wrath of the public would not have been towards the police and the Bar Association would not have taken up the cause. ... The possibility of the police having caused serious injuries cannot be ruled out altogether. Since the local police at the highest level have taken a stand that the assault on the deceased was by members of the public and not the police after the apprehension of the deceased it is futile to expect an independent and wholly objective investigation by the State police. Even otherwise, the people will have little confidence in the investigation no matter how honest and objective the investigation be.

Accordingly the Court directed that an investigation be carried out by the CBI, which was to hear the allegations of the wife and other relatives of the deceased without being influenced by the claim that the assault was carried out by the members of the public. The order was concluded:

> The Registrar General will write a letter to the Director of CBI to take immediate steps to take over the investigation of the crime from the local police and try to complete the same at an early date and bring the real culprits to book. The petition will stand so disposed of.

## Firings and Encounter Deaths

***W P (Cri) Nos 55, 62 and 68 of 1982***

***Chaitanya Kalbagh and others* v. *State of U.P. and others***

Petitions were filed under Article 32 of the Constitution regarding the killing of many people after 'encounters' with the police. W P No 55 filed by journalist Chaitanya Kalbagh related to the massacre of 24 Harijans on 18/11/81 in Dehuli, Manipuri, U.P. This petition stated that as many as 299 innocent people had been killed in an effort to eliminate dacoitism. W P No 62 was filed by Rajni Kothari and K. Manoharan relating to the killing of a number of people in Tamil Nadu in 1980-81 in Districts Dharmapuri and North Arcot. Most of the people killed were young activists engaged in the cause of rural development, especially Harijans and other landless labourers, so the petitioners contended that the encounters were not genuine but formed part of a massive drive by the state police to eliminate such activists believed to be Naxalites. This petition also asked the Court to direct the State of Tamil Nadu to define what was meant by the term 'Naxalite'. W P No 68 related to the killing of a number of people in Andhra Pradesh.

Stating that these killings were illegal and violated Article 21 of the Constitution, the petitioners asked the SC to institute an impartial agency, not under the control of the state government, and with the authority to launch prosecutions against the concerned police officers.

In an order D/-29/3/89 by Chief Justice R.S. Pathak and Justice Ranganath Misra
[reported AIR 1989 SC 1452]
An objection to the admission of the petition had been filed by the Additional Solicitor General who stated that Article 32 of the Constitution would not be applicable in cases of this kind as a remedy was available under the Cr P C, 1973. Moreover, as the facts were of a complex and political nature, it was claimed that a commission would need to be appointed by the government, to which the respondents replied that the state governments should first be addressed on the question of appointing a commission to inquire into the deaths. The Court therefore directed the petitioners to petition the concerned state governments, which should dispose of the grievances within three months, at 1453:

> Having given the matter careful consideration we think that these three writ petitions relate to matters which properly fall within the domain of the State Governments, and that in the first instance the State Governments should be petitioned. The facts mentioned in the three writ petitions call for a complete review of what has been described as "encounter" and in conditions of disturbed law and order of the magnitude reflected in these writ petitions we cannot preclude the

possibility of personal feuds and enmities being settled and other motives being satisfied by recourse to the use of force under the guise of maintaining law and order. There is the imperative requirement of ensuring that the guardians of law and order do in fact observe the code of discipline expected of them and that they function strictly as the protectors of innocent citizens.

The Court stated that if the State Governments did not act, then the Court would.

☆ ☆ ☆

***W P (Cri) No 369 of 1986***
***People's Union for Democratic Rights v. State of Bihar and others***

A petition was filed under Article 32 of the Constitution stating that the police opened fire on 19/4/86 at a peaceful meeting of 600-700 poor peasants and landless people within the compound of the Gandhi Library, Arwal. Most of the people at the meeting were from the backward classes of District Gaya, Bihar. The petition stated that the police opened fire without warning or provocation. Twenty-one persons including some children had died.

In an order D/-19/12/86 by > Justice Ranganath Misra and Justice M.M. Dutt
[reported AIR 1987 SC 355]
The Court acknowledged the report of B.D. Sharma, the Assistant Commissioner for Scheduled Castes and Scheduled Tribes. It was decided to dispose of some aspects of the case in the SC and leave the rest to the HC and the petitioner's discretion. Compensation of Rs 10,000 had already been paid by the State, but the Court held that this amount could be increased. The Court directed that Rs 20,000 be paid for each death and Rs 5,000 for each injured person, and for the rehabilitation of the dependants of the deceased.

After the firing the organization that held the meeting, the MKSS (Mazdoor Kisan Sangram Samiti), was banned. Although the Court had granted compensation, it could not be claimed as it would have been dangerous to admit to being a member of a banned organization.

☆ ☆ ☆

***C W No 3393 of 1990, Delhi***

***P.V. Kapoor and another v. Union of India and another***

A petition was filed under Article 226 of the Constitution by two advocates after the Mandal Riots based on the October 1990 issue of the video magazine *Newstrack*. The petition alleged that the police firing on a crowd of unarmed students on 25/9/90, in and around INA market in Delhi was illegal. A student, Devinder Kumar, was killed in the firing, and the petition submitted the video film shot by M/s Living Media India Ltd., as evidence. The petition stated that after he was shot, the student was not provided with immediate transportation to a hospital by the police. The petition asked for Rs 5 lakhs as compensation for this death and that of Aditya Narain, aged fifteen, on 25/9/90 in Sarojini Nagar.

In an order D/-6/9/91 by > Justice B.N. Kirpal and Justice D.K. Jain

[reported 1991 (3) Delhi Lawyers 391 (DB)]

Referring to *People's Union for Democratic Rights* v. *Union of India*, *S.P. Gupta*, *Fertilizer Corporation*, *Bandhua Mukti Morcha* and *Bangalore Medical Trust*, the Court held, at 400-1:

> An analysis of the aforesaid decisions shows that PIL is a new brand of litigation which is not meant to be adversarial in nature. It is intended to vindicate public interest where fundamental and other rights of people who are poor, ignorant or are in a socially or economically disadvantageous position, go unredressed. PIL is meant to be a cooperative and collaborative effort of the parties and the court to secure justice for the poor and the weaker sections of the community. Causes of public nature can be espoused by public spirited citizens having faith in the rule of law. Writ petitions in the nature of PIL can be filed where substantial issues of accountability of those entrusted with the responsibility of the administration are raised. Public Interest Litigation, in other words, means nothing more than what the words themselves state viz., it is a litigation in the interest of the public. PIL is not that type of a litigation which is meant to satisfy the curiosity of the people but it is a litigation which is instituted by public spirited organizations or people with a desire that the court could be able to give effective relief to the whole or a section of the society.

The Court also held that PIL is not just a remedy for the infringement of the fundamental rights for the poorer and weaker sections but can also be used for issues of public concern, at 397-8:

> This is a new type of litigation which has come into existence as a result primarily of, judicial activism. This type of litigation has been given impetus by the Supreme Court. The Court was conscious of the fact that cases of gross violation of fundamental rights were going unnoticed and no relief was being granted by the executive or the Court. This was particularly true in cases involving the weaker and poorer sections of society. The plight of such persons was made known to the public by another institution, which also developed a certain amount of activism and that institution was the press. Social organizations and intellectuals began taking notice of articles appearing in the national dailies, whereby the general public was informed, as a result of investigative journalism, about the plight of certain sections of the suffering masses. One of the first cases which the Supreme Court took up, as an instance of public interest litigation, was when a writ petition was filed by an advocate of the Supreme Court based on a series of articles in the national dailies pertaining to long pre-trial detention of the undertrial prisoners in Bihar. It had been pointed out in the newspapers that in some cases the pre-trial detention had been for a longer period than the period for which the persons would have been sentenced, if they had been convicted after being charged. Soon there was a flood of such type of litigation to the Supreme Court, which is evident from the fact that it appears that between 1980 and 1982, about 75 public interest litigation cases were filed in the Supreme Court by activists, individual lawyers and lawyers' groups.

The Court identified the issues with which it should concern itself, at 401:

> Firstly, what is the extent and manner of force which should be used by the police in effecting control of a crowd and secondly, the manner in which the persons who are injured as a result of the police firing should be handled or treated. Excessive use of force can be arbitrary and can even result in violation of Article 21 of the Constitution.

Noting that a problem arises when there are disputed questions of fact in PILs, at 402:

> It is not possible to lay down a general rule or proposition as to the manner in which facts can be ascertained in such cases. However, it is not unknown that in petitions under Article 226, occasions do arise where facts have to be determined. It is not necessary that in every case, oral evidence has to be recorded in order to arrive at the correct finding of facts. In petitions under Article 226 facts are determined on the basis of the affidavits and documents on the record. But in all the cases merely resorting to the records before the Court may not be sufficient. The Court may have to innovate procedures in order to ascertain correct facts. In view of the fact that proceedings in public interest litigation are not adversarial in nature, perhaps more reliance can be placed on the affidavits which are filed before the Court. The petitioner, be it an individual or organization, approaches the court not with a view to gain advantage for itself but comes with a spirit of pubic service. There could be, ordinarily, little incentive for the petitioner not to set out the correct facts. But even then the averments made in the petition may be based on second hand information or knowledge which may not be wholly correct. Therefore, even though the petitioner may honestly state in the petition the facts as known to him it may transpire that those facts are either not complete or are wholly or partly untrue. Unless the facts, as alleged in the petition, are admitted by the respondents in their affidavit, the Court should, even in public interest litigation cases, try and have other information or evidence.

On an analysis of the present case, the Court held that compensation cannot be awarded because of the firing as, at 413:

> One wrongdoer cannot ordinarily benefit from the other party's wrongful act, unless it can be shown that the use of force was so grossly disproportionate to the injured party's wrongful act so as to lead one to believe that the use of excessive force was mala fide or vindictive.

and Devinder Kumar Sharma was part of an armed crowd. However, the Court did award Rs 50,000 compensation to his next of kin because of the manner in which the police handled him after he was injured. Compensation of Rs 2,50,000 was directed to be paid to the next of kin of Aditya Narain who was not a member of an unlawful assembly and was only fifteen years of age. Both these amounts were to be paid by the Delhi Police.

☆ ☆ ☆

***W P (Cri) Nos 1118 of 1991 and 1141 of 1991***
***R.S. Sodhi, Advocate, People's Union for Civil Liberties v. State of U.P. and others***

A petition was filed under Article 32 of the Constitution regarding the killing of a number of people in encounters with the police in Pilibhit. Ten alleged terrorists were killed on the night of 12-13/7/91.

In an order D/-21/8/91 by Chief Justice Ranganath Misra and Justice Kuldip Singh
[reported 1991 (2) SCALE 81 [463]]
The Court declined to admit W P No 1141 of 1991 as it contained the same allegations as W P No 1118 of 1991. The Court noted that the state of U.P. had been providing protection to the legal representatives and other persons who would like to appear before the Commission.[10] The Union of India was to be impleaded as a party to the petitions after which the matter was to be fixed for 25/9/91. The Court directed, at 464:

> As an ad interim measure of compensation we direct that in respect of each of the deaths (total number being ten) an interim compensation of Rs 50,000 (Rupees fifty thousand) shall be paid within four weeks from today.

An open letter was sent to Chief Justice Ranganath Misra and Justice Kuldip Singh from Chittaranjan Singh D/-30/8/91 on the Pilibhit incident. The letter stated that Chittaranjan Singh had filed a petition which was rejected because of the pendency of another petition by advocate R.S. Sodhi, on which the Court awarded Rs 50,000 to the dependants of the dead in fake encounter killings. In the letter it was requested that this second petition be co-joined with the petition filed by Sodhi, a Sikh, as the existence of a petition by a Hindu would increase goodwill. Moreover the letter stated that the

[10] No details of this Commission were given in the order.

cost of filing of Chittaranjan Singh's petition had been borne by the labourers. The letter cited earlier cases to support his plea:

> in 1982, on 12/13 March in Gonda district of U.P. there was a fake encounter in which a Deputy SP, K.P. Singh and 12 other villagers were killed. I had filed a petition in the Supreme Court for a CBI enquiry. Hon'ble Judges cojoined my petition to the already filed petition of the widow of K.P. Singh, Mrs Vibha. My petition was heard with hers, an enquiry was ordered and the culprits, after a long battle, are undergoing trial at Lucknow.

An article reported that after the order in R.S. Sodhi's petition:

> The BJP government has filed a review petition praying that the payment of interim compensation be made conditional upon a finding by the commission of inquiry headed by Justice K.P. Singh that the encounters were fake. The petition claims that this interim compensation sets a bad precedent which could be grossly abused in terrorist-affected states like Punjab, Kashmir, the North-East and some districts of U.P. The petition cautions that the morale of the police, who are fighting against terrorists must not be damaged at any cost.[11]

The State filed an appeal against the order of 21/8/91 awarding compensation. It was stated that because those killed were terrorists, no compensation should be given for their death.

In an order in 1992, the Court directed that Rs 20,000 be given to each of the dependants and that the remaining Rs 30,000 be held as a deposit in the Court.

The Rs 20,000 was not disbursed because an application was filed by the State questioning the identity of those killed. It was stated that the identity of the next-of-kin needed to be verified. Accordingly, in another order in 1992, the Court directed that a criminal investigation be conducted by the CBI to verify the identity of those killed and stayed the disbursal of the compensation pending the findings of this inquiry.

☆ ☆ ☆

[11] "Newsfile: BJP Opposes Compensation for Pilibit Victims", *The Lawyers*, Vol. 6, No. 10, October 1991, 11.

***W P (Crl) No 612 of 1992***
***People's Union for Civil Liberties (PUCL) v. Union of India and others***

A petition was filed under Article 32 of the Constitution. Two persons, Sri Seikaplen and Sri K. Bheeieklian, were picked up by the police in Manipur on 3/4/92. The petition alleged that they were killed by the police on 15/4/92 in an "encounter". As no postmortem details were available, a request was made to the Chief Minister of Manipur to enquire into this fake encounter. Having received no response from him, a petition was filed asking for an enquiry into the killings and the payment of compensation.

Admitting the petition the SC issued notice to the Manipur Government.

☆ ☆ ☆

***W P (C) No 635 of 1992***
***All India Democratic Women's Association v. the State of Tamil Nadu and others***

Two letters were sent to the Court as well as to the SCLAC by a womens organization. On 27-28/1/92 the Tamil Nadu Police had opened fire on a gathering of Harijans in Village Nalumunai Kenaru. Eight people were seriously wounded, including two children aged 6 and 12 years. Properties of the Harijan families were looted and 'terror and violence were unleashed'. The police visited the neighbouring villages and repeated the same arbitrary firing and arrested various persons. The villagers were forced to flee and one woman had to give birth in the forest. In response to the letter, the SCLAC then filed a regular writ petition under Article 32 of the Constitution. However, before filing the petition, the SCLAC had written to the concerned authorities to see what action had been taken. No replies to these letters were received. The petition stated that no action had been taken against the police officials, that no compensation had been given and it was contended that the attack had been instigated by the Deputy Inspector of Police, Madras. The petition detailed the properties lost by the villagers, together with their value. The Court was asked to appoint a commission of enquiry, to direct the payment of compensation, to issue directions that the erring police officials and other state officials be brought to book and to make an order for costs.

In an order D/-5/5/93 by Chief Justice M.N. Venkatachaliah and Justice S. Mohan

It was noted that in an earlier order D/-1/3/93 the Court had ordered that an independent inquiry should look into the allegations. In the present order, the Court directed that the inquiry be carried out by the Secretary, Public (Special) Department, Government of Tamil Nadu, and not by the Home Secretary as it had indicated earlier. It was also noted that the Revenue Commissioner had himself described the police as careless.

The "Enquiry Report on the Police Firing in Nadunalumoolaikinaru Village" was submitted to the Court.

The report stated that those injured and treated in a government hospital should be given Rs 2,000 each as an ex gratia payment, to 'mollify' the grievances of the villagers. It was held that as the loss to properties could not be verified, no compensation could be given. It was noted that some other grievances of the villagers emerged in the visit of the commissioner, and the District Collector had been asked to look into these matters. The report stated that the State had no responsibility and no liability for the events and that the villagers had run amok.

After this PIL petition was filed, the Government also made an *ex gratia* payment of Rs 10,000 to each of those who had suffered bullet injuries.

"Objections to the Report Submitted by the Enquiry Officer by the Petitioner" was submitted to the Court.

The petitioner stated that the enquiry report was not categoric on the action of the police and there was no recommendation for any action to be taken against police officers. Many objections were raised about the manner of conducting the enquiry and the conclusions reached thereby.

In an order D/- 29/10/93 by Justice J.S. Verma, Justice N.P. Singh and Justice S.P. Bharucha

The Court ordered:

> It is pointed out by Shri Mukhoty, learned counsel for the petitioner that the enquiry report has been submitted by Shri P Bhaskar Doss, Secratary (Public Department) Government of Tamil Nadu who is the officer who had earlier filed the counter-affidavit on behalf of respondents one to four. In these circumstances, without meaning to cast any reflection on Shri

> Bhaskar Doss or his report, we consider it appropriate that the enquiry be conducted and a report on that basis be submitted by the Government. Both sides agree that in such a situation, Shri Muni Raman, Law Secretary, Government of Tamil Nadu may be directed to conduct a fresh enquiry into the matter and submit his report within six weeks.

The "Report on the Enquiry Conducted by Thiru M Muniram, Secretary to the Government, Law Department, Government of Tamil Nadu in the Matter Relating to the Police Firing on the Villagers on 28/1/92 at Nalu Moolaikinaru, Tiruchendur Taluk, Chidambaranar District and the other Matters Relating Thereto" was submitted to the Court on 6/1/94.

In an order D/-28/2/94 by Justice J.S. Verma and Justice S.P. Bharucha

The Court acknowledged the receipt of the report, and found the criticism of the report filed by S. Muralidhar, advocate for the petitioner, to be justified:

> The report does not properly advert to the matters in respect of which the enquiry was required to be made, and the material available on record merely places reliance on the version of the police officials and the Government doctors whose conduct was the subject matter of the enquiry. The report does not refer to or consider the statement of any villager who was a victim of the alleged atrocity. It goes further to recommend that 'no separate action is necessary against the police officials who are responsible for ordering firing on that date'. In short, the report does not serve any useful purpose nor does it satisfy the requirement of the desired report. We are constrained to observe that such an unsatisfactory report made pursuant to the directions of the Court is, to say the least, highly unsatisfactory and not up to the level expected from an officer holding that rank. The report is accordingly rejected.

The Court directed the Chief Justice of the Madras High Court to nominate a judicial officer of the rank of district judge to make a fresh enquiry and submit a report within eight weeks of nomination as the Enquiry Officer. All the material in the case was to be made available to the District Judge. The matter was to be listed after receipt of the report by the SC.

## Negligence

***W P (Cri) No 303 of 1989***

***Supreme Court Legal Aid Committee, through its Hon'y Secretary v. State of Bihar and others***

A petition was filed under Article 32 of the Constitution based on a newspaper report in the *Illustrated Weekly of India* on 2/7/89 detailing the negligence of police officials in failing to give proper medical aid to Mahesh Mahto who had been injured and died in police custody. The petition stated that his death was caused by the delay in getting help, and that therefore, Article 21 of the Constitution was violated.

In an order D/-4/3/91 by Chief Justice Ranganath Misra and Justice P.B. Sawant

[reported (1991) 3 SCC 482]

The Court held that it was the obligation of the police to ensure appropriate protection to any person taken into custody, and stressed that any necessary medical care must be provided. The state of Bihar was directed to pay Rs 20,000 compensation to the legal representatives of the deceased, as this is the compensation ordinarily payable in case of a death of this kind.

## Investigations and Corruption

***C A No 570 of 1983 with S L P (Cri) No 2671 of 1983***

***State of West Bengal and others v. Sampat Lal***

An appeal was filed under Article 136 of the Constitution from the judgement and order D/-27/9/83 of the Calcutta High Court. Two letters had been sent to the Chief Justice of the Calcutta HC asking him to intervene as the police investigation in connection with the unnatural death of two young boys was not proper and above board. The letters referred to newspaper reports in *Anand Bazar Patrika* which had detailed a parallel investigation by Secret Eye, a private detective agency. The letters were registered as petitions under Article 226 of the Constitution. As the findings of this private investigation had not been denied by the respondents, the HC had ordered that an independent investigation be conducted by a special officer. The petition discussed the provisions of the Cr P C, 1973.

In an order D/-4/12/84 by Justice P.N. Bhagwati, Justice A.N. Sen and > Justice Ranganath Misra
[reported (1985) 1 SCC 317]
The SC held that the HC should not have appointed a special officer as the matter fell within the jurisdiction of the police, as the conduct of such an investigation is a police power, and noted that the HC order had implied that all was not well. It was held that possible exceptions to the investigative powers of the police were not applicable in this case and that the HC should have allowed the appellants a hearing and not taken evidence *prima facie*. Referring to the pendency of the criminal case, the SC stated, at 336:

> We have, therefore, thought it a proper exercise of discretion not to enter into the facts and express any opinion one way or the other so as not to prejudice the trial that might take place. It is sufficient to indicate that there is a residuary jurisdiction left in the Court to give directions to the investigating agency when it is satisfied that the requirements of law are not being complied with and investigation is not being conducted properly or with due haste and promptitude. The Court has to be alive to the fact that the scheme of the law is that the investigation has been entrusted to the police and it is ordinarily not subject to the normal supervisory power of the Court.

In the present case, however, the Court did suggest, hope and trust, at 339:

> We would ... suggest that the Director-General of Police, West Bengal will appoint a competent supervisory officer from the higher ranks of the State Police with expertise in investigation to supervise the investigation in the present case. The police authorities will, we hope, avail of any credible material collected by Secret Eye, if such material is made available to the police authorities.

The appeal was allowed.

☆ ☆ ☆

***Civil Writ Jurisdiction Case No 7696 of 1989, Bihar***
***Association for Protection of Public Rights and Interest through its Secretary* v. *State of Bihar and others***

A petition was filed under Article 226 of the Constitution by an organization in Bihar. There were allegations of misappropriation of crores of rupees by certain police officers in Bihar, ostensibly for the purchase of clothing and other materials for the Department. The media exposed this corruption by members of the Indian Police Force and reported that the Director-General of Police was involved in the criminal conspiracy. The Government of Bihar referred the matter to the CBI for investigation and five cases were registered. The petition was filed challenging the investigation in the five cases on the grounds of *malafides* and questioning the jurisdiction of the CBI to investigate. It was contended that documents had been fabricated, that all the facts had not been disclosed and that the inquiries were conducted by relatives and friends of the Director General of Police. The Court was asked to quash the FIRs and investigate into the matter. Certain newspaper reports were annexed to the petition.

In an order D/-26/3/90 by Justice Prabha Shanker Mishra and Justice Bhuvaneshwar Prasad

After a detailed discussion, the Court concluded that the contentions challenging its jurisdiction to hear the matter were rejected. The FIRs in all five cases were quashed and directions were issued to the CBI to re-investigate the role of the DIG and to investigate the allegations in respect of the Commandants and the SSP of the districts concerned. The Court described its trust that the CBI inquiry would be conducted irrespective of the attitude of the State Government or its officers, and would disregard any links or connections with the officers under scrutiny.

The petition was allowed.

***S L P (C) No 2380 of 1991***
***Union of India and another* v. *Association for Protection of Public Rights and Interest through its Secretary Shri Sachidanand Singh and another***

An appeal was filed against this order of the HC. It was contended that the HC unnecessarily considered some evidence in the case, without going through the whole evidence, and that the HC should, therefore, not have given any order in the case.

The SC ordered a CBI enquiry into this matter.

☆ ☆ ☆

***C A No 7243 of 1993, arising out of S L P (C) No 13066 of 1993 Punjab and Haryana High Court Bar Association Chandigarh through its Secretary v. State of Punjab and others***

An appeal was filed under Article 136 of the Constitution against the order of the Punjab and Haryana HC in C W P No 2376 of 1993. Advocate Kulwant Singh, his wife and a young child had apparently been abducted and murdered. Many details emerged about this incident, and as the Bar Association was not satisfied with the police investigation, it demanded a judicial enquiry by a sitting judge of the HC, a district judge or a vigilance judge of the higher judiciary. This demand was not acceded to, so the members of the Association went on strike on 6/2/93. The District Bar Associations of Punjab, Haryana and Chandigarh joined in the strike. A petition was then filed by Suresh Kumar as a PIL asking for a judicial enquiry, especially as the interests of the litigating masses were suffering as a result of the strike. The HC issued a notice in this petition to the HC Bar Association as a respondent to the petition. An attempt was made to withdraw the petition at which point the advocate for the Bar Association and Bar Council stated that as the petition was a PIL it could not be withdrawn. It was also argued that as the lawyers had been on strike for more than six weeks, it would be in the interest of justice to finally adjudicate on the points raised. The HC had rejected the petition, stating:

> In our view, there is a vital distinction between the original petition filed by the petitioner and the stand taken by the added respondents. Reading between the lines, the reference of the former is to save the "litigant" and that of the latter is to save the "lawyer". In one case the relief is claimed against the members of the Bar and in the other the relief is claimed against the State. We do not think that we could be justified in permitting the proxy war in the name of litigation styled as public interest litigation when the real sufferer is the litigant public. … whereas any person can set the criminal law into motion, no stranger can challenge conviction or other adverse order recorded against a person under the garb of public

> interest litigat.on. ... the mere fact that the Motion Bench has admitted the writ petition of Suresh Kumar for consideration of the Full Bench does not necessarily conclude the question whether, in fact, the writ petition relates to a matter of public interest litigation. ... the admission of the writ petition by itself will not convert the petition of Suresh Kumar into public interest litigation.

It was then that this appeal was filed.

In an order D/-7/12/93 by Justice Kuldip Singh and Justice S C Agrawal
[reported 1993 (4) SCALE 147 [636]]
The Court stated, at 641:

> The High Court was wholly unjustified in closing its eyes and ears to the controversy which shocked the lawyer fraternity in the region.

Observing that the HC should have directed an independent investigation/enquiry. The Court then stated, at 641-2:

> We are conscious that the investigation having been completed by the police and charge-sheet submitted to the Court, it is not for this Court, ordinarily, to reopen the investigation. Nevertheless, in the facts and circumstances of the present case, to do complete justice in the matter and to instill confidence in the public mind it is necessary, in our view, to have fresh investigation in this case through a specialized agency like the Central Bureau of Investigation.

The Court directed that a CBI investigation be conducted which was to be completed within three months. The proceedings in this case before the Additional District and Sessions Judge, Ropar, were stayed till 31/3/94. The appeal was allowed.

# CASE CHAPTER 3

# The Armed Forces

## Framing the Issue

Most of the cases in this chapter relate to the armed forces stationed in areas of the north-east. The chapter is separated into three categories — challenge to enactments, the Oinam issue and the rest of the cases. Although there have been cases from other areas of the country where the army has been deployed, information on these has not been readily available. In addition to the cases in this chapter, petitions have been filed in response to incidents of rapes committed by members of the armed forces in the north-east,[1] to prevent women from being abused while in custody or during interrogation[2] and the detention of children.

A survey of the relevant statutory law reveals the extent of the powers conferred on the armed forces in the north-east. Both the Assam Disturbed Areas Act, 1955 and the Armed Forces (Special Powers) Act, 1958 give wide ranging powers to the army. The term 'disturbed area' is not defined and protection is afforded to those acting under the Acts. Similarly, members of the Assam Rifles, one

[1] See the chapter on 'Injustices Specific to Women' for two such cases, one filed by Niloy Dutto and the other as a *suo moto* petition.

[2] The order of the SC in Editor *Boodhbar* has been included in this chapter but the order of the Guwahati High Court in *Niloy Dutto* has only been included in the chapter on 'Injustices Specific to Women' — this order stated that no woman should be expected to go to an army camp for interrogation.

of the major batallions of the Army stationed in the North-East, have been empowered by the Assam Rifles Act, 1941 to act in place of the police.

The Assam Disturbed Areas Act, 1955 was enacted to make better provisions for the restoration and maintenance of public order in those areas of Assam considered to be disturbed. With the division of the state of Assam, the Act has subsequently been adopted by other states like Nagaland and Meghalaya. Reproduced below are relevant sections of this Act:

> Section 3. **Power to declare areas to be disturbed areas.** — The State Government may, by notification in the Official Gazette, declare that the whole or any part of any district of Assam may be specified in the notification as a disturbed area.
>
> Section 4. **Power to fire upon person contravening certain orders.** — Any Magistrate or Police Officer not below the rank of Sub-Inspector or Havildar in case of the Armed Branch of the Police or any officer of the Assam Rifles not below the rank of Havildar, may, if in his opinion it is necessary so to do for the maintenance of public order, after giving such warning, if any, as he may consider necessary, fire upon, or otherwise use force even to the causing of death, against any person who is acting in contravention of any law or order for the time being in force in a disturbed area, prohibiting the assembly of five or more persons or the carrying of weapons or things capable of being used as weapons or fire-arms, ammunition and explosive substances.
>
> Section 5. **Power to destroy arms, fortified positions, etc.** — Any Magistrate or Police Officer not below the rank of Sub-Inspector or any officer of the Assam Rifles not below the rank of Jamadar may, if in his opinion it is necessary so to do, destroy any arms dump, prepared, or fortified or shelters from which armed attacks are made or attempted, structures used as training camps for armed volunteers or utilized as hide-outs or shelters by armed gangs or absconders wanted for offences in connection with the disturbances.
>
> Section 6. **Protection of persons acting under sections 4 and 5.** — No suit, prosecution or other legal proceeding shall be instituted except with the previous sanction of the state Government against any person in respect of anything done or

purporting to be done in exercise of the powers conferred by sections 4 and 5.

The Armed Forces (Special Powers) Act, 1958, as amended in 1972 and 1986, empowers the Governors of the States of Arunachal Pradesh, Assam, Manipur, Meghalaya, Mizoram, Nagaland and Tripura to declare any area within their states to be a 'disturbed area', in protection against internal disturbance. Sections of this Act, relevant for the study of PIL cases, state:

Section 3. **Power to declare areas to be disturbed areas.** — If, in relation to any State or Union Territory to which this Act extends, the Governor of that State or the Administrator of that Union Territory or the Central Government, in either case, is of the opinion that the whole or any part of such State or Union Territory, as the case may be, is in such a disturbed or dangerous condition that the use of armed forces in aid of the civil power it necessary, the Governor of that State or the Administrator of that Union Territory or the Central Government, as the case may be, may, by notification in the Official Gazette, declare the whole or such part of such State or Union Territory to be a disturbed area.

Section 4. **Special powers of the armed forces**. — Any commissioned officer, warrant officer, non-commissioned officer or any other person of equivalent rank in the armed forces who may, in a disturbed area, —

(a) if he is of the opinion that it is necessary to do so for the maintenance of public order, after giving such due warning as he may consider necessary, fire upon or otherwise use force even to the causing of death, against any person who is acting in contravention of any law or order for the time being in force in the disturbed area prohibiting the assembly of five or more persons or the carrying of weapons or of things capable of being used as weapons or as fire-arms, ammunition or explosive substances;

(b) if he is of the opinion that it is necessary to do so, destroy any arms dump, prepared or fortified position or shelter from which armed attacks are made or are likely to be made or are attempted to be made, or any structure used as training camp for armed volunteers or utilized as a hide-out by armed gangs of absconders wanted for any offence;

(c) arrest, without warrant, any person who has committed a cognizable offence or against whom a reasonable suspicion exists that he has committed or is about to commit a cognizable offence, and may use such force as may be necessary to effect the arrest;

(d) enter and search without warrant any premises to make any such arrest as aforesaid or to recover any person believed to be wrongfully restrained or confined or any property reasonably suspected to be a stolen property or any arms, ammunition or explosive substances believed to be unlawfully kept in such premises, and may for that purpose use such force as may be necessary.

Section 5. **Arrested persons to be made over to the police.** — Any person arrested and taken into custody under this Act shall be made over to the officer in charge of the nearest police station with the least possible delay, together with a report of the circumstances occasioning the arrest.

Section 6. **Protection to persons acting under Act.** — No prosecution, suit or other legal proceeding shall be instituted, except with the previous sanction of the Central Government, against any person in respect of anything done or purported to be done in exercise of the powers conferred by this Act.

In the north-east these enactments have been used by the state in aid of civil power in the sensitive border areas to protect national security, and manage the problems raised by demands for secession, corruption, tribal identity and the influx of people from outside the area, in particular refugees from Bangladesh. The increased presence of army and inability of the people in the area to vent grievances against army personnel, has led to the use of the writ jurisdiction of the HC.

The constitutionality of both the 1955 and the 1958 enactments have been challenged in petitions filed by human rights organizations and individuals in the Guwahati HC. In response to a growing feeling of discontent with the extent and reality of the army presence and powers, lawyers in urban areas as well as the residents of different states have used the power of judical review vested in the courts. Writ petitions have been filed in response to specific occurrences, as in Oinam in 1987, asking the Court not just to strike down the enactments but to vindicate the rights of the people, provide compensation and punish the guilty men.

As those challenging the legitimacy of state power do so with a particular vision of civil society, and at a considerable personal risk, the network of human rights activists is connected throughout the region. Most of the petitions are also connected in some way, and the court orders received in one case, have informed and determined the content of other petitions filed. Care has been taken to frame petitions carefully and in detail so as to ensure that the case will be given due consideration by the Court.

## Access to Justice

The standing of the petitioners to bring these issues, relating to army powers, to the courts has not been questioned at all. Mostly filed with the help of a supportive advocate, or by advocates themselves, the grievances were framed for adjudication by the Court and in a form acceptable to it. Access to justice issues were raised, when the Naga People's Movement for Human Rights asked the Guwahati HC to prevent the Assam Rifles from prolonging the procedure for the provision of legal aid, and in *Vanlalhruala, Chairman, Aizawl Bazar/Town Damaged Committee*, when the petitioner noted that rich and powerful petitioners had been able to get legal redress. Nonetheless, there was one instance of a telegram being registered as a petition in the Guwahati HC during the proceedings of the case filed by the *Manipur Baptist Convention Women's Union*.

## The Court's Response

The petitions filed challenging enactments are still pending, as are those filed on the Oinam issue. The only order given regarding the constitutional validity of an enactment was in the case filed by Inderjit Barua in which the Delhi HC upheld the Assam Disturbed Areas Act, 1955. Although pending in appeal in the SC, the order in this case has prevented other petitions challenging the constitutional validity of this enactment from being filed in the Guwahati HC.

The Oinam litigation has been protracted by the procedure of hearing evidence and the miscellaneous petitions filed by the Assam Rifles in the cases of the *Naga People's Movement for Human Rights* and the *Manipur Baptist Convention Women's Union*. In an order in the former case, the Guwahati HC did not accept newspaper reports as evidence as they had not been verified by the journalists concerned, and the Court contradicted itself on the criteria for the institution of an inquiry by the Court. In the appeal filed by the editor, "*Boodhbar*", an important judgement was given by the SC which tacitly acknowledged the excesses committed by the armed forces. This order has been widely referred to in the Oinam cases and provided a point of reference when the case was taken to the United Nations.[3]

Only one *habeas corpus* petition has been included in this chapter — that filed by Sebastian Hongray. The importance of this judgement to PIL has been great. Exemplary costs were awarded and the Court held the respondents in civil contempt of court. In the petitions filed in the Jammu and Kashmir HC, inquiries have been instituted, and in the case filed by *Gautam Uzir*, without deciding on the legality of the firing by the Border Security Force (BSF), the Guwahati HC directed that the injured persons receive any necessary specialized treatment. Similarly, in the cases from Mizoram filed by the *People's Union for Civil Liberties* and *Vanlalhruala, Chairman, Aizawl Bazar/Town Damaged Committee*, the Court acknowledged the illegality of certain acts carried out by members of the armed forces and simply ordered that the pending compensation be paid.

## The Contribution of PIL

The Court has been constrained by the paramount considerations of national security and law and order when giving its orders. The

[3] See Haksar, Nandita, "Armed Forces (Special Powers) Act 1958. A Report on Human Rights Violations in North East India", New York, March 1991. This unpublished paper described how between 27/11/90, when Assam was declared to be a disturbed state under the Act, and 10/3/91 ninety-nine *habeas corpus* petitions had been filed on behalf of people arrested and tortured by the Armed Forces.

restrictions have meant that very few substantive results have been realized. Even where inquiries have been instituted and orders given, the administration has been recalcitrant in implementing these orders. An example of this may be seen in the petitions filed by H.N. Wanchoo, a noted activist from Jammu and Kashmir who died in December 1992, after being shot:

> His petitions to the High Court of Jammu and Kashmir were for judicial enquiry into the killing of innocent Kashmiris by the security forces, the troture of detainees in custody, rapes committed by soldiers, information regarding numbers and identities of detainees and conditions in jails.
>
> It is a matter of shame that he met with no success. Even when the High Court passed directory or mandatory orders in response to his petitions, the local administration simply did not obey them. The orders of the High Court were ignored brazenly, unblushingly and insolently.[4]

Some of the petitioners have used law, through PIL and *habeas corpus* petitions as a mechanism to expose the injustice of the system of governance, including the courts. The existing feeling that the Constitution has little relevance to the peoples of the border areas, for example of the north-east, has been reinforced by the ineffective use of PIL, perceived the last resort. For many, approaching the courts for redress has been untenable, and even when gaining access to the Court has been possible, the delays in hearings have been unacceptable to the petitioners. When asked why he was unable to secure the compensation requested in the PIL cases from Mizoram, the advocate for the petitioners stated that if he tried to speed up the proceedings of the case in Court, the judges would assume that he has a financial stake in the outcome of the litigation.

Little has been gained from the use of PIL in these areas. In a paper presented to the UN Committee on Human Rights, Nandita Haskar, the advocate for the Naga People's Movement for Human Rights, stated:

> There is no possibility for the vast majority of people living

[4] Varadarajan, P.M., "H.N. Wanchoo", *PUCL Bulletin*, Vol. 13, No. 1, January 1993, 16. See also Sachar, Rajinder, "Kashmir — Need for a Better Understanding", *PUCL Bulletin*, Vol. 13, No. 7, July 1993, 15-16.

> in disturbed areas to reach either a lawyer or the court. The High Court is too far, the expenses are prohibitive and justice is slow. There is also an anti-tribal bias in the Bar and Bench. The Court is slow to give relief when rights of tribal peoples are affected. Even when the High Court gives relief it is limited.[5]

She noted that the now deceased Major General responsible for the atrocities committed on Nagas in Manipur during Operation Bluebird had been given Republic Day honours, inspite of the cases pending against him in the Guwahati HC. Even the national Human Rights Commission set up by the Government in 1993 has not been empowered to hear complaints against the armed forces. Certainly the framework within which the courts have felt able to operate has been limited, but PIL can really be described as a last resort for people who feel the force of the strong arm of the State.

## Challenge to Enactments

***C R No 182 of 1980, Guwahati***

***Inderjit Barua* v. *State of Assam and another***

A petition was filed under Article 226 of the Constitution by a resident of Guwahati. On 5/4/80 two notifications were issued by the Government of Assam, through the Governor, under the Assam Disturbed Areas Act, 1955 and the Armed Forces (Assam and Manipur) Special Powers Act, 1958. These notifications declared most areas of Assam to be "disturbed areas", allowing the armed forces to be used in aid of civil power. The petition asked for a stay on the notifications of the Government of Assam on 5/4/80 under the two Acts.

In an order D/-7/4/80 by Justice Hansaria

The Court passed an order staying the operation of the notification declaring areas of Assam as "disturbed areas". The Court asked the respondents to show cause why the petition should not be allowed.

The State moved an SLP in the SC which was not admitted, but

5 Haksar, Nandita, "Armed Forces (Special Powers) Act 1958. A Report on Human Rights Violations in North East India", New York, March 1991, at 27.

the case was transferred to the HC of Delhi along with other petitions.

***C W P Nos 832 to 834 of 1980 and L P A No 108 of 1980, Delhi***
***Inderjit Barua* v. *State of Assam and another***

Petitions were filed under Article 226 of the Constitution. The petition (C R No 832 of 1980) filed by Inderjit Barua, again asked for a stay on the notifications of the Government of Assam on 5/4/80 under the Assam Disturbed Areas Act, 1955 and the Armed Forces (Assam and Manipur) Special Powers Act, 1958. A similar petition was filed in the Guwahati HC by Hem Kant Sharma (C R No 192 of 1980). Another petition (C R No 203 of 1980) was filed by Jatin Goswami challenging the proclamation and orders of the President D/-12/12/79 and Ordinance No 3 of 1980 regarding these enactments. The petitions not only challenged the *vires* of the two Acts as being violative of Articles 14, 19 and 21 of the Constitution, but also the legislative competence of the Assam Legislature and the Lok Sabha in passing these legislations. The notifications by the Governor declaring certain areas to be disturbed were described as unjust, unfair and an unreasonable exercise of power. The petitions stated that as the concept of a "disturbed area" had not been defined, the declaration of an area as disturbed is without any basis and irrational. The petitions also challenged the Armed Forces (Assam and Manipur) Special Powers (Amendment) Act, 1972.

In an order D/-3/6/83 by > Chief Justice Prakash Narain and Justice B.N. Kirpal
[reported AIR 1983 Del 513]
The Court discussed Assam, describing it as a border state with a troubled history. It was held that the right of private defence, a right recognized in criminal law, can no longer be restricted to a person under attack or subjected to assault, and that even a stranger to a crime can approach the Court to prevent an attack or assault on another. Having upheld the standing of the petitioner, the Court held, on the substance of the petitions, that because of the social purpose of the enactments to uphold the rule of law, they are valid, at 526:

> if the circumstances warranted by the historical background as pleaded before us are examined, in our view, a social purpose is fulfilled by the impugned statutes. The question is whether this is permissible. The answer must be clearly in the

affirmative. It is the state's duty to see that the rule of law enunciated by Article 21 is available to the greatest number.

It was held that the legislators must be presumed to know what a disturbed area is, and that guidelines do exist in the enactments. The Court held that the power to kill conferred by the Acts was not unreasonable on the grounds that there are no safeguards, and that the immunity from prosecution provided by section 5 of both Acts is to prevent officers and officials from facing frivolous litigation for acts done in the course of duty. Partially allowing the petitions the Court did provide a fresh interpretation of parts of sections 4 and 5 of the Assam Disturbed Areas Act, 1955 regarding the powers of officials. The parties were left to bear their own costs.

An appeal has been filed under Article 136 of the Constitution in the Supreme Court against this judgement of the High Court.

☆ ☆ ☆

***W P No 5328 of 1980***

***Human Rights Forum, Manipur and another* v. *Union of India***

A petition was filed under Article 32 of the Constitution challenging the constitutional validity of the Armed Forces (Special Powers) Act, 1958.

***W P No 550 of 1982***

***Naga People's Movement for Human Rights* v. *Union of India***

A letter was sent to Justice O. Chinnappa Reddy of the SC by Ahu Sakhrie, Convenor of the Naga People's Movement for Human Rights (NPMHR) and a research student at JNU. A detailed report sent along with the letter formed the basis of the petition which was registered under Article 32 of the Constitution. The report described the reign of terror inflicted upon the Nagas by the army, describing how entire villages had been razed, boys kidnapped, girls raped, and elders beaten. After trying to raise the issue in Parliament, the NPMHR said that they had approached the Court in desperation. Admitting the petition, the Court appointed Kapil Sibal, advocate, as *amicus curaie* and asked him to submit a detailed list of the missing persons.[6]

6 Bhaumik, Subir, "Reign of Terror in Nagaland", *Sunday Mid-Day*, Dak edition, 20/6/82.

***W P Nos 9229-30 of 1982***
***People's Union for Democratic Rights (PUDR)* v. *Union of India***

A petition was filed under Article 32 of the Constitution by the PUDR challenging the constitutional validity of the Armed Forces (Special Powers) Act, 1958, on the grounds that the Act gave wide, unfettered and oppressive powers to even the juniormost officers of the armed forces. The petition alleged that the Act was beyond the legislative competence of Parliament as it provided for the use of the armed forces in aid of civil power. The petition noted that although the Cr P C had not been notified in many areas of the north-east, its spirit was enforced. The 1958 Act was also challenged on the grounds that when it was enforced, provisions of the the Cr P C, 1973 could no longer apply as the civil authorities could have no control over the militrary. The petition also asked that the Cr PC be made applicable in the north east, so that the rule of law could prevail. In support of this claim the petition cited an example: in the absence of the Cr P C, women do not get the usual protection of being searched by women officers. Further challenges to the 1958 Act were made questioning the legality of provisions which permitted searches and arrests without warrant, allow the army to detain people for indefinite periods for interrogation, and gave army personnel near immunity from judicial proceedings. The Act was also challenged on the grounds that it gave powers to the armed forces to virtually take over the administration and the constitutional scheme.

***W P Nos 9229-30 of 1982, with W P No 5328 of 1980, with W P No 550 of 1982***

In an order D/-14/2/83 by Chief Justice Y.V. Chandrachud, Justice R.S. Pathak and Justice A.P. Sen

Referring to the allegations by the petitioners that churches and educational establishments have been used and are being used by the army as camping grounds for interrogation of people, the Court held, at 2:

> It is impossible for us at this stage to examine whether the allegation made by the petitioners is well-founded, but we direct, on the supposition that it is well-founded … that the army authorities shall not use any church or educational institutions for the purpose of setting up any camp and for the purpose of detaining people.

The matter was to be listed before the Constitution Bench for hearing.

☆ ☆ ☆

***C R Nos 2314, 2238, 2415 of 1990 and 11 of 1991, Guwahati***
***People's Union for Human Rights (represented by Ramesh Kumar Jain and others) v. Union of India and others***

Petitions were filed under Article 226 of the Constitution challenging the promulgation of President's rule in Assam for the fourth time on 27/11/90. Sections 4 and 5 of the Armed Forces (Special Powers) Act, 1958 and section 3 of the Assam Disturbed Areas Act, 1955, were described as violative of Article 21 of the Constitution. The petition also referred to the preamble of the Central Reserve Police Force Act, 1949. One petition was filed by the People's Union for Human Rights (PUHR) represented by its members, and others by Nibaran Bora, a local journalist and by the editor of *Boodhbar*, an Assamese weekly. The latter petition challenged the *vires* of the 1958 Act, and described certain provisions of the enactment as violative of fundamental rights.

In an order D/-20/3/91 by > Chief Justice A. Raghuvir and Justice S.N. Phukan
[reported AIR 1992 Gau 23]
Referring to the Armed Forces (Special Powers) Act, 1958, the Court stated at 36:

> ... actually there are no rules to guide the actions of the authorities under the Act. The ordinary protection guaranteed under the laws to life and limb are not regulated under the 1958 Act. Therefore, we hold the quality of life in the area where the Act is enforced by notification the citizen's life stands radically changed to his detriment in view of the actual practices followed.

It was held that the notification of Central rule was only to apply to the specified areas listed by the Court and that the notification enforcing both Acts was to be reviewed every two months. The Court directed that any person, arrested by the armed forces, be handed over to the nearest police station with the least possible delay and be produced before the nearest Magistrate within twenty-four hours from the time of arrest. It was also held that only those who have committed cognizable offences or against whom reasonable suspicion exists could be arrested, and that the Central Reserve Police Force could not exercise any extraordinary powers under the notification.

An appeal has been filed under Article 136 of the Constitution in the Supreme Court by the petitioners.

☆ ☆ ☆

***C A No 2551 of 1991***

***Editor, "Boodhbar" v. Union of India and another***

An appeal was filed under Article 136 of the Constitution against the order of the Guwahati HC on 20/3/91. The writ petition challenged the constitutional validity of the Armed Forces (Special Powers) Act, 1958. One of the directions sought for in the petition was that the army should not be allowed to search women.

In an order in 1992 by Justice S. Ratnavel Pandian (Vacation Judge)

The full text of the Court order stated:

> Heard both counsel for a considerable length of time and gone through Annexure "A" under the caption "List of Do's and Dont's while acting under Armed Forces (Special Powers) Act, 1958" annexed with counter-affidavit filed on behalf of the respondents and also vide the order of this Court dated 23/4/91 made in SLP (C) No.6811-13/91.
>
> In addition I give the following directions:
>
> The Army Officers while effecting the arrest of a woman or making search of woman or in searching the place in the actual occupancy of a female shall follow the procedure meant for the police officers as contemplated under the various provisions of the Code of Criminal Procedure, namely the proviso to sub-section (2) of section 47, sub-section (2) of section 51, sub-section (3) of section 100 and proviso to sub-section (1) of section 160 of the code.[7]

☆ ☆ ☆

[7] This order has been reproduced in the chapter on 'Injustices Specific to Women'

The above challenges to the Armed Forces (Special Powers) Act by the PUDR, the NPMHR, Inderjit Barua and the Manipur Human Rights Forum have been pending in the Supreme Court since 1983 and are due to be listed before a constitutional bench. The appeal filed by the PUHR has been tagged onto these petitions, together with that filed by the Editor, '*Boodhbar*', which was tagged onto the PUHR petition.

☆ ☆ ☆

## The Oinam Cases

Three petitions and many applications were filed in the Guwahati HC after the Army operation in Manipur District, called Operation Bluebird. The petitions were tagged together by the HC for final hearing. Members of the Naga People's Movement for Human Rights and the Manipur Baptist Convention Women's Union, the petitioners in two of the cases, formed a common platform, the Co-ordinating Committee on the Oinam Issue (COCOI), along with others, from which they were able to deal with issues of concern to all the groups.

☆ ☆ ☆

***C R No 1043 of 1987 with Misc C No 1127 of 1987, Guwahati***
***Naga People's Movement for Human Rights (NPMHR) v. Union of India and others***

A petition was filed under Article 226 of the Constitution on behalf of the people of Senapati District, Manipur, who were subject to 'mindless violence by the armed forces'. On 9/7/87 the Assam Rifles Camp at Oinam village, Senapati District, Manipur, was attacked by certain unknown persons, believed to be members of the National Security Council of Nagaland (NSCN), an organization committed to the secession of Nagaland from the Union of India. In that attack nine jawans were killed, three others were seriously injured and the raiders took away a large quantity of arms and ammunition. After this the Assam Rifles launched "Operation Bluebird" to recover the arms and ammunition. This army operation was begun even though the FIR, reporting that arms had been looted, was not filed until a week after the attack. The petition stated that the operation lasted for three months, during which time, in the name of counter-insurgency, a reign of terror was let loose in the entire area of Oinam by the Assam Rifles. It was contended that in the course of just a few weeks fifteen people were shot dead after being subjected to inhuman torture. All the villagers, including pregnant women, the sick, and paralysed persons were made to stand in playgrounds exposed to torrential rains and scorching heat for months. Six babies died, as did many others, hundreds were beaten, people were subjected to the most horrific kinds of torture and degradation, labour was extracted from the residents of the area, women were raped and assaulted ... The petition listed these and many other offences. For example, it was claimed that houses were looted and burnt, crops were destroyed and that no one was allowed to tend to their cattle or fields for months. The petition stated that as the area was declared to be disturbed under section 3 of the Armed Forces (Special Powers) Act, 1958:

> the security forces have taken over the administration of Senapati District and have wrongfully detained the Superintendent of Police and Deputy Commissioner of the District. Thus the villagers have no way left to redress their grievances under the ordinary law of the land. The fundamental rights guaranteed under Articles 14, 19, 21, 22, 23, 25 and rights under Article 300-A of the Constitution have been rendered meaningless for the people of this District.

The petition alleged:

> The armed forces have not allowed anyone to enter the area so it is difficult for the petitioner organization to furnish this Hon'ble Court with all the facts.

And stated that by taking over the administration, the army did more than simply act in aid of civil power, as mandated by the 1958 Act:

> The most glaring example of the abuse of military power was the recent raid by the armed forces on the office of the Sub-Divisional Magistrate of Paomata when they took away the official seal of the Sub-Divisional Magistrate along with a bunch of judicial and non-judicial stamp papers.

The petition invoked Articles 19(1), 21, 22, 23 and 25 of the

Constitution together with other constitutional and legal rights. A number of reliefs were requested from the Court:

(1) that the notification declaring Senapati District as a disturbed area under the Armed Forces (Special Powers) Act, 1958 be revoked.

(2) that guidelines be framed to ensure that the civil administration can effectively check misuse of power by the armed forces during combing operations.

(3) that section 6 of the 1958 Act be declared to be unconstitutional.

(4) that exemplary damages be paid to the families of those tortured to death; to women who were assaulted or raped; to house owners whose houses were dismantled or burnt; to those who were tortured or illegally detained; to those whose goods were looted or destroyed; and to all those who were forced to work without any payment.

(5) that criminal cases be filed against the guilty men and the officers of the Assam Rifles.

The petition with annexures amounted to over a thousand pages.

In an order D/-28/10/87 by > Chief Justice K.N. Saikia and Justice T.C. Das
[reported AIR 1990 Guwa 1]
The Court held that the Governor has immunity from legal action under Article 361 of the Constitution and is not answerable to any Court. Having ensured that the name of the Governor was deleted from the petition, the Court held that the petition could now be admitted.

In a judgement and order D/-15/12/87 by > Justice B.L. Hansaria and > Justice J. Sangma
The main judgement of the Court was given by Justice Hansaria. The Court noted that because it was not possible to file individual suits for those affected, a PIL had been filed. Referring to previous instances where the courts had awarded compensation, the Court expressed its concern at the recalcitrance of the respondents, at 5:

> The learned Advocate-General, Manipur, however submitted that not to be killed by torture and not to be raped are not fundamental rights available to the citizens of this country. We are flabbergasted at this submission.

Discussing the question of whether an inquiry should be

instituted, the Court held that it is competent to order an inquiry in a case where fundamental rights have been infringed. In the present case, the Court acknowledged that although many people had refuted the allegations of the petitioner, these statements may have been obtained by force or coercion — the example given by the petitioner, of a person who had given two affidavits to the Court — one in support of the case for the petitioner and the other in support of the case for the respondents, was cited. The Court refused to accept the newspaper articles annexed to the petition as they were not accompanied by affidavits of any of the reporters ensuring their veracity. Justice Hansaria concluded, at 15:

> There is no doubt in our mind that in a case of the present nature, we would be justified in ordering enquiry only on existence of two conditions: (i) compelling circumstances; and (ii) full satisfaction about establishment of a *prima facie* case relating to violation of fundamental rights. This apart, an enquiry to be ordered by us cannot be omnibus; it has to be confined to specific act(s). Further, it has to be by a person, body or agency which commands confidence of both the sides. Though the first condition seems to exist in the present case, we are not satisfied, in view of our aforesaid analysis of the materials on record, about the existence of the second of the aforesaid conditions. We have pointed out about the dearth of materials put on record which is in sharp contrast with those supporting the case of respondents No. 1 and 2. The prayer for enquiry is therefore presently rejected.

Justice Sangma agreed with Justice Hansaria, stating that security forces should have no objection to an inquiry into the detention of the District Collector and the Superintendent of Police, and that as these allegations were not denied, an inquiry would be in order. However, noting that the security forces had not filed any objection in their affidavit, Justice Sangma also concluded that no enquiry was needed, at 3:

> Though at one stage of the affidavit, the State of Manipur stated that an enquiry may be conducted by the CBI, at another stage they also stated that the government has directed the district administration to assess the alleged damages to the property etc. and that the report thereof was being awaited. I

believe that by the word "etc." they mean to include the alleged excesses to the lives and limbs of innocent people.

In an order D/-6/7/88 by Chief Justice A. Raghuvir and Justice Sangma

The pleadings in the case had been completed as counter-affidavits and rejoinders had been filed. Accordingly the Court said that it could not sustain the objection by the respondents to the institution of an enquiry into the killing of 27 persons, the rape of three and sexual assault of five women, the torture of 300 people, the detention of fifteen people, the burning and dismantling of over one hundred houses, the dismantling of schools and churches, the looting of property and the use of forced labour. The Sessions Judge, Manipur, Imphal, was directed to record, expeditiously, the evidence of witnesses at Imphal offered by the petitioners, at 3:

> Ms N. Haksar, the learned counsel for the petitioner expressed that it may not be possible for her to visit the villages without the assistance of the State of Manipur. If assistance is sought for, the State of Manipur will provide assistance.

The case was transferred to the Court of the Sessions Judge, Imphal to ensure compliance.

On 22/8/88 the Sessions Court began recording the evidence of witnesses for the petitioner on a day to day basis. As the Assam Rifles continuously interfered in the proceedings before the Sessions Judge by intimidating, arresting, detaining and torturing witnesses, and by threatening the petitioners and their advocate, the petitioners filed a miscellaneous case in the High Court asking that the Assam Rifles be prevented from interfering.

In the five and a half months during which the Sessions Court recorded evidence, the petitioners were able to produce only 22 witnesses. Each witness was cross-examined for days by the advocates for the respondents. After this period, the petitioners did not produce more witnesses, because of the continuing harassment.

On 29/1/89 the Assam Rifles raided the room of the advocate for the petitioners, Nandita Haksar. She was staying in the girls' hostel

[8] "Civil Liberties: Civil Rule Threatened In The North- East", *The Lawyers*, February 1989, 24-25.

of the Manipur Baptist Convention Centre Church at the time. Her room was searched and documents relating to the case were taken.[8]

In February 1989, the petitioners filed a contempt petition in the HC against the Assam Rifles. The petitioners again filed a contempt petition in 1991, both to no avail.

In 1988 and 1989, a number of miscellaneous petitions were filed in the HC by the Assam Rifles. Amongst other things, the Court was asked to stay the proceedings before the Sessions Court, to transfer the proceedings to another court because of the alleged bias of the Sessions Judge and to vacate the order of the Sessions Court directing Assam Rifles not to bring their own chairs and tables into the court room.

In an order D/-2/2/89, the High Court dismissed all the miscellaneous cases filed by the Assam Rifles.

An article in the PUCL Bulletin in 1989 described the three sets of problems which the NPMHR encountered when approaching the courts — the availability of money for travel to villages; the rumours spread by the Assam Rifles that the Co-ordinating Committee on the Oinam Issue (COCOI) was anti-national and had political links; the rumours and suspicion spread by the Assam Rifles among villagers that the members of the COCOI are from one particular tribe and intend to create trouble.[9]

In March 1989 the Assam Rifles began producing their witnesses before the Sessions Court, Imphal. They filed a list of more than 700 witnesses.

A miscellaneous case was filed on 12/9/89 by the petitioners asking the Court to direct the Government of Manipur to deposit all files and documents relating to Operation Bluebird with the Court. In an order D/-13/9/89 the HC directed the Government of Manipur to deposit the files. Only five files were deposited, and that too after a wait of one year. The state of Manipur claimed that the rest of the files had been lost.

Another miscellaneous case was filed on 25/9/89 by the petitioners asking the Court to restrain the respondents from prolonging the process for legal aid.

In January 1990 the HC directed the Assam Rifles to limit the number of witnesses to 32, all of whom were to be heard within three months. By April 1990, the Assam Rifles had produced 41 witnesses

9 "Manipur: The Oinam Issue", *PUCL Bulletin*, Vol. 9, No.3, March 1989, 4-6 and 9.

and the recording of evidence at the Sessions Court, Imphal ended. The papers were sent back to the Guwahati HC by July 1990.

On 3/9/90, the petitioner filed the report of Drug Action Forum, West Bengal, entitled, "Post Torture State of Mental Health". For the first time in India a team of doctors carried out a study of the effects of torture. They examined the victims of the torture inflicted on the residents of Senapati District during Operation Bluebird, two years after the event. It was found that most were suffering from post-traumatic stress disorder. The report was filed in the HC on 3/9/90 and by 1992, no counter-affidavit had been filed in reply to these findings.

Although the petition was ready for final hearing in October 1990, it was not listed. Accordingly in July 1991, the petitioners requested the Court to transfer the petition to the Imphal Bench of the HC as this was their home state. In an order D/-9/1/92, the HC directed the final hearing to begin from March 1992, in the Imphal Bench.

☆ ☆ ☆

***C R (HC) No 2 of 1987, Guwahati***
***Civil Liberties and Human Rights Organization (CLAHRO)* v. *State***

A petition was filed under Article 226 of the Constitution. This was the first petition to be instituted after the events in Senapati District during Operation Bluebird, and was filed on behalf of eight illegally arrested village leaders. The petition asked for their immediate release.

In an order in 1987 the HC directed the release of all the leaders and the villagers. Rs 5,000 was awarded to each of those who were illegally detained, and Rs 20,000 to the families of the two people who were tortured to death.[10]

☆ ☆ ☆

***Misc C No 1461 of 1987 in connection with C R No 1355 of 1987, Guwahati***
***Manipur Baptist Convention and another* v. *Union of India and others***

A petition was filed under Article 226 of the Constitution in the Guwahati HC in 1987 by the Manipur Baptist Convention Womens'

10 "Manipur: The Oinam Issue", *PUCL Bulletin*, Vol. 9, No. 3, March 1989, 4-6 and 9.

Union (MBCWU) on behalf of the women who were sexually assaulted and forced to work without any wages or payment by the Assam Rifles during Operation Bluebird.

In an order D/-7/3/88 by > Justice B.L. Hansaria and Justice S.N. Phukan

The Court discussed the application filed regarding the extraction of forced labour from the women of four named villages, including Oinam, and their sexual exploitation. In response to the plea for interim orders directing that these activities be prevented, the Court stated, at 6:

> We are of the considered view that in a public interest litigation of the present type, where serious allegations relating to violation of the human rights have been made, this Court may not treat the proceeding as adversarial in nature leaving it to the parties alone to file such documents as they may deem fit to establish their cases. We do think that this Court as a protector of fundamental and human rights would be justified in a case of the present nature to collect relevant materials through its own agencies.

The Registrar (Judicial) was asked to investigate, even though the petitioners had not asked the Court to enquire into the incidents. The Registrar was directed to visit Imphal and submit a report within one month from the date of the order. The Court stated that it would be open to the parties involved to produce relevant persons before the Registrar other than those mentioned already in the petition. The Court again stressed the importance of the army in fighting anti-secessionism and insurgency.

On 25/3/88, nine persons from Ngamju (including five women who were sexually exploited) were detained by the Assam Rifles. The petitioners, through their advocate, informed the HC of this. The respondents were then asked to produce the detained persons in Court by 8/4/88. As five persons were not produced, contempt proceedings were initiated. The petition was to be listed on 2/5/88.

Although the Court had directed the Registrar (Judicial) to conduct an immediate enquiry, it was postponed because of the Prime Minister's visit to the region. In May 1988, after his first visit to Imphal and Oinam, the Registrar left without recording any statements, but reported to the Court that 'the fear psychosis to which the villagers seem to have been subjected is shocking to one's conscience.' On 17/5/88 the Registrar (Judicial) again went to Imphal and found that Major Ravindra of the Assam Rifles had intimidated the villagers.

On 10/6/88 a telegram was sent to the HC by the village Secretary Khondei Khuman complaining that witnesses were being threatened. The telegram was received by the Chief Justice and treated as a writ petition under Article 226 of the Constitution.

Meanwhile a petition was filed under Article 32 of the Constitution in the SC on 14/6/88 by the Assam Rifles asking for a stay on the visit of the Registrar to Manipur. The petition was dismissed by the Vacation Judge.

Nine petitions were then filed by the Assam Rifles before the Registrar in an attempt to delay the recording of statements by the Registrar (Judicial).

Members of the COCOI, which comprised members of the NPMHR and the MBCWU amongst others, had been harassed and detained. Accordingly, in mid-1988, the Registrar (Judicial) directed the District Magistrate to provide security for COCOI members and gave notice to the Standing Counsel for the Central Government that he would begin contempt proceedings against him. At the request of the petitioners, in June, 1988 the Registrar (Judicial) was directed by the HC to protect the petitioner's witnesses from the Assam Rifles.

On 19/6/88 the Registrar (Judicial) examined 13 witnesses of the petitioners and ten of the Assam Rifles. The proceedings were then closed.

From 1989 to 1992 each time the cases came up for the final hearing the counsel for Assam Rifles asked for an adjournment.

☆ ☆ ☆

Common legal submissions were filed in the HC by the NPMHR and MBCWU. The petitioners referred to the order in *The Editor, "Boodhbar"* and cited international law to ask the Court to direct the payment of exemplary costs and to frame guidelines which would protect the people of the north-east from: extra-judicial killing and deprivation of liberty; illegal searches and seizures; forced labour; destruction of property during counter-insurgency operations; illegal occupation of land and destruction of forests. These legal submissions stated that:

> The petitioners have incurred enormous debts in order to continue these cases. Several members of the petitioner organizations namely the Naga People's Movement for Human Rights (NPMHR) and Manipur Baptist Convention Women's Union (MBCWU) have set aside their other work for more than four years to work on this case. Under the circumstances they pray that this Hon'ble Court may direct the respondents to pay costs.

Common written submissions and arguments were filed in the High Court in 1991 by the NPMHR and MBCWU. Referring to the two cases filed and the CLAHRO petition, it was noted:

> The evidence in all three cases is substantial. In NPMHR's petition the evidence is contained in 12 volumes with over 10,000 pages. However, despite all this evidence the full record of the atrocities committed by the Assam Rifles during Operation Bluebird is still not available. The evidence in support of the petitioner's charges against the Assam Rifles can be broadly divided into five categories:
>
> 1. affidavits of victims of atrocities committed by the Assam Rifles
> 2. testimony given by victims before the Sessions Court, Imphal and cross-examined by the respondents
> 3. statements recorded by the Registrar (J)
> 4. documents like press cuttings, memos and appeals by villagers to various official authorities and
> 5. documents and correspondence of the Government of Manipur with regard to the atrocities committed by the Assam Rifles during Operation Bluebird.

There were many evidentiary problems during the course of the litigation.

While not a party to the main petition filed by the NPMHR, all the affidavits for the respondents in all three cases were filed by the Assam Rifles. By 1991, no counter-affidavit had been filed by the Government of Manipur. Refuting the charges against them, the Assam Rifles claimed that all the people in support of the petition were sympathisers of the National Security Council of Nagaland. In written submissions to the HC in 1991, the petitioners noted:

> The then Chief Minister, in a Memorandum to the Union

Home Minister wrote that 'The Civil Law has, unfortunately, ceased to operate in Senapati District of Manipur due to excesses committed by the Assam Rifles with complete disregard shown to the Civil Administration. The Assam Rifles are running a parallel administration in the area. The Deputy Commissioner and Superintendent of Police were wrongfully confined, humiliated and prevented from discharging their official duties by the Security Forces'.

The petitioners had submitted evidence in support of the allegations. For example, the fact that women and girls were used by the Assam Rifles for doing forced labour had been recorded in messages sent to the Deputy Commissioner by the SDO, Pacenta; the use of forced labour had been recorded in the small chits sent by the Assam Rifles to the Headman of Maram Khullen, New Maram, directing him to send men to report at the Battalion Headquarters of the 21st Assam Rifles at Lairouching every day along with their tools. The Assam Rifles did not deny the charge that they had used forced labour, but stated that the villagers had already been paid. The petitioners replied to this stating:

> They have in fact given the paltry sums of Rs 1,500 to some villagers and some of them were compelled to accept these sums. And these sums of money were given after a year and during the pendency of petitions and can be seen more in the nature of interference in the judicial process.

The petitioners also described how Major Ravindra took fines from the village leaders if he was not provided with women, and detailed the ways in which evidence had been fabricated by the army.

The allegation that 1500 jawans and officers of the Assam Rifles had recklessly cut down the forests without permission from the owners or giving any payment was refuted. However, the petitioners noted that during the deposition of witnesses for the respondents, it had been admitted that although each jawan and officer is entitled to 900 grams of firewood, no firewood was provided. Moreover the jawans and officers of the Assam Rifles were not given sufficient rations, according to the evidence — the person in charge of rations admitted that none of the personnel were supplied with eggs or chicken during Operation Bluebird.

With the exception of the order in *The Editor, "Boodhbar"* little had resulted from the challenge to the enactments. Moreover, the petition on the Oinam issue was pending. Despairing of the legal process, the NPMHR went to the United Nations with its grievances. Hearings before the Human Rights Committee lasted for two days, on March 26 and 27, 1991. After the hearings, members of the NPMHR documented the event:

> We went in the hope that the Government of India might modify its attitude under international pressure. We were successful in raising concern among human rights organizations about the anguish of our people. But we are not sure whether the attitude of the Government of India will change.
>
> At the Human Rights Committee we discovered that although India has acceded to the International Covenant on Civil and Political Rights which guarantees the Right to Self-determination it has interpreted it to mean the right is only for people 'under foreign domination and that these words (Article 1) do not apply to sovereign independent States or to a section of the people or nation — which is the essence of national integrity'.[11]

## The Rest of the Cases

***W P (Cri) No 148 of 1983***
***Sebastian M Hongray v. Union of India***

A *habeas corpus* petition was filed under Article 32 of the Constitution on behalf of two people who were taken from their home and not returned. The petitioner, a Naga from Manipur who was a student of political science at Jawaharlal Nehru University, petitioned the Court on behalf of C. Daniel, of the Manipur Rifles, and C. Paul, Assistant Pastor of the Baptist Church·in Huining Village who were detained by the Officer-in-charge of the 21st Sikh Regiment on 10/3/82.

In an order D/-24/11/83 by > Justice D.A. Desai and Justice

[11] "NPMHR goes to the United Nations", 1991.

O. Chinnappa Reddy
[reported AIR 1984 SC 571]
The Court held, at 580:

> When a petition for a writ of *habeas corpus* under Article 32 of the Constitution is moved before the Court, ordinarily the Court would not issue *ex parte* a writ of *habeas corpus* unless the urgency of the situation so demands or issuing a notice of motion was likely to result in defeat of justice. Further the Court will be reluctant to issue a writ of *habeas corpus ex parte* where the fact of detention may be controverted and it may become necessary to investigate the facts.

And stated that in this case it was agreed that both the men had been taken by army jawans, so, at 581:

> The burden was obviously on the respondents to make good the defence

The petition was allowed, and the Court directed that the two men be produced before the Court on 12/12/83. Referring to certain allegations against army personnel made in the petition, which were dependent upon confidential documents, the Court held that as the documents were not relevant to the case, it did not need to decide on the claim by the respondents that the documents were protected by privilege.

In an order D/-23/4/84 by Justice D.A. Desai and Justice O. Chinnappa Reddy
[reported AIR 1984 SC 1026/1984 (1) SCALE 106 [629]]
It was directed that the two men be produced before the Court by 12/12/83. The Court held that the respondents had wilfully disobeyed the writ of *habeas corpus*, as they had misled the Court and distorted the facts when responding to the writ. Accordingly, the Court held that this amounted to civil contempt of court under the Contempt of Courts Act, 1971, section 2(b), and directed, at 1028:

> in the facts and circumstances of the case, we do not propose to impose imprisonment nor any amount as and by way of fine but keeping in view the torture, the agony and the mental oppression through which Mrs C. Thingkhuila, wife of Shri C. Daniel and Mrs C. Vangamla, wife of Shri C. Paul had to pass and they

> being the proper applicants, the formal application being by Sebastian M. Hongray, we direct that as a measure of exemplary costs, as is permissible in such cases, respondents nos. 1 and 2 shall pay Rs 1 lac to each of the aforementioned two women within a period of four weeks from today.

The Registrar (Judicial) was directed to forward all the papers of the case accompanied by a writ of *mandamus* to the Superintendent of Police, Ukurul, Manipur. The papers were to be treated as information of a cognizable offence and the Superintendent of Police was directed to commence an investigation as prescribed by the relevant provision of the Cr P C, 1973.

☆ ☆ ☆

***C M P No 4311 of 1991 in W P No 1612 of 1991, J & K***
***H.N. Wanchoo* v. *State of J & K***

A petition was filed under Article 226 of the Constitution by a civil liberties activist claiming that the paramilitary forces deployed in the Kashmir Valley had taken unauthorized occupation of the houses of the minority community in the city of Srinagar. As this has affected the privacy of the inhabitants and curbed their liberty as citizens, the petition asked for an enquiry into bunkers that had been raised in these houses, and into the deployment of paramilitary forces in this way.

In an order D/-3/12/91 by Justice S.M. Rizvi
The Court held, at 2:

> The prime concern of the state should be the safety and security of the people and it is the duty of the forces to ensure the same. The forces for doing so should not adopt any illegal means by forcibly occupying the houses of the inhabitants or act in such a manner as to endanger the life and liberty of the people.

Mr Ghulam Nabi Wani Gowhar, District and Sessions Judge, Srinagar was appointed as the inquiry officer by the Court and was asked to submit a report as soon as possible.

☆ ☆ ☆

***C M P No 5465 of 1991 in W P No 1733 of 1991, J & K***
***H.N. Wanchoo* v. *State of J & K***

Another petition was filed under Article 226 of the Constitution by this activist regarding the torture of Muzafar Ahmad Mirza and other persons by the security forces, and the consequent death of Showkat Ahmad Bhat. The petition was based on an inquiry, conducted by the Srinagar People's Union for Civil Liberties (PUCL), and asked for a judicial inquiry into these incidents.

In an order D/-19/11/91 by Justice S.M. Rizvi

The Court noted that Mirza had died during the pendency of the petition. An investigation was directed to be made by a gazetted police officer into some of the issues raised:

> In view of the seriousness of the allegations in respect of the unnatural death, ... it would be just and proper to direct the police concerned to register cases in this respect so as to find out who is responsible for causing their deaths. It is also directed that the investigation of the said cases shall be conducted by some gazetted police officer. The DIG, Srinagar shall supervise such investigations and submit progress reports thereof to the court fortnightly.

Other issues were to be dealt with by the Court after a counter-affidavit had been filed.

☆ ☆ ☆

A petition was filed under Article 226 of the Constitution in the J & K High Court in 1991 or 1992 by the PUCL, Srinagar, seeking the prosecution of K. K. Verma, Additional Director-General of the BSF and the person in charge of Hari Niwas interrogation centre. The petition also sought the prosecution of Mr Kadat, Deputy Commandant of the 7th Battalion and of Mr K.K. Sharma, Commandant of the 5th Battalion, for causing death of a detenu during interrogation. Apparently Mushtaq Ahmad Shora alias Noorul Hassan was subjected to physical torture in Hari Niwas, after which he died in the Army Hospital, Srinagar, in March 1992. While the hospital records showed that Mushtaq had died because of renal failure, the petition referred to the post-mortem report of the deceased which apparently stated that the death of the detenu had been caused by "traumatic injuries inflicted on various parts of the deceased's body and death was due to torture and not by renal failure."

In its order the Court heard the arguments of the PUCL counsel and directed the senior government advocate U.K. Jalali, present in the Court, to receive the notice and file objections to admissibility of the petition wthin four weeks. The petition was ordered to be listed for further hearing immediately after expiry of four weeks.[12]

☆ ☆ ☆

***W P No 2506 of 1992, J & K***
***H.N. Wanchoo* v. *State***

Another petition was filed under Article 226 of the Constitution in the High Court of Jammu and Kashmir stating that many innocent people had been killed in custody or otherwise by the armed forces. The petition listed 79 such persons who were killed in July 1992 and 15 persons who were killed the same month in interrogation centres alone.[13]

☆ ☆ ☆

***C R No 3627 of 1991, Guwahati***
***Gautam Uzir* v. *State of Assam and others***

A petition was filed under Article 226 of the Constitution by an advocate on the basis of a newsapaper report. The BSF had opened fire at Dipila Chowk near Sipajhar in District Darrang, Assam, killing five people and injuring three others. The petitioner had gone to see two of the injured, Dilip Kalita and Girindra Kalita, who were admitted in the MMC Hospital, Guwahati, and was told that the firing took place after an explosion under a nearby wooden bridge. When the explosion occurred there had been two vehicles on the bridge, one belonging to Patharighat Tea Estate and the other to the

[12] "Srinagar PUCL files petition in Court", *PUCL Bulletin*, Vol. 12, No. 8, August 1992, 13.

[13] Tarkunde, V.M., "Innocent persons allegedly killed in custody in Kashmir (letter d/-6/2/93 to Mr. Chavan, Minister for Home Affairs)", *PUCL Bulletin*, Vol. 13, No. 3, March 1993, 2-3. This letter mentions other petitions filed under Article 226 of the Constitution by Mr H.N. Wanchoo listing those who had died in the months of August (79 people) and September (37 people) 1992.

BSF. The injured persons claimed that members of the BSF, assuming that the bomb was meant for their vehicle, started firing and beating people after the explosion. The petition challenged the legality of this firing and asked that security be provided to the two people in the hospital, that the Chief Judicial Magistrate of Guwahati should record the statements of the injured persons immediately, that specialized medical treatment be provided for the injured and that the respondents be directed not to use handcuffs on the injured in hospital as this would be violative of Articles 21 and 22 of the Constitution.

In an order D/-2/8/91 by Justice Phukan and Justice Srivastava The Court ordered that the statements of the injured be recorded and sent to the Chief Judicial Magistrate, Mongoldoi, as the matter would be under his jurisdiction. The Court held that the provision of adequate security is a duty of the state and shall be given to the two injured persons. The hospital authorities were directed to do the needful with regard to specialized treatment. The Court also noted:

> Mr Uzir has stated that there is an apprehension that the above named persons may be handcuffed. This Court has repeatedly held that handcuffing in hospital is not in accordance with law.

The matter was directed to be listed on 5/8/91.

The Government of Assam, after conducting a Magisterial Inquiry, held that the firing was improper and called for proper compensation. The BSF has not conceded to this and has stated that the firing was proper. The case is awaiting decision.

☆ ☆ ☆

***C R No 342 of 1990, Guwahati***

***C. Thangmura* v. *Union of India***

A petition was filed under Article 226 of the Constitution by a member of Amnesty International and President of the PUCL in Mizoram, asking for compensation for the families of those killed in an army action on 28/3/88. The Assam Rifles had opened fire on two occasions — firstly at 9 pm killing one person instantly and injuring thirteen, and later at 11.30 pm killing two people instantly and injuring many others. A magisterial inquiry had been instituted by a government order D/-31/3/88. In this petition the facts of the incident were disputed. The official version of events contended that a total of six persons had died and twenty-seven injured on 29/3/88 and 30/3/88. However, according to the medical report recorded in the Civil Hospital, Aizawl, 90 persons had been injured. The petition stated that a total of twelve people died, and asked for adequate compensation of Rs 5 lakhs each to the next of kin of the 12 victims, and a payment of Rs 50,000 each to those who were seriously injured in the incidents.

In an order D/-26/2/90

The petition was admitted and notice was issued, and the HC directed the State to file a counter-affidavit. The petition was ordered to be listed within one month. It had not been listed by mid-1993.

☆ ☆ ☆

***C R No 564 of 1990, Guwahati***

***People's Union for Civil Liberties (PUCL)* v. *Union of India and others***

A petition was filed under Article 226 of the Constitution claiming that the government should pay compensation to all the victims of army atrocities during an army operation in the state of Mizoram in 1966.

In an order D/-28/3/90 by Acting Chief Justice S. Haque and Justice H.K. Sema

The Court held:

> Upon hearing the learned counsel of the parties, we direct the government of Mizoram to retain the undisbursed amount with the Rehabilitation Department of Mizoram and not to surrender it so that the Department would be in a position to disburse the amount to the persons entitled in the event of orders from this Court. List after a month.

☆ ☆ ☆

***C R No 4693 of 1991, Guwahati***

***Vanlalhruala, Chairman, Aizawl Bazar/Town Damaged Committee* v. *Union of India***

A petition was filed under Article 226 of the Constitution on behalf of 155 businessmen from Aizawl, Mizoram whose claims for compensation had been assessed and verified, by the Relief and Rehabilitation Department of the Government of India, but who had not been paid. Before it received statehood, Mizoram was a District of Assam called Lushai Hills. On 22/9/69 an order was issued by the District Magistrate, Mizoram, that all buildings and huts in the area specified under the order should be destroyed or rendered useless before 15/10/69. At the time of the order, Lushai Hills had been declared to be a "disturbed area". The petition claimed that this order had caused those living in Aizawl town to be put through miseries:

> The army authority in the name of combing operation assaulted the innocent citizens, burnt down their houses, destroyed properties worth crores of rupees as if they were in an occupied territory.

On 26/3/73 another notification was issued by the Administrator of Mizoram (by then a Union Territory) declaring the whole of Mizoram to be a "disturbed area" under the Assam Disturbed Areas Act, 1955 and under section 13 of the Assam Maintenance of Public Order Autonomous District Act, 1953. This notification ordered that all persons residing in the villages specified remove themselves to places specified in Column No.2 of the order. Moreover, for "the public interest in the interest of the safety and security of the whole of the Union Territory of Mizoram" all persons residing in places in Column No.2 of the order were directed to remain there for a period of six months and were only to leave the place with the permission of the Administrator of Mizoram. The petition contended that again the homes and properties of those who had to leave were burnt down by the army in the name of the combing operation. The petition noted that the incident was acknowledged by the administration, at 7-8:

> the facts are being admitted by the present Government of Mizoram and also by the representatives of the Union of India, Ministry of Home Affairs, New Delhi which would be revealed from the fact that in the minutes of the meeting of the team constituted for looking into the problems of compensation/rental charges on account of properties damaged/destroyed by Security Forces since 1966 which was held at Aizawl on 25th August, 1981 … it was held that 655 persons were paid compensation amounting to Rs 21,71,457 which was sanctioned by the Government of India.

The total claims received by the government amounted to Rs 2,83,89,506.50, whereas the petitioner estimated that the total claims from 41,921 out of 69,457 families in Aizawl town including the business community of Aizawl town, amounted to Rs 70,45,11,964. It was alleged that nothing had been paid to the villagers, and only 655 inhabitants of Aizawl town had received any compensation. This situation was described in the light of the provisions in the Mizoram Accord between the Mizo National Front and the Government of India. However the Government of India had acknowledged the loss to the business community and, in 1974, had sanctioned Rs 62,57,900 for rehabilitation loans to 368 businessmen of Aizawl. The government had stated that the claims of those in rural areas would take time, the people who, according to the petitioner, had suffered the most. An earlier petition was referred to (C R No 2285 of 1988 *Aizawl Town Damage Compensation Committee and others* v. *State of Mizoram and others*) filed by 374 people of the business community from Aizawl under Article 226 of the Constitution to get compensation. In its judgement D/-17/7/89, the Guwahati HC awarded Rs 1,95,71,160.50 as compensation. The State then appealed to the Supreme Court under Article 136 of the Constitution (C M P No 18567 of 1989). The SC rejected the special leave petition and the compensation was paid. The present petition stated that this victory of the businessmen in Aizawl demonstrated that those who were rich and powerful and able to approach the court were able to get compensation, whereas those who were economically backward have not received anything. The petition claimed that Articles 14 and 21 of the Constitution were being violated because many people were on the verge of starvation having lost their livelihood. It was also claimed that Articles 15, 16 and 19 of the Constitution were being violated, and the petition asked that each family whose claim is pending disposal be paid at least Rs 30,000 and that alternative land be awarded in lieu of that which had been spoilt. Annexed to the petition was the order D/-28/3/90 by the Guwahati HC in C R No 564 of 1990 (see above).

In an order D/-26/2/92 by > Chief Justice U.L. Bhat and Justice D.N. Baruah

The Court noted that the amount which had been made available had not been paid and stated, at 2:

> We are not prima facie satisfied that there is any reason to withhold the money from distribution. However, we allow the respondents to file a counter-affidavit within one month. At the same time we direct the respondents 2 to 4 to ensure that 50% of the balance amount now lying with the Rehabilitation Department be paid to the victims as determined by the Revenue Department.

## CASE CHAPTER 4

# Injustices Specific to Women

### Framing the Issue

This chapter has been divided into a number of sections: violence (general, harassment for dowry, sati, rape,[1] the army and the police); challenge to enactments; discrimination; prostitution; the rest of the cases. Each case documents an injustice that is specific to women. Many of the cases were filed in response to the broad-based failure of the legal system to resolve the grievances of women. With unsatisfactory investigations into crimes against women, biased laws and an unsympathetic judiciary, the writ jurisdiction of the Court in PIL has been mobilized for some of the worst instances of injustice. These cases were filed in tandem with the growth of the women's movement and investigative journalism, and with the support of some legal successes[2] and an increasing tendency of looking towards the Court.

It is women's groups who have most often framed the issues for the Court, or have intervened in cases to give them a PIL character.[3]

[1] One of the earliest PIL cases on rape was in the form of a letter sent by advocate R.S. Sodhi to the *Hindustan Times*, which was registered as a petition in the SC.

[2] See for example in *Air India* v. *Nargesh Meerza and others*, 1981 (3) SCALE 192 [1275]/AIR 1981 SC 1829.

[3] In addition to the cases documented, other petitions have been filed. For example, the Women's Legal Aid Cell, Guwahati, filed a petition in the Guwahati High Court on

One of the strategies of the All India Democratic Women's Association (AIDWA) and of non-political organizations, like Saheli and the Joint Women's Programme, has been to activate the judiciary and use law to get specific reliefs.[4] Framing the issues for resolution within the existing legal framework has often been difficult. The petition filed by *Manushi* for the women of the Ho tribe asked for the Court to confer individual property rights on the women, a concept alien to the tribe.

By focusing on certain issues, the media has been an important factor in inspiring the petitioners and courts. The attention given to the death of Roop Kanwar on the funeral pyre of her husband and reports on the privacy of nuns are instances that have brought sati and the right to privacy to the fore.[5] Many of the cases in this chapter have been filed in response to newspaper articles, for example those filed after the sale of Kamala and after reports of rape in the press.

Women have been abused in a variety of ways, as demostrated by the cases on violence. The harassment of young women for dowry has become an increasing problem, because of the expectation of substantial 'gifts' of money and material goods from a woman's natal family. Not just at the time of marriage, but for years later, these demands have led to numerous, alarming reports on 'dowry deaths'. The cases on sati and rape reveal other patterns of violent behaviour. All but one of the cases compiled on rape are concerned with gang-rape by policemen or members of the armed

behalf of a woman who was raped and murdered. A relative of the woman had approached the cell but did not want to be involved in legal proceedings. On production of a false medical certificate the accused had been allowed to go out on bail until his illness was cured. The High Court responded to the writ petition by cancelling the bail, and transferred the petition to the original District Court. See also the chapter on 'The Police' for *SAHELI, a Women's Resource Centre through Ms Nalini Bhanot and others* v. *Commissioner of Police, Delhi and others* AIR 1990 SC 513 and *All India Democratic Women's Association* v. *State of Tamil Nadu and others* W.P. (C) No. 635 of 1992] for examples of other cases filed by women's organizations.

4 In addition to the documented cases, a petition was filed in the Madras High Court 1992 or 1993 by a Joint Action Committee of Women's groups regarding the increasing numbers of posters in films and cinema theatres [Geeta Ramaseshan, advocate, interview, Madras, 4/93].

5 For a case specifically relating to the girl-child, see the chapter on 'Children' for: *Brinda Karat and another* v. *The State* [Cr Misc (M) No. 1819 of 1991, Delhi] — the case of Ameena.

forces. The need for accountability and legality in the actions of police and army personnel is highlighted in the last set of cases on violence.

The petitions filed challenging enactments provide an insight into the problems and inequities of the existing legal framework. Similarly, the cases on discrimination provide an insight into the many forms that discrimination can take. The cases on prostitution demonstrate how not all the cases have been filed in support of women. The contention in *People's Council for Social Justice* paid little attention to the needs of prostitute women, many of whose circumstances have compelled them to earn their living in this profession. By grouping prostitutes with *goondas* and hooligans, this case did little for women in need of greater protection of the law and not further marginalization.

## Access to Justice

The *locus standi* of women's groups has been upheld by the Court, both as petitioner and as intervenor. The case of the dowry death of Sudha Goel, *State (Delhi Administration)*, although not a PIL, has been included because women's organizations intervened compelling the Supreme Court to reconsider the verdict of the High Court.[6] Other interventions by such groups can be found in the case of the rape of Rameezabee and in the petitions challenging Muslim Women (Protection of Rights on Divorce) Act, 1986. Petitions challenging this particular enactment have been filed both as PILs and as cases by aggrieved women, raising issues beyond the scope of the individual grievance.

In the section on rape there are cases filed by advocates and women's organizations and taken up *suo moto* by judges. After the rape of two nuns in Gajraula, two petitions were filed, one by an

[6] In the case of the rape of Mathura, the accused head constable, Tukaram and the constable, Ganpat were acquitted of the charge of rape in the SC: *Tukaram* (1979) 2 SCC 143. There was a public outcry after the judgement which prompted Upendra Baxi, Vasudha Dhagamwar, Raghunath Kelkar and Litika Sarkar to write "An Open Letter to the Chief Justice of India", d/-16/9/79 [(1979) 4 SCC J [7] complaining of the "cold-blooded legalism" of the SC. Although nothing resulted in this particular case, the law of rape was subsequently amended.

advocate in Madras and the other by a women's organization. While hearing the petition by the advocate, the Court rejected the petition filed by the AIDWA. This was in disregard of the attempts made by the organization to resolve the case locally, before filing the petition. Moreover, the Court failed to acknowledge that the nuns on whose behalf the petitions were filed, had given thier consent and support to AIDWA's petition. It was felt that the Court had not considered all the relevant factors when considering the merits of the petitions.

Letters have been sent to the Court in the cases of *Brij Bala* and *Anjalakshmi.* Although these two only relate to access to justice, they were described by the registries of the HCs concerned as being PILs.[7] Not having been defined, the distinction between the letter-petition and PIL has remained blurred and any innovation in the procedure continues to be described as PIL.

The case filed by *Mary Roy* is interesting because of the developments after the SC judgement on the validity of the Travancore Christian Succession Act, 1902. Initially not a PIL petitioner, she was made into one by the continuing harassment she faced after her success in the courtroom. The petition filed in the High Court of Kerala on behalf of Corpus Christi School was as a PIL.

The judicial process itself has been one of the major obstacles in getting effective access to justice. The SC itself noted the five month delay in listing the letter sent by *Bholanath Tripathi*, and similarly the petition filed for the Ho Tribe women was delayed by incorrect listings and as a result of the Supreme Court registry having lost some of the papers relating to the case. Moreover, in *Kasturi Lal Sharma*, the Court directed that the petitioner approach the Allahabad HC, as a more suitable forum.

## The Court's Response

One of the most striking characteristics of all the cases challenging enactments has been a consistent delay in listing. All the petitions on the Muslim Women (Protection of Rights on Divorce) Act, 1986, have been grouped together and are pending, as are the petitions

[7] Both cases were registered as PIL letter petitions in the High Court registries, involved a relaxation of procedure and were accorded preference in listings.

challenging the Chhota Nagpur Tenancy Act.[8] Similarly, the petitions filed on sati have been pending inspite of the efforts of the advocates dealing with the cases. The complexitity and sensitive nature of these cases — in political and social terms — provides a plausible explanation for the continued delays. Individual relief to those petitioners with a personal stake in the outcome of the litigation has not been forthcoming.

In a number of cases relating to violence, the Court has taken up the issue and monitored the progress of the case. In the dowry case filed by the Joint Women's Programme the Court, in an *obiter dicta*, suggested that dowry cells be established. Recognizing the failure of the lower judiciary to deal with instances of dowry violence, in the *All India Democratic Women's Association* v. *State of Haryana* the Supreme Court directed that the verdict of the lower court be implemented, echoing the report that the two convicted of the murder of Sudha Goel had not been imprisoned. Commissions of inquiry have been appointed by the Court, recognizing that the collection of evidences alone may otherwise be insufficient.[9] For example, in the case of *Catholic Association of Bombay and others* the Court directed the Government to appoint a commission.

In the Guntaben rape case, *P. Rathinam*, the investigation ordered by the Court took the evidence of 584 persons. In spite of this, the CBI investigation took many years to be completed and the Court had to concede that there may have been a deliberate delay in the proceedings by the State. Moreover, there is no evidence that the policemen found guilty were prosecuted, and it is notable that, although the rape took place in 1986, it was not until 1993 that the Court awarded compensation. Similarly *In the matter of: Judicial Enquiry into Gang-Rape Demanded, and, Concerted Demand for Judicial Probe*

[8] Petitions have also been filed challenging the constitutional validity of guardianship laws under Article 14 of the Constitution by *Manushi* and by the People's Union for Civil Liberties together with the Indian Council of Legal Aid. These are pending in the SC [see *Manushi*, No. 35, 1986 at 32-36 and the *PUCL Bulletin*, Vol. 12, No.4, April 1992 at 5].

[9] In addition to those documented, another petition was filed in the High Court of Madras in 1983 or 1984 asking the Court to inquire into a suspected dowry death. An inquiry was ordered. Pennurimai Iyakkam, an organization working in the slums and the Democratic Women's Association were impleaded in the petition. Meanwhile the husband was convicted for life in the Sessions Court, acquitted in appeal to the High Court and an appeal was filed in the SC by the State.

the Guwahati HC awarded an "ad hoc interim *ex-gratia* payment" without waiting for the guilty police officers to be punished.[10] In the Gajraula rape case the Court did not award compensation, and even refused to suggest that the CBI investigate the incident.

In a series of three orders, two in the Supreme Court and one in the Guwahati HC, on the extent of army and police powers, the courts have tacitly accepted the sexual abuse and harassment of women by members of the forces. Inspite of the general pliant approach in dealing with cases filed against the army and the police,[11] the Court has ordered that guidelines be framed and has issued directions on the treatment of women so as to ensure their safety.

The petition filed on behalf of unwed mothers, asking the Court to order the government to conduct DNA testing, was dismissed on the hope that the tests would be conducted. This discretion, exercised by the courts in dealing with PIL petitions, is most apparent in the case *Anjalakshmi* when the Madras HC sat out of hours to hear about the plight of a young bride.

As in cases brought to the Court as regular matters, the courts' response to the PIL petitions relating to prostitutes has also been not to consider the women as people in need of sympathetic treatment. In *Gaurav Jain* the children of prostitutes were ordered to be separated from their mothers and in *Bholanath Tripathi* the Court ordered that the woman in question be put in a rescue home, without considering the conditions that persist in such homes.[12] However, in *Vishal Jeet*, while refusing to direct that a CBI inquiry be conducted, the SC did direct the enforcement of Acts that would safeguard the interests of the girl-child and asked the government to inquire into the *devadasi* and *jogin* traditions.

## The Contribution of PIL

With the exception of the orders given on the army and the police,

[10] See the chapter on 'Environment and Resources' for the case of *Rajasthan Kisan Sangathan* v. *State of Rajasthan and others* AIR 1989 Raj 10.

[11] See the chapters on 'The Armed Forces' and 'The Police'.

[12] See the chapter on 'Prisons and State Institutions', in particular the section on institutions for women.

the Court has limited its role to reacting to injustices brought before it in a piecemeal fashion. When petitioning the Court, many of the women's groups hoped to vindicate the injustices done by getting a favourable court order. This has been possible in few of the cases. Even where the Court has directed inquiries and/or awarded compensation, this has taken many years. The cases speak for themselves, indicating the ways in which resort to law can be a futile exercise. The importance of the media in highlighting issues and informing the courts has been noted in *State (Delhi Administration)*, when the Supreme Court expressed its concern that the High Court had been affected by the publicity given to the case. In *In the matter of: Judical Enquiry into Gang-Rape Demanded, and, Concerted Demand for Judicial Probe*, the response of the State Government was described as a gesture of respect to the Court's anticipated verdict. The Rameezabee case is a discouraging example of the use of law. Rameezabee herself has become disillusioned with the "interference" of women's organizations, the press and the legal system.

The dynamics of the sati case reveal some of the reasons for the erratic and tentative response of the Court to the cases filed. Subsequent to the last documented order in 1989, the respondents made a statement that while they do not believe in *Sati-dah* (sati burning), they do believe in "Sati". This position has been echoed by the National Commission for Women. Women's organizations then vehemently protested against what was perceived as an endorsement of the worship of the "pure woman".[13] The SC has refused to become embroiled in this issue, simply by not hearing the case.

At the time when the amniocentesis petition was filed, proposed amendments and bills were introduced in the Lok Sabha and the Maharashtra Assembly to ban amniocentesis tests. Nothing happened as a result of the petition or the bills. Without any mobilization on the issue and any support for a ban on popular sex determination tests, there is little that can be done by the Court. In a seemingly supportive decision in *Brij Bala* the Court directed that the woman be allowed to compete fairly for the post of patwari through the District Employment Exchange. It is unlikely that Kumari Brij Bala will ever get to the interview stage given the numbers of people registered in the exchange.

[13] Kirti Singh, advocate, interview, 12/93.

The limitation of the courts in dealing with injustices specific to women have to be seen in the light of the cases in the rest of the book. The petitions that relate to women in other contexts are found in all the other chapters on urban space, labour, the environment etc. The inconvenience of having to deal with the legal system and its actors has been accentuated in this chapter as the biases of the legal profession, and the legal system against women have added complexities that transcend social or economic class.

## Violence

### General

***W P No 2229 of 1981***

***Coomi Kapoor, Ashwini Sarin, Arun Shourie v. State of MP and others***

A petition was filed under Article 32 of the Constitution by three journalists five days after a woman by the name of Kamala was purchased and brought to Delhi. She had been bought as a test-case, to demonstrate the commonplace sale of women. Newspaper reports had appeared in the national press exposing the sale, and the petitioners asked the Court to provide relief for Kamala and other women in the "flesh trade" in the Morena and Dholpur regions. The petition stated that traffic in women violates the fundamental rights, under sections 362, 365, 366, 367, 370, 371 and 372-374 of the the Indian Penal Code, 1860, and the Suppression of Immoral Traffic in Women and Girls Act, 1956. Asserting that they should be given *locus standi*, the petitioners stated that as Kamala was unable to move the Court because of her bondage, fear and ignorance of the duties of the state, it was the Court's duty to realize Articles 39(a), 39(e), 39(f), 51A(a), 51(e), 51(g) and 51(j) of the Constitution. As this was an early PIL petition, the petitioners had also to ask the Court to fulfil the mandate of Article 32 of the Constitution, by relaxing procedural rules.

Before the petition could be heard, Kamala disappeared.

☆ ☆ ☆

A petition was filed under Article 226 of the Constitution, in the Kerala HC in 1992, by advocate A.X. Verghese, on behalf of the unwed mothers in Thiruvelli, in the Wynad District of Attapadi in the hill districts of northern Kerala. These are predominantly tribal areas and the petition concerns about 250 tribal women who bore about 1000 children. The petition described how the women were raped or enticed into sexual activity by forest/police officials and settlers in the area. Once pregnant, the women were not only ostracized in their community, but were also unable to claim any maintenance from the fathers of their children as paternity was not established. A Malayalam language newspaper and the *Indian Express* published a series of articles on the trauma of these tribal women. The matter was taken up on the floor of the Assembly, at which point the Minister in charge of Tribal Welfare promised that DNA tests would be conducted at the expense of the government to identify the fathers of the children. As the government did not fulfil its promise to conduct the tests, the petition was filed. Annexed to the petition were newspaper articles, one of which reported:

> There are more than 300 unmarried tribal mothers in the hundred-odd tribal colonies in Thirunelli alone, according to

social activists in the area. The number of children with no records of their fathers would cross more than a thousand.[14]

Dismissing the petition, the HC expressed its "hope" that the state would do the necessary tests.

Advocate A.X. Verghese hopes to file another petition in which a few of the women, who have declared their willingness to come forward, would be the petitioners.

## Harassment for Dowry

A petition was filed under Article 32 of the Constitution in 1982 by Amrita Chhachi of Saheli, a women's organization based in Delhi. The petition asked for an inquiry into Vimla's death, which was suspected to be because of demands for dowry. Vimla had been burned to death in Hyderabad and a women's organization there, Stree Shakti Sangathana had investigated the case and found that the Deputy Superintendent of Police conducting the inquiry was watering down the evidence. The petition cited strong medical evidence to show that it was not possible for Vimla to have burned herself to death.

The petition was admitted and the Supreme Court ordered a CBI inquiry.[15]

☆ ☆ ☆

***W P (Crl) No 51069-1076 of 1983***
***Neelam Varma and others v. Union of India***

A petition was filed under Article 32 of the Constitution by seven "dowry victims" and two women's organizations. The petitioners claimed that the police authorities had refused to register their complaints of dowry harassment and had not carried out the necessary investigations as specified by the Criminal Procedure Code. Referring to SC decisions, it was contended that the right to life included the right to live with human dignity and that the

[14] Chekutty, N.P., "The Trauma of Thirunelli's Tribals", *Indian Express*, 17/11/91.

[15] "Appeal to Supreme Court — Enquiry into Vimla's Death in Hyderabad", *Manushi*, Number 20, 1984, 41-42.

fundamental rights under Articles 14 and 21 of the Constitution were being violated.

☆ ☆ ☆

***Crl A Nos 93 and 94 of 1984***
***State (Delhi Administration)* v. *Laxman Kumar***

This criminal case referred to Sudha Goel, who was burned to death by her husband, Laxman Kumar, mother-in-law and brother-in-law when in the ninth month of pregnancy. The three accused were sentenced to death under the IPC, 1860, for a dowry offence by the Additional Sessions Judge but then acquitted in the Delhi HC. There was an uproar after the judgement, during which time the media and women's organizations vociferously protested against the acquittal. An appeal was then filed in the SC under Article 136 of the Constitution. The Indian Federation of Women Lawyers was a petitioner in this appeal and women's groups including Janwadi Mahila Samiti, Karmika and Mahila Dakshata Samiti intervened in the case, protesting against the HC verdict.

In a judgement D/-23/9/85 by Justice A.N. Sen and > Justice Ranganath Misra
[reported AIR 1986 SC 250]
The Court noted, at 266:

> We were, however, disturbed by the fact that the High Court took notice of publicity through the news media and indicated its apprehension of a flutter in the public mind. It is the obligation of every Court to find out the truth and act according to the law once the truth is discovered. ... What happens outside the courtroom when the Court is busy in its process of adjudication is indeed irrelevant and unless a proper cushion is provided to keep the proceedings within the courtroom, dissociated from the heat generated outside the courtroom either through the news media or through flutter in the public mind, the cause of justice is bound to suffer.

The SC absolved the elder brother of the husband and sentenced Laxman Kumar and his mother Smt Shakuntala to life imprisonment. The death sentence was not restored because of the delay in the proceedings and "intervening circumstances" (Laxman Kumar had remarried after his acquittal in the HC).

A Hindi Sunday newspaper later published an article stating that on 1/1/88, news reporter Dhirendra Kumar and advocate Arvind Jain discovered that neither of the accused were in jail. No arrests had been made after the SC judgement and there was no functioning machinery to follow up the judgement.[16]

☆ ☆ ☆

***W P No 707 of 1986***

***Joint Women's Programme v. State of Rajasthan***

A petition was filed under Article 32 of the Constitution asking for an investigation into the unnatural deaths of Mrs Kantha and Mrs Prasani Devi.

In an order D/-24/3/87 by Justice M.P. Thakkar and Justice B.C. Ray

[reported AIR 1987 SC 2060]

The SC ordered that investigation be conducted by an officer not below the rank of Superintendent of Police. In this interim order the Court directed the states of Rajasthan and Haryana to create a special dowry cell at the state level, with which women social workers were to be associated.

☆ ☆ ☆

***W P No ?? of 1992***

***All India Democratic Women's Association v. State of Haryana and others***

A petition was filed under Article 32 of the Constitution on the basis of a newspaper report in the *Times of India* on 13/7/92 stating that even three months after the SC held Satish Kumar guilty of murdering his wife Shashi Bala for dowry, he was yet to be put in jail. The petition asked the Court to direct the District Magistrate, Hissar and the District and Sessions Judge, Hissar, to ensure the immediate arrest of Satish Kumar, in accordance with the SC decision on 10/4/92. As this was not an isolated case of non-implementation of a judgement of the SC, more general directions were asked for — that there should be immediate

16 "Who is afraid of the Supreme Court", *PUCL Bulletin*, Vol. 8, No. 3, March 1988, 16.

compliance with any sentence of the SC and that this compliance should be communicated to the Registrar within one month.

## Sati

The sati issue came to the fore after Roop Kanwar died on the funeral pyre of her husband in Jhunjhunu in 1987. Two petitions were then filed by women's organizations on sati. In both AIDWA is the main petitioner, with six national women's organizations and other national and autonomous groups as parties to the petitions. The first petition was filed one year after Roop Kanwar was killed. The second petition relates to the Jhunjhunu temples in Rajasthan where sati is glorified, and to the trust which is responsible for the wealth of the temples.

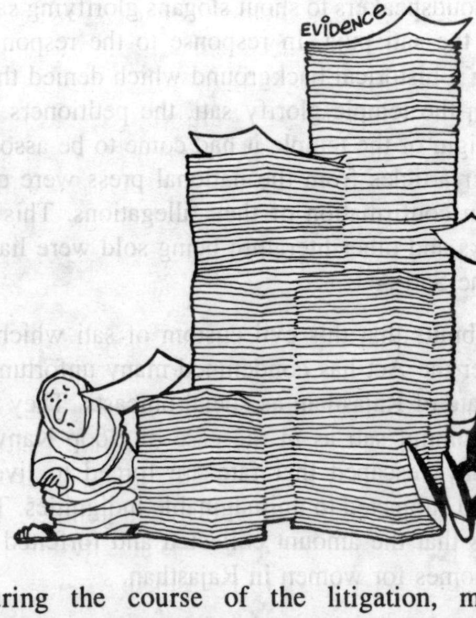


During the course of the litigation, many miscellaneous applications were filed by the parties involved, and other petitions were initiated. There are many small orders in these cases, together with dozens of affidavits and rejoinders. Some of these are documented below.

☆ ☆ ☆

***W P No 913 of 1988***

***All India Democratic Women's Association and Janwadi Mahila Samiti v. Union of India and others***

A petition was filed under Article 32 of the Constitution, invoking the Commission of Sati (Prevention) Act, 1987, the Rajasthan Sati (Prevention) Act, 1987, and Articles, 14, 25, 26, 51A(e) of .the Constitution. The petition asked for the sati *puja* in Sri Rani Satiji Mandir to be prohibited as it glorifies sati. It also asked for the prohibition of the preparation for the *Mela* to be held on 10/9/88, and the implementation of the provision of the Sati Act in Rajasthan.

An application was filed by the petitioners, during the pendency of the writ petition, in response to the claim made by the second respondent, Sri Rani Satiji Mandir, Jhunjhunu, that preparations for the usual sati *mela* were not taking place. The petitioners alleged that the preparations had begun with the sale of *chunries* and glossy booklets, the use of loudspeakers to shout slogans glorifying sati and the performance of the sati puja. In response to the respondent's arguments providing a historical background which denied that the rituals undertaken in the temple glorify sati, the petitioners stated that whatever the origin of the temple it had come to be associated with sati. Newspaper articles from the national press were quoted by the petitioners, in confirmation of their allegations. This CMP also stated that books and other literature being sold were liable to be forfeited under the Sati Act:

> The petitioner submits that this evil custom of sati which is now banned under the Act has condemned many unfortunate widows in the State of Rajasthan as social outcasts. They are either forced to commit sati as in the case of Roop Kanwar and those who have escaped that fate are forced to live a sub-human life and subjected to unimaginable indignities. The petitioner submits that the amount collected and forfeited be used for shelter homes for women in Rajasthan.

The Court was asked to issue a show cause notice to the respondents asking them why contempt should not be issued.

Another application was filed by the petitioners asking the Court to prohibit the performance of the *chunri* ceremony in Sri Rani Satiji Mandir, on the grounds that it glorifies sati. Dr L.M. Singhvi, the advocate for the respondents, had contended that the ceremony did not glorify sati but was part of a traditional form of offering worship known as "Sodash Upachar".

In an order D/-17/3/89 by Justice Ranganath Misra and Justice M.N. Venkatachaliah
[reported AIR 1989 SC 1280]
An earlier interim order prohibiting the performance of the ceremony was upheld, but the Court declined to make a definitive judgement stating, at 1281:

> We do not think it would be appropriate for us to express any view beyond this point at this stage as the same may embarrass the Bench which would ultimately hear the matter.

The demand by the petitioners for the conversion of the temple into rehabilitation camps for uncared for ladies was rejected by the Court in the absence of any statutory provision for such a change of user. In the order, the Court stressed the heterogeneity of religious practices.

***Shree Rani Satiji Mandir and others v. Union of India***

A petition was filed under Article 226 of the Constitution in the Calcutta HC by a temple registered under the Societies Registration Act, 1906, at Calcutta. The petition contended that the temple does not glorify sati as widow burning, but is a Shiva-Shakti temple in which prayers are offered to a Trishul. The petition further claimed that it was incorrect to state that this glorifies sati in contravention of the Rajasthan Sati (Prevention) Act, 1987, and that such allegations offend religious sentiments.

An article on this petition noted:

> The Calcutta High Court is known for its ever expanding jurisdiction. Its jurisdiction now extends to Rajasthan. The order of the Collector in Rajasthan banning the sati mela in Jhunjhunu was successfully challenged in Calcutta. The Rajasthan Government promptly appealed to the Supreme Court, pointing out that the Supreme Court had on several occasions criticized the Calcutta High Court for exceeding its jurisdiction.[17]

[17] Devil's Advocate, "Adaalat Antics: An Omnipotent Court", *The Lawyers*, Vol. 3, No.9, September 1988, 24.

Another petition was filed after Swami Agnivesh had tried to lead a band of Arya Samajees on a *padyatra* to Deorala in December 1987, to counter the myth that sati is a religious practice:

> First, on December 18, Shri Bhagirath Singh Shekawat, a member of the Dharma Rakshaa Samiti, moved the Court in a writ petition seeking a ban on the anti-sati march into Deorala.
>
> The government, in a bid to thwart the march, had earlier imposed orders under Section 144 of Cr P C. Later the Sub-Divisional Magistrate of Amber served orders on Swami Agnivesh prohibiting the *padyatra* group from entering Chomu tahsil. Swami Agnivesh moved a public interest petition before the High Court on Monday, December 21. It was a court holiday. The acting Chief Justice, Shri Ghuman Mal Lodha and Justice Panachand Jain took up the petition. Justice Lodha cancelled an appointment for the purpose. The Court observed that the SDM's order was directed against those who were working for the re-establishment of the constitutional law. The authorities, instead, should move against those who were threatening the law abiding groups. 'It is the duty of the government to protect peaceful citizens who were doing right work', observed the judges. It expressed a hope that the government would monitor the *padyatra* to Ajitgarh, adjoining Deorala, and allow it to enter Chomu tahsil.

It is strange that the prohibitory orders were served on Swami Agnivesh and not on those who were threatening him in the face of the recent state and central laws on sati. From the very beginning the state government has indirectly strengthened the pro-sati upsurge in the state. This episode is yet another expression of its resolve not to enforce the existing laws — old and new — against sati.[18]

### Rape

A petition was filed under Article 226 of the Constitution in the

[18] Chibbar, Y.P., "Rajasthan High Court Restores Right to Oppose Sati", *PUCL Bulletin*, Vol. 8, No. 1, January 1988, 6.

Karnataka HC in 1984 by Streelekha, a women's organization in Bangalore. A woman by the name of Rameezabee had been raped by several policemen in Andhra Pradesh. There had been riots after the rape and the government responded by appointing the Mukhatadar Commission, with Justice Mukhatadar, a Sitting Judge of the Hyderabad HC, as the sole commissioner. The accused had been acquitted in the Sessions Court in Raichur, Andhra Pradesh. Members of Stree Shakti Sangathana in Andhra Pradesh had wanted to appeal against the order in the High Court of Andhra Pradesh, but as the case had been transferred to Karnataka, it could only be filed by an organization there. It was then that Streelekha was asked to petition the Court.

In an order the HC acquitted the policemen of the rape.

Streelekha then filed an appeal in the SC in 1984 or 1985, members of the organization became disillusioned with the lack of response both from its lawyers and from the Court, and no longer felt able to follow the case. The appeal is still pending in the Supreme Court.

Rameezabee continues to live in Andhra Pradesh, and work there as an agricultural worker. Activists of Streelekha described her as a "broken woman" because of her fear, having been harassed by the legal process and the communal tensions. She now refuses to meet local women's groups.[19]

☆ ☆ ☆

***W P No 92 of 1986***

***P. Rathinam* v. *Union of India and another***

A petition was filed under Article 32 of the Constitution by an advocate after the gangrape of Guntaben of Gujarat by policemen. On 5/1/86 Guntaben Behn was taken from her home in connection with the kidnapping of a relative. She was stripped naked by the police before a crowd and subsequently raped by several policemen in the cabin of a truck when it was stopped en route to a local police station. She was again assaulted and raped at the police station.

19 See *Sangarsh*, an occasional magazine published by Vimochana, Bangalore: Vasantha, Kannabiran, "More About Rameeza", Vol. 1 at 1; Donna, "Rameeza Bee — Justice Denied", Vol. 2, at 3.

Initially the police refused to record the complaint of rape but did so on 12/1/86. The petition demanded an inquiry into the incident.

In an order D/-13/2/86

The SC appointed its own Commission of Inquiry with a senior police officer from outside the state, K.V. Joseph and Ela Pathak, a social worker, as commissioners.

The commissioners recorded the statements of 584 persons, and submitted their report by 27/2/86.

In an order D/-27/10/86 by Chief Justice P.N. Bhagwati, Justice V. Balakrishna Eradi and Justice Ranganath Misra

The Court noted that the report on the CBI investigation had still not been received inspite of the two extensions granted, so the report of investigation was directed to be produced before 5/11/86:

> It will be for us to decide what action should be taken on the basis of the report of CBI. We hope and trust that the report will be submitted within the extended time.

In subsequent orders in 1986 and 1987, the Supreme Court repeatedly adjourned the case. The State was urged to file an affidavit and take action against the persons found guilty in the report. The CBI was asked to submit a report to the Court indicating the proceedings initiated by it. Details on the grant of sanction under section 6 of the Prevention of Corruption Act for prosecution of police officers were asked for from police officials.

In an order D/-7/12/87 by Justice S. Natarajan and Justice M.N. Venkatachaliah

[reported 1987 (2) SCALE 317 [1464]]

The CBI inquiry directed to be conducted by the Court had found that there was a *prima facie* case against the police and that Guntaben had been illegally detained. Six policemen were arrested in March 1986 but were released on bail on the technical ground that the CBI had not charged them within the prescribed time. The Gujarat State Government had still failed to take any action on the report of the Joseph Commission. The Court described the attitude of the state government in not taking action against those named as responsible for the rape and its subsequent cover-up as disclosing a "pathetic state of affairs". The Court noted that, nearly two years after the incident had taken place and despite two investigation commissions identifying the culprits, the state government had failed to take any action, stating:

In the affidavit of 20 January 1987, a statement was made by the Deputy Secretary of the State Government indicating the stage at which proceedings have been taken in respect of the several officers mentioned in the report submitted by the Joseph Commission. Thereafter an affidavit dated 16 November 1987 was filed by the Joint Secretary of the State Government. On a comparison of the contents of the two affidavits it is clear that no serious attempt has been made to pursue the matter.

The Court ordered the Gujarat Government to bring all original records of the case to the Court and to have submitted to the Supreme Court any charge sheets issued to the policemen held responsible.

In later orders, the Court asked for an affidavit from the respondents regarding the progress made in the prosecution launched, and appointed a Special Judge to try the accused persons and to submit a report to the Court on the progress in the cases.

In an order D/-13/9/88 by Justice B.C. Ray

The Court acknowledged receipt of the affidavits of the state and of the petitioner, stating:

> We do not propose to make any comment on the affidavits at this stage, but we do feel that there is good ground for both the Commissions of Enquiry and the Criminal Court conducting and completing the proceedings in pursuance of the orders made by us as expeditiously as possible. Accordingly, we direct the Commission of Enquiry to conduct the proceedings from day to day and to complete the proceedings within three months from today. Upon the completion of the enquiry, a Report of the Enquiry will be furnished to this Court. As regards the criminal trial against the several officers, we think it appropriate to direct the Criminal Court taking those proceedings to complete them, if possible, also within three months from today. In the event of the proceedings not being completed within that period the trial court may request for further time, but while doing so it will indicate in sufficient detail the progress of the proceedings from stage to stage.

In an order D/-2/4/93 by Justice B.P. Jeevan Reddy and Justice N. Venkatachala

[reported 1993 (2) SCALE 126 [631]]

The Court acknowledged receipt of the report of the second Commission which stated that departmental inquiries have been commenced against the various officers, most of which were still pending. The Court had asked the state of Gujarat and other concerned officers to deal with these inquiries quickly. Although this has happened on a few occasions, the Court stated, at 631:

> The Government of Gujarat has since filed an affidavit explaining the stage of enquiry against various officers and the reasons for the pendency of the enquiry. While we do not propose to deal with the reasons assigned for delay in finalization in respect of each of the enquiries, we must say that we are not satisfied with the reasons assigned. The enquiries have been pending over the last several years. The petitioner alleges that the delay is deliberate. We would like to think the petitioner is not right but, it must be said, the undue delay in concluding the enquiries is giving room for such belief and comment.

The Court directed that pending inquiries be concluded within three months. Rs 50,000 were directed to be paid as compensation to Guntaben, and she was to be immediately intimated of this order.

☆ ☆ ☆

***C R No 292 of 1988, Misc Case No 310 of 1988, Guwahati***
***In the matter of: Judical Enquiry into Gang-Rape Demanded, and, Concerted Demand for Judicial Probe***

A petition was filed under Article 226 of the Constitution as a *suo moto* action at the instance of the Chief Justice of the Guwahati HC on the basis of a PTI news report published under the caption "Gang Rape in Kokrajar Village" and "Judicial Enquiry into Gang-Rape Demanded", detailing the rape of women from the Bodo tribe by policemen. Justice Guman Mal Lodha was Chief Justice in the Guwahati High Court for fifteen days and it was at his initiative that the case came up.

In an order D/-14/3/88 by > Chief Justice Guman Mal Lodha and Justice Sangma
[reported (1988) 1 Guwa LR 489]
The Court stated, at 499:

> After issuing of the notice and the rule in this public interest litigation to the state functionaries, the very next date a Judicial Commission appointment has been announced by the state and a day earlier to the final hearing, 8 arrests of the police personnel have been made on the charge of rape and certain other offences in these incidents. The State's response, though belated according to the "Bodos", shows respect to the Court's anticipated verdict.

Accepting what it described as the *bona fide* help of lawyers, women's organizations, student's unions and social groups, the Court went on to state, at 506-7:

> The people of Assam, especially the tribal people nearby and women throughout this country have once again established, the utility of encouraging Public Interest Litigation, without insisting upon formal writ petition or questioning *locus standi* for justice to the down-trodden. By now in this country this new innovation in public interest has become successful and its utility well established and proved, and it has come to stay.

Chief Justice Lodha felt that it was unfortunate that forty years after independence this kind of incident should occur. He quoted from the Sastras, Manu and ancient vedic texts, stated that the state "should" initiate its own inquiry, but nonetheless appointed a Judicial Commission. Regarding the payment of compensation, the Court held, at 502:

> We feel that payment of money in the form of compensation is wholly misconceived and would rather be undermining the honour of the ravished family.... An *ad hoc* interim *ex-gratia* payment for the purpose of rehabilitation should be granted without prejudice to either of the parties.

The amounts awarded by the Court were:

> Rs 25,000 made to seven proven victims; Rs 15,000 made to two other victims, to be increased to Rs 25,000 when investigation proves they are victims; Rs 10,000 made to one victim, also to be increased later.

The Court also directed that, at 505:

> Unless the Government for some very strong compelling reasons

to refuse to refer the matter to the CBI the investigation of the criminal case(s) and the prosecution should be expedited and it is expected that the police force in future would take remedial measures to improve their lot. It is the fairness of the State Government that has not taken any rigid stand whatsoever so far in this litigation.

The judicial inquiry took place, but no details were available about a report. However, one incidental result of this case, known as the "Boomka rape case" is the confidence it created amongst the Bodos and the mobilization point it provided.[20]

☆ ☆ ☆

***W P (C) No 385 of 1988, W P (Crl) No 366 of 1988***
***All India Democratic Women's Association and another*** **v.** ***State of Tripura and others***

Petitions were filed under Article 32 of the Constitution by a women's organization and its President. In early June, 1988, newspaper articles in local and national newspapers reported the rape of twenty-five tribal women in the village of Ujay Maidan in the Khowai Sub-Division of Western Tripura by jawans of the Assam Rifles. On reading these reports a team of six members of the All India Democratic Women's Association went to Tripura and visited village Ujay Maidan to find out what had happened. They interviewed thirteen of the women who had been raped, six of whom had separately and voluntarily affirmed affidavits stating that they were raped by jawans of the Assam Rifles. The Chief Minister of Tripura held a press conference on 21/6/88, in which he admitted having received complaints from four women who had been raped. He stated that an FIR had been lodged and the State Police had been instructed to inquire into the matter. An executive inquiry was conducted by a fact-finding committee constituted of the District Magistrate and Collector, West Tripura District, Sub-Divisional Officer, Khowai, Deputy Superintendent of Police of the Government of Tripura and Major S.K. Raina. The report of the inquiry stated that the women lived in an inaccessible area, were illiterate and were unable to mention any dates. It admited that it is

20 Niloy Dutta, advocate, interview, Guwahati, 5/93.

possible that two women were raped according to the report, but held that the allegations of mass rape were baseless. The petitions were then filed as no action had been taken after the report, and because the issue had been dismissed by the state government as political propaganda to malign the army. The petition stated:

> as soon as the aforementioned incidents of gang rape was brought to the notice of the State Government, the Chief Minister, and the Home Minister of Tripura and army officers outright started saying that it was a baseless political propaganda of the opposition and the CPI(M) in particular maligning the army. They threatened to take action against those who complained and described the criticism of the army as an anti-national act.

The petitioners asked for an order directing that all records relating to the rape be produced, that financial help be given to the victims of rape, that an inquiry be conducted under the orders and directions of the SC, and that criminal cases be initiated against the culprits who had committed rape. Several newspaper cuttings were annexed to the petition, as was a copy of the enquiry conducted by the fact-finding committee.

In an order D/-22/3/90

The Court acknowledged receipt of the report of the Commissioner, S.C. Dab, earlier appointed by the Court to look into the allegations. The report concluded that at least four women had been gang-raped, two were raped and one molested. The report also held that the State of Tripura and the army officers were trying to hush up the crimes and that the police investigation had proceeded in that direction.

A judgement has not been given and the case is pending — waiting for the state of Tripura's reply. The advocate for the petitioner, Kirti Singh, has been asked by the new CPI(M) government in Tripura to take over as counsel for the State of Tripura. As the incident happened when the State of Tripura had a Congress Government, there is hope that a conclusion to the case will be reached.

☆ ☆ ☆

***Crl W P No 22 of 1991***

***All India Democratic Women's Association* v. *Union of India and others***

A petition was filed under Article 32 of the Constitution by a women's organization. On 13/7/90 in Gajraula in UP, two nuns were raped and sodomized when St. Mary's Convent School was raided. The culprits also stole Rs 1,10,000. After the incident the two nuns were treated shoddily by the police, administrators and doctors who refused to document the case correctly. The police then arrested the wrong people for the crime. The petition filed on behalf of the nuns, asked the Court to institute an inquiry into the incident. The petition detailed the incident and the subsequent events in which the action of the police, administration and doctors were found lacking. It recounted the many representations made by the nuns to different officials, and described a further incident in which in spite of the presence of members of the Uttar Pradesh Police, the nuns were again threatened and the convent raided, though no one was hurt. The petition stated:

> The petitioner has been constrained to file the present petition at the request of the sisters of St. Mary's Convent Gajraula as the UP Administration and police have deliberately not investigated the case properly.

and noted that:

> The petitioner has come to know that an advocate from Madras, Mr Cherian has filed a writ petition in this Hon'ble Court concerning the rape but no notice of the same has been sent to the sisters of Gajraula.

The petition asked for a judical inquiry into the lapses of the police and administration of UP. It also asked for the investigation to be expedited, the case in Moradabad against the arrested accused to be quashed, compensation to be awarded, reimbursement of things lost made, and for guidelines to be issued by the Court for the investigation, collection of evidence by the police and preparation of medical reports in the case of assaults/rape.

When the case came up for hearing it was tagged with the case of Mr Cherian's petition, as the Court refused to entertain the petition filed by AIDWA separately.

***W P (Crl) No 1753-55 of 1990***

***Gudalure M.J. Cherian and others v. Union of India and others***

Petitions were filed by three prominent Chistians on the rape of the nuns at Gajraula in UP, asking for a CBI enquiry.

In an order D/-9/12/91 by Justice Kuldip Singh and Justice Fathima Beevi
[reported 1991 (2) SCALE 241 [1305]]
The Court stated, at 1307:

> The investigation having been completed by the police and charge-sheet submitted to the Court, it is not for this Court, ordinarily, to re-open the investigation specially by entrusting the same to a specialized agency like the CBI. We are also conscious that of late the demand for CBI-investigation even in police cases is on the increase. Nevertheless — in a given situation, to do justice between the parties and to instill confidence in the public mind it may become necessary to ask the CBI to investigate a crime. It only shows the efficiency and the independence of the agency.

However, the case from Moradabad was not transferred or quashed and AIDWA was asked to withdraw its petition because relief had been given and the petition disposed of.

## The Army and the Police

Women have suffered violence by members of the army and the police, as can be seen in most of the rape cases documented above. The Supreme Court and the Guwahati High Court have acknowledged the abuse of the powers of these state institutions in three PILs:

***Crl W P No 221 of 1988***
***Janwadi Mahila Samiti and another* v. *Union of India***

A petition was filed under Article 32 of the Constitution by a women's organization. A demonstration of women activists was held in support of the Bharat Bandh on 15/3/88. Volunteers were peacefully demonstrating in central Delhi at 11.30 a.m. when policemen arrived and made a lathicharge on the women. Brinda Karat, the secretary of Janwadi Mahila Samiti was taken into custody and beaten by police constable Jai Gopal. Her hand was fractured, and she was prevented from registering an FIR against the constable. As this action by a police officer was illegal, a petition was filed with Brinda Karat as the second petitioner. The petition invoked Articles 14, 15(3) and 21 of the Constitution, section 192 of the Criminal Procedure Code, 1973 and the police acts and rules, all of which provide minimum safeguards to demonstrators. The petition stated that the state has a duty to frame appropriate guidelines in the matter. The preliminary inquiry which was conducted was considered to be an "eyewash" and based on a fictitious medical test, so the petition stated:

> every citizen has a right to register a complaint and by not allowing the second petitioner to register her complaint the police have acted against all provisions of law. The police have also acted contrary to law by not taking *suo moto* cognizance of a crime committed in front of them. ... the police have cooked up a fictitious story that the said constable was surrounded and attacked by women in the police station, and in the ensuing melee, the second petitioner's forearm was fractured.

The petition asked that this and other such lathicharges be declared as illegal, and that action be taken against the named police constable and other policemen.

A counter-affidavit was filed on behalf of the respondents in September 1988 by Kanwaljit Deol, Deputy Commissioner of Police, New Delhi in which the averments made in the petition were denied. It alleged that some of the women demonstrators were throwing stones, that women police, assisted by male police, had rounded up the demonstrators, that there was no lathicharge and that constable Jai Gopal was hurt in an attack by women demonstrators and had to be hospitalized. The counter-affidavit also stated that a FIR had been lodged against Brinda Karat for attacking constable Jai Gopal and causing obstruction in the discharge of his duty.

In an order D/-23/1/89
The SC said that the State should formulate proper rules for the conduct of members of the police force in conjunction with women's organizations.

Following this order the petitioners filed seven pages of suggestions regarding police conduct in relation to women demonstrators, in terms of the court order.

The case is now pending.

☆ ☆ ☆

***C A No 2551 of 1991***
***Editor, "Boodhbar" v. Union of India and another***

An appeal was filed against the order of the Guwahati HC in a litigation on the extent of army powers in the north-east of India.[21]

In an order in 1991 by Justice S. Ratnavel Pandian (Vacation Judge) The full order of the Court stated:

> Heard both counsel for a considerable length of time and gone through Annexure A under the caption "List of Do's and Dont's while acting under the Armed Forces (Special Powers) Act, 1958" annexed with counter-affidavit filed on behalf of the respondents and also vide the order of this Court dated 23/4/91 made in SLP(C) No.6811-13/91.
>
> In addition I give the following directions:
>
> The Army Officers while effecting the arrest of a woman or making search of a woman or in searching the place in the actual occupancy of a female shall follow the procedure meant for the police officers as contemplated under the various provisions of the Code of Criminal Procedure, namely the proviso to sub-section (2) of section 47, sub-section (2) of section 51, sub-section (3) of section 100 and proviso to sub-section (1) of section 160 of the Code.

The concerned sections of the Code state:

Section 47(2). If ingress to such a place cannot be obtained under sub-section (1), it shall be lawful in any case for a person acting under a warrant and in any case in which a warrant may issue, but cannot be obtained without affording the person to be arrested an opportunity of escape, for a police officer to enter such a place and search therein, an in order to affect an entrance into such a place, to break open any outer or inner door or window of any house or place whether that of the person to be arrested or any other person if after notification of his authority and purpose and demand of admittance duly made, he cannot otherwise obtain admittance (Proviso…)

> Section 51(2). Whenever it is necessary to cause a female to be searched, the search shall be made by another female with strict regard to decency.
>
> Section 100(3). Where any person in or about such place is

21 Details of the larger litigation have been given in the chapter on The 'Armed Forces'.

> reasonably suspected of concealing about his person any article for which search should be made, such person may be searched and if such person is a woman, the search shall be made by another woman with strict regard to decency.
>
> Secion 160(1) Proviso. Provided that no male person under the age of fifteen years or woman shall be required to attend at any place other than the place in which such male person or woman resides.

☆ ☆ ☆

***C R (HC) No 24 of 1991, Guwahati***
***Niloy Dutta v. District Magistrate, Sibsagar District***

A newspaper report appeared in an Assamese daily on 24/1/91 "Suspected ULFA female members detained", stating that on 22/1/91, two women were taken into custody for interrogation. This article was read out in Court on 24/1/91 by Pranab Pathak, advocate and the Court requested Hrishikesh Roy and Niloy Dutta to file a writ petition under Article 226 of the Constitution. The question of the constitutional protection of women from interrogation at police station houses was raised.

In an order D/-5/2/91 by Chief Justice A. Raghuvir and Justice S.N. Phukan
[reported in (1991) 2 Guwa LR 217]
The Court expressed its limitations, at 220:

> we term the instant order subject to full orders of this Court in Civil Rules 2238, 2341, 2415, of 1990 and Civil Rule No. 11 of 1991 as in the above group of cases larger issues are pending decision amongst others including the subject of protection of women from police and army officials.

before going on to say, at 223:

> whenever army officials have to deal with women under Act 28 of 1958 as offenders before arrest or as witnesses or "otherwise" when women are to be interrogated, no woman is expected to be taken to the Army Camp for interrogation. In simple words a woman is not to be requisitioned by the Army officials for attendance at any place other than the woman's residence, as provided in Section 160(1) of the Code of

> Criminal Procedure.... The learned Advocate General stated once a person male or female is handed over to the police authorities by the army authorities, such arrested person cannot be taken again into the custody by the army officials. The elucidation is recorded for guidance and compliance by the army officials and police establishment.

## Challenge to enactments

There are a number of writ petitions pending in the Supreme Court which challenge the constitutional validity of the Muslim Personal Laws (Application) Act, 1937. Many of the petitions were precipitated by the passing of the Muslim Women (Protection of Rights on Divorce) Act, 1986. In the now famous Shah Bano judgement (*Mohammed Ahmed Khan* v. *Shah Bano Begum and others* AIR 1985 SC 945) the Court had stated that although Muslim Personal Law limits the liability of the husband to provide maintenance to the divorced wife during the period of iddat, section 125 of the Criminal Procedure Code, 1973 had to be taken into account. This section provides for the maintenance of divorced wives, children and parents and for penalties if such maintenance is not paid (note that the onus is on the wife to prove the income of her husband). In Shah Bano, the Court held that if the divorced wife is able to maintain herself, the husband's liability to pay maintenance would cease when the period of iddat expired, as envisaged in the Muslim Personal Laws. However, the Court also held that if a divorced wife is unable to maintain herself after the period of iddat, she is entitled to recourse under section 125 of the Criminal Procedure Code, 1973.

This judgement caused a furore as it was felt that the judiciary was directly "interfering" in the realm of the personal laws of Muslims. Taking this opportunity the Muslim Women (Protection of Rights on Divorce) Act, 1986, was enacted to specify the rights which a divorced Muslim woman is entitled to at the time of divorce. In the event that she is unable to maintain herself, nor are her dependants or inheritors, the State Wakf Board were to provide funds on the direction of a Magistrate. Unless both husband and wife agree to be governed by section 125 Cr P C, 1973, the Muslim husband was no longer required to support his wife after divorce beyond the period of iddat, as long as the requisite amounts according to Muslim Personal Law are paid.

Seven petitions, relating to the application of Muslim Personal Law and the 1986 Act in particular, have been grouped together by the SC, and have yet to come up for hearing.

Petitions were filed by: Daniel Latifi and Sona Khan; Tara Ali Baig; the Islamic Shariat Board; the National Federation of Indian Women; Rashidaben; Susheela Gopalan and Shehnaaz Sheikh. The latter two are detailed below:

### *W P No 1055 of 1986*
### *Ms Susheela Gopalan and others v. Union of India*

This petition was filed by the General Secretary of AIDWA, with eight other petitioners, all of whom were divorced Muslim women from Kerala and Kanpur. The petition stated that AIDWA welcomed the SC judgement in the *Shah Bano* case, but it challenges the Muslim Women (Protection of Rights on Divorce) Act, 1986 as unjust and discriminatory. As the divorced woman needs maintenance, the petition described the procedure prescribed by the Act as unreasonable and arbitrary. The petition asserted that the exclusion of the divorced Muslim woman from the purview of section 125 of the Criminal Procedure Code, 1973 is discriminatory and violative of Article 14 of the Constitution. The petition provided a detailed examination and critique of the provisions of this Act.

### *Shehnaaz Sheikh and others v. Union of India*

A petition was filed under Article 32 of the Constitution on 14/12/83 by a Muslim woman who had suffered a two year ordeal of torture, humiliation and unilateral divorce by her husband. The petition challenged the constitutional validity of the Muslim Personal Laws (Application) Act, 1937 and described Muslim Personal Law as discriminatory, male-dominated, unconstitutional and "redundant to the true spirit of Islam" on several counts. It invoked Articles 13, 14, 15, 44 of the Constitution and provisions of the Criminal Procedure Code, 1973, the Indian Penal Code, 1860 and various other enactments.

The petition pinpointed practices of polygamy, *purdah* (veil) and *talaaq* (divorce of wife by husband), and the rules governing maintenance and inheritance, stating that such practices are no more or less Islamic than the ban on drinking, entertainment and the giving and taking of loans with interest, which Muslims freely violate.

Applications for intervention in this petition were filed by the Lawyers' Collective of Bombay, in support of the petition, and the Jamaat-ul-Ulema-e-Hind, opposing it. The latter application was rejected.[22]

☆ ☆ ☆

**C W P No 22133 of 1982**

**Madhu Kishwar and others v. State of Bihar and others**

A letter was sent to Justice Bhagwati in his capacity as the Chairman of CILAS and admitted as a writ petition under Article 32 of the Constitution, soon after which a regular petition was submitted. The letter had been written by a woman activist and editor of the magazine *Manushi*, challenging sections 7, 8 and 76 of the Chhota Nagpur Tenancy Act, 1908 as violative of Articles 14 and 15 of the Constitution. The petition noted that the 1908 Act prevented women of the Ho tribe from acquiring proprietary rights and the right to acquire, hold and transfer any family land, as it confines succession of property to the male line. The second and third petitioners in the case were both women of the Ho tribe, residing in Lonjo village, Sonua Block, District Singhbhum in Bihar. The second petitioner, Maku Bui was a woman whose husband had died leaving her at the goodwill and mercy of her husband's male relatives, and the third petitioner was her daughter. The petition asked for the provisions in the impugned Act to be struck down and a direction issued to the effect that the land records relating to the Ho tribe be amended to show the Ho women as having equal shares in land belonging to their families, at 4:

> In theory, a widow has usufructuary rights in the family's land for her lifetime. But in practice, when there are adult male heirs, the land is often taken over by them and there is no guarantee that the usufructuary rights will be respected by the male heirs.

22 Mitra, Nirmal, "The Shehnaaz Sheikh Petition. Sunni Girl's Daring Crusade Against Muslim Personal Law", *Onlooker*, 23/5/84-7/684, 13-38.

Particular reliefs relating to the petitioners were also asked for, including the provision of free legal aid, and the petition noted that the women were made to feel unsafe and insecure and have cases pending in the lower courts to secure succession rights. Detailing a socio-economic history of the area and of the 1908 Act, the petition stated, at 10:

> The petitioners however say that they have good reason to believe that the alleged customary law, which prevents Ho women from owning and inheriting property and land is not in fact customary and not established in long and immemorial use.

When the petition came up for hearing the judge tried to apply the Hindu Succession Act, 1956 to these women, under which each woman would get very little.[23] Madhu Kishwar described how the notion that property is alienable and can be willed away does not appear in the Ho tribal customs because of legal and customary limitations. She also told how two years were wasted because of a wrong listing and when the case was finally admitted, a typist's error put it on the admissions list instead of the hearing list. Speaking after ten years she said:

> I feel criminal now for having raised hopes and expectations. I hoped something new would happen but it did not, the people feel let down and betrayed and we have blackened our own faces.

Another petition was filed under Article 32 of the Constitution by women of the Oraon tribe of the Chhota Nagpur area. The petition, which also challenged the 1908 Act, was tagged to the one filed by Madhu Kishwar.

In an order D/-11/10/91 by Chief Justice Ranganath Misra and Justice Kuldip Singh
[reported 1991 (2) SCALE 148 [794]]

The Court discounted a decision of the Patna HC which supported the arguments of the petitioners, as the order in that case was confined to the particular facts. The state of Bihar was asked

[23] Madhu Kishwar, interview, Delhi, 12/1/91.

to carry out a feasibility study on amendments to the 1908 Act, and the Court noted, at 796:

> A Committee appears to have been set up by the State of Bihar to examine this question and it has come to the conclusion that by custom prevalent amoung the scheduled tribes, a female heir is excluded from succession and in case the law was otherwise interpreted or changed and property was allowed to go into the hands of female heirs, there would be great agitation and unrest in the area among the Scheduled Tribe people who have custom-based living.

and went on to state, at 796:

> Scheduled Tribe people are as much citizens as others and they are entitled to the benefit of the guarantees of the Constitution. It may be that the law can provide reasonable regulation in the matter of succession to property with a view to maintaining cohesiveness in regard to Scheduled Tribes and their properties. But exclusion from inheritance would not be appropriate. Since this aspect of the matter has not been examined by the State of Bihar, and the feasibility of permitting inheritance and simultaneously regulating the inheritance for the purpose of ensuring that the property does not go out of the family by way of transfer or otherwise, we are of the view that in the peculiar facts of the case the State of Bihar should re-examine the matter.

The matter was adjourned for three months and ordered to be next listed before a bench of which Justice Kuldip Singh is a member.

During the pendency of the petition, the Court ordered that the second petitioner, Maku Bui, be offered protection by the state of Bihar. As this was not done, *Manushi* filed a petition for contempt. Writing in 1994, Madhu Kishwar described the reaction of the Court to this petition, in statements that were not included in the written record of the Court. She claimed that Justice Ranganath Misra said:

> We can pass a contempt order if you insist. But what good will it do for the petitioner? The Bihar government or its police are not going to heed it any more than they did our original order. Better that you advise that old woman to continue staying with her daughter so at least she is more safe than in

her own village. Or else bring her to Delhi and keep her with you so she is safe.

By 1993, both Maku Bui and her daughter, Sonamuni, had died, but nonetheless, the case is still pending.

☆ ☆ ☆

***W P (Civil) Nos 8260 of 1983, 651-52 and 657 of 1985, 15174-79 of 1984 and 11692 of 1985***

***Mary Roy v. State of Kerala and others***

A petition was filed under Article 32 of the Constitution challenging sections 24, 28 and 29 of the Travancore Christian Succession Act, 1902 as unconstitutional under Article 14 of the Constitution and void in the light of Part B States (Laws) Act, 1951 and the Indian Succession Act, 1925. The question raised was whether after the 1951 Act was passed, the 1902 Act still governed intestate succession to the property of a member of the Indian Christian community. Under the 1902 Act, a woman gets a maximum of Rs 5000 of her father's property if he dies without leaving a last will and testament. This Act had been passed by the Maharaja of Cochin when Rs 5000 was a considerable sum. However, on her father's demise, Mary Roy was effectively made destitute. Her brother denied her an equal share of the inheritance by giving her Rs 5000 and asking her to leave the family home, even though her father's property was worth over Rs 1 crore and she was earning very little at the time. Her brother had decided to sell the house so that he could go on a holiday.

In a judgement D/-24/2/86 by > Chief Justice P.N. Bhagwati and Justice R.S. Pathak
[reported 1986 (1) SCALE 36 [250]]

The Court held that the 1902 Act automatically stands repealed by the coming into force of the 1925 Act. It was further held that the 1925 Act is now applicable to Christian intestate succession, so the question of the constitutionality of sections of the 1902 Act no longer needed to be explored. The judgement was made retrospective, so all inheritance claims settled between 1951 and 1986, when the judgement was given, could be challenged if the bequeathor died intestate.

Many Christian women had initially supported the judgement, but a backlash ensued. Legislation which is pending in the Kerala Legislative Assembly will alter the judgement, taking away its retrospective nature. More Christian men have already begun to write wills and few women have been able to claim their share of their father's property because of the difficulties of going to court and pervasive social pressure. Even Mary Roy had petitioned the Court in the face of opposition from her mother.

Mary Roy, who runs Corpus Christi School in Kottayam, again had to petition the Court, this time the HC of Kerala in the form of a PIL. Each year the children of the school enact a drama and in 1990 "Jesus Christ Superstar" was chosen. Opposition to this grew as Mary Roy had antagonized many in the State with her Supreme Court victory, and the production was considered to be blasphemous. The church was mobilized and Mary Roy was threatened, but the school went ahead with the production. An article on the cases stated:

> the role of the district collector in the incident was not above board either. According to Mary Roy, similar reasons could be behind the Kottayam District Collector's enthusiasm in issuing a ban order and search warrant on the school. She alleges that a few months prior to the incident, the collector, Mr K.J. Alphonse had requested admission for his cousin into the school. Going through the proper admission channels, the cousin had failed to meet the standard expected and was consequently denied admission. In a writ petition before the Kerala High Court against the District Collector, Kottayam, and others, the petitioner Mary Roy has challenged that since then, the respondent has been hostile towards the school and intended to have it shut down.
>
> The petition in the High Court prays that the respondent be prohibited from misusing his powers to interfere in the peaceful functioning of the school. Consequently, the High Court passed an interim order to that effect on 26 October 1990.[24]

In another incident, Mary Roy's brother had apparently begun to malign the school and spoil its reputation, because of which the school had to be closed down for a week until the furore calmed down. In an interview, Mary Roy spoke of her continued harassment:

24 D'Mello, Pamela, "Report: Jesus Christ Superstar — Banned", *The Lawyers*, June 1992, Vol. 7, No. 6, 12.

> Strangely enough, I have received notice to pay tax on the 1/6th share which I may receive from my father's estate.
>
> In spite of being fully aware of the legal impediments during income tax appellate hearings, the department has insisted on payment now. For land that is occupied by my mother and my brother! Strangely enough, the other heirs (my brothers and sister) have not been served similar notices.[25]

Extracts from two newspaper articles some years after the judgement show the blatant hostility to the idea of conferring an equal status upon women:

> Mary Roy's single-handed fight against the Christian law of succession is not yet over. Six years after the Supreme Court declared the law invalid, resistance among Kerala Christians, if anything, has increased.
>
> "Very few women are fighting for their property rights," laments Roy, because they face "tremendous social pressure and even veiled threats." In fact, she points out, many women are now being forced to say they do not want the new law, despite the fact that many of them, especially pensioners, are dependent on their brothers' bounty to survive. ...
>
> Roy's stubborn fight for her rights outraged her whole family, including her mother. "With this atrocious claim you are draining your brother of his manhood", her mother told Roy. Her family was not the only one who was outraged. "The verdict will open up floodgates of litigation and lead to social tension and economic ruin", warned a Member of Parliament P.J. Kurien, who introduced a private member's bill seeking to revalidate the law on Christian succession after the Supreme Court struck it down in 1986.
>
> The staunchly conservative church, dependent upon the landed gentry for its revenue, also joined the fight against Roy. "They now have this announcement in church after the Sunday sermon that free legal services will be provided to any man who wants to make a will", says Roy.
>
> ...
>
> While the former regime in the state was unsympathetic,

25 Roy, Mary, "First Person: The Wages of Dissent", *The Lawyers*, June 1992, Vol. 7, No. 6, 12.

> the Christian lobby appears to be having better luck with the current coalition government backed by the pro-church Kerala Congress. The first signs of this emerged three months ago when the Revenue and Law Minister K.M. Mani announced in the state legislature that the government was "considering the innumerable requests of individuals and organizations to have the law changed".[26]

The second article in 1992 demonstrates how years after the judgement its impact is still being felt:

> The Supreme Court ruling made all titles to property, which contain even a single inheritance according to the Travancore Christian Succession Act ... in the period between 1951 and 1986 defective, and in some cases worthless.
>
> This caused immense problems for the traders, farmers, etc. who form the mainstay of the Christian community because they found it difficult to raise loans from banks and other financial institutions for their operations in the absence of a clear transferable title to property which can be sold, pledged or hypothecated.
>
> Realizing the gravity of the situation, the Joint Christian Action Council has sought the scrapping of the retrospective clause in the SC order.[27]

## Discrimination

### *C W P No 211 of 1983, Simla*
### *Brij Bala* v. *State of HP and others*

A letter D/-22/7/83 was sent to Chief Justice V.D. Misra of Himachal Pradesh HC by Kumari Brij Bala, a woman belonging to the Scheduled Caste of Village Patta Mahlog, Tehsil Kasauli, District Solan, Himachal Pradesh. She had applied for Patwari training on 18/3/83 and received a letter in reply from the Director of Land Records, Shimla-2, HP (letter No R.6.6-III (LR)/82-5371, D/-27/5/83) which stated:

[26] J. Gita, "Fighting for right of equality", *Indian Express*, 7/3/92.

[27] Venugopal, P., "Undoing the 'excess' of a SC verdict", *Indian Express*, 12/6/92.

> This is with reference to her application dated 18/3/83 addressed to the Hon'ble Revenue Minister. She is hereby informed that there is no provision in the Land Records Manual under which a girl can be imparted Patwari training and recruited as a Patwari, as the field duties of a Patwari are not congenial to girls. The Patwari has to safeguard the public record like a Chowkidar in a Patwar Khana which is generally not a lovely place and is frequently visited by litigants. As such it is not possible to accede to her request.

Kumari Brij Bala's letter, annexing the letter she had received from the Director of Land Records, was converted into a writ petition under Article 226 of the Constitution.

In an order D/-26/7/83 by Chief Justice V.D. Misra and Justice H.S. Thakur

The full order of the Court stated:

> This petition by Kumari Brij Bala, who is a Harijan, was received by post. She alleges that she has been refused Patwari training since the Director of Land Records, Himachal Pradesh, had written to her to say that the training and duties are not congenial to girls. *Prima facie* discrimination on the basis of sex which is prohibited by the Constitution, has been made. We have decided in the interest of justice and keeping in view the fact that the petitioner is a poor Harijan girl, to treat it as a civil writ petition.
>
> Rule D.B. [Division Bench]
>
> The State is directed to file the return within two weeks from today. The matter to be listed for arguments on 22nd August 1983.
>
> Since the petitioner is not represented by a counsel and since Miss Kamlesh Sharma is anxious to defend the rights of the woman, she is requested to help the Court on behalf of the petitioner. The petitioner may also be informed about the date of hearing so that she may be present in Court, if she so desires.

A reply affidavit on behalf of respondents from the Director, Land Records, HP was attested on 3/8/83 and filed in the HC on 6/8/83. The affidavit stated that the earlier contention of the Director regarding the suitability of a woman for the post of Patwari, was, at 2:

> a personal opinion of the undersigned. The recruitment rules of Patwari candidates do not provide any bar for the recruitment of girls.... In this particular case, there was no occasion for the selection of the applicant and the opinion expressed in the impugned letter is a personal opinion of the undersigned. If any vacancy of Patwari candidate arises in the district of the applicant and if she gets her name registered with the Employment Exchange, and the same is sponsored by the District Employment Exchange, the District Collector would consider her for selection along with other candidates.
>
> It is prayed that there are no grounds for writ petition and the same may be dismissed.

In a judgement D/-22/8/83 by Chief Justice V.D. Misra and Justice H.S. Thakur
[reported (1984) 2 SLR 408]
The Court ordered, at 410-11:

> As the government has already conceded in their return that there could be no discrimination on the ground of sex, we need hardly pass any direction. The petitioner can get herself registered with the Employment Exchange in her district for the Patwari training. We have no doubt that the District Employment Exchange would sponsor her name to the District Collector for selection along with other candidates according to rules.

and directed that the petitioner be sent a copy of the judgement free of cost.

☆ ☆ ☆

A petition was filed under Article 226 of the Constitution in the Bombay HC by the Mahila Dakshita Samiti Trust seeking to prevent prenatal amniocentesis or any other sex determination tests, and selective abortions on the basis of the sex of the foetus. The impetus for filing a case came when Sunita Chaturvedi died after having an amniocentesis test and abortion, which she was persuaded to undergo by her husband and his family. The test, conducted half-way into her fifth month of pregnancy, showed that she was carrying a female foetus. This would have been her third female child, so there was considerable family pressure to abort. She died of secondary peritonitis after an abortion was carried out. The petition stated that sex determination tests and selective abortions violate Articles 14 and 21 of the Constitution. Moreover, as most amniocentesis tests were performed in the sixteenth week of pregnancy, they were illegal under the Medical Termination of Pregnancy Act, 1971. The petition also wanted those who conducted the test and subsequently underwent abortion to be punished.

In an order D/-20/10/86 by Justice Jahagirdhar

The petition was admitted, but no interim orders were given.[28]

☆ ☆ ☆

***W P ?? of 1990***

***Catholic Association of Bombay and others* v. *State of Maharashtra and others***

A petition was filed under Article 226 of the Constitution in 1990 in the Bombay High Court by the Catholic Association of Bombay invoking the right to privacy. Two nuns in Bombay were found dead on 16/11/90 with multiple stab wounds on their bodies. They had looked after a group of homeless boys in Sneha Sadan. Newspapers reported that the examination of the bodies by the Coroner indicated that the nuns were used to sexual intercourse and that one of them appeared to be suffering from a venereal disease. The petition stated that these reports could bring the nuns into disrepute and violate their right to privacy.

In an order D/-28/2/91 by Justice S.W. Puranik and Justice M.F. Saldhana

The respondents denied the newspaper reports. The Court noted:

> *Prima facie*, we find it difficult to accept the case made out before us which is to the effect that none of the government authorities had disclosed the material that formed the subject matter of the post-mortem of the nuns.

The Court directed the Director General of Police to hold a

[28] Gopinath, Deepthi, "Comment: Amniocentesis Petition Admitted", *The Lawyers*, Vol. 1, No. 10, October 1986, 14.

thorough inquiry and submit a report into the case for the purpose of fixing responsibility for the publication of the 'obnoxious and scandalous' reports that appeared in the newspapers, stating:

> Opinions expressed in the course of a post-mortem are subject to scrutiny and are invariably to be tested in the course of subsequent proceedings, and it appears both dangerous and reckless to spout conclusions which often find their way to the press.
>
> It was significant that the Additional Coroner had pointed out that nobody from the press was present at the time and, therefore no question of the disclosure of any of the findings of the post-mortem examination can arise ... the lingering doubt, that arises, therefore, is as to whether some individuals had made statements in addition to the official communications.
>
> In our view, the irresistible inference is that somebody in authority who was connected with the case and to the investigation must have made the disclosures to the press, as otherwise, newspapers of some status would not have accepted the material.

The Court went on to direct the Government of Maharashtra to constitute a committee comprising representatives of the Home and Police departments, the Coroner of Bombay, representatives of Bombay University's Department of Law, and a representative from the Press Council of India to look into this matter and take appropriate steps to ensure that there was no recurrence of such incidents.[29]

## Prostitution

### *W P No 608 of 1984*

A petition was filed under Article 32 of the Constitution by journalist and activist, Sheela Barse, seeking to ensure a minimum level of fundamental rights to prostitutes. The petition was based on the living conditions of prostitutes in four states: Maharashtra, Andhra Pradesh, Tamil Nadu, and Karnataka. The petitioner had

[29] Reddy, Chidananda, "Warrants Attention: Piety of Privacy after Death", *The Lawyers*, Vol. 6, No. 8, August 1991, 12.

appealed to the police authorities many times to help individual women trapped in prostitution. She found that while senior police officials appeared to be sympathetic, the people responsible for buying and selling the girls and using them as bonded labour remained free and untroubled, as the police just would not act and officers were covering up for brothel-keepers.[30]

☆ ☆ ☆

***W P (C) No 824 of 1988***

***Gaurav Jain* v. *Union of India and others***

A petition was filed by advocate Gaurav Jain under Article 32 of the Constitution asking for the establishment of special schools for the children of prostitutes

In an order D/-15/11/89 by Justice Ranganath Misra and Justice M.N. Venkatachaliah and Justice P.B. Sawant
[reported AIR 1990 SC 292]

The Court stated that the segregation of children from their peer group is not a good idea, however, they do need to be segregated from their mothers for which hostels and reformatory homes are needed. A Committee was set up to examine the material aspects of the problem and report to the Court. The Committee was to constitute of: Mr V.C. Mahajan, Mr Gaurav Jain, and Mr R.K. Mehta, together with Dr Deepa Das, Women's Studies and Development Centre, Chhatra Marg, University of Delhi, Delhi, 110007, Smt Sarla Mudgal, Kalyani, 5030, Kalidas Marg, Darya Ganj, New Delhi, 110002, and Smt Krishna Mukherji (later replaced by Usha Ramanathan), All Bengal Women's Union, Research and Development Committee, 89, Elliot Road, Calcutta, 700016. Mr M.N. Schroff was appointed as the convenor.

In an order D/-14/5/91 by Chief Justice Ranganath Misra and Justice Kuldip Singh
[reported 1991 (1) SCALE 201 [963]]

The Court acknowledged receipt of the Report of the Committee of lawyers and social activists and observed, at 963-4:

Initially the petitioner's application was confined to Delhi area

30 "Petition: To Break a Cycle of Oppression", *PUCL Bulletin*, Vol. 4, No. 8, August 1984, 8.

but later noticing the nature of reliefs sought, its impact on society and the fact that the problem is common to several parts of India, the States and Union Territories were impleaded and notice was ordered to them.

In an order D/-10/4/91, the Court had asked for affidavits from each state. It was noted that only the state of Orissa had filed an affidavit initially, and that the standing counsel for several states were absent during the hearings. Even by 3/5/91 the Delhi Administration, and the States of Uttar Pradesh, Madhya Pradesh, Maharashtra, Tamil Nadu, Andhra Pradesh, Karnataka, West Bengal, Bihar and Gujarat had not yet filed affidavits, and still many of the standing counsel were not present. Noting their "callous attitude", the Court stated, at 964:

> In this proceeding a social problem is being considered by the Court. It is the obligation of the standing counsel retained by the States and who are officers of the Court to comply with the directions of the Court. We are [not] in a position to appreciate the attitude of various standing counsel nor are we in a position to tolerate indiscipline.

The Court stated that only those states which have filed affidavits, that is Orissa, Punjab, AP, Rajasthan, will help with the case and that all other states would be precluded from participating in the Court proceedings. However, the Court stressed that the decision of the Court would bind every state and Union Territory.

The matter was directed to be called on 9/7/91 when a date of hearing was to be fixed.

☆ ☆ ☆

***O P No 2983 of 1988-E, Kerala***

***People's Council for Social Justice* v. *State of Kerala and others***

A petition was filed under Article 226 of the Constitution stating that the 36th Division of Cochin Corporation, extending from the Ernakulam Junction Railway Station in the east to Park Avenue in the west, is highly infested with prostitutes, goondas and hooligans. The petition contended that people were unable to walk through the roads freely after 8 p.m. and that daylight robberies and burglaries were regular feature in the area. The petition asked the Court to direct the respondents to discharge their duties under sections 7, 8, 13, 15, 16, 20 and 21 of the Suppression of Immoral Traffic in Women and Girls Act, 1956, to take cognizance of offences committed under the Opium Act, Cochin Dangerous Drugs Act, Kerala Abkari Act and to take steps to curb the illegal and antisocial activities of women of loose character and other antisocial elements.

In a judgement D/-10/7/92 by Justice K. Sreedharan
The Court held that the prevention of prostitution under statutory law was being effected, and similarly steps were already being taken to prevent the sale of ganja. This was noted despite the respondents not having filed any counter-affidavits. The Court did urge the state of Kerala to act, at 5:

> I impress upon respondents in this case to take effective remedial steps with full co-ordination between the Police and Excise to curb the activities of the antisocial elements. ... A copy of this judgement will be forwarded to the City Commissioner of Police for follow up action.

☆ ☆ ☆

***W P (Crl) No 421 of 1989***
***Vishal Jeet* v. *Union of India and others***

A petition was filed under Article 32 of the Constitution by advocate Vishal Jeet, exposing the sexual exploitation of children in the flesh trade and seeking directions to the CBI to inquire into the matter. Nine statements from girls were given to the Court as evidence of the plight of many. The petition invoked the Suppression of Immoral Traffic in Women and Girls Act, 1956 and sections 366-A, 366-B, 372 and 373 of the Indian Penal Code, 1860.

In an order D/-2/5/90 by > Justice S. Ratnavel Pandian and Justice K. Jayachandra Reddy
[reported AIR 1990 SC 1412 / (1990) 3 SCC 318]
The Court quoted from the Declaration of the Rights of the Child, Principle No 9, adopted by the UN General Assembly which says: "The child shall be protected against all forms of neglect, cruelty and exploitation. He shall not be the subject of traffic, in any form". Also discussed were Articles 23, 35 and 39 of the Constitution. The Court stated that it would be neither practicable nor possible nor desirable to carry out a CBI inquiry throughout the country.

Directions were issued to the State Governments and Union Territories to enforce the Acts, establish advisory committees to suggest programmes and measures, and to provide rehabilitation homes with proper staff. The Union Government was also directed to set up an Advisory Committee which would go deep into the *devadasi* system and *jogin* tradition and to establish more machinery for implementation of the Acts.

☆ ☆ ☆

***W P (Cri) No 473 of 1989***
***Bholanath Tripathi v. State of UP***

A letter D/-23/6/89 sent by a journalist Bholanath Tripathi to the Chief Justice was treated as a writ petition under Article 32 of the Constitution. The letter detailed the plight of Kanchan Devi, a woman held in captivity and forced into prostitution by Janak Dulare Srivastava. The letter-petition invoked Article 21 of the Constitution.

In an order D/-6/11/89 by Justice M.N. Venkatachaliah and Justice K. Ramaswamy
[reported 1990 (Supp) SCC 151]
The Court acknowledged the unfortunate five month delay in listing the matter. The SCLAC was asked to appoint a Commissioner in the case and Shri Mahesh Prasad Saxena was appointed. The Court directed that if the complaint was found to be authentic then the woman was to be placed in a Rescue Home and produced before the Court on 9/11/89.

## The Rest of the Cases

A petition was filed under Article 32 of the Constitution in 1985 or 1986 by Stree Shakti Sangathana and two other women's organizations. Members of these organizations had visited the Patancheru Primary Health Centre near Hyderabad, which had been selected for a Phase IV trial of the contraceptive drug Net-Oen by the Osmania Medical College. After this visit the petition was filed asking the Court to prevent the Union of India, the State of Andhra Pradesh and the Indian Council for Medical Research from further testing, recommending for use, and administration of the injectible contraceptive Net-Oen (Nor-esthisterone oenanthat). The petition stated that the drug had not been proven to be safe for long term use, and in fact had been found to be a definite health hazard when used even for a short term under Indian conditions. The petition invoked Articles 21 and 51A of the Constitution.

Notice had been issued by the SC.[31]

A letter sent by a Delhi-based women's group, Saheli, to a magazine, stated:

> The case did not progress much in court. However, when we came to know that ICMR [Indian Council for Medical Research] plans to introduce other hazardous contraceptives (while withholding NET-EN) we filed another affidavit in December 1990, bringing all these other contraceptives which are hazardous, such as sub-dermal implants, vaginal rings, anti-fertility vaccines, nasal sprays etc. into the ambit of the NET-EN case. Our main argument was that ICMR and other respondents (drug controller, ministry of health and family welfare) had not taken concrete measures to improve the way in which contraceptives were being hastily tested and introduced without adequate regard to women's health. Once again there was no progress in court.[32]

☆ ☆ ☆

***W P (Civil) No 329 of 1990***
***Kasturi Lal Sharma v. State of UP***

A letter sent to the Supreme Court based on a newspaper article appearing in *The Tribune* relating to the agonies of Vrindaban widows. The letter was treated as a writ petition under Article 32 of the Constitution.

In an order D/-9/4/90 by Justice Ranganath Misra, Justice V. Ramaswami and Justice P.B. Sawant
[reported 1990 (Supp) SCC 748]
The Court transferred the petition to the Allahabad High Court

31 Moray, Raju Z., "Special Report: Net-Oen: Trials and Errors", *The Lawyers*, Vol. 1, No. 6, June 1986, 21.

32 Saheli, "Letters: Fighting NET-EN", *The Lawyers*, Vol. 7, No. 2, February 1992, 2.

within whose jurisdiction the matter lay, under Article 226 of the Constitution.

☆ ☆ ☆

***H C P No 561 of 1993, Madras***
***In the matter of Ayyanar***
***Anjalakshmi v. State of Tamil Nadu and others***

A woman wrote a letter to the Law Minister, enclosing a letter to the Chief Justice of the High Court. This letter was treated as a *habeas corpus* writ petition under Article 226 of the Constitution. Anjalakshmi's marriage had been fixed for 29/3/93 but the bridegroom had been detained by the police, under suspicion of being involved in terrorist activities. The letter asked for the release of the detainee so that the marriage could take place. The letter-petition was sent to the Court on the 16th or 17th March 1993, reaching the HC on 19th. The intervening court holidays caused a delay in listing the letter, but on the 26th March the LAB appointed a counsel to prosecute on the basis of the letter. Although a *habeas corpus* petition had been filed in the regular manner, there were no requests for parole on record. Accordingly, the letter was treated as a *habeas corpus* petition. The Registry noted that no records of request for parole in the earlier petition were on file, so the application by the woman should be admitted. A Special Bench was constituted which sat at 5.45 p.m. when the usual time for the court business to end was at 4.30 p.m.

In an order D/-26/3/93 by > Justice Arunachalam and Justice Somasundaram

The Court ordered Ayyanar to be released for his marriage on 28/3/93 and for two nights thereafter, stating, at 3:

> Though it is settled law that power of parole should normally be exercised only by the State Government and courts very rarely step in, in this area, we are inclined to approach the request made in this petition in a humanitarian way, for a marriage fixed should not be allowed to be thwarted. Orders passed in this petition shall stand restricted to the facts of the instant case alone and it cannot be treated as a precedent.

The Court thanked the counsel appointed by the SLAAB, and directed a special messenger to be sent to the jail so that he may be released in time for his marriage.

## CASE CHAPTER 5

# Children

### Framing the Issue

The cases on children have been divided into sections on prisons, institutions, child labour, inter-country adoption and the girl-child.[1] As children are unable to litigate for themselves, these cases form a distinct category, separate from other PILs. Most of the children on whose behalf petitions have been filed do suffer from the social and economic disabilities that were identified by the courts in the early PILs. However, children form an even more disadvangated class. Unable, by definition, to petition the courts themselves, they have had to rely on the *parens patriae* role of the state. The cases for children have mobilized PIL in an attempt to force the state to acknowledge this role by focusing on the non-implementation of statutory and constitutional provisions for children.

The Constitution has recognized the special needs of children in Articles 15(3), 24, 39(e), 39(f) and 45. It was using the mandate provided by these articles and by the Children's Acts of different states,[2] that the cases on prisons were filed. It was only in 1986 that juvenile justice issues were codified in a central enactment, the

[1] For other cases relating to children see the chapter on 'Injustices Specific to Women' for: *Gaurav Jain* v. *Union of India and others* AIR 1990 SC 292 and 1991 (1) SCALE 201 [963] and the cases challenging enactments. See also the chapter on 'Education' in volume two.

[2] Also see the chapter on 'Prisons and State Institutions'.

Juvenile Justice Act. All the cases in the section on prisons were filed before 1986, and reflect the concerns that were later to form the basis of the legislation. The illegal confinement of children in jails for long periods, the treatment of mentally and physically handicapped children and the conditions in jails were all brought to the attention of the Court by journalists or because of news reports.[3] Similar issues were raised in the cases relating to institutions, again at the instance of a journalist or of news reports.[4]

The Juvenile Justice Act, 1986 was passed to provide a uniform legal framework for juvenile justice and to prevent children from being lodged in jails and police lock-ups. It provides for the specialized treatment of children who are victims of social maladjustment, delinquency or neglect, and sets up a machinery for the treatment and care of such children, including Juvenile Courts, Juvenile Welfare Boards and Observation Homes. Norms and standards of juvenile justice administration, different from the usual criminal procedures, have been established for the investigation, trial and detention of children; special offences have been defined. Voluntary agencies are included in the care and treatment of these children.[5]

Another special legislation, the Child Labour (Prohibition and Regulation) Act, 1986, was passed ostensibly to protect the rights of the child. This Act prohibits the employment of children in certain industries and regulates their employment in others. For the purposes of the Act, a child is defined as a person who has not completed fourteen years of age. This Act allows child labour to continue in certain industries, repealing the Employment of Children Act, 1938. By lowering the age of a child to fourteen, the new Act denies the protection of legisation to those between fourteen and fifteen years of age. No minimum age of employment is set, so it is possible that a child as young as four may be employed in

[3] *Ibid.*

[4] The petition filed by advocate M.C. Mehta on children in Orissa jails was the first of many PIL cases to be filed by this advocate. See the chapter on 'Environment and Resources' in volume two.

[5] For a discussion of children in prisons see the "National Expert Committee on Women Prisoners' Report" 1987 in 2 volumes, Ministry of Human Resource Development, V.R. Krishna Iyer (Chairperson).

permissible industries, and no regulation is made of children working in the unorganized sector, for example domestic workers.

A Schedule is annexed to the Child Labour Act specifiying the occupations and processes prohibited under it. Both these sections can be supplemented by the Central Government. When the Act was notified, the following list of prohibited areas was annexed:

**Part A, Occupations:**

(1) Transport of passengers, goods or mail by railway.

(2) Cinder picking, clearing of an ash pit or building operation in the railway premises.

(3) Work in a catering establishment at a railway station, involving the movement of a vendor or any other employee of the establishment from one platform to another or into or out of a moving train.

(4) Work relating to the construction of a railway station or with any other work where such work is done in close proximity to or between the railway lines.

(5) A port authority within the limits of any port.

**Part B, Processes:**

(1) Bidi-making.

(2) Carpet-weaving.

(3) Cement manufacture, including bagging of cement.

(4) Cloth printing, dyeing and weaving.

(5) Manufacture of matches, explosives and fireworks.

(6) Mica-cutting and splitting.

(7) Shellac manufacture.

(8) Soap manufacture.

(9) Tanning.

(10) Wool-cleaning.

(11) Building and construction industry.

Read in conjuction with Article 24 of the Constitution, this schedule permits the employment of children in industries not specifically mentioned, even though they may be hazardous.

Apart from these enactments, other labour laws are applicable to child labour and the issues that have been raised are complex.[6] Used

[6] For references to child labour see the chapter on 'Labour': *Labourers Working on Salal Hydro Project* v. *State of Jammu and Kashmir and others* (1983) 2 SCC 181 and (1984) 3 SCC 538; the chapter on 'Public Policy and Administration' in volume two: *Kishen Patnayak and another* v. *State of Orissa* AIR 1989 SC 677/1989 (1) SCALE 4 [32]] and the chapter on 'Bonded Labour'.

in specific industries, child labour displays all the features present in the adult labour force. Many are working in bondage or in the unorganized sector and there are labour touts and contractors. A study published in 1992 noted the links between caste, illiteracy and bondage in the incidence of child labour:

> Indications are that most child labourers belong to the illiterate groups, small and middle peasants, most of whom are from among the Scheduled Castes and Tribes. These are also the groups to which most bonded labourers belong.[7]

A distinction was made between the child worker and the child labourer. Whereas the latter is one who is involved in full-time work in order to survive and makes a direct contribution to the economy of the family, the child worker works part time within the family but does make a full time direct contribution to its economy. The exact number of child labourers is not known, but:

> Their working conditions, the process through which they enter the work force, the exploitation and hazards under which they work, their low wages and efforts made to keep them illiterate and poor, show that it is a vested interest and not a harsh reality that some would like to call it.[8]

The litigation on child labour began in 1983, before the legislation was passed. A series of newspaper reports appeared investigating child labour in the fireworks and match factories of Sivakasi, in Tamil Nadu.[9] The reports noted that children were employed illegally despite both industries having been scheduled as hazardous for children in the 1938 Act. A national debate, on Sivakasi in particular and child labour in general, began, after which a petition was filed by M.C. Mehta. Again in April 1984, news reports exposed the forced child labour employed in the Mirzapur carpet industries. These reports detailed the abduction and sale of children from Palamu district of Bihar to a carpet weaver of

7 Fernandes, Walter; "Child Labour and, the Processess of Exploitation", *Indian Journal of Social Work*, April 1992, Vol. LIII, No. 2, 171-190, at 171-172.

8 *Ibid* at 186.

9 See Varghese, Jose; "Law Relating to the Employment of Children in India", Socio-Legal Resource Centre, Secunderabad, 1989 at 4.

Mirzapur District of UP and prompted Bandhua Mukti Morcha to file a petition.[10]

Access to correct information and data is a perennial problem in PILs. It is however, more insidious, when examining child labour, as children have no way of letting their situation be known. The state has denied the incidence of child labour in industries where it is known to be common.[11] Many of the petitions in this chapter have relied on newspaper reports in the expectation that the Court would take up the injustices perpetrated upon children. Advocate M.C. Mehta was first prompted to file a PIL petition when the number of children in the Orissa jails caught his attention. Advocate Laxmi Kant Pandey petitioned the Court for an issue that had remained unresolved: inter-country adoption. With the exception of *Pratul Kumar Sinha* and the petition filed by *Brinda Karat and another*, there have been few cases relating to the girl-child in particular.[12]

## Access to Justice

Reacting to news reports and to letters sent by Sheela Barse and Rajangam, it appears that the Court has not permitted any obstacles to dealing with the cases on children. Even in a disposed of matter filed by M.C. Mehta on child labour, the Court took *suo moto* notice of newspaper reports of an accident in the area.

## The Court's Response

In procedural terms the Supreme Court has responded flexibly to the petitions filed. In the *Sheela Barse* case on prisons and in *Rajangam,*

10 *Ibid* at 4.

11 See *ibid* at 6 — whereas the Union Labour Minister stated that there were no children below the age of 14 years working in the potteries of Khurja, social worker Neera Burra had identified about 5,000 children below 14 years of age in those very potteries.

12 For another case relating to the girl-child, see the section on prostitution in the chapter on 'Injustices Specific to Women': *Vishal Jeet* AIR 1990 SC 1412/(1990) 3 SCC 318. Also see the case on amniocentesis testing.

*Secretary, District Beedi Workers' Union*, the scope of the litigation was extended. Enlarging the import of the petition, the Court has admitted to the existence of problems relating to children on a large scale. In all the prison cases inquiries were ordered and the Court has monitored the progress of the case and the implementation of its orders. This also happened in *Gautam Uzir and another*, and in *Brinda Karat and another* the Court ensured that Ameena's well-being was looked after. However, in *Sanjay Suri and another* the Court expressed its limitations, stating that it was able to monitor implementation of its orders only because Tihar jail was located in Delhi, indicating that proximity to the Supreme Court would ensure better implementation.

It is not only the implementation of the Supreme Court's own orders that were monitored, but also the implementation of the existing statutory framework. In *Munna and others*, the SC directed that the children's Acts be implemented and in the *Sheela Barse* case on prisons the implementation of the Juvenile Justice Act, 1986 was ordered. Having extended the scope of the litigation in *Sheela Barse and another*, the Court ensured that each state government responded to its orders. Certain interesting directions were given. For example, in the case of the Children's Home in Bombay, the SC held that the home could be treated as "the state" within the meaning of Article 12 of the Constitution, thus making all the fundamental rights available against the state also available against the administrators of the Home. This was an important statement because there have been few instances where the Court has been prompted to discuss the scope of Article 12 of the Constitution in PIL matters, most of which have been filed against the state or its instrumentalities. In *Sanjay Suri and another*, the Court discussed in detail the character of an ideal jail and in the Sivakasi case filed by advocate M.C. Mehta, the Court not only directed that the children be insured, but that the insurance be paid to them.

In the area of child labour, notwithstanding the innovations of procedure, the Court has responded with a rhetoric in support of the child that has been discredited by its actual orders. Even the available statutory framework has not been endorsed, inspite of the Court's stated commitment to the objects of enactments. Although the employment of children in the manufacture of matches had been banned by the Child Labour (Prohibition and Regulation) Act, 1986, the Court justified it in the context of packing matches away from the site of manufacture, because the "tender hands of the young workers" were more suitable to the task. Ignorance of working conditions led the Court to assume that separation of the processes of manufacture and packing was possible. In *Rajangam, Secretary, District Beedi Workers' Union*, the Court permitted, without exception, the employment of children in an industry in which child labour had been prohibited, and directed that children be paid only a percentage of the minimum wage. Moreover, the Court tacitly permitted illegal practices to continue by directing that the state decide whether contract labour be employed, thus leaving the responsibility of phasing out child labour to the state, which itself should have been held answerable for the existence of child labour in the bidi industry. Moreover, the liability of the Sivakasi industries to ensure the well-being of the labourers was translated simply into the payment of compensation,[13] absolving other responsibilities for the safety of workers.

The case of *Laxmi Kant Pandey* led the Court to frame detailed principles and norms for inter-country adoption, and allow intervention by specialist organizations. Even in this case, renowned for the Court's policy-making, certain areas of concern were not resolved. Although the question of the future of the children after they reach majority was raised, the Court did not pass any direction providing for a support framework for these young people.

Although none of the orders detailed in this chapter have been from the HCs, there is evidence that the HCs have responded to issues relating to children. In *Munna and others* and *Sanjay Suri and another* the SC alluded to the HC proceedings but took over the case in the absence of positive or effective action. In the appeal filed by Sheela Barse on the basis of the order of the Bombay HC on a children's home in Bombay, the SC expanded the scope of the HC's orders.

It is not just in the case of the children's home that journalist and activist, Sheela Barse, faced the brunt of the courts' displeasure. When approaching the Court to get relief for children in prisons, she was compelled to make repeated trips to Delhi only to find that the case had been adjourned. Her frustration led to a disagreement with the advocate-on-record for the case, who applied to the Court to be discharged from the case. Taking over the case as a petitioner-in-person, Sheela Barse faced repeated adjournments.

13 See the chapter on 'Environment and Resources' in volume two.

Expressing frustration with the Court's inability to ensure compliance and the unbearable delays, four years after filing the appeal she attempted to withdraw her case. Disregarding this protest, which highlighted the ineffectiveness of judicial proceedings, the Supreme Court admonished the petitioner for attempting to thwart the public interest and asked the SCLAC to take over the case. The Court failed to acknowledge Sheela Barse's efforts in bringing the case to Court and giving detailed information. The litigation was subsequently dealt with by lawyers who were not able to give the case the kind of attention that it had previously been given. However, in the case brought by Sheela Barse on the Children's Home in Bombay, the SC admonished the HC for its disparaging remarks against the petitioner, and ordered that she be paid costs.

## The Contribution of PIL

If the cases are examined within the framework of judicial activism, then it can be observed that the Supreme Court has responded to the needs of children. Conversely, if the cases are examined from the perspective of the needs of children, then the SC's response would have to be described as superficial. It is only through using the courts that statutory institutions were set up under the Juvenile Justice Act, 1986. However, like most petitioners to the Court for children in prisons, M.C. Mehta was unable to follow up the case after the children were released from jail and the question of rehabilitation of the released children was never raised.

In the cases on prisons and institutions, the Court has been willing to assert its judicial role vis-a-vis the state authorities. The superficiality of the Court's response is most apparent in the cases on child labour, both through the orders themselves and an examination of the legal process itself, with its delays. The Court has been unable to mobilize the state to the necessary extent, as is apparent from the petition filed by Rajangam. The legislation that regulates rather than abolishes child labour, has allowed the violations of the rights of the child to go unchecked. Thus with a compromising legal framework and a judiciary which has proven its unwillingness to tackle the causes and consequences of child labour, it is unsurprising that these cases are still pending in the Supreme Court.

International Covenants have been an important reference point for the courts in discussing child labour. The mobilization of the issue outside the Court has focussed on these covenants and on the foreign exchange issue by encouraging importers of finished products, like carpets to refuse to purchase goods made through the employment of child labour. The importance of education and other welfare provisions has also been highlighted. The expansion of standing in the courtroom has led to the inclusion of liberal procedures in the Child Labour (Prohibition and Regulation) Act, 1986. Aside from these incremental gains, it is impossible to gauge the effects of litigation on the extent of child labour. For the same reason the situation of children released from prisons needs more in-depth study. In real terms it would seem that the situation of the girl-child as prisoner, labourer and sexual object remains much the same.

## Prisons

***W P Nos 9133 & 8974 of 1981 and 6 of 1982***

***Munna and others* v. *State of Uttar Pradesh and others***

A petition was filed under Article 32 of the Constitution based on a news report in the *Indian Express* D/-2/12/81. Madhu Mehta of Hindustan Andolan had gone to the Kanpur Central Jail and discovered that juvenile prisoners were being sexually exploited by adult prisoners. The petition contended that the children should be in a Children's Home and not in the Kanpur Central Jail, and alleged that the provisions of the Uttar Pradesh Childrens' Act, 1951 and Rules, 1962 were not being implemented.

In an order D/-19/2/82 by Justice P.N. Bhagwati and Justice R.S. Pathak

[reported (1982) 1 SCC 545]

The SC noted that a PIL petition to the same effect had also been filed in the Allahabad HC by an organization called Human Rights Organization. The HC had ordered the seniormost Sessions Judge, Kanpur, to visit the Kanpur Central Jail and to make a report detailing the numbers, ages and treatment of the children there. This report had been submitted to the HC on 22/12/81. Although the SC did not go into the details of the report, it observed that out of the seven undertrial prisoners in the jail below the age of sixteen, all except one had been released between 7/12/81 and 16/12/81. These children had been released before the HC order on 18/12/81 but after the newsreport and the filing of the petition. The SC noted that although the allegations had been denied by the Assistant Jailor, it would not dismiss the petition *in limine*, stating, at 548:

> Juvenile delinquency is, by and large, a product of social and economic maladjustment. Even if it is found that these juveniles have committed any offences, they cannot be allowed to be maltreated. They do not shed their fundamental rights when they enter the jail. Moreover, the object of punishment being reformation, we fail to see what social objective can be gained by sending juveniles to jails where they would come into contact with hardened criminals and lose whatever sensitivity they may have had to finer and nobler sentiments. That is the reason why Children's Acts are enacted by states all over the country and the UP legislature has also enacted the UP Children's Act, 1951.

As the six released children could not be interviewed by the Sessions Judge, the Court directed the Secretary of the Uttar Pradesh SLAAB to contact them, to find out how they were treated in the jail and to report to the Court by 27/1/82. The state of UP and the Superintendent of Kanpur Central Jail were directed to submit an affidavit detailing the circumstances of the release of the six children and the procedure adopted. They were also asked to explain how the one remaining boy was suddenly transferred on 19/12/81 to the Children's Home, Kanpur. Concluding, the Court held, at 551:

> We would strongly impress upon the Magistrates in the state of Uttar Pradesh — and what we say here must apply *mutatis mutandis* to the Magistrates in the other parts of the country where the Children's Acts are in force, that they must be extremely careful to see that no person apparently under the age of 16 years is sent to jail but is detained in a Children's Home or other suitable places of safety set up by the government for the purpose of providing a place of detention for children under the age of 16 years. No words we can use could be strong enough to convey our feelings in this respect.

A nation which is not concerned with the welfare of its children cannot look toward a bright future.

☆ ☆ ☆

***W P (Cri) Nos 2546-47 of 1983***

***Sanjay Suri and another v. Delhi Administration, Delhi and another***

A petition was filed under Article 32 of the Constitution by a news reporter and a trainee sub-editor regarding the treatment of juvenile undertrial prisoners because of the maladministration in the Tihar Jail.

In an order D/-9/12/87 by > Justice Ranganath Misra and Justice Murari Mohon Dutt
[reported 1987 (2) SCALE 276 [1257]]
The SC quoted from its earlier order D/-28/10/83, at 1257:

> When these writ petitions came up for hearing before us we had certain hesitation in entertaining them because another petition was pending in the High Court of Delhi in regard to juvenile prisoners in Tihar Jail when some directions had been given by the High Court, and we were anxious to avoid a parallel investigation particularly since in matters of this kind it is desirable that the High Courts should be activised. But since no inquiry into the conditions prevailing in the Tihar Jail, so far as prisoners in the juvenile ward are concerned, had been ordered and what was ordered was only a limited enquiry relating to medical examination of seven juvenile prisoners who were directed to be produced in court, we thought that we would be failing in our constitutional duty if we do not take judicial action and direct the District Judge to visit Tihar Jail in so far as the prisoners in the juvenile ward are concerned.

In the present order the Court made many suggestions about the way in which an ideal jail should be run, at 1259:

> Those who are in charge of the jail administration from bottom to top must develop the proper approach to deal with the prisoners and undertrials. It is true that a considerable number of hardened prisoners live in the jail and more who have longer terms of sentence to suffer, stay on for quite a part of

> their life behind the prison bars. Longer stay at one place brings in familiarity and familiarity generates a number of human reactions. There is no provision in the jail manuals and, perhaps it is difficult as a rule to adopt, that the long-term prisoners should keep on shifting from jail to jail. Whatever may have been the philosophy of punishment in the past, today the prison house is looked upon as a reformatory and the years spent in jail should be with a view to providing rehabilitation to the prisoner after the sentence is over. … the Prison House, in case the true purpose is to be achieved, has to provide the proper atmosphere, leadership, environment, and situations of circumstance for the regeneration. Members of the staff of the jail from bottom to top (we have purposely not said top to bottom) must be made cognizant of this responsibility and that awareness must be reflected in their conduct. Judicial notice can be taken of prevailing conditions of our jails and what we have stated above is still utopian. But if a change has to be brought about it has to start from somewhere and Tihar Jail, in our opinion is probably most suited for that purpose, being located at the seat of the national capital and being under the direct management of the Union of India (through, of course, Delhi Administration). This can be the institution to set the move in motion.

W1%1The Court continued in this vein and went on to hope and trust that a sense of humanism would be generated. The Court held that every warrant of detention should specify the age of the person to be detained in order to be accepted as valid, and that this warrant should be used to determine whether the prisoner should be lodged at the Juvenile Jail or at Tihar Jail. Directions were made to the prison warders and the Court directed that a visitor's board be constituted with social activists, media people, lady social workers, jurists and retired public officers from the Judiciary and the Executive. The need for a new jail to alleviate the overcrowding was stressed. Disposing of the petition, the Court observed, at 1259:

> Monitoring the affairs of a jail is a difficult job for this Court but on account of the fact that Tihar Jail is in the capital of the country and on account of the advantages of publicity available through the media and otherwise, the affairs of the jail have received due publicity over the last four years where

> these matters have been pending before this Court and it is time that we should dispose of them finally

and stated, at 1261:

> We place on record our appreciation of the services rendered by the petitioners by bringing the matter before the Court.

The petition was disposed of with no order for costs.

☆ ☆ ☆

***W P (Cri) No 1501 of 1984***
***M.C. Mehta v. State of Orissa and others***

A petition was filed under Article 32 of the Constitution by advocate M.C. Mehta on the basis of reports in the *Indian Express* and in a local newspaper in Orissa. The reports stated that 197 children were lodged in Orissa jails and were being maltreated, sodomized and used by hardened criminals. Twenty children were reported to be living in each small cell. Apparently, poor children were picked up by the police for petty offences and put into jail. Having confirmed the press reports through sources in Orissa, Mr Mehta filed a PIL petition. The SC appointed a commission and Mr Pramod Mishra, social activist and bank manager, was appointed Commissioner on the recommendation of Mr Mehta. The Report confirmed the allegations and ultimately the children were released from the jails.

☆ ☆ ☆

***Cri W P No 1508 of 1984***
***Kamaladevi Chattopadhyay v. State of Punjab and another***

A petition was filed under Article 32 of the Constitution on behalf of those detained in the Central Jail and the Special Security Jail, Ludhiana. The petition stated that several devotees and pilgrims including children had been rounded up in an army action in the Golden Temple.

In an order D/-21/9/84 by Justice O. Chinnappa Reddy and Justice V. Khalid
[reported AIR 1984 SC 1895]
In an earlier order D/-28/8/84 the Court had directed the District Judges of Ludhiana and Amritsar to visit the jails, determine

whether any children were detained and, if so, to arrange for their removal, safe custody and well-being. In the present order, the Court noted that it had still not received a report from the state of Punjab and the District Judge, Amritsar but had received reports from the Superintendent of the Central Jail, Ludhiana and the District Judge Ludhiana. Stating that the latter report revealed a sad state of affairs and that no reason for the detentions had been forwarded, the Court ordered that all the children listed be released, together with women who had been detained. Further orders were to be made on receipt of report from the District Judge Amritsar.

☆ ☆ ☆

***W P (Cri) No 1541 of 1985***
***Sheela Barse and another* v. *Union of India and others***

A petition was filed under Article 32 of the Constitution by journalist and social activist, Sheela Barse regarding mentally and physically handicapped children who were lodged in jails. The petition asked for the release of children below the age of sixteen and for information on the numbers of such children. The Court was asked to ensure that adequate facilities were provided for the children in the form of juvenile courts, homes and schools, that District Judges should be directed to visit the jails and sub-jails to ensure that the children were being properly looked after, and to direct the SLAABs to ensure the availability of legal protection for the children.

There were many orders in this petition from September 1985. All the States and Union Territories had been made respondents and the Court referred to Articles 21 and 39(f) of the Constitution along with section 5 of the Children Act, 1960, and twenty-one other Childrens Acts from different states. Later, when the Juvenile Justice Act, 1986 came into force, the Court took heed of its provisions.

After a disagreement with the advocate-on-record for the case, both the petitioner Sheela Barse and the advocate R. Venkataramani agreed that the case should no longer be dealt with by him. An application was made to the Court asking that Mr Venkataramani be discharged from the case.

In an order D/-12/7/86 by Chief Justice P.N. Bhagwati and Justice Ranganath Misra
[reported 1986 (2) SCALE 1 [1]]
The Court ordered, at 1:

Mr Venkataramani is discharged from this case at his request.

The petition was adjourned so that the petitioner-in-person could analyse the reports of the District Judges that had been submitted to the Court. The Court expressed its surprise that not all the districts had submitted reports. In this order the Court only dealt with urgent matters, directing that the state take care of the mentally and physically handicapped children by providing them with medical treatment, vocational treatment, and moving those abandoned out of jails to places of safe custody. The Court held that if there were not enough places for these children in homes then social service organizations were to be entrusted with the task of rehabilitating the children. Accordingly, the Social Welfare Board was ordered to provide a list of non-governmental, governmental and semi-governmental organizations to the Registrar. The Court also asked the Director-General of All India Radio and Doordarshan to publicize the Court's request to non-governmental and service organizations asking them to offer their services and rehabilitate the children. The Court further directed that two girls in the Jalpaiguri District Jail, aged eight and ten, be transferred to a home immediately as recommended by the District Judge of Jalpaiguri.

In orders D/-5/8/86 and 13/8/86 by Justice P.N. Bhagwati and Justice Ranganath Misra
[reported AIR 1986 SC 1773/(1986) 3 SCC 596 and 632]
In the order D/-5/8/86, the Court stated, at 1776:

> Article 39(f) of the Constitution provides that the state shall direct its policy towards securing that children are given opportunities and facilities to develop in a healthy manner and in conditions of freedom and dignity and that childhood and youth are protected against exploitation and against moral and material abandonment. Every state except Nagaland has a Children's Act. It is a fact that some of the Acts have been in existence prior to the inclusion of the aforesaid clause in article 39 by the amendment of 1976. Though the Acts are on the Statute book, in some states the Act has not yet been brought into force. This piece of legislation is for the fulfilment of a constitutional obligation and is a beneficial statute. Obviously the state legislatures have enacted the law on being satisfied that the same is necessary in the interest of the society particularly of children. There is hardly any

> justification for not enforcing the statute. For instance, in the case of Orissa though the Act inforce now is of 1982, for four years it has not been brought into force. Ordinarily it is a matter for the state government to decide as to when a particular statute should be brought into force but in the present setting we think that it is appropriate that without delay every state should ensure that the Act is brought into force and administered in accordance with the provisions contained therein. Such of the states where the Act exists but has not been brought into force should indicate by filing a proper affidavit by August 31, 1986, as to why the Act is still not in force.

Directions were given with reference to the physically and mentally handicapped and to abandoned and destitute children. The Directors-General of All India Radio and Doordarshan were again asked to publicize the Court's observations about the need for co-operation from the non-governmental organization and social service organization in the rehabilitation of the children. The Court stated, at 1776:

> The Court had intended that the reports of the District Judges would be sent to the Registry of this Court through the Registrars of the respective High Courts. This obviously meant that the Registrars of the High Courts were to ensure compliance. We are both concerned and surprised that a direction given by the apex Court has not been properly carried out by the District Judges who are an effective instrumentality in the hierarchy of the judicial system. Failure to submit the reports within the time set by the Court has required adjournment of the hearing of the writ petition on more than one occasion. We are equally surprised that the High Courts have remained aloof and indifferent and have never endeavoured to ensure submission of the reports by the District Judges within the time indicated by the order of this Court.

In its order D/-13/8/86, the Court suggested that a central legislation be passed to replace the state Acts. Describing the child as a national asset, the Court held that children must not be imprisoned but must be kept in remand homes set up by the state. The need for Juvenile Courts with a specialized cadre of magistrates in every district was indicated, as was the need for a different procedure and approach when dealing with cases relating to children. It was held that the time between the filing of the FIR and the completion of investigation must be no more than three months, and that there must be a limit on the amount of time for which a child can be imprisoned. The Court stressed the importance of the National Policy Declaration for the Welfare of Children, 1974 in this context.

In an order D/-21/11/86 by Chief Justice P.N. Bhagwati and Justice Ranganath Misra
[reported (1987) 1 SCC 76]
The Court reviewed its earlier orders as follows:

- On 15/4/86 the Judicial Magistrate was directed to visit the District Jail and sub-jail in their respective districts to find out how many children were detained and whether they have been produced before the Children's Court.
- On 5/8/86 the Court directed that every defaulting District Magistrate should submit a report by 31/8/86.
- On 5/9/86 allegations were made before the Court regarding the institution run by the Gajanan Maharaj Sikshan Sansthan, which was described as being in a dubious state of affairs. The SC directed that these allegations be looked into and that in the meanwhile records relating to the inmates should be taken by the Chief Judicial Magistrate and remain with him till the SC gave further orders.

In the present order, the Court noted, at 78:

> Notwithstanding our expression of anguish and concern and the specific directions referred to above, it transpires that there has been no compliance from certain quarters.

Listing the instances of non-compliance, the Supreme Court directed the High Courts to ensure that enquiries were conducted. The Court noted that allegations against Ferozabad and Amravati Jails had been made and stated that these would be considered later.

A miscellaneous petition was filed by the petitioner, Sheela Barse, asking the Court to allow her to withdraw the PIL petition she had filed on behalf of children suffering custodial restraints. In this application she stated that the Court was dysfunctional as the petition was not disposed of expeditiously and the directions of the Court were not effective. She contended that she could withdraw the petition which she had filed voluntarily, and referred to the events in the courtroom which cast slurs on her integrity and dignity.

In an order D/-29/8/88 by > Justice Ranganath Misra and Justice M.N. Venkatachaliah
[reported AIR 1988 SC 2211 / (1988) 4 SCC 226]
The Court stated that PIL doesn't mean that the petitioner has rights like *dominus litis*, and as the matter is of public interest, the petition cannot be withdrawn. The SCLAC was requested to take over the case and the name of the SCLAC was to be substituted in place of the petitioner.

In all subsequent orders, the case is cited as

***Supreme Court Legal Aid Committee* v. *Union of India and others***

In an order D/-17/3/89 by Justice Ranganath Misra and Justice M.N. Venkatachaliah
[reported (1989) 2 SCC 325 / AIR 1989 SC 1278]
The Court noted that the Juvenile Justice Act, 1986 came into force on 2/10/87 and that certain provisions are relevant to the litigation, namely, sections 2(e), 2(h), 5, 9, 10, 11 and 62. The Act empowered the state governments to make rules to carry out the purposes of the Act, however, in spite of the Court's directions, it was observed that many states had not framed rules. District Judges were directed to furnish details of implementation of the Act and the homes constituted under it, and the Court stated, at 326-7:

> We would like to place on record that on the earlier occasion response to directions by this Court had taken more than six months; repetitive adjournments had become necessary and compliance was effected by indicating coercive steps. We hope and trust there would be no repetition.

The Court further stated that Juvenile, Special and Observation Homes should be set up to deal with delinquent juveniles, and further ordered that rules should be framed under section 62 of the 1986 Act by each state government. A group of advocates was entrusted with the work of making a draft scheme for the proper implementation of the Act, which was to be placed before the SC for review. A.S. Nambiar, senior advocate, was appointed as commissioner to visit jails in three districts of Bihar (Deogarh, Patna and Bhagalpur) and report on the number of "delinquents" in the jails there. A fund, created from the central and state funds, was instituted in the Registry to meet the expenses incurred.

A commission of advocates was established to work out the

modality of the Act and make overseeing convenient. The commission constituted of advocates V.C. Mahajan, Yogeshwar Prasad, R.K. Jain, Tapas Roy and Mukul Mudgal. The Union of India was directed to deposit Rs 50,000 and the states of Bihar, West Bengal and Uttar Pradesh to deposit Rs 15,000 each with the SC Registry, to meet the expenses of the commission. The SC stated that further such orders may follow for all the states.

In an order D/-5/9/89 by Justice Ranganath Misra and Justice G.L. Oza

[reported 1989 (2) SCALE 73 [400]]

The Court noted that affidavits had been filed by all the states including Nagaland and directed that Boards be set up at state level under the scheme but not at district level for the time being. All the states, including Jammu and Kashmir, were directed to set up Advisory Boards under the scheme and lists of between fifteen and twenty Board members were to be drawn up. Compliance reports were directed to be filed with the Registry within eight weeks. The Court directed that the first meeting of the newly-constituted Boards were to be held within four weeks, and the first proceedings were to be sent to the Registry as part of the compliance report.

## Institutions

***Cri A No 300 of 1985***

***Sheela Barse v. Secretary, Children's Legal Aid Society and others***

A letter D/-22/8/84 sent to the HC of Bombay, by activist and journalist Sheela Barse, was registered as a writ petition under Article 226 of the Constitution. The letter exposed conditions in the New Observation Home at Mankhurd, maintained and managed by the Children's Aid Society, Bombay. It was alleged that children were illegally detained and harassed, that there was no repatriation of children to their parents as orders were not carried out and follow up action was not taken. It was also contended that children were forced to take up hazardous employment and that the Society was making a profit of about four lakh rupees each year. In its order the HC had found some of the allegations to be without justification, while others were accepted. The directions of the HC were considered to be inadequate as the Court failed to consider several of the contentions raised in the writ petition, therefore an appeal under Article 136 of the Constitution was filed in the SC by the petitioner. The appeal stated that the HC had lost sight of the provisions of the Bombay Children Act, 1948 and Articles 21, 24, 39(e) and 39(f) of the Constitution, and that the society should be treated as "the state" under Article 12 of the Constitution, not as a voluntary organization.

In an order D/-20/12/86 by > Chief Justice P.N. Bhagwati and > Justice R.S. Pathak (concurring)
[reported (1987) 3 SCC 50 / AIR 1987 SC 756]
As during the pendency of the petition the Juvenile Justice Act, 1986 had been passed, the Court directed that Juvenile Courts be set up presided over by Judicial Officers with special training according to the special needs of the children. The Court noted that the Chief Minister of Maharashtra was, at the time of the order, the ex-officio President of the Society and that the Minister for Social Welfare was the Vice-President of the Governing Council of the Society. As the Society was receiving grants from the state, the Court then stated, at 56:

> We agree with the appellant that the respondent-Society should have been treated as a state within the meaning of Article 12 as it is undoubtedly an instrumentality of the state on the basis of the test laid down by this Court. The respondent-Society has, therefore, to regulate its activities not only in accordance with the statutory requirements of the constitutional provisions in Articles 21 and 24 as also the Directive Principles of state Policy.

The HC had made disparaging remarks about the petitioner Sheela Barse, regarding her lack of acquaintance with court procedure. Censuring the High Court, the Supreme Court stated that she is a social worker and a freelance journalist and that the observations against her were unjustified. The state of Maharashtra was directed to pay the appellant costs of Rs 5,000.

☆ ☆ ☆

***C R No 2258 of 1988, Guwahati***
***Gautam Uzir and another* v. *Assam Seva Samity and others***
A petition was filed under Article 226 of the Constitution by two advocates on behalf of seventy-five children living in Noonmati Sisu Kaylan Kendra, a home for destitute children run by the Assam Seva

Samity. The petition was filed in response to an article in a local newspaper *Dainik Asom* on 13/12/88 entitled "Children fasting due to non-receipt of food". The petition claimed that this charitable organization received funding and paid a salary to three office holders of the Samiti, and stated:

> That although the Noonmati Sisu Kaylan Kendra receives a good amount of money, it appears that, the said Kendra is in a very deteriorated condition. The house is not properly maintained and it needs many urgent repairs. The conditions of the beddings of the childrens are very poor and most of the children are now living without warm clothes and mosquito nets.

The petitioners stated that Article 21 of the Constitution was being violated and asked the Court to order that the Home be supplied with food, that the records of the Home be made available by the respondents, that a Special Officer and a committee be appointed to investigate the whole matter, and that the petition be considered as a PIL. Another submission asked the Court to direct that the management of the Samity be put under a committee of advocates and doctors, set up for this purpose and that the court supervise the funds of the Samithy.

The Court admitted the petition and set up an inquiry committee. On receipt of the committee report, a steering committee was formed to run the Home, under the Court's supervision. It was then ordered that the funds of the Home be deposited in the Court. On two subsequent occasions, the Court asked the Samity to take over the running of the Home from the Court but no-one responded. Accordingly the petitioners formed a committee to run the home.

## Child Labour

***W P (C) No 13064 of 1983***
***Rajangam, Secretary, District Beedi Workers' Union v. State of Tamil Nadu and others***

A letter was sent to the Court by a Trade Union in Tirunelevi and registered as a petition under Article 32 of the Constitution. The letter referred to three factories manufacturing beedis and contended that the records relating to employees were being manipulated, appropriate dues for work done were not being paid, relevant provisions of the labour laws were not being implemented and that the contract labour system was still prevalent. The petition invoked Article 21 of the Constitution and referred to the Beedi and Cigar Workers (Conditions of Employment) Act, 1966.

In an order D/-19/11/91 by > Chief Justice Ranganath Misra and Justice Yogeshwar Dayal
[reported (1992) 1 SCC 221]
The Court noted that a connected petition was heard along with Rajangam's petition as it related to the same subject but asked for different ancillary reliefs regarding the employment of child labour and the non-implementation of the 1966 Act. Notice had initially been issued to the three factories, but this was later extended to other beedi manufacturing units in the state.

In an earlier order D/-24/10/89 the Court appointed the Society for Community Organization (SOCCO) Trust to investigate and submit a report. After the report was received and circulated, the Government of Tamil Nadu and the manufacturers were given time to file their response by way of affidavits. The Court then directed that a scheme be formulated for the implementation of the relevant enactments, which would be put before the Court for consideration.

In an earlier order D/-24/7/91 the Court stated, at 222:

> We gather from the submissions made at the bar that in the meantime some exercise has been undertaken for the purpose of finalizing the Scheme. Initially the state of Tamil Nadu had taken the lead but later the Union of India has also got interested and a meeting on a bigger scale for the purpose of finalizing the Scheme is being arranged. The Attorney General is present in Court today. We have also suggested to him that he may participate in the proceedings to help the Scheme to be finalized as quickly as possible.

Two schemes were then framed, one by the petitioners and the other by the state of Tamil Nadu. In an order D/-8/10/91 after getting the consent of the counsel for both sides, the Court directed that a conference be held to settle the terms so that one scheme could be adopted. Then, in an order D/-10/10/91 the Court directed, at 223:

Pursuant to our earlier direction, the employers, employees and the State Goverment through their representatives have met and have sorted out some of the differences. Matters which are agreed to by all and aspects which are not agreed to by the employers have been separately shown. A copy of this may be served on counsel for the Union of India present in the Court today and he is given three weeks time to indicate the responses. The appropriate Ministry of the Government of India is to respond to the relevant aspects.

In the present order the Court noted that the affidavit received from the Under-Secretary in the Ministry of Labour of the Union Government does not apply because the objections raised are concerning matters which fall within the power of the State Government. Certain directions were passed as listed below:

- The Rules framed in 1968 under the 1966 Act were to be implemented, along with other labour laws.
- The 1966 Act was to be implemented by the Regional Provident Fund Commissioner, who was asked to set up an establishment which was to start functioning within three months.
- The Court held, at 224:

  Tobacco manufacturing has indeed health hazards. Child labour in this trade should therefore be prohibited as far as possible and the employment of child labour should be stopped either immediately or in a phased manner to be decided by the State Governments but within a period not exceeding three years from now. The provisions of the Child Labour (Prohibition and Regulation) Act, 1986 should be strictly implemented.
- The Court noted the respondents' claim that the contract labour system was indispensable to this industry. The Union of India was directed to look into this claim and decide whether contract labour was to be permitted, within six months.
- As the beedi trade was flourishing and labour exploitation rampant, the Court held that the government labour establishment be located in the area, so that it could deal with the requirements of the industry.
- As most of the beedi manufacturing takes place outside the factory, registers were to be maintained for the regulation of labour. Pass books were to be maintained in the names of

workers and the welfare fund was to be properly administered, and help extended quickly on the death of a worker. The Court held, at 224-5:

> In view of the health hazard involved in the manufacturing process, every worker including children if employed, should be insured for a minimum amount of Rs 50,000 and the premium should be paid by the employer and the incidence should not be passed on to the workmen.

The TNSLAAB was asked to monitor the scheme for three years from January 1992 and to receive full co-operation from the concerned authorities. Mr Raja, Secretary of TNSLAAB was to be paid Rs 1,500 each month as an allowance for any expenses incurred. Disposing of the cases, the Court stated, at 225;

> We ... hope and trust that the authorities as also the employers and the employees would try to implement the directions in true spirit.

☆ ☆ ☆

### *W P No 12125 of 1984*
### *Bandhua Mukti Morcha v. Union of India and others*

A petition was filed under Article 32 of the Constitution by a bonded labour organization invoking the Employment of Children Act, 1938 and Article 24 of the Constitution. The petition stated that carpet manufacturers in Mirzapur were employing children.

Admitting the petition, the Supreme Court appointed a Commissioner — Sri Prembhai of Banwasi Sewa Ashram, Mirzapur District — to submit a report on the state of child labour in the carpet industry in the Mirzapur-Bhadhoi belt. The incidence of child labour was found to be high.[14] In addition to the thirty children mentioned in the original petition, he found another 114 children in the forced custody of loom owners. These children were then released through the office of the District Magistrate on 16/4/84. As the loom owners refused to co-operate, the District Magistrate had to conduct raids on the premises with the help of the police. The Commissioner also visited 42 villages in the area with 884 looms and found that 42 per cent of the total work force engaged in those

[14] As was the incidence of adult bonded labour.

looms were children below the age of fourteen years. The total number of such children was 369, 95 of whom were between the ages of six and eleven years and most were from Scheduled Caste and Scheduled Tribe communities. The Commissioner was unable to ensure the release of these 369 children. As many children were being taken away from District Mirzapur to avoid the investigations, the SC extended the jurisdiction of the Commissioner so that more investigations could be, and were, made. When the SC issued notice to the state of Bihar in September 1984, the Deputy Director of Social Security informed the Court that all the confined, kidnapped children were identified and released by the District Magistrate under the Bonded Labour System (Abolition) Act, 1976. The police later filed two criminal cases in the matter, against those who were offending under the Act. The existence of child labour was never denied.[15]

In an order D/-1/9/86 by Chief Justice P.N. Bhagwati and Justice Ranganath Misra
[reported 1986 (Supp) SCC 553]
The Court expressed its "regret" that the UP state government had flouted the Court's earlier directions, and said that it would give the state another opportunity to implement the directions. The Court also noted that the state of UP had not yet responded with the lists of children employed or with a scheme for their rehabilitation.

☆ ☆ ☆

***Sheela Barse* v. *Union of India***

A petition was filed under Article 32 of the Constitution by a journalist and social activist bringing the use child labour, in the glass factories of Firozabad in the Agra District of UP, to the attention of the Court. A study of the case highlighted the disparity between the findings of the petitioners and those of the state:

> Ms Sheela Barse, a freelance journalist made a thorough study of the area and reported that thousands of boys between the ages of six and sixteen years were playing with fire in the multi-crore glass industry of Firozabad. The bare-foot children

[15] See Varghese, Jose; "Law Relating to the Employment of Children in India"; Socio Legal Resource Centre, Secunderabad, 1989 at 4 and 65.

stand and move around gigantic furnaces containing maunds of boiling glass at a temperature maintained at 1400° Centigrade. The work environment is heavily polluted with heat, chemical fumes, soot and coal dust, while the floor is littered with broken glass. Children between the age groups of eight and twelve years were found dealing with loams of glass stuck on the tips of four feet long three centimeter thick iron rod without handles, known as "labias"....

Alarmed by the reports, the then Union Minister of State for Labour Mr P.A. Sangma and some of the MPs made a surprise visit to Firozabad but since the visit was pre-announced, most of the child workers were either whisked away or locked in rooms by their employers successfully so as to escape notice. One of the MPs who chanced to notice them through a window grill, had to force his entry into the room to rescue the children. Later on a petition of PIL was filed in the Supreme Court and the District Judge who was appointed by the Supreme Court to report with regard to the allegations of the working children below 14 years, has recently submitted his report confirming the incidence of child labour.[16]

☆ ☆ ☆

### *W P (C) No 465 of 1986*

### *M.C. Mehta* v. *State of Tamil Nadu and others*

A petition was filed under Article 32 of the Constitution by advocate M.C. Mehta, invoking sections 3 and 4 of the Minimum Wages Act, 1948 and sections 67, 71 and 75 of the Factories Act, 1948. The petition detailed the illegal use of child labour in the match and fire cracker factories at Sivakasi, in the Kamaraj District of Tamil Nadu. Also invoked were Articles 24, 39(f) and 45 of the Constitution.

In an order D/-31/10/90 by Chief Justice Ranganath Misra and Justice M.H. Kania

[reported (1991) 1 SCC 283 / AIR 1991 SC 417]

The Court noted, at 284:

16 *Ibid* at 6.

> From the affidavit of the state it appears that as on December 31, 1985, there were 221 registered match factories in the area employing 27,338 workmen of whom 2941 were children.

and stated that these would be used for the disposal of the petition. Discussing Articles 39(f) and 45 of the Constitution, the latter which has particularly remained a "far cry", the Court stated that while no children may be employed in the manufacturing operations, they can be employed for packaging, at 285:

> Children can, therefore, be employed in the process of packing but packing should be done in an area away from the place of manufacture to avoid exposure to accident. We are also of the view and learned counsel for both sides have agreed that a minimum wage for child labour should be fixed. We take note of the fact that the tender hands of the young workers are more suited to sorting out the manufactured product and process it for the purposes of packing. We are, therefore, of the opinion that in consideration of their special adaptability at least 60 per cent of the prescribed minimum wage for an adult employee in the factory doing the same job should be given to them. Our indicating the minimum wage does not stand in the way of prescription of a higher rate if the state is satisfied that a higher rate is viable.

The need for education and recreation to improve the quality of life of the children was stressed, and the Court stated, at 285:

> We are happy to notice that the learned counsel for the state of Tamil Nadu has suggested the creation of a Welfare Fund to which the registered match factories can be asked to contribute. The government can decide as to whether the contribution should be at a fixed rate per factory or made commensurate to the volume of production.

and noted that the state of Tamil Nadu had offered to contribute to the fund which was directed to be set up by 1/1/91. The Court held that the statutory requirement under the Factories Act, 1948, for providing facilities for recreation and medical attention must be implemented. As mobile medical vans from UNICEF were already being sent to the area, the state was directed to provide additional facilities. A compulsory insurance scheme was framed by the Court, holding the employer liable for the payment. A Committee was appointed with the District Judicial Magistrate, a public activist, a Union representative and the local labour officer to oversee the implementation of the Court's directions. The state of Tamil Nadu was directed to pay Rs 3,000 as expenses to Mr Mehta, at 284:

> It is a fact that the problem has been in existence for over half a century, if not more, and no appropriate attention has been focused on it either by the government or the public. We are, therefore, thankful to Mr Mehta for having brought this matter before the Court for receiving judicial consideration.

Disposing of the petition, the Court stated, at 286:

> Though we are disposing of this petition with these directions we are cognizant of the position that all the problems relating to employment of children are not covered by the present directions. We leave it open either to Mr Mehta or some other agency to move the Court as and when necessary for further orders.

In an order D/-14/8/91 by Chief Justice Ranganath Misra and Justice Kuldip Singh
[reported 1991 (2) SCALE 82 [464]]
The Court stated, at 464:

> In a disposed of case, we took *suo moto* proceedings when information about the unfortunate accident in one of the Sivakasi cracker factories was published.

Notice was issued and an affidavit received by the Court showed that insurance was effected for the 39 people dead, and that the insurers had agreed to pay Rs 50,000 per person. The Court directed that the insurance money be deposited with the District Judge, Kamraj who was to distribute the money, and noted that Rs 10,000 had already been paid, to the families of the deceased, out of the Chief Minister's Relief Fund. As the level of compensation for injuries was difficult to decide upon, the Court asked the Tamil Nadu SLAAB to take over the inquiry, so that the proceedings should not continue as specified under the Workmen's Compensation Act, 1923. An Advocates' committee including advocates R.K. Jain and Indira Jaising was established to inspect the area. They were to go to Sivakasi and four other areas mentioned in the scheme. The Court directed K.C. Dua, advocate for the state of TN to arrange for Rs 20,000 to be deposited in the Court to go towards the expenses of the Committee, and the matter was directed to be listed after the report was received.

The Court also noted, at 464-5:

> It is stated that though our Scheme did not permit children to be employed in the factory area except for the packing portion, it may be that some of the deceased who died inside the factory had been children. It is difficult at this stage to institute an enquiry as to the age of the people who died, but for the future as a general direction we are prepared to call upon the employers to maintain a list of employees indicating their age in their registers, and we would require the Public Officer concerned, immediately after an accident of this type, to verify the names of the dead people with reference to the age indicated and also to enquire as to whether the place of employment was within the permissible area in the case of a child being involved in the accident

## Inter-Country Adoption

***W P (Crl) No 171 of 1982***
***Laxmi Kant Pandey* v. *Union of India***

A petition was filed under Article 32 of the Constitution by advocate Laxmi Kant Pandey, alleging malpractices and trafficking in children by social organizations and voluntary agencies who offer Indian children for adoption overseas. The petition was filed on the basis of a report in the foreign magazine *The Mail* and invoked Articles 15(3), 39(e) and 39(f) of the Constitution.

In an order D/-6/2/84 by > Justice P.N. Bhagwati, Justice R.S. Pathak and Justice A.N. Sen
[reported (1984) 2 SCC 244]
The Court laid down detailed principles and norms to be followed for the adoption of children by people overseas. Many foreign examples were cited while discussing the issue, along with statutory provisions and international standards — the Guardians and Wards Act, 1890, the Adoption of Children Bill, 1972, the Adoption of Children Bill, 1980, the UN Declaration on the Rights of the Child,

1959, the 1978 Geneva Convention and other conventions. Stressing the fact that the child and its welfare is a matter of national importance, the Court expressed its gratitude to the many respondents involved in this case.

Applications were filed by the Indian Council for Child Welfare, the Karnataka State Council for Child Welfare and the Delhi Council for Child Welfare asking the Court for directions as to when they were required to act as a scrutinizing agency. Money for the extra expenditure was also requested.

In an order D/-3/12/86 by > Chief Justice P.N. Bhagwati and Justice Ranganath Misra
[reported (1987) 1 SCC 66]
In the light of these applications, the Court clarified earlier orders and directions issued to the scrutinizing agencies involved. Stating that if it was not possible to provide these children with a decent family life in India, it was held that adoption abroad was consistent with the National Policy on Children. However, the Court did state that every effort must first be made to see if the child can be rehabilitated by being placed within the country, thus sparing the child from going through the adjustments to a new culture and race. Exemption from the Court's guidelines was made for those children living with their biological parents who then give their children for adoption abroad.

More applications were filed asking the Court for further directions, including a direction that children in inter-country adoption should retain Indian nationality till they reach majority.

In an order D/-14/8/91 by Chief Justice Ranganath Misra, Justice M.H. Kania and Justice Kuldip Singh
[reported AIR 1992 SC 118]
Notice had been issued on these petitions on 21/9/90 regarding the implementation of the Children's Act, 1960 and the Juvenile Justice Act, 1986. Accordingly, Welfare Boards should have been constituted under both legislations, but as the Court noted, at 120:

> Though these two statutes in recognition of the importance of children to society have made these beneficial provisions, nothing concrete and substantial appears to have been done yet for implementing either statute in a serious way...
>
> The Union of India has set up a Department of Women and Child Development and most of the states and Union Territories have corresponding departments, yet the full

co-ordination has not been achieved. The responsibility of administering the two statutes is not properly shared. Monitoring seems to be very much wanting.

The petitioner had asked that those children with no or unknown parents be transferred from statutory homes to recognized agencies for placement. The Court stated that as these recognized agencies have not been set up everywhere, this cannot be directed as a rule. The Court ordered that when such a request is made by a recognized agency, then a Juvenile Court or Board may consider it, saying, at 122:

> A strait-jacket formula may very often be injurious to the interests of the child.

The request that adopted children should retain Indian citizenship was not acceded to by the Court on the basis that the children would need to be assimilated in their new society. The Court commented on the Acts and raised the question of the future of the children, when boys reach the age of sixteen and girls the age of eighteen. However, after posing the question, the Court did not go into the issue.

## The Girl-Child

***W P (C) No 185 of 1989***
***Pratul Kumar Sinha* v. *State of Orissa***

A letter was sent to the Court by an advocate from Nadia in West Bengal bringing a newspaper article, published in the Calcutta edition of the daily newspaper *Amrit Bazar Patrika*, to the attention of the Court. This article detailed the sexual exploitation of blind girl students in the Red Cross Blind School, in Berahmpur, in the District Ganjam of Orissa. The letter was registered as a writ petition under Article 32 of the Constitution.

In an order D/-12/5/89 by Justice Ranganath Misra and Justice M.N. Venkatachaliah
[reported AIR 1989 SC 1783]
In an order D/-6/4/89 the Court had directed the Chief Judicial Magistrate of Berahmpur to inquire into the allegations and record the statements of the inmates of the school. The inquiry report was submitted to the Court, along with the affidavit filed by the Union of India.

In the present order, the Court referred to the report which detailed the allegations that one girl had been sexually exploited, been compelled to have an illegal abortion and expelled from the school. The report concluded that it was difficult to hold that the girl was sexually exploited, at 1784:

> though a suspicion in the matter still exists.

Referring to the need to ensure that blind children are well provided for, the Court held, at 1784:

> While we do not propose to enquire further into the matter on the basis of the newspaper report, in view of what the Chief Judicial Magistrate has indicated, we are of the opinion that certain directions are necessary for the proper management of the institution.

Notice was issued to the Union of India, and the matter adjourned till 18/7/89.

☆ ☆ ☆

***Cri Misc (M) No 1819 of 1991, Delhi***
***Brinda Karat and another* v. *State***

A petition was filed under Article 226 of the Constitution by a member of AIDWA. Ameena, a girl of eleven or twelve years of age had been married to a man much older than herself. While being taken on an aeroplane from Hyderabad to Delhi on 10/8/91, she was crying. When the crew and passengers noticed this, it was brought to the attention of this women's organization. Ameena was brought before a Magistrate and sent to Nari Niketan, a home for destitute women. It was at this point that a petition was filed under section 482 of the Criminal Procedure Code, 1973 asking for Ameena to be shifted to a children's home, as Nari Niketan was not a suitable place for a child. The petition stated that the procedure for sending her there was incorrect, that the action of the Magistrate was unlawful and that Ameena should have been produced before a board constituted under the Juvenile Justice Act, 1986 which would then have sent her to a proper safe place of custody. The petition also asked for access to the child.

While at first the petitioners did not want Ameena to return to her parents, they were persuaded to support Ameena's own wishes to return home after learning about the circumstance of her marriage during the legal proceedings. It was discovered that Ameena came from a very poor family in Hyderabad, which had only taken four or five thousand rupees from the Sheikh, all of which they had spent on the wedding of their daughter. At the same time the air hostess Amrita Ahluwalia who had become very involved with Ameena, to the extent that she wanted to adopt her, had also filed a writ petition about Ameena. Ameena, however, continued in her desire to return home, so when written securities and assurances were given to the Court by her parents and officials in Hyderabad that her well-being would be monitored, she was sent back to her family.

# CASE CHAPTER 6

# Labour

## Framing the Issue

The cases on labour have been divided into sections on closure of industry, the unorganized sector, health and safety, and the rest of the cases. These cases should be examined together with the cases in the chapters on Bonded Labour and Urban Space, in which cases relating to bonded labour, hawkers and street vendors can be found.[1]

Most of the PIL cases filed for workers have been for those in the unorganized sector, where the structure of the industry is not easily identifiable. In this sector, the State has taken upon itself a *parens patriae* role, assuming that labour cannot take care of itself even when empowered by legislation. For example, provisions in the Contract Labour (Regulation and Abolition) Act, 1970, and the Inter-State Migrant Workmen (Regulation of Employment and

[1] For cases on Industrial Tribunals and Labour Courts see the chapter on 'Judges, Courts and Lawyers' in volume two: *Inder Mohan* v. *Union of India etc.* [C W P No. 2646 of 1982, Delhi] and *M.C. Mehta* v. *Union of India and others* 1986 (Supp) SCC 562. For cases on prison labour, see the chapter on 'Prisons and State Institutions': *In the matter of: Prison Reforms Enhancement of Wages of Prisoners etc.* AIR 1988 AP 295; *Gurdev Singh and others etc.* v. *State of Himachal Pradesh and others* AIR 1992 HP 76. For a case of forced labour in police custody, see the chapter on the 'Police': *Peoples Union of Democratic Rights through its Secretary and another* v. *Police Commissioner, Delhi Police Headquarters and another* 1989 (1) SCALE 114 [599]. For cases on child labour see the chapter on 'Children'.

Conditions of Service) Act, 1979, confer a duty upon the State to look after the well-being of workers. Inspite of this the State has been the worst offender.[2] Far from realizing the rights of these workers, enactments such as the Rajasthan Famine Relief Works Employees (Exemption from Labour Laws) Act, 1964, permitted labour laws and minimum wage standards to be legally suspended.[3] Thus in the cases such as filed by *Labourers Working on Salal Hydro Project* and by the advocate A.X. Verghese, PIL has proven to be a necessary check on breaches of the rights of workers which would otherwise remain unchecked.

The blurred distinction between class action and PIL is apparent in many of the cases. The two cases relating to closure of industry, *Fertilizer Corporation Kamagar Union* and *Workers of M/s Rohtas Industries Ltd.* are both class actions which have been included because of the importance of the Court's judgements to PIL. Similarly, the case filed by the *Sand Carriers' Owners' Union and others* has been included because of the Court's pronouncements on PIL. Thus, even the few cases relating to labour in the organized sector have been brought by the workers themselves and do not form a separate body of case law in PIL. Numerous class actions, for example on equal pay for equal work[4] and the regularization of

[2] In addition to the documented cases, a petition was filed in the SC in 1982 by the People's Union for Democratc Rights invoking the Inter State Migrant Workers Act, 1979 on behalf of over 1.5 lakh migrant labourers from Orissa, employed by contractors at the behest of the State Government. Provisions of the 1979 Act had been suspended by the State Government.

[3] In order to avoid paying minimum wages and provide facilities, projects were deliberately conducted under this Act.

[4] For examples of class action cases on equal pay for equal work see: *Randhir Singh* v. *Union of India and others* AIR 1982 SC 879; *Inder Pal Yadav and others* v. *Union of India and others* (1985) 2 SCC 648; *Surinder Singh* v. *Engineer-in-Chief, CPWD* (1986) 1 SCC 639; *Ram Kumar and others* v. *Union of India and others* AIR 1988 SC 390; *Daily Rated Casual Labour employed under P&T Department through Bharatiya Dak Tar Mazdoor Manch* v. *Union of India and others* (1988) 3 SCC 354; *Federation of All India Customs and Central Excise Stenographers* v. *Union of India* (1988) 3 SCC 91; *Halli Gowda and others* v. *Managing Director, KSRTC and another* AIR 1989 SC 1117; *Bhagwati Prasad* v. *Delhi State Mineral Development Corporation* AIR 1990 SC 371; *Ram Sukh and others* v. *State of Rajasthan and others* AIR 1990 SC 592; *Food Corporation of India Workers' Union* v. *Food Corporation of India and others* AIR 1990 SC 2178; *Grih Kalyan Kendra Workers' Union* v. *Union of India and others* AIR 1991 SC 1173; *Sandeep Kumar and others* v. *State of Uttar Pradesh and others* AIR 1992 SC 713.

labour have been filed. The easily identifiable nature of industries in this sector, extensive unionization and the precedent of class actions set by PIL had laid the foundations for using law in this way. The petition filed by M.K. Sharma on behalf of the workers of Bharat Electronics Ltd., is another example of a case which has been included as it is perceived as a PIL, but is in fact a class action.

Organizations and social action groups have played a significant role in bringing the situation of workers in the unorganized sector to the Court. Sanjit Roy of the Social Work and Research Centre (mistakenly called the Special Works and Research Centre in the reported judgement), at Tilonia in Rajasthan, has filed two cases, both on the payment of minimum wages. Similarly, the cases filed by the People's Union for Democratic Rights and the Lok Adhikar Sangh, were filed in response to written and oral reports of injustice. Those filed by the latter organization were both in response to newspaper articles, as were the petitions filed for the workers on the Salal Hydroelectric Project and in the Kandla Port. Other petitions filed by SEWA[5] and the Vidhayak Sansad[6] resulted from a long-term involvement with the people represented. Without the awareness of their rights and the duty of their employers and the State, the unorganized labourers needed to have cases fought for them.

## Access to Justice

Allowing letters as writ petitions meant that early PIL cases filed by Sanjit Roy and the People' Union for Democratic Rights were admitted by the Court. Other cases such as *Workers of M/s Rohtas Industries Ltd.*, *Ram Kumar Misra* and *Rohit Vasudava* originated in letters. Again the difference between letter-petitions and PIL cases has to be noted, as the letter in the case of *Workers of M/s Rohtas Industries Ltd.* was sent by the workers themselves, but the PIL character of the litigation is affirmed when examining the nature of the grievance and the fact that access to justice was only possible for these workers after procedural rules had been relaxed.

5 See the chapter on 'Urban Space'.

6 See the chapter on 'Bonded Labour' for cases filed together with the parallel organization, the Shramjeevi Sangathana in Thane District, Maharashtra.

In one of the earliest expositions of PIL, *Fertilizer Corporation Kamagar Union*, Justice Krishna Iyer discussed standing and linked it with the nature of the grievance brought to Court. Even though the petition in question was dismissed on the facts of the case, the right of a worker to approach the Court questioning the closure of an industry was upheld. The Court also discussed the scope of PIL and *locus standi* in its notable judgement in the *Asian Games* workers case. However, in the case of the *Sand Carriers' Owners' Union* the Calcutta HC limited the availability of standing by denying it to an unincorporated association.

Only one case was rejected on the grounds that an alternative forum was available. In the petition filed by *Vidyulatta Vivek Pandit*, after originally asking the Labour Commissioner to appear in Court, the Bombay HC asked the petitioners to approach the Industrial Tribunal. Similarly, in *Valiben Bhikhabhai Parmar and others*, although the Gujarat HC granted interim relief in the petition, the grievance was to be resolved in the Industrial Tribunal.

## The Court's Response

One of the first cases in which the Court ordered an inquiry and monitored the implementation of its orders was in the case filed by the People's Union for Democratic Rights, notable for the Court's innovative treatment of the procedural impediments to access to justice and also for the Court's order in which importance was given to the Directive Principles of State Policy. The scope of forced labour in Article 23 of the Constitution was expanded to include the compulsion of economic circumstances. The judgement in the first case filed by Sanjit Roy was another striking development in the law relating to Article 23 of the Constitution. Justice Bhagwati, relying on his judgement in the *People's Union for Democratic Rights*, held that the Rajasthan Famine Relief Works Employees (Exemption from Labour Laws) Act, 1964, was unconstitutional under Article 23 of the Constitution. This was the first time that this Article had been used in this way. In a concurring judgement, Justice Pathak upheld the order but stated that the Act had violated Article 14 and not Article 23 of the Constitution. This difference of perspective between the judges reflects a general and continuing disparity about how to deal with issues relating to the poor. Few later judgements have been as resourceful when analysing fundamental rights for workers.

Commissions had been appointed in *Hira Lal*, in the case of workers at the Kandla Port Trust, *Nagendra Dutt Jagudi* and in *Social Work and Research Centre*. In the case filed for the workers of Sabarmati Coal site, two commissions were appointed. The need for information and insight that would otherwise not be available, either from the State or from the petitioners, led the courts to institute their own investigation. Not only has the Court been unable to rely on the State for adequate information, in the cases of the workers of M/s Rohtas Industries Ltd., the Kandla Port trust and of the migrant sugarcane cutters, the Court has itself taken on the responsibility of monitoring the implementation of its orders.

Although, in *Hira Lal* and *Special Works and Research Centre*, the government has been praised for its co-operation during the Court's inquiries and in implementing the Court's orders, most of the cases have been characterized by a reluctance to cooperate. Even the praise for the government in *Special Works and Research Centre* seems misplaced in the context of the Court's order in Sanjit Roy. The imperative for the former case came when the government flouted the directions in the latter. The obduracy of the State machinery is more glaringly apparent in other cases, such as that of the Sabarmati coal workers, when the government was unwilling to frame a statutory scheme on the grounds that it would not be successful, without analysing or attempting to rectify the causes of the anticipated failure. The Court could only trust that necessary action would be taken by the State, but was disappointed by the results. The Court was compelled to monitor the implementation of its order, to appoint a committee and directed the sugar factories to pay the costs of the litigation.

The Court has had to analyse various enactments before giving orders, and decide which of the many labour laws would be applicable in the case under consideration, as in the Sabarmati case. Before assigning responsibility for the implementation of its judgements, decisions had to be made as to which party would be responsible for the implementation of the provisions of the Acts. In the case of the *Labourers Working on Salal Hydro Project*, the contractors and sub-contractors were directed to register themselves as contractors under the Contract Labour (Regulation and

Abolition) Act, 1970, so that provisions of the Act would apply to them. Similarly, in the case of the migrant sugarcane cutters, the Court had first to decide who were the principal employees before determining their duties.

Reference was made in *Labourers Working on Salal Hydro Project* to the employment of children,[7] and to the applicability of the Bonded Labour System (Abolition) Act, 1976. Without considering that the Labour Commissioner may be hiding the existence of bonded labour from the Court, the statement that there was no bonded labour was accepted at face value. The nebulous distinction between bonded labour and other forms of exploitation was made apparent in the cases of *Ram Kumar Misra* and *Rohit Vasadava.* These cases, along with *People's Union for Democratic Rights* and *Sanjit Roy,* were decided on the basis that the labour involved was forced labour. The Court described the form of labour as bonded, without reference to the Bonded Labour System (Abolition) Act, 1976. In many instances, the courts' comprehension of labour issues has lacked clarity and sensitivity to the workers themselves.

Certain other legal developments have taken place. In *M. K. Sharma* the Court held that while there was no immediate danger to the workers from radiation, Bharat Electronics Limited should nonetheless provide insurance for its workers.[8] Conversely, in *Nagendra Dutt Jagudi,* the Court ordered that criminal proceedings be initiated against the management of Chahal Engineering and Construction (P) Ltd., vindicating the stand taken by the workers upon whom "atrocities" had been committed. And in *Vivek Raghunath Pandit,* the right of workers to demonstrate was upheld.

## The Contribution of PIL

Just as the issues brought to the Court related to the non-implementation of labour laws, PIL has resulted in the non-implementation of the Court's judgements. There has been

[7] See the chapter on 'Children'.

[8] See the section on health in the chapter on 'Public Policy and Administration' in volume two for a case filed by M.C. Mehta on radiation in which the SC directed that insurance cover be provided for employees at risk.

sympathy for the workers, and, in some cases this has resulted in dynamism in the Court too, but this in itself brought little in the way of substantive results.

The landmark judgement in *People's Union for Democratic Rights*, received much attention at the time and has been quoted in innumerable later cases. Despite this there was no change in the working conditions on the Asiad construction sites. By the time orders had been passed by the SC, few workers remained, as the time taken for the Court to act was just too long. The ombudsmen visited the construction sites when most of the work had been completed and the majority of the unskilled migrant labourers had already left. When, following the main SC order, labour inspectors started supervising the work, they found that the contractors were still bypassing the laws, that they were preventing the workers from reporting their situation to the ombudsmen and that they were attempting to hide major accidents. At least 100 major accident cases were treated at one nursing home alone during the eighteen-month period ending in July 1982.[9]

In legal terms, the orders on labour have displayed little innovation. With the exception of the ruling in *People's Union for Democratic Rights* which clarified the scope of Article 23 of the Constitution and used the Directive Principles of State Policy, there have been few incisive comments. Conspicuous, as in most of the other chapters, it is the lack of comment or criticism of the statutory framework which govern labour relations. Relief has been provided on a case-by-case basis, as in *M.K. Sharma*, when the broader issue of liability and the duty to protect workers was reduced to the payment of insurance premiums. The innovation of PIL for workers has been procedural, in the wide acceptance of class actions.

The way in which the case on the workers of Sabarmati coal site was brought to Court reflected on the eventual outcome, as has the differences in the approach of activist groups working in the area. The petition had been filed by a group of lawyers, the Lok Adhikar Sangh, apparently without consulting or informing the Ahmedabad Women's Action Group, a social action group which was already working in the area.[10] Members of the women's group felt that the

[9] op. cit, note 11 at 5.

[10] In addition to this case, another petition from Gujrat involved a number of activist groups. It was filed in the Gujrat HC by a co-operative society in Ahmedabad constituted

petitioner's focus was to secure a legal victory, but not on the implementation of that victory. Reports indicate that the case was eventually withdrawn at the request of the management, who had superficially fulfilled the requirements of the Court order.

Far from improving the situation of the migrant sugarcane cutter, the other case brought by the Lok Adhikar Sangh, worsened it. Even before the case was filed, the State Government was aware of the conditions of work. In May 1986, the Rural Commissioner for Labour in Gujarat had stated in a memo:

> ... if some public interest litigation were to be filed for and on behalf of these migrant workers, the Government could be placed in the most embarrassing position.[11]

Even after the intervention of the HC, the State Government did not co-operate. Moreover, as noted by an analyst of the case:

> The biggest problem seems to me to be the fact that the Lok Adhikar Sangh was not content with the role of advocate, but in the second instance started to negotiate with the employers as the defender of the migrants' interest. Once they had succumbed to this predilection they found themselves in a position in which they entered into agreements on behalf of clients who had not given them permission to do so and who were scarcely aware of what was being done in their name.[12]

The Court's orders were flouted and the factory owners became more sophisticated in the methods of exploitation of the workers. An appeal was filed by the management of the co-operative factories, and the litigation continues. It seems that many of the

of persons plying handcarts for carrying bales of cloth in the Maskati Cloth Market, challenging the constitutional validity of the Cloth Markets or Shops Unprotected Workers (Regulation of Employment and Welfare) Rules, 1981, because certain areas were excluded from the scheme, which was framed without any application of mind as it can only operate if workers/employees are registered. The HC appointed a Commissioner to look into the matter. An application was then filed stating that the petitioners were not handcart pullers and the petition was not filed *bona fide*. Another organization in Ahmedabad, SEWA, then intervened in the petition.

[11] Quoted in Breman Jan, 'Agribusiness and Labour in South Gujrat', Institute of Commonwealth Studies, London, unpublished paper for discussion, presented on 21/10/88, at 9.

[12] *Ibid.* at 17-18.

workers have lost the employment they had. It is in this case that the strength of intrenched business interests in the maintenance of the cheapest possible labour force is most visible.

The judgements in *Sanjit Roy* and *Special Works and Research Centre* mobilized a lot of social action groups within Rajasthan and resulted in a series of judgements on minimum wages in the Rajasthan HC. The SC judgements were also used in lower courts, provided standards in support of those who approached the government and gave institutional support to the real problems addressed by the petitioning organization. Implementation of the judgements themselves were monitored by this organization, which had prepared the ground for a successful outcome in the Supreme Court. In the cases that have had some success, this can be attributed to the work of the non-governmental organizations, rather than to the administration.

## Closure of Industry

***W P No 3804 of 1980***
***Fertilizer Corporation Kamagar Union (Regd.) Sindri and others* v.**
***Union of India and others***

A petition was filed under Article 32 of the Constitution by a Union of workers at a factory, and by a Member of Parliament from Dhanbad, A.K. Roy, who was also the President of the Union. The third and fourth petitioners were both working in the factory. The petition challenged the legality of the sale of certain plants and equipments of the Sindri fertilizer factory. Objections were made on the grounds that this would mean losses of money for the public exchequer because of the method and results of the tenders for sale, and because the sale would jeopardize the employment of over 11,000 workers. The petition stated that this would amount to depriving the workers of their Fundamental Right to carry on their occupation as industrial workers under Article 19(1)(g) of the Constitution. Moreover the sale was described as arbitrary, unfair and therefore violative of Article 14 of the Constitution.

In an order D/-13/11/80 by > Chief Justice Y.V. Chandrachud, Justice P.N. Bhagwati, > Justice V.R. Krishna Iyer, Justice S. Murtaza Fazal Ali and Justice A.D. Koshal
[reported AIR 1981 SC 344]

Preliminary objections were raised to the petition, one being that the petitioners did not have *locus standi*, the other being that no fundamental rights were infringed. In a discussion of the scope of Articles 32 and 226 of the Constitution, Justice Krishna Iyer held, for Justice Bhagwati and himself, at 354:

> Law, as I conceive it, is a social auditor and this audit function can be put into action only when someone with real public interest ignites the jurisdiction. We cannot be scared by the fear that all and sundry will be litigation-happy and waste their time and money and the time of the Court through false and frivolous cases. In a society where freedoms suffer from atrophy and activism is essential for participative public justice, some risks have to be taken and more opportunities opened for the public-minded citizen to rely on the legal process and not be repelled from it by some narrow pedantry now surrounding *locus standi*.

and went on to say, at 356:

> If a citizen is no more than a wayfarer or officious intervener without any interest or concern beyond what belongs to any one of the 660 million people of this country, the door of the Court will not be ajar for him. But if he belongs to an organization which has a special interest in the subject matter, if he has some concern deeper than that of a busybody, he cannot be told off at the gates, although whether the issue raised by him is justiciable may still remain to be considered.

The Court held that fundamental rights were not violated and the petition was dismissed on the facts of the case. The Court reasoned that although old plants were shut down, no employee was deprived of employment on this account as surplus workers were absorbed into alternative employment in the same complex. Moreover, the Court held that the closure of an establishment in which workmen are employed does not by itself infringe the Fundamental Right to carry on an occupation. Observing that Article 32 is a basic feature of the Constitution, which cannot be taken away by amendment, Justice Chandrachud stated, at 347:

> The jurisdiction conferred on the Supreme Court by Article 32 is an important and integral part of the basic structure of the

> Constitution because it is meaningless to confer fundamental rights without providing an effective remedy for their enforcement, if and when they are violated. ... The violation of a fundamental right is the *sine qua non* of the exercise of the right conferred by Article 32.

After quoting B.R. Ambedkar, in the Constituent Assembly Debates, Justice Krishna Iyer held, at 353:

> *locus standi* must be liberalized to meet the challenges of the times. *Ubi jus ibi remedium* must be enlarged to embrace all interests of public-minded citizens or organizations with serious concern for conservation of public resources and the direction and correction of public power so as to promote justice in its triune facets

and went on to state, at 355:

> Public interest litigation is part of the process of participative justice and "standing" in civil litigation of that pattern must have liberal reception at the judicial doorsteps

and at 356:

> In the present case a worker, who clearly has an interest in the industry brings this action regarding an alleged wrongdoing by the Board of Management. Article 43A of the Constitution confers, in principle, partnership status to workers in industry and we cannot, therefore, be deterred by technical considerations of corporate personality to keep out those who seek to remedy wrongs committed in the management of public sector.

☆ ☆ ☆

***W P No 5222 of 1985***
***Workers of M/s Rohtas Industries Ltd. v. M/s Rohtas Industries Ltd.***

A letter D/-8/7/85 was sent to the Chief Justice from workmen after the closure of four plants of M/s Rohtas Industries. These plants, where paper and boards, cement, asbestos and vegetable ghee were manufactured, were located in Dalmianagar in Rohtas, Bihar. The letter also asked that the wages owed to the workers be paid, that their electricity supply be restored, and that they should be paid compensation under the 1984 amendment to the Industrial Disputes Act. The petition referred to the Bihar Relief Undertakings (Special Provisions) Act, 1981, the Sick Textile Undertakings (Taking Over of Management) Act, 1972, the Industries (Development and Regulation) Act, 1951, and the Industrial Disputes Act, 1947.

In an order D/-27/4/87 by Justice Ranganath Misra and > Justice G.L. Oza
[reported (1987) 2 SCC 588]
The Court held that payment of salaries and wages due to the workers will have priority over payment to creditors like the Banks and financial institutions. The Court directed that the goods lying in stock be sold to pay the workers their salary up to the date of the closure.

The official liquidator moved the Court to ask for more time to make the sales and raise funds.

In an order D/-22/7/87 by Justice Ranganath Misra and Justice M.M. Dutt
[reported 1987 (Supp) SCC 462]
Further time was granted for the disposal of the goods etc.

In an order D/-24/10/89 by Justice Ranganath Misra, Justice P.B. Sawant and Justice K. Ramaswamy
[reported AIR 1990 SC 481]
The Court recalled its order D/-27/4/87 regarding the payment of arrears of wages by sale of assets. In an order D/-22/5/89 the High Court of Patna appointed a Provisional Liquidator to rehabilitate the industry quickly as the livelihood of 10,000 workmen and their families were at stake.

The Court directed that a senior member of the IAS cadre be appointed by the state of Bihar as the Rehabilitation Administrator. The assets of the company were directed to be put in his control and the Court held that he could not be proceeded against by financial and other institutions for one year. This would give the company a chance to rehabilitate itself. The dues against the company of Rs 15 crores were directed to be paid by the State of Bihar out of its plan assistance funds. A committee was appointed by the Court and the case was adjourned till 1/3/90. The Court noted, at 483-4:

> If the Company is not revived and gets liquidated, the liabilities would turn out to be far in excess of the assets and notwithstanding the first or second charge on the assets, the creditors may not appreciably benefit. This Court cannot lose

> sight of the fact that living has been denied to about 10,000 families for over five years and apart from the national loss, the workmen have been put to serious jeopardy. In these circumstances we are satisfied that it is of paramount importance that the Company in respect of the viable units should be revived and allowed to come into production.

## The Unorganized Sector

***W P No 1869-70 of 1981***

***Hira Lal and another* v. *Zilla Parishad, Kanpur and others***

A petition was filed under Article 32 of the Constitution on behalf of workers belonging to Scheduled Castes who were employed in the flaying of carcasses. The petition invoked section 239(2) of the Uttar Pradesh Kshetra Samiti and Zilla Parishad Act, 1961.

In an order D/-5/3/82 by Justice P.N. Bhagwati and Justice Baharul Islam

[reported 1982 (1) SCALE 123 [545]]

In an earlier order D/-1/5/81 the Court had appointed Upendra Baxi and Krishan Mahajan as commissioners to undertake a socio-legal investigation of the flaying of carcasses in Sarsaul District of UP. They were to inquire into the way in which the flayers (chamars) were paid and the details of the contract system. In the present order, the Court noted that the petitioners had expressed their willingness to join a co-operative society to carry out the flaying operations, if one were formed. The Court directed the State Government to consider the directions and suggestions made by Court in this regard and to work out a proper scheme before the next hearing of the petition. The Court acknowledged the help of the counsel for the State, at 546:

> It must be said to the credit of Mr Bhardwaj that he has extended fullest support to the cause of the poor chamars and other backward classes engaged in flaying of carcass and adopted the right approach to a problem of this kind. This is not a litigation of an adversary character but it is really in the nature of Public Interest Ligitation which seeks to bring about amelioration in the life conditions of a large number of people who are victims of exploitation and the approach in such a

litigation has therefore to be of a totally different kind. Public interest litigation of this character must be looked upon as a collaborative or co-operative effort on the part of the State Government and its officers, for example, lawyers appearing for parties and the Court for the purpose of making basic human rights available to the weaker sections of the community and reaching to them socio-economic justice.

☆ ☆ ☆

***W P No 6816 of 1981***
***Sanjit Roy* v. *State of Rajasthan***

The Director of a social action group, the Social Work and Research Centre, Tilonia, Ajmer District, an organization working for the uplift of Scheduled Castes and Scheduled Tribes, wrote a letter to the Supreme Court. It stated that the Public Works Department was violating the Minimum Wages Act, 1948, and that inequal payments were being made to those employed in the department. It contended that the workers on the construction of the Madanganj Harmara Road were being paid less than the minimum wage of Rs 7 per day. The letter challenged the constitutional validity of the Rajasthan Famine Relief Works Employees (Exemption from Labour Laws) Act, 1964, as violative of Articles 14 and 23 of the Constitution and the 1948 Act. It also challenged the Rajastan Act which legitimized the suspension of minimum wage and other labour laws. The letter was treated as a writ petition under Article 32 of the Constitution.

In an order D/-20/1/83 by > Justice P.N. Bhagwati and > Justice R.S. Pathak
[reported AIR 1983 SC 328]
Justice Bhagwati held that the Rajasthan Act is violative of Article 23 of the Constitution, because it excludes the applicability of the Minimum Wages Act, 1948, to workmen employed on famine relief work by permitting the payment of less than the minimum wage to such workmen. Discussing the term "forced labour", Justice Bhagwati stated, at 329:

> The state cannot be permitted to take advantage of the helpless condition of the affected persons and exact labour on service from them on payment of less than the minimum wage. No

> work of utility and value can be allowed to be constructed on the blood and sweat of persons who are reduced to a state of helplessness on account of drought and scarcity conditions.

Justic Pathak, concurring, said at 355-6:

> But while he [Bhagwati] has found substance in the contention that the case is one of "forced labour" within the meaning of Article 23 of the Constitution, I prefer to rest my decision on the ground that there is a breach of Article 14 of the Constitution... The rights of all the workers will be the same, whether they are drawn from an area affected by drought and scarcity conditions or come from elsewhere... Because he belongs to a distressed area, is he liable, in the computation of his wages, to be distinguished from the other by the badge of his misfortune? The prescription of equality in Article 14 of the Constitution gives one answer only, and that is a categorical negative.

The petition was allowed and the impugned Act struck down.

☆ ☆ ☆

### *W P No 8143 of 1981*
### *People's Union for Democratic Rights (PUDR) and others v. Union of India and others*

A letter was sent to Justice Bhagwati, based on a report made by a team of three social scientists who were commissioned by the PUDR to inquire into the conditions of work on the various Asiad construction projects where labour laws were being flouted.

In an article entitled "ASIAD-82",[13] the President of the PUDR and advocate in the case, noted that the labourers working at the construction sites were not directly recruited by the contractors, but had been enlisted by jamadars who either went to villages to recruit them, or collected them from the migrants who came to Delhi. Having visited the site, he stated that almost all the labourers were migrants — recruited from Bihar, Orissa, Bengal, Tamil Nadu,

[13] "ASIAD 82", published by Gobinda Mukhoty, President, PUDR, Delhi, October 1982.

Andhra Pradesh, Madhya Pradesh and Rajasthan. Most of them were from the "backward" districts of these states and were mainly landless and poor peasants. With large families to feed, unproductive lands, poor wages and no employment they agreed to come to Delhi to work at sites.

In an order D/-11/5/82 by Justice P.N. Bhagwati and Justice Baharul Islam
[reported 1982 (1) SCALE 158 [817]]

The Delhi Development Authority was directed to carry out weekly inspections and to ensure the payment of minimum wages and implementation of other labour laws. The Court stated, at 817:

> We would also like to appoint two independent institutions to act as ombudsmen for protecting the interests of the workers and ensuring observance of the Contract Labour (Regulation and Abolition) Act, 1970, the Minimum Wages Act, 1948, the Equal Renumeration Act, 1976, the Employment of Children Act, 1938, and the Inter-State Migrant Workmen (Regulation of Employment and Conditions of Service) Act, 1979, by the contractors.

The Court directed Walter Fernandes and Alfred D'Souza, Directors of the Indian Social Insitute, and Shri Das Gupta, Director of the People's Institute for Development and Training to visit the sites on a weekly basis and report to the Court. Copies of the report were to be sent to the second petitioner (advocate Mr Gobinda Mukhoty) and government offices so that any necessary action could be taken against the contractors. The Court decided that it would give reasons for its order at a later date. No costs were awarded because a letter had been sent and the second petitioner had appeared in person. However, the Court did express its gratitude to the petitioners.

In an order D/-18/9/82 by > Justice P.N. Bhagwati and Justice Baharul Islam
[reported AIR 1982 SC 1473 / 1982 (1) SCALE 159 [818]]
The contentions of the petitioners were denied by the respondents and preliminary objections were filed. *Locus standi* was questioned and it was alleged that no petition could lie against the respondents, because, at 1482:

> the workmen whose rights were said to have been violated were employees of the contractors and not of the respondents and the cause of action of the workmen, if any, was therefore against the contractors and not against the respondents.

The Court conferred standing on the PUDR, saying, at 1483:

> Where judicial redress is sought of a legal injury or legal wrong suffered by a person or class of persons who by reason of poverty, disability or socially or economically disadvantaged position are unable to approach the Court and the Court is moved for this purpose by a member of the public by addressing a letter drawing the attention of the Court to such legal injury or legal wrong, the Court would cast aside all technical rules of procedure and entertain the letter as a writ petition on the judicial side and take action upon it. That is what has happened in the present case. Here the workmen whose rights are said to have been violated and to whom a life of basic human dignity has been denied are poor, ignorant, illiterate humans who, by reason of their poverty and social and economic disability, are unable to approach the Courts for judicial redress and hence the petitioners have under the liberalized rule of standing, *locus standi* to maintain the present petition espousing the cause of the workmen. It is not the case of the respondents that the petitioners are acting *mala fide* or out of extraneous motives and in fact the respondents cannot so allege, since the first petitioner is admittedly an organization dedicated to the protection and enforcement of Fundamental Rights and making Directive Principles of State Policy enforceable and justiciable. There can be no doubt that it is out of a sense of public service that the present litigation has been brought by the petitioners and it is clearly maintainable.

Discussing the Equal Renumeration Act, 1976, the Employment of Children Act, 1938, the Contract Labour (Regulation and Abolition) Act, 1970 and the Inter-State Migrant Workmen (Regulation of Employment and Conditions of Service) Act, 1979, the Court held that the enactments are available against the respondents, that is the Union of India, the Delhi Administration and the Delhi Development Authority. Articles 14, 23, 24, 39 and 226 of the Constitution were also discussed and the Court expanded the definition of "forced labour" in Article 23 to include the compulsion of economic circumstances stating, at 1490:

> It may be physical force which may compel a person to provide labour or service to another or it may be force exerted through a legal provision for imprisonment or fine in case the employee fails to provide labour or service or it may even be compulsion arising from hunger and poverty, want and destitution. Any factor which deprives a person of choice of alternatives and compels him to adopt one particular course of action may properly be regarded as "force" and if labour or service is compelled as a result of such "force", it would be "forced labour".

Referring to the allegation of the existence of child labour and that minimum wages were not being paid, the respondents claimed that there was no violation and that therefore the laws were not applicable. However the Court noted, at 1479:

> The Union of India in the affidavit in reply, filed on its behalf by Madan Mohan, Under Secretary, Ministry of Labour, asserted that the contractors did pay the minimum wage of Rs 9.25 per day but frankly admitted that this minimum wage was paid to the jamadars through whom the workers were recruited and the jamadars deducted rupee one per day per worker as their commission and paid only Rs 8.25 by way of wage to the workers.

The public sector corporations were told to ensure that labour laws were being observed without waiting for a complaint, and that periodic inspections should be carried out to ensure implementation of the laws. The respondents were asked to conduct an inquiry to ensure that the minimum wage was being paid and make up the shortfall if it was not. The Court suggested that the wages should be paid directly by the contractor in the future.

The Court went through the reasons for its order D/-11/5/82. Unable to adjudicate upon the dispute between the petitioners and the respondents on the implementation of labour laws, the Court held, at 1491;

> Since it would not be possible for this Court to take evidence for the purpose of deciding this factual dispute between the

parties, and we also wanted to ensure that in any event the provisions of these various enactments were strictly observed and implemented by the contractors, we by our order dated 11th May, 1982, appointed three ombudsmen and requested them to make periodical inspections of the sites of the construction work for the purpose of ascertaining whether the provisions of these labour laws were being carried out.

☆ ☆☆

***W P (Cri) No 1179 of 1982***

***Labourers Working on Salal Hydro Project v. State of Jammu and Kashmir and others***

A letter was sent to Justice D.A. Desai of the Supreme Court enclosing a news item from the *Indian Express* D/-26/6/82. This was registered as a petition under Article 32 of the Constitution. The news item detailed the exploitation of migrant workers on the Salal Hydroelectric project, which was a government undertaking. These workers were subjected to difficult working conditions, labour laws were flouted and they were exploited by contractors.

In an order D/-2/3/83 by > Justice P.N. Bhagwati, Justice R.S. Pathak and Justice A.N. Sen
[reported (1983) 2 SCC 181]
The Court noted that protection to workers is implicit in the labour laws and cited the Contract Labour (Regulation and Abolition) Act, 1970, the Minimum Wages Act, 1948, the Inter-State Migrant Workmen (Regulation of Employment and Conditions of Service) Act, 1979, the Employment of Children Act, 1938, and also invoked Articles 14, 21, 23 and 24 of the Constitution. As the Labour Commissioner of the State Government had stated that no bonded labour was being used in the project, the Court held that it would proceed on the basis that there was no violation of the Bonded Labour System (Abolition) Act, 1976. Referring to the incidence of child labour, the Court observed, at 191:

> We must concede that having regard to the prevailing socio-economic conditions, it is not possible to prohibit child labour altogether and in fact, any such move may not be socially or economically acceptable to large masses of people. That is why Article 24 limits the prohibition against

> employment of child labour only to factories, mines or other hazardous employments and no child below the age of 14 years can therefore be allowed to be employed in construction work by reason of the prohibition in Article 24, and this constitutional prohibition must be enforced by the Central Government. The Central Government would do well to persuade the workmen to send their children to a nearby school and arrange not only for the school fees to be paid but also provide, free of charge, books and other facilities such as transportation. We would suggest that whenever the Central Government undertakes a construction project which is likely to last for some time, the Central Government should provide that children of construction workers who are living at or near the project site should be given facilities for schooling and this may be done either by the Central Government itself or if the Central Government entrusts the project work or any part thereof to a contractor, necessary provision to this effect may be made in the contract with the contractor.

Directions were issued to the Central Government as the enforcing authority regarding the implementation of labour laws. It was to ensure that the "piecewagers" or sub-contractors obtain licences under section 12(1) of the Contract Labour (Regulation and Abolition) Act, 1970, so that they did not escape their obligations under sections 16-21 of the Act, read with rules 41-62, to provide facilities to the workmen and to ensure that canteens, restrooms and washing facilities were provided by the contractors and sub-contractors as under the Act. An enforcement machinery was to be established by the Central Government to ensure that labour laws were being properly observed, to investigate at regular intervals and to ensure that payments were being made to the workers in the presence of a representative appointed by the National Hydroelectric Power Corporation or by the Central Government. This payment was to be free from the intervention of *khatedars* (middlemen) except those authorized by law. The Central Government was also directed to report to the Court on the implementation of these directions on 30/4/83 and to ensure that workers were given a day off.

In an order D/-25/4/84 by > Justice P.N. Bhagwati and Justice R.B. Misra
[reported (1984) 3 SCC 53]

In a letter D/-22/3/83 to the Manager of the National Hydroelectric Power Corporation, the Central Government pointed out that registration under section 12(1) of the Contract Labour (Regulation and Abolition) Act, 1970, and section 8 of the Inter-state Migrant Workmen (Regulation of Employment and Conditions of Service) Act, 1979, was being carried out; canteen facilities had already been provided to the workmen, instructions for the provision of restroom facilities had been given by 30/4/83; arrangements for sufficient supply of drinking water had been made at work places; latrines and urinals had been provided and additional ones ordered; directions had been issued regarding payment of wages with double rate for overtime; wages had been increased from Rs 9 to Rs 10 as of 1/12/83; and instructions had been given regarding employment of children below the age of fourteen and provision for a weekly off day which was to be compulsorily provided.

In a letter D/-23/3/83 to the contractors, the Manager of the National Hydroelectric Power Corporation passed the directions on to the contractors who were instructed to act within two days. The Court held, at 546:

> It is not necessary to set out in detail the facts showing compliance with the various directions given by the Court in its interim judgement, but suffice it to state that it is clear from the documents and statements produced by the National Hydroelectric Power Corporation that the directions have been substantially complied with by the National Hydroelectric Power Corporation as also by the contractors and sub-contractors or piecewagers.

To avoid future recurrence of violations, the Central Government was ordered to carry out close and detailed inspections by fairly senior inspection staff at frequent intervals, as it was held that without judicial intervention implementation may become slack. The Central Government was directed to pay Rs 5,000 as costs to advocate Gobinda Mukhoty of the PUDR who brought this matter to the Court through a letter.

☆ ☆ ☆

***Crl W P No 53 of 1983***

***Ram Kumar Misra v. State of Bihar and others***

A letter was sent to the Court by the President of the Free Legal Aid Committee, Bhagalpur. The letter stated that the owners of public ferries of Bhagalpur and Sultanganj were not paying the minimum wages to their workmen. The letter was registered as a petition under Article 32 of the Constitution.

In an order D/-21/9/83 by > Justice P.N. Bhagwati, Justice A.N. Sen and Justice Ranganath Misra
[reported AIR 1984 SC 537]
Allowing the petition the Court invoked the Minimum Wages Act, 1948, and section 2(6) of the Bihar Shops and Establishments Act, 1953. The Court stated that the employers were establishments as in the 1948 enactment and in the notifications made under it in 1975 and 1979. The allegations made of the existence of bonded labour were not found to be correct by the District Magistrate of Bhagalpur who had been directed to inquire into the matter. The Court held that arrears in wages were to be decided by an appropriate authority appointed by the Labour Department of the government of Bihar. The state of Bihar was directed to pay costs of Rs 2,000 to the petitioner.

☆ ☆ ☆

A letter was sent to the High Court of Gujarat in April 1983 relating to contract workers in Kandla Port. The letter, based on a report in the newspaper Jansatta, was sent by a local municipal councillor. It was treated as a writ petition under Article 226 of the Constitution.

Admitting the petition, the Court appointed a commission of inquiry. The report of the commission recommended that the Kandla Port Trust should be responsible for the entire range of labourers working in the dock premises and that the Dock Labourers Act be suitably amended to provide for this. The report also suggested that the authorities ensure that the contractors were registered so that minimum benefits guaranteed under the Contract Labour (Regulation and Abolition) Act, 1970, can be given to the workers.[14]

☆ ☆ ☆

***Spl Crl A No. 1007 of 1983, Gujarat***
***Rohit Vasavada and another v. General Manager, IFFCO, Kalol and others***

A letter was sent to the Court by the IFFCO Karamchari Sangh

14 Patel, Sujata "Contract Labour and Public Interest Litigation", (1983) 18 EPW 2151-3.

bringing the working conditions of contract labourers on the premises of the IFFCO (Indian Farmers and Fertilizers Cooperative Ltd.) factory to the notice of the Court. A proper petition was asked for and submitted under Article 226 of the Constitution, invoking Articles 21 and 23 of the Constitution

In an order D/-13/10/83 by > Chief Justice P.S. Poti and Justice S.B. Majumdar

[reported 1983(2) GLR XXIV(2) 1529]

The Court appointed a commissioner to determine suitable action to free bonded labourers. The commissioner in his first report D/-4/10/83 reported that safety measures were not adhered to even though the work involved handling of dangerous chemicals. Many problems were identified, for example food was cooked on *chulas* near the chemicals. In this order the HC examined the SC cases on bonded labour, and noted that settled principles had been established in the cases of the *People's Union for Democratic Rights* (supra) and *Sanjit Roy* (supra). The Court directed that sections 7 and 10(2) of the Contract Labour (Regulation and Abolition) Act, 1970, and the Contract Labour (Regulation and Abolition) (Gujarat) Rules, 1972, be enforced by an ex-officio member of the State Board. The Court ordered that a list of unlicensed contractors be prepared quarterly by the Labour Commissioner, that all licensed contractors be inspected periodically, and that surprise checks be carried out. The Commissioner was then directed to report to the Court.

☆ ☆ ☆

***W P (Cri) No 1608 of 1984***

***Nagendra Dutt Jagudi v State of UP***

A petition was filed detailing atrocities committed on workmen in Tehri.

In an order D/-10/4/87 by Justice A.P. Sen and Justice V. Balakrishna Eradi

[reported 1987 (2) SCALE 306 [1301]]

The Court noted that the State Government had not complied with its earlier orders stating, at 1301:

> We strongly deprecate the approach of the State Government.

The report of the inquiry ordered to be conducted by a District Judge showed that atrocities were committed on the workmen of the

Chahal Engineering and Construction (P) Ltd., Tehri. A copy of the report was directed to be given to the State of Uttar Pradesh so that criminal proceedings could be initiated against the management of the company and other persons responsible. The Court decided to hear the application for intervention at a later date and adjourned the case for two weeks.

☆ ☆ ☆

***Spl C A No 391 of 1984, Gujarat***

A petition was filed in the High Court of Gujarat under Article 226 of the Constitution by the Lok Adhikar Sangh, an Ahmedabad based organization committed to the protection of civil liberties and democratic rights of the people. It was filed in response to an article "Slaves of Sabarmati" by Ramesh Menon, published in *India Today* on 15/10/83. The petition invoked the Contract Labour (Regulation and Abolition) Act, 1970, and asked the Court to provide the benefit of labour legislations to labourers on the Sabarmati coal site in Ahmedabad. The journalist had entered the site by contacting Ila Pathak, an activist of the Ahmedabad Women's Action Group (AWAG), who was working with women and children of the area.

In an order D/-15/10/86 by > Justice A.M. Ahmadi and Justice S.A. Shah

In an earlier order D/-2/2/84 the Court had appointed senior advocate P.V. Hathi as the Court Commissioner to report on the health hazards under which women labourers were working and the hazards to their children; accommodation facilities provided for women and facilities provided to them to tend to their children; whether the provisions of the Contract Labour (Regulation and Abolition) Act, 1970, and the Inter-State Migrant Workmen (Regulation of Employment and Conditions of Service) Act, 1979, were applicable to these workers; the amount, method of disbursement and record kept of the wages; the responsibility taken by the principal employee (the railway) for these workers, if any; the facilities provided to the workers as codified in the labour laws; and any difference in the position of the workers and any matters requiring immediate attention.

The Court noted the findings of the Commissioner, at 4:

> The working conditions at the said two railway yards is, to say the least, appalling and betray little or no concern for the quality of life of these unfortunate men and women.

It was held that the 1979 Act was not attracted, but the Court was unclear whether the 1970 Act would be applicable to these workers. In earlier orders D/-27/4/84 and 20/9/84 the Court had issued interim directions. In another order the Court had stated, at 5:

> It appears that thereafter the matter was placed for the first time before this bench on 6th February 1986 and having regard to the interim orders passed ... the time was now ripe to take some positive and effective action to implement the earlier orders which had been hitherto ignored by the concerned authorities.

Two Court Commissioners had therefore been appointed, and assurances were given by the Railway Administration that drinking water would be provided. Further assurances made by the respondents, were recorded in an order D/-12/3/86, as was the promise that gum-boots would be provided to the workers. According to the advocate for the petitioners this had not been done. In the present order the Court analysed the legislative background and noted that Articles 14, 15, 16, 19, 21, 23, 24, 30, 38, 41, 43 and 47 of the Constitution were applicable to the case. As the applicability of the 1970 Act was unclear, the Court allowed the petitioners to invoke the Gujarat Unprotected Manual Workers (Regulation of Employment and Welfare) Act, 1979. After analysing the provisions of this Act the Court dismissed the pleas of the respondents who did not want to frame the required scheme, at 14-15:

> Merely because one scheme framed in relation to employees working in cloth markets and shops has not been fully successful, it is no reason to fold up the Act and refuse to frame any other scheme, thereby frustrating the legislative intent...
>
> We, therefore, direct the State Government to prepare a draft scheme as contemplated by Section 4 of the Act and produce the same before this Court within one month from today. Further directions in regard to the scheme will be made hereafter.

In an order D/-29/4/87 by Justice A.M. Ahmadi and Justice D.M. Shukla

The Court declined to make certain directions at the request of the petitioners in view of the statement put forward for the respondents. The Court directed notification to be issued under Section 4(1) of the Gujarat Manual Workers (Regulation of Employment and Welfare) Act, 1979, in the Official Gazette regarding the scheme.

The matter was directed to be listed on 1/7/87.

☆ ☆ ☆

***W P (C) Nos 279, 282, 337 of 1986***
***Special Works and Research Centre through Sanjit Roy and others v. State of Rajasthan***

A petition was filed under Article 32 of the Constitution by the Director of a social action group, the Social Work and Research Centre, Tilonia, Ajmer District, Rajasthan. The petition stated that workers on famine relief operations were not being paid the minimum wages.

In an order D/-29/9/86 by Chief Justice P.N. Bhagwati, Justice G.L. Oza and Justice M.M. Dutt
[reported 1986 (Supp) SCC 561]

A committee had already been appointed by the Supreme Court, so in this order the Court noted that the report of the committee was being considered by the State Government. The report stated that the minimum wages were required to be paid for famine relief operations. The Court held, at 561:

> But since acceptance of the recommendations of the Committee and issue of notification in accordance therewith as well as implementation of the interim order made by this Court for payment of the minimum wages to workers engaged in drought relief work will involve a financial burden of almost rupees twenty crores, we hope and trust that the government will provide necessary assistance to the State Government at an early date since the minimum wages required to be paid are for work given by way of famine relief operations.

In an order D/-14/11/86 by Chief Justice P.N. Bhagwati and Justice Ranganath Misra
[reported 1986 (2) SCALE 232 [905]]

The Court noted that the Government of Rajasthan had fixed the minimum wages according to the recommendation of the committee, which was constituted under the Minimum Wages Act, 1948. The Court directed that the workers be paid this amount from 16/10/86, and adjourned the case for two weeks, stating, at 905-6:

> We are glad to find that the State Government has accepted the suggestion made in paragraph five of the Report of the committee constituted for fixing the minimum wages, except in regard to the provision of tools and plants which is under consideration of the State Government. We are happy that this public interest litigation has provided relief to a large number of needy poor persons and we also note with a sense of satisfaction as to the manner in which the State Government has responded to this litigation.

☆ ☆ ☆

***Spl C A No 6685 of 1986, Gujarat***
***Lok Adhikar Sangh v. State of Gujarat and others***

A petition was filed under Article 226 of the Constitution by an organization in Ahmedabad committed to the protection of civil liberties and democratic rights of the people, particularly the poor and disadvantaged sections of society. The petition invoked Articles 14, 16, 21 and 23 of the Constitution, the Inter-State Migrant Workmen (Regulation of Employment and Conditions of Service) Act, 1979, the Inter-State Migrant Workmen (Regulation of Employment and Conditions of Service) Rules, 1980, the Contract Labour (Regulation and Abolition) Act, 1970, and the Contract Labour (Regulation and Abolition) Rules, 1971. It concerned migrant workers in the cooperative sugar factories in South Gujarat, where labour laws were openly violated. In particular the petition detailed the labour and wage conditions of those involved in the process of sugarcane cutting.

The petition was based mainly on three articles. One was a news report by Mahesh Vijaypurkar published in *The Hindu* on 13/12/86 entitled "Exploitation continues despite the law", the other two were reports by Indukumar Jain published in *Naya Marg* on 16/11/86 and 1/12/86 entitled "Mithi Khandni Kadvi Vato". The petition stated, at 5:

> These articles clearly point out that over a lakh inter-state migrant agricultural labourers who have migrated from Maharashtra and other places are being crushed simultaneously with the crushing of the sugarcane and they are

> being exploited. Payment of wages to them is far below the prescribed minimum and the payment is being made only once, at the time of their return to their native place.

The petition detailed the method of payment of wages, through agents known as "mukkaddams" and pointed to the fact that no records of the work done were kept by the agents. It also detailed the lack of facilities provided to the workers and stated that although the minimum wage at the time was Rs 11 per day, at 11:

> Each and every worker is being paid Re 1 plus 1 kg of *jowar* which is worth Rs 1.60 every day and they are told that the remaining amount will be finalized afterwards which is being calculated at Rs 4.50 or Rs 5.50 per day.

The petition went on to state that as the sugar factories employ labourers through the mukkaddams on behalf of the farmers, who form the cooperative societies, it can be said that the farmers and the sugar factories are principal employers and the mukaddams are contractors under the 1970 Act. It was contended that reports and decisions of the state government regarding these workers which have detailed their rights, have not been implemented. The petition therefore asked that labour laws be implemented, that the government constitute a special cell for supervision, enforcement and implementation of the provisions of the relevant enactments, and that the State Government submit bi-monthly reports on enforcement. The petition also asked for interim reliefs: that a commission be appointed to inquire into the conditions of the workmen, that the Court prevent information from being suppressed as this would frustrate the commission's work, and that the Commissioner be provided with all the necessary help and cooperation. Other interim reliefs were also asked for, including that the Commissioner of Police, Surat, take immediate steps for the protection of workmen, and that every sugar factory be directed to deposit Rs 1 lakh in the High Court to go towards the unpaid amount due to the workers under the various labour laws.

In an order D/-7/1/87 by Justice R.A. Mehta

As the petition was based mainly on press reports, the Court appointed a committee to investigate the facts of the case. The Committee was to be constituted with advocate Mahesh Bhatt, social activist Medha Patkar and a special officer of the Court, M.P. Buch. In an order D/-26/2/87

The Court gave a number of interim reliefs on the basis of the report submitted by the committee. These reliefs aimed at ensuring payment of the minimum wages to the workers. The nine sugar factories examined all agreed to pay the minimum wage of Rs 11 per day.

In an order D/-9/3/87

In this second interim order, the sugar factories postponed the payments ordered to be made to the workers on the plea that the matter had first to be approved by the Board of Directors of the concerned factories.

In an order D/-19/3/87 by Justice R.A. Mehta

The matter came up for admission and since the case related to labour laws, it was directed to be heard before a division bench.

In an order D/-14/4/87 by > Justice A.M. Ahmadi and Justice D.H. Shukla

The respondents challenged the maintainability of the petition on a number of grounds — that the minimum wages were being paid, that each group of workers, known as a koyta, has no more than two persons (an important point in the calculation of wages), that the newspaper articles were distorted and incorrect, — and the article by Jan Breman[15] produced by the petitioners in the affidavit in rejoinder was described as outdated. Many other challenges were made on legal grounds and the Court examined the relevant enactments and found that the minimum wages were not being paid according to the committee report. It was held that the sugar factories were the principal employers, even though they recruited labour through intermediaries. The Court stated that even in cases where an employee was employed on a piece-rate basis, his renumeration must not be less than the wage payable to a worker on a time-rate basis. The Court directed that minimum wages be paid to the workers and an interest of 12 per cent per annum be paid on the outstanding amount. The method of disbursement and monitoring of the wages were specified. Compliance reports were ordered to be submitted to the Court within a week after disbursement of the payment. Referring to the other reliefs asked for, for example the provision of drinking water and other facilities, the Court stated that as the season was almost over, it would not make any directions, as, at 32:

15 Breman, Jan "Sessional Migration and Co-operative Capitalism. Crushing of Cane and of Labour by Sugar Factories of Bardoli" *EPW* Special Number, August 1978, 1317-1360.

> the learned counsel for the sugar factories has assured us that these arrangements will be made forthwith. As pointed out earlier, the respondents themselves have suggested the appointment of a tripartite committee to look into the grievances of the petitioners along with the viewpoints of the sugar factories with a view to finding a long-term solution to the problem. We think this suggestion is quite positive and we are, therefore, of the opinion that a high level committee should be appointed, comprising a chairman and two members, to look into the grievances and make recommendations for redressing them well before the next harvesting season begins.

The committee consisting of a chairman and three members was directed to be appointed and its recommendations submitted by 15/8/87 at the latest. The Court recommended that the State Government start a cell in the Labour Department to collect and collate the relevant material and place it before the committee. An application for a stay of the order was rejected.

In an order D/-22/4/87 by Justice A.M. Ahmadi and Justice D.H. Shukla

Modifications were made to the earlier order of the HC, regarding the specific methods of calculating wage payments. The Court agreed to an ad hoc fixation of payments agreed upon by the factory owners. The Court made it clear that this would not affect the interim order passed on 14/4/87.

In an order D/-27/4/88 by > Justice A.M. Ahmadi and Justice D.H. Shukla

The Court noted that it had hoped that the wage issue had been resolved, but at 6:

> Our hopes are belied and here we are called upon to deal with the complaints that the powerful sugar lobby has by its manoeuvres and manipulations tried to systematically efface and nullify the impact of our said interim order [of 14/4/87]. In this behalf two Civil Applications Nos 1275 and 1276 of 1987 have been moved by the petitioners. It is pointed out in these Civil Applications that when the current harvesting season began, attempts were made to change the entire system of recruitment, conditions of service, wage pattern etc. to the detriment of labour and in disregard [of] … the provisions of

the Bombay Industrial Relations Act, 1946, and/or the Industrial Disputes Act, 1947, notwithstanding the fact that the High Level Committee was inquiring into the matter.

The petitioners pointed out that the recruitment offices of the factories were closed down, so that recruitment would be done by farm members and the interim order would no longer apply. After considering the pleas of the respondents, the Court held that the changes were made with the purpose of frustrating its earlier order. The Court appointed a committee to enforce its interim order of 14/4/87 and conferred powers upon it to enable it to do so effectively. The sugar factories were directed to deposit Rs 20,000 in the Court within one week for the renumeration/expenses of the Court Committee. The application for a stay of the order was rejected.

In an order D/-1/5/87 by Justice A.M. Ahmadi and Justice D.H. Shukla

Modifications were made to certain details in the previous order. Members of the High Level Committee as ordered on 14/4/87 were appointed and its modalities were defined. The Court directed that statements by the parties to the petition should be submitted within three weeks. The sugar factories were asked to deposit Rs 50,000 in the HC to meet costs.

☆ ☆ ☆

***Spl C A No 2005 of 1987, Gujarat***

***Valiben Bhikhabhai Parmar and others* v. *Dena Bank and others***

A petition was filed under Article 226 of the Constitution, invoking Articles 14, 19 and 21 of the Constitution, the Payment of Wages Act, 1936, and the Minimum Wages Act, 1948. The first eleven petitioners, members of the Self Employed Women's Association (SEWA) based in Ahmedabad, all belonged to Scheduled Castes. The twelfth petitioner was SEWA, a trade union working for and on behalf of the petitioners. The petitioners challenged the termination of their cleaning contract with the Bank as illegal and asked that the contract be reinstated. They also asked that the Court direct the minimum wages to be paid to the women, along with the back wages they were owed.

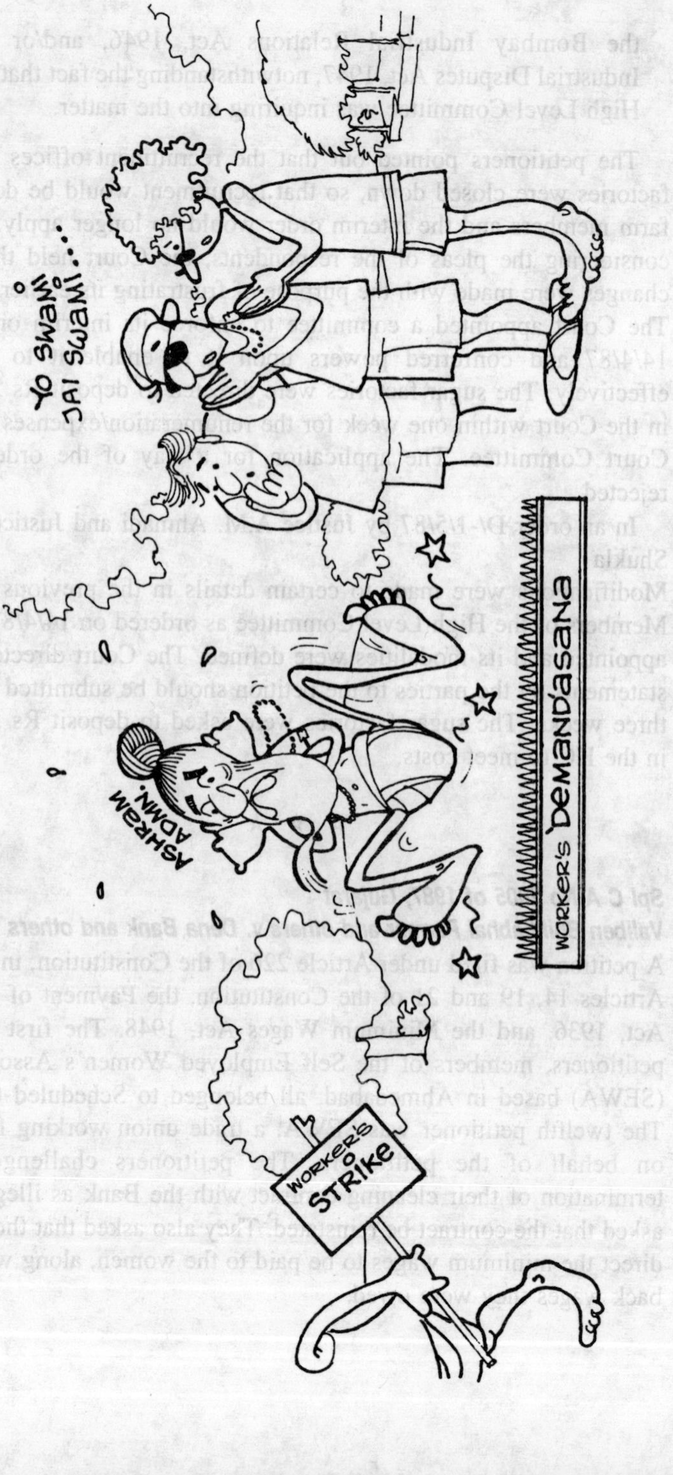
YO SWAMI
JAI SWAMI....
ASHRAM ADMN.
WORKER'S 'DEMANDASANA
WORKER'S STRIKE

In an order D/-11/9/87 by Justice A.M. Ahmadi and Justice N.B. Patil
The Court stated (order given in full):

> Interim relief not to recruit and appoint candidates already selected by the Bank other than the petitioner until further orders. The Industrial Court to go ahead with the proceedings and dispose the same of at an early date.

☆ ☆ ☆

**W P No ?? of 1987, Bombay**
**Vidyulatta Vivek Pandit and others v. State of Maharashtra and others**

A petition was filed under Article 226 of the Constitution by an activist of the Vidhayak Sansad and Shramjeevi Sangathana, organizations working with tribals in Thane District. The petition detailed the violation of labour laws at the Gurudev Siddhapith, Ganeshpuri, Taluka Bhiwandi, District Thane (the fourth respondent) in Maharashtra. Known as a meditation centre, with branches all over the world, many of the visitors to the *ashram* were foreigners. Established in 1962 this centre had 114 acres of land with guest houses and buildings for the residence of permanent settlers and visitors, together with bungalows, flats and two canteens. At the time of filing the petition there were altogether thirty-seven permanent employees both in the canteens and for maintenance of buildings. The women were paid Rs 7 and men were paid Rs 10 per day. There were a total of 211 other employees, so the petition stated that the *ashram* was an industry within the meaning of the Industrial Disputes Act, 1947. All the employees working in the canteens, gardens and for various purposes were adivasis or tribals from the locality.

In an incident on 18 or 19/4/87 a group of foreigners assaulted some labourers. In protest against this there was a strike, and the petition narrated how, at 7:

> As a part of the peaceful and constitutional method to achieve these aims there were *Satyagrahas*, "*Morchas*", *Uposhen* and indefinite *Uposhana*. The principal demands were enforcement of the Minimum Wages Act and Equal Renumeration Act.

An agreement was reached on 24/5/87 as the *ashram* agreed to pay the minimum wages to the workers and not to victimize anybody, but in reality this did not happen. The minimum wages were not paid and sixty-one labourers had their services terminated after the agreement. The petition invoked Articles 12, 14, 16, 38, 41, 43 and 46 of the Constitution while asking for the enforcement of labour laws and reinstatement of the sixty-one workers.

The petition was admitted one morning and Justice Dharmadikari asked the government advocate to produce the Labour Commissioner before the Court in three hours. However, when the hearing recommenced in the afternoon, the judge held that the High Court was not the correct forum for a grievance of this nature and directed the petitioners to go to the Industrial Tribunal.

***Cri W P No 1050 of 1987, Bombay***
***Vivek Raghunath Pandit and others* v. *Inspector Incharge, Ganeshpuri Police Station and others***

Another petition was filed under Article 226 of the Constitution, complaining that the workers of Siddhapith Ashram had been prevented from lawfully asserting their rights. Notice had been issued to the the leaders of the workmen under section 111 of the Cr P C, 1973.

In an order D/-13/7/88 by > Justice Pendse and Justice Tipnis The Court held, at 3:

> It is no offence to lead the workmen who desire to achieve their legal rights and which according to the workmen, were denied. It is now an accepted principle that workmen are entitled to hold demonstrations and even go on strike, and enforcement of the legal right cannot be defeated by issuing notice under section 111 against the leaders of the workmen.

## Health and Safety

***W P (C) No 761 of 1986***
***M.K. Sharma and others* v. *Bharat Electronics Ltd. [BEL] and others***

A petition was filed under Article 32 of the Constitution by an employee of BEL and secretary of the Bharat Electronics Union, with the Union as the second petitioner. The petition referred to the Radiation Protection Rules, 1971, and claimed compensation under

Article 21 of the Constitution and the Atomic Energy Act, 1962, for employees of this public sector undertaking who were exposed to the ill-effects of radiation. The manufacture of big radars in BEL involved the use of the Klystron Tube, which emits high density x-rays, harmful to human beings. The petition stated that there was no lead shielding between the workers and the x-rays. It was only when a team of scientists from the Division of Radiological Protection, Bhabha Atomic Research Centre, Bombay visited the plant that the dangers were accidentally discovered. The workers had subsequently petitioned the management to act and asked for medical details and testing information. The results of the investigation were not made known and very few workers were sent for medical tests:

> The petitioners state that they have a right to know about the radiation hazard faced by them and other workers/employees in the respondent No. 1 factory at Ghaziabad. The employees/workers also have a right to get full reports of the test carried out by the scientists of respondent No. 2 in the transmitter assembly room and have a right to get a detailed medical report of the four employees. The petitioners also have a right to know about any other information which the respondent No. 1 has in its possession regarding the said radiation hazard, which may be included in their records, correspondence with the respondent No. 2 or otherwise.

Articles 19(1)(a), 19(1)(e), 19(1)(g), 39(e) and 43 of the Constitution were invoked. The petitioners asked for compensation and that the transmitter assembly room workers be monitored by medical experts for the rest of their lifetime due to exposure to X-rays.

In an order D/-29/4/87 by > Justice Ranganath Misra and Justice G.L. Oza

[reported (1987) 3 SCC 231]

The Court held that no ill-effects of the radiation were found on medical examination of the employees. However, the Court recorded BEL's promise to pay compensation to its workers, if and when any ill-effects were found. The Court directed bi-annual checks for safety and insurance cover for the employees.

☆ ☆ ☆

A writ petition under Article 226 of the Constitution was filed in the Kerala HC in 1993 by advocate A.X. Verghese in the name of Niyamavedi, the law firm of which he was a member. The petition was filed after the advocate read a press report on the death of a girl worker called Sheeja, aged sixteen or seventeen years, under mysterious circumstances. At the same time, five others got infected with an unknown disease. Sheeja was one of the workers brought from South Kerala to Kozhikode to work in a factory. The majority of the workers in the factory were children between the ages of fourteen and sixteen years who were not paid the minimum wages and had to live in a hall which was intended to be a resting place and was damp and cold etc. The death occurred because of violations of the health and safety regulations in the Factories Act. The authorities had inspected the place after the incident but said that they could not do anything because there had been no individual complaints from those affected. The petition asked for a judicial inquiry by a sitting judge, for compensation and for a direction that minimum wages be paid. The case was admitted and notices were issued.[16]

## The Rest of the Cases

***C O No 3270(W) of 1988, Calcutta***
***Sand Carrier's Owners' Union and others* v. *Board of Trustees for the Port of Calcutta and others***

A petition was filed under Article 226 of the Constitution by an association of truck owners, challenging the enhancement of the dock permit fee in respect of vehicles operating inside the dock area.

In an order D/-21/4/89 by Justice B.P. Banerjee
[reported AIR 1990 Cal 176]

The maintainability of the petition was questioned by the respondents, and the Court noted that normally, at 179:

> The writ application can only be filed by the person concerned whose legal right has been affected by the action of the respondents. There may be cases where a large number of persons are affected by a common order and such a composite application is also maintainable when a common order is

16 A.X. Verghese, interview, Kochi, September, 1993.

> challenged on any ground. In the instant case, the writ application was filed by three different associations out of which two were registered and one unregistered, and the members of the association are unascertained or in other words, not disclosed in the writ application. The writ application can be filed by the persons affected and there may be cases where the writ application is maintainable by any third party as public interest litigation... In such cases the person concerned should not have any interest in the matter but he can espouse the cause of the other but the condition is that the persons concerned for whose benefit the writ application is filed, must be specially socially and/or economically backward and not aware of their rights.

The Court summarized the law relating to standing, discussing individual standing, statutory standing, public interest and citizen participation, and representative or class actions. Noting that one of the petitioners was an unincorporated association, the Court held at 177-78:

> The members of such an association may be affected by a common order and may have common grievance, but for the purpose of enforcing the rights of the members, a writ petition at the instance of such association is not maintainable. The door of the writ court could be made open at the instance of persons and authorities under the aforesaid four categories and to hold that every Tom, Dick and Harry can move the writ application would render the standing requirement meaningless and would introduce a procedure which is not judicially recognized.
>
> In the instant case, no right has been conferred on the association of truck owners under any law, and they have no individual standing. They cannot move the writ application as a public interest litigation or in a representative character.

The Court went on to clarify, at 183:

> In my view, the public interest litigation can only be moved where a section or whole community is involved with such an organization and where the persons concerned for whose benefit it is moved, are socially and educationally backward and are not aware of their legal rights.

The petition was dismissed *in limine* because the requirements of *locus standi* were not fulfilled.

# CASE CHAPTER 7

# Bonded Labour

## Framing the Issue

The cases in this chapter are categorized as: the Bandhua Mukti Morcha cases; the Raipur cases; the Thane cases; the rest of the cases. All the cases invoke the Bonded Labour System (Abolition) Act, 1976, which was enacted to give effect to Article 23 of the Constitution by providing for the release and rehabilitation of bonded labourers.[1] The Act states that a bonded labourer is one who has incurred a bonded debt under the bonded labour system. Section 2(g) defines the bonded labour system as operating when the labourer works under certain conditions:

(i) in consideration of an advance obtained by him or by any of his lineal descendants (whether or not such advance is evidenced by any document) and in consideration of the interest, if any, due on such advance, or

(ii) in pursuance of any customary or social obligation, or

(iii) in pursuance of an obligation devolving on him by succession, or

[1] For other cases in which bonded labour has been discussed see the chapter on 'Labour': *Ram Kumar Misra* v. *State of Bihar and others* AIR 1984 SC 537; *Rohit Vasavada and another* v. *General Manager, IFFCO, Kalol and others* 1983(2) GLR (2) 1529; *Labourers Working on Salal Hydro Project* v. *State of Jammu and Kashmir and others* (1983) 2 SCC 181 and (1984) 3 SCC 538.

(iv) for any economic consideration received by him or by any of his lineal ascendants or descendants, or

(v) by reason of his birth in any particular caste or community, he would —

(1) render, by himself, or through any member of his family, or any person dependent on him, labour or service to the creditor, for a specified period or for an unspecified period, either without wages or for nominal wages, or

(2) forfeit the freedom of employment or other means of livelihood for a specified period or for an unspecified period, or

(3) forfeit the right to move freely throughout the territory of India, or

(4) forfeit the right to appropriate or sell at market value any of his property or product of his labour or the labour of a member of his family or any person dependent upon him.

The Act stated that any worker to whom the Inter-State Migrant Workmen (Regulation of Employment and Conditions of Service) Act, 1979, and the Contract Labour (Regulation and Abolition) Act, 1970, would apply and who is working in conditions specified in section 2(g) would be classified as a bonded labourer under the Act. The Act also provided for the establishment of vigilance committees at the district level for the implementation of the Act and for punishments for offenders under the Act.[2]

Bonded labour exists in many industries and can take many forms. In a study of bonded labour in agriculture published in 1981, 26,17,000 bonded labourers were identified in ten states. The study described how 97.5 per cent of the bonded labourers identified were men and 2.3 per cent women.[3] The five most common ways to end

2 Punishments are laid out in Sections 16-20: for enforcement of bonded labour or for advancement of bonded debt—up to three years imprisonment and also a fine up to Rs 2,000; for extraction of bonded labour—up to three years imprisonment and also a fine up to Rs 2,000 (out of which a payment of Rs 5 is to be made to the bonded labourer for each day worked); failure to restore the property of a bonded labourer—up to one year of imprisonment or a fine up to Rs 1,000 or both (out of which a payment of Rs 5 per day is to be made to the bonded labourer for the time that property was not restored); abetment has the same punishment as the offence.

3 See Sarma, Marla, "Bonded Labour in India: A National Survey on the Incidence of Bonded Labour, Final Report, January 1981"; (Academy of Gandhian Studies, Hyderabad, 1981).

up in bondage were detailed as: inter-generational bondage; child bondage;[4] loyalty bondage; bondage through land allotment; and widow bondage. Two types of bondage were identified in the study — customary (traditional) bondage where the relationship between the bonded labourer and the landlord is characterized by a high degree of paternalism and personalization, and modern bondage in which the relationship between debtor and creditor is more impersonal and complex. It was found that bonded labour was a phenomenon which could be structurally identified with the Scheduled Castes and Scheduled Tribes, as 86.6 per cent of the bonded labourers came from the under-privileged sections of Harijans and Adivasis (Scheduled Castes: 61.5 per cent, Scheduled Tribes: 25.1 per cent).

Together with labour laws, the Bonded Labour System (Abolition) Act, 1976, provides legal protection and support for those labourers recognized as bonded labour under the Act. However, it was not until the social action groups, working for the release and rehabilitation of bonded labour, began to petition the Supreme Court that the protection of this Act was used. Nothing had been done for such labourers by the local administration, which at best denied the existence of bonded labour and often supported its use. The labourers themselves, unaware of their rights and unable to engage with the legal process, were not in a position to petition the court. Journalists and organizations took note of the powerlessness of these labourers, and of their legal rights. Approaching the Supreme Court became the only solution to a structurally entrenched problem.

Bandhua Mukti Morcha began working with bonded labour in 1981 and was immediately successful in releasing some of the bonded labourers working in the stone quarries of Haryana. The release of these labourers generated reactions both in Parliament and the media and gave the labourers themselves a sense of their rights.[5] As no money was made available for rehabilitation of the released labourers and the administration was unresponsive, the organization decided that a case should be filed.[6] Hopes about what could be

4 See the section on child labour in the chapter on 'Children'.

5 "Agnivesh rescues bonded labour", *PUCL Bulletin,* Vol. 1, No. 2, May 1981, 20.

6 In addition to the documented cases, other petitions have been filed. W P No. 1628 of 1983 was filed by Bandhua Mukti Morcha in the SC on behalf of bonded brick kiln workers in Haryana.

gained from the Court were high as it was envisaged that the labourers would be identified, released and rehabilitated.

A similar situation arose at about the same time in Thane District of Maharashtra. While working with bonded labourers in 1981, Vivek and Vidyulatta Pandit found that the administration was both apathetic and ignorant about the existence of bonded labour.[7] The Government of Maharashtra, without constituting Vigilance Committees to investigate the existence of bonded labour, claimed that there were no bonded labourers in the state.[8] Through their organization, Vidhayak Sansad, attempts were made to mobilize the administration and the labourers themselves. Unable to make any changes, the Pandits decided to take recourse to law. Two letters were sent to the Court — one asking for the identification of bonded labourers and the other for their release.

In Chattisgarh (Raipur) political and organizational activity developed together as a struggle was begun by bonded labourers and activists both inside and outside the courts. It is only in this group of cases that bonded labourers were themselves parties to the petitions. All the petitions were similar in content as the petitioners are linked through social action groups and organizations.

The definition of bonded labour has given rise to confusion. The administration itself has not been clear about who is a bonded labourer. It was the SC that was then approached for a number of reliefs, first to identify the bonded labourers, then to order their release and provide them with proper rehabilitation.

## Access to Justice

The only major obstacle to gaining access to the courts has been the limited knowledge of the writ jurisdiction of the courts and of the statutory and constitutional provisions available. Letters from Bandhua Mukti Morcha, Vivek Pandit, Neeraja Chaudhary, Mukesh Advani and Hav P. Sivaswamy have been admitted by the Court.

7 When the commissioners appointed by the Court visited the area, they found that the Collector of Thane District was not aware of the Bonded Labour Act and that no provisions for rehabilitation had been made.

8 The denial of the existence of bonded labour was reported in several newspapers of the time including the *Nagpur Times* on 2/1/83.

The letter sent by Mukesh Advani was registered on the basis of a newspaper article. With the encouragement of judges like Justice Bhagwati and the national media, letters were sent to the SC from all over the country.

The cases from Tamil Nadu are an example of the kinds of cases filed outside the SC. Filed by the HCLAC, these petitions have often taken the form of *habeas corpus* petitions, asking for the release of labourers from bondage.

## The Court's Response

The letter sent to the SC in 1981 by Bandhua Mukti Morcha led to one of the most important judgements in PIL. Delivered on 16, December 1983, many months after the hearings had concluded, the main judgement was given by Justice Bhagwati, with concurring judgements by Justice R.S. Pathak and Justice A.N. Sen. Dismissing objections to the admissibility of the petition, the Court stated that there would be a presumption of bondedness if it were found that the labour in question was forced. The Court realized that to ask each labourer to provide proof of debt-bondedness would be untenable, and held that whenever the existence of forced labour is proven, the onus would be on the employer to discredit this claim. After a detailed examination of the relevant enactments, the labourers in question were defined as inter-state migrant labourers as well as bonded labourers. Twenty-one directions were issued outside the scope of the original petition and the state of Haryana was informed of the need to be more responsive and to perform the role of a welfare state. During the course of the litigation the Court monitored its directions and appointed a number of commissions of inquiry. Even with the Court's efforts, the case has been protracted, marked by the continuing intransigence of the employers and the administration.

The appointment of commissions and the resistance of the administration form a common theme that runs throughout the orders. In the later cases filed by Bandhua Mukti Morcha and in the Raipur cases the Court also monitored the progress of the litigations. In *Neeraja Chaudhary* the Court was compelled to monitor the rehabilitation of labourers it had released, noting the terrible choice between freedom and hunger forced upon most of the labourers who had been released. Monitoring rehabilitation became a more onerous task than was anticipated. In the main case filed by Bandhua Mukti Morcha, the Court's limited capacity to monitor its own directions was noted, as it was the administration which was to ensure release and rehabilitation. Implementation of the Act by the establishment of an administrative machinery in the form of vigilance committees was ordered.

Although the terms of reference of the commissions appointed were clearly defined, the method of conducting the inquiry and the conclusions reached often limited the Court's directions. In the inquiry ordered in *Vivek Pandit* all the allegations about the existence of bonded labour were found to be true but no criticisms were directed at the administration or the District Magistrate who was openly flouting provisions of the Act. In *Mukesh Advani*, the inquiry commission appointed found that although there was no bonded labour, labour laws were being flouted, a situation to which the Court responded with hopes and prayers.

That courts are restricted by the information that is made available is most apparent in the case of *Kameshwar Prasad Sharma*. Originally concerned with providing protection and rehabilitation to released bonded labourers, the attention of the Court became focussed on allegations that the petitioner-organization had misappropriated funds. Without examining the matter in detail, the Court accepted in full the report of the District Judge, closed the monitoring of the case and refused to allow the petitioner to file any more applications in the case. Problems relating to the inquiry ordered by the Court also arose in the case filed by the *Chattisgarh Krishak Mazdoor Sangh*. While it is impossible to gauge the real causes of the reluctance to investigate, one can surmise that the inquiry officers were disinclined to antagonize the local administration. Similarly in *T. Chakkalackal*, the administration refused to testify to the existence of bonded labourers despite its earlier declaration.

In spite of the evidentiary problems and the burden of monitoring, one important result of the Court's intervention was the support given to the work of social action groups. In the main judgements in *Bandhua Mukti Morcha* and *Neeraja Chaudhary* the value of the work of such organizations was stressed. As in *Hav P. Sivaswamy* these groups were used to monitor the implementation of the Court's order and given an important role on the vigilance committees.

Another feature of the Court orders in this chapter has been the tendency to direct the states concerned to pay the costs of the investigations ordered by the Court, as in *Upendra* and *Hav P. Sivaswamy*. In *Bandhua Mukti Morcha* (W P No 7139 of 1982) and *Mukesh Advani*, CILAS was asked to pay the costs. The links between legal aid and PIL, both methods of securing access to justice, were used to the advantage of bonded labourers.

## The Contribution of PIL

There have certainly been a number of benefits from using PIL for bonded labourers. In Raipur, it was only after the Court's intervention that the bonded labourers were released for the first time in 1983.[9] Migrant bonded labourers from other states were returned home and there was a widespread feeling that law could be mobilized for the disadvantaged. The growth of activist groups, and credibility lent by successes in the form of Supreme Court judgements meant that more bonded labourers became aware of their rights and the obligations of the state towards them. It is certainly true that without the courts, the Act would not have been implemented at all, nor would its provisions have become known. For the first time bonded labourers were made visible, the activist groups were given the much needed support for their activities, and the Court did have initial success in identifying, releasing and rehabilitating some bonded labourers.

The interpretation of the Bonded Labour System (Abolition) Act, 1976, through the documented PIL orders permitted uncertainties as to what conditions determined the applicability of the Act. In the main judgement in *Bandhua Mukti Morcha*, Justice Bhagwati defined bonded labour as any labour which was forced by economic hardship, but did not define force. As the administration has largely identified bonded labour with physical force, it was felt that indebtedness is not bondedness — a situation that was not helped by the lack of definitional clarity.

The procedural mechanisms for identifying bonded labourers have proven inadequate and innovative methods of manipulating the

9 Sail, K. Rajendra, "Madhya Pradesh: Released bonded labourers form a Trade Union", *PUCL Bulletin*, Vol. 9, No. 4, April 1989 7-9 at 9.

Act have been found.[10] The need for evidence and proof have been a heavy burden on the Supreme Court. Moreover, the rehabilitation payments and packages were not realized for those labourers who were actually released. The courts could only provide a one-time solution. By setting in motion the process of release and rehabilitation, and by monitoring the case, the courts attempted to sensitize the administration. As bonded labour is not just a social or political issue, but also an economic issue, what was needed was a fundamental change in labour relations. That could not be done solely by the courts.

Even though punishments have been provided for by the Act, few bonded labour keepers have been punished.[11] None of the Court orders in PIL have directed that any action be taken by the lower judiciary against those who have flouted the provisions of the Act. In the main judgement in *Bandhua Mukti Morcha*, the Court analysed the Act without mentioning the punishments for crimes committed in relation to bonded labour. It is not just landlords, but the administrators and the legislators themselves who are violating the laws.[12] A study of the Act noted that the cases against bonded labour keepers are kept pending for many years.[13]

10 Another petition (WP (C) No. 13450 of 1983) was filed in the SC by the Santhal Pargana Antyodaya Ashram on behalf of 3457 bonded labourers from three blocks in the Santhal Pargana region of Bihar. The Court appointed an enquiry commission. Documentation from the Ashram described the problems in verification of debt-bondedness, which was done by community workers in the face of opposition from vested interests. Because of the fear instilled by the organization and its support from the SC, the commissioners reported an increase in the prevailing wage. However, since the SC order, many local landlords began enrolling bonded labour so that they could trade in 'rehabilitation aid'. The Ashram reported three cases of well-to-do farmers being officially enrolled as bonded labourers.

11 The first ever reported conviction under the Bonded Labour System (Abolition) Act, 1976, was not until 27/2/87 when a landlord from Thane was sentenced to three months' rigorous imprisonment and fined Rs 2,000. See "3-month RI for landlord", *Indian Express*, 12/3/87; R. Vinayak, "Liberated", *Illustrated Weekly of India* 10/5/ 87; "Loosening the Knot", *India Today*, 15/4/87.

12 A petition was filed in the Karnataka High Court regarding landlords who kept bonded labourers in their field and garden works. One such landlord was an MLA.

13 Pandit, Vivek, "Bonded Labour System: Is there will to abolish it?", New Delhi, 8/2/90. See also Pandit, Vivek, "Bonded Labour and Voluntary Agencies", *People's Action* Vol. 5 No.6 (CAPART) in which Lok Sabha question No. 2842 on 14/3/88 was referred to. Replying to a query about bonded labour, the government stated that 64 bonded labourers in Gujarat and 823 in Kerala were identified and released. Pandit states that not a single case was registered against the culprits.

## The Bandhua Mukti Morcha cases

Petitions filed by Bandhua Mukti Morcha, a social action group set up by Swami Agnivesh and working for the release and rehabilitation of bonded labourers.

### *W P (Crl) No 1366 of 1982*
### *Kameshwar Prasad Sharma, "Slave" President, Bandhua Mukti Morcha, Bihar v. State of Bihar and others*

A petition was filed under Article 32 of the Constitution for the rehabilitation of 445 families of Village Banda in Bihar. The petition also asked that the petitioner and the families be protected from harassment and be removed from the village.

In an order D/-6/5/83 by Justice P.N. Bhagwati and Justice A.N. Sen
[reported 1983 (2) SCALE 160 [897]]
As an interim measure, the Court directed that armed police be used to protect the villagers and plain clothes policemen be used to protect the petitioner.

In an order D/-10/11/83 by Justice P.N. Bhagwati and Justice A.N. Sen
[reported 1983 (2) SCALE 161 [897]]
The Court noted that the State of Bihar had decided to rehabilitate the weaker sections and give them land within six months. It was held that until such rehabilitation was complete, the earlier decision on security would apply. Making a distinction between a decision and its implementation, the Court stated, at 898:

> We would like the state of Bihar to consider favourably the question of implementation of this decision of the government. We have no doubt that the government will also proceed to consider favourably the question of implementation of this decision for the proper rehabilitation of these families in the same spirit in which the government has decided to rehabilitate these 445 families on 22.25 acres of acquired land.

During the course of the litigation, a contempt petition was filed by the petitioners as the respondents had disobeyed the Court's earlier orders. Moreover, the undertaking given by Mr Giridhar Mishra, Joint Secretary, Department of Land Reforms, Government of Bihar, that the families of released bonded labourers would be rehabilitated, had not been adhered to. The Court issued notice on the contempt petition. In response, the State of Bihar said that the orders of the Court regarding implementation had been complied with. In its reply the State of Bihar also contended that the petitioner was at fault and that public funds, given for the construction of housing, had been misappropriated by the petitioner. In response to this accusation, the petitioner filed further allegations against Mr Bhaskar Banerjee, the Land Reforms Commissioner and other officers in Bihar.

***C M P No 3473-3474 of 1991 in W P (Crl) No 1366 of 1982***

In an order D/-19/3/93 by Justice Kuldip Singh and Justice N.M. Kasliwal

[reported 1993 (2) SCALE 31 [127]]

In an earlier order D/-30/7/91 the Court had stated, at 128:

> Ordinarily a petition of this type should not have been entertained. The petitioner narrated a series of events which if found true require a serious view to be taken. The counter-affidavit of the state alleges mis-appropriation of public money by the petitioner himself. Both aspects need investigation. We have considered it appropriate that the matter should be examined by a senior judicial officer of the state. We direct the District Judge, Samastipur, to look into the matter and submit a comprehensive report to this Court.

In the present order, the Court acknowledged the report which had been submitted on 31/1/92. The report stated that 445 houses had been erected, that land distribution had not taken place, that there were irregularities in dealing with government money by the co-operative society and that proper accounts were not maintained, at 129:

> The houses have not been properly distributed. In some cases the son, father, brother etc. are occupying different houses. The petitioner himself is in occupation of two twins (four houses) allotted in the name of two nephews, his brother's wife and himself. All the four houses have been amalgamated within one boundary wall.

The report went on to state that the petitioner received costs for the case from the SC and collected Rs 12 lakhs from the 445 families for litigation costs between 1975 and the time of the report, however no accounts or banking facilities were available. The Court directed the State Government to distribute the houses and land properly and to get the petitioner's accounts, of the Rs 21.25 lakhs spent on construction of houses, examined by the Auditor-General. The Court rejected the petitioner's claim for litigation expenses as frivolous, given that he had collected Rs 12 lakhs, stating, at 131:

> We, therefore, dismiss the contempt petition. We also close the monitoring of this case and direct the Registry not to entertain any miscellaneous petition or interlocutory application in these proceedings.

☆ ☆ ☆

***W P No 2135 of 1982***
***Bandhua Mukti Morcha* v. *Union of India and others***

A letter D/-25/2/82 was sent to Justice Bhagwati claiming that bonded labour was being used in some mines of Faridabad, and that the labourers were migrant workers from MP, Rajasthan and UP. The letter detailed the appalling conditions in which these labourers had to work, without even being paid the minimum wage. Labour laws were being flouted, there were serious injuries, basic facilities were not provided and an illegal system of "Thekedars" or middlemen was common. The labourers mentioned in the letter were working in Cutton, Anagpur and Lakkaarpur areas of Faridabad District in Haryana State. The letter was treated as a writ petition under Article 32 of the Constitution.

In an order D/-16/12/83 by > Justice P.N. Bhagwati, > Justice R.S. Pathak and > Justice A.N. Sen
[reported AIR 1984 SC 802 / (1984) 4 SCC 161]

In a long and detailed order the Court discussed the following enactments:

Bonded Labour System (Abolition) Act, 1976, Ss 2(d), 12
Mines Act, 1952
Inter-State Migrant Workmen (Regulation of Employment and Conditions of Service) Act, 1979
Workmen's Compensation Act, 1923
Payment of Wages Act, 1936
Employees' State Insurance Act, 1948

Employees' Provident Funds and Miscellaneous Provisions Act, 1952

Maternity Benefit Act, 1961

Contract Labour (Regulation and Abolition) Act, 1970

Mines Vocational Training Rules, 1966

Minerals (Vesting of Rights) Act, 1973

Minimum Wages Act, 1948

The Code of Civil Procedure, 1908, Order 26

Supreme Court Rules, 1966, Order 46

Also discussed was the scope of Articles 21, 23, 39, 41, 42, 226 and 256 of the Constitution.

Preliminary objections to the petition were raised. The State of Haryana claimed that the petition should not be allowed as there was no breach of fundamental rights. On this point Justice Bhagwati stated, at 811:

> We can appreciate the anxiety of the mine lessees to restrict the writ petition on any ground available to them, be it hyper-technical or even frivolous, but we find it incomprehensible that the state government should urge such a preliminary objection with a view to stifling at the threshold an inquiry by the Court as to whether the workmen are living in bondage and under inhuman conditions…
>
> The Government and its officers must welcome public interest litigation, because it would provide them [with] an occasion to examine whether the poor and the down-trodden are getting their social and economic entitlements or whether they are continuing to remain victims of deception or exploitation at the hands of strong and powerful sections of the community and whether social and economic justice has become a meaningful reality for them or has remained merely a teasing illusion and a promise of unreality, so that in case the complaint in the public interest litigation is found to be true, they can discharge their constitutional obligation, root out exploitation and injustice and ensure to the weaker sections their rights and entitlements. When the Court entertains public interest litigation, it does not do so in a cavilling spirit or confrontational mood or with a view to tilting at executive authority or seeking to usurp it, but its attempt is only to ensure observance of social and economic rescue programmes,

> legislative as well as executive, framed for the benefit of the have-nots and the handicapped and to protect them against violation of their basic human rights, which is also the constitutional obligation of the executive. The Court is thus merely assisting in the realization of the constitutional objectives.

Justice Bhagwati also noted, at 806:

> It is not uncommon to find that the administration in some states is not willing to admit the existence of bonded labour, even though it exists in their territory and there is incontrovertible evidence that it does so exist. We fail to see why the administration should feel shy in admitting the existence of bonded labour, because it is not the existence of bonded labour that is a slur on the administration but its failure to take necessary steps for the purpose of putting an end to the bonded labour system by quickly identifying, releasing and permanently rehabilitating bonded labourers.

The Court recalled its earlier orders:

In an order D/-26/2/82 the Court issued notice and appointed two advocates, Ashok Srivastava and Ashok Panda to look into the allegations.

In an order D/-5/3/82 the petition came up with another filed by Bandhua Mukti Morcha asking for the release of other bonded labourers. The Court ordered that copies of the Report submitted by the advocates should be supplied to all mine lessees and stone crushers, so that they could reply. The Court also appointed Dr Patwardhan of the Indian Institute of Technology to carry out a social-legal investigation. An investigation on the working conditions was conducted by him and journalist Krishan Mahajan. The report was furnished on 28/6/82. Responding to the findings of this report it was held, in the present order, that the bonded labourers were migrant workers for the purposes of the 1959 Act. It was this report, that the Court relied on when making the present order, analysing, in detail, the issues involved and the various enactments.

Appearing for the respondents, the Advocate-General contended that the labourers had not been proved to be bonded under the Bonded Labour System (Abolition) Act, 1976. Justice Bhagwati noted that if this contention were allowed by the Court it would defeat the object of the Act, at 826:

> … the state authorities as also the employer would be entitled to insist that the bonded labourers must first prove that they are providing forced labour in consideration of an advance or other economic consideration received by them and then only they would be eligible for the benefits provided under the Act and this would make it extremely difficult, if not impossible for the labourers to establish that they are bonded labourers because they would have no evidence …

Accordingly, he held, at 827:

> whenever it is shown that a labourer is made to provide forced labour, the Court would raise a presumption that he is required to do so in consideration of an advance or other economic consideration received by him and he is therefore a bonded labourer. This presumption may be rebutted by the employer and also by the State Government if it so chooses but unless and until satisfactory material is produced for rebutting this presumption, the Court must proceed on the basis that the labourer is a bonded labourer entitled to the benefit of the provisions of the Act. The state government cannot be permitted to repudiate its obligation to identify, release and rehabilitate the bonded labourers on the plea that though the concerned labourers may be providing forced labour, the state government does not owe any obligation to them unless and until they show in an appropriate legal proceeding conducted according to the rules of the adversary system of justice, that they are bonded labourers.

Discussing the need to realize economic and social rights of the majority of people, Justice Bhagwati noted that although the Directive Principles of State Policy are not justiciable, if statutory provisions exist then at least, at 812:

> the State can certainly be obligated to ensure observance of such legislation, for inaction on the part of the state in securing implementation of such legislation would amount to denial of the right to live with human dignity enshrined in Article 21, more so in the context of Article 256 which provides that the

> executive power of every State shall be so exercised as to ensure compliance with the laws made by Parliament and any existing laws which apply in that State.

The importance of the education of workers was stressed by Justice Bhagwati, at 830:

> The knowledge of their rights and entitlements will give them the strength to fight against their employers for securing their legitimate dues and it will go a long way towards reducing, if not eliminating, their exploitation. We have fortunately in our country the Central Board of Workers Education which is entrusted with the function of educating workers in their rights and entitlements.

Also indicated was the importance of non-governmental organizations, at 828:

> non-political social action groups and voluntary agencies and particularly those with a record of honest and competent service for Scheduled Castes and Scheduled Tribes, agricultural labourers and other unorganized workmen should be involved in the task of identification and release of bonded labourers, for it is primarily through such social action groups and voluntary agencies alone that it will be possible to eradicate the bonded labour system, because social action groups and voluntary agencies will be able to penetrate through the secrecy under which very often bonded labourers are required to work and discover the existence of bonded labour and help to identify and release bonded labourers. We would therefore direct the Vigilance Committees as also the District Magistrates to take the assistance of non-political social action groups and voluntary agencies for the purpose of ensuring implementation of the provisions of the Bonded Labour System (Abolition) Act, 1976.

The concept of rehabilitation was discussed, as was the sophisticated scheme set up by the Ministry of Labour, which had not yet been implemented.

Twenty-one directions were issued by the Court, many of them outside the scope of the initial petition. These directions were:

1. That the government of Haryana was to constitute a Vigilance Committee under the 1976 Act, within six weeks.

2. That the government of Haryana was to instruct the District Magistrates to identify bonded labour as a top priority, to map out the areas of concentration of bonded labour and to assign task forces for their identification and release. Labour camps were to be held, with the assistance of the National Labour Institute, to educate the labourers.

3. That the state government, vigilance committees and district magistrates were to take the help of non-political social action groups, and voluntary agencies, to ensure the implementation of the 1976 Act.

4. That the government of Haryana draw up a scheme or programme, within three months, for the rehabilitation of freed bonded labourers, using the guidelines set out by the Government of India, and to implement the scheme or programme to the extent found necessary.

5. That the Central Government and the government of Haryana take all necessary steps to ensure that the minimum wages were paid to the workers of the stone quarries and crushers, within six weeks.

6. In the event that payment of wages is done on a truck basis, the Central Government was to direct the appropriate officer of the Central Enforcement Agency, or any other appropriate authority or officer, to determine the quantity of stone each truck could hold, and to print or inscribe the measurement taken on the truck so that appropriate and adequate wage would be received by the workers for the work done.

7. That the Central Government direct the inspecting officers of the Central Enforcement Agency or any other appropriate inspecting officer to carry out surprise checks at least once a week to ensure that the trucks are not overloaded. Any defaulting mine-owners, thekedars or jamadars were also to be reported to the appropriate authorities, and necessary action initiated.

8. That the Central Government and the government of Haryana ensure that wages were paid directly to the workmen by the mine lessees and stone quarry owners, or if not, that representatives of the lessees, owners and inspecting officers of the Central and State Government carry out periodic checks to ensure that the stipulated wage was being paid to the workers.

9. That the Central Board of Workers Education organize periodic camps near the sites of the stone quarries and crushers to educate

the workers of their rights and benefits as conferred by social welfare and labour laws. The progress made in this was to be reported to the Court at least once in every three months.

10. That the Central Government and the government of Haryana immediately take steps to ensure that the stone crusher owners do not continue to pollute the air, and that they either keep a drum of water above the stone crushing machine to continuously spray the machine, or that they install a dust sucking machine. A compliance report was to be made to this Court on or before 28/2/84.

11. That the Central Government and the government of Haryana ensure that the mine lessees and the stone crusher owners immediately begin to supply at least 2 litres of pure drinking water to each worker every day. This water was to be kept in suitable vessels at shaded and conveniently accessible points and the vessels were to be kept in a clean and hygienic condition, to be emptied, cleaned and filled every day. The government of Haryana was to supervise, strictly, the enforcement of this direction and initiate necessary action in the case of default.

12. That the Central Government and the government of Haryana ensure that the minimum wage is paid to women and/or children who look after the vessels in which the water is kept.

13. That the Central Government and the government of Haryana immediately direct the mine lessees and stone crusher owners to obtain drinking water from any unpolluted source(s) of supply and to transport by tanker with enough frequency to ensure adequate supply. The Chief Administrator, Faridabad Complex, was to set up points from where the mine lessees and stone crusher owners could obtain a supply of potable water for the tankers.

14. That the Central Government and the government of Haryana ensure that conservancy facilities (latrines and urinals) be provided by 15/2/84, under section 20 of the Mines Act, 1952, and rules 33 to 36 of the Mines Rules, 1955.

15. That the Central Government and the government of Haryana take immediate steps to ensure the provision of appropriate and adequate medical and first aid facilities as under section 20 of the Mines Act, 1952 and rules 40 to 45-A of the Mines Rules, 1955, by 31/1/84.

16. That the Central Government and the government of Haryana ensure that every worker blasting with explosives be trained under the Mines Vocational Training Rules, 1966, and carry a first aid outfit while on duty, as required by rule 45 of the Mines Rules, 1955.

17. That the Central Government and the government of Haryana take immediate steps to ensure that proper and adequate medical treatment is provided, free of cost, to the workers and their families by the mine lessees and stone crusher owners. The workers and their families were also to be provided with the cost of transportation, doctor's fees, medicines and hospitalization charges.

18. That the Central Government and the government of Haryana ensure that the provisions of the Maternity Benefit Act, 1961, the Maternity Benefit (Mines and Circus) Rules, 1963, and the Mines Creche Rules, 1966, be implemented, where applicable, by the mine lessees and stone quarry owners.

19. That concerned mine lessee or stone quarry owner immediately report any worker who is injured or becomes ill to the Chief Inspector or Inspecting Officers of the Central Government and/or state government. These officers were to provide the worker with legal assistance to enable a claim of compensation to be made and to ensure that the claim is pursued vigorously and that the amount awarded be secured to the workers.

20. That the Inspecting Officers of the Central and the State Governments visit each stone quarry or stone crusher, at least once a fortnight, to ascertain whether there is any worker who has been injured or is suffering from any illness or disease. If so necessary steps were to be taken immediately for the provision of medical and legal assistance.

21. That if the Central Government and the government of Haryana fail to ensure that the directions given in clauses 11, 13, 14 and 15 be implemented by the mine lessees and the stone crusher owners within the time specified, the obligations shall be carried out by the Central and State Governments.

The Court directed another inquiry to be conducted by Laxmi Dhar Misra, Joint Secretary, Ministry of Labour, Government of India, at 828:

> for the purpose of ascertaining whether any of the labourers working in the stone quarries and stone crushers in Faridabad District are bonded labourers in the light of the law laid down by us in this judgement.

The numbers of contract labourers were also to be analysed by the Commission.

In a concurring order, Justice Pathak expressed certain reservations about the procedure to be followed in PILs, stating, at 842:

> If there is a statute prescribing a judicial procedure governing the particular case the Court must follow such procedure. It is not open to the Court to bypass the statute and evolve a different procedure at variance with it. Where, however, the procedure prescribed by the statute is incomplete or insufficient, it will be open to the Court to supplement it by evolving its own rules. Nonetheless, the supplementary procedure must conform at all stages to the principles of natural justice.

and anticipated problems, at 844:

> The successful implementation of the orders of the Court will depend upon the particular social forces in the backdrop of local history, the prevailing economic pressures, the duration of the stages involved in the implementation, the momentum of success from stage to stage and acceptance of the Court's action at all times by those involved in or affected by it.

The Court later asked Dr Mahavir Jain to report on how far the twenty-one directives had been implemented and the latest position on each particular directive. His report was presented in the Supreme Court in March 1989: *Stone Quarry and Crusher Workers of Faridabad: A Report on the Position of 21 directives of the Supreme Court. A Summary.*

The report noted that the fifty-nine educational camps that had been conducted since January 1984 had failed to fulfil their stated objectives, and that:

> In the process of conducting his field investigation, the commissioner became increasingly aware of the lack of basic facilities such as drinking water, medical, sanitary, educational facilities and the like. He also came to appreciate that the extreme degree of exploitation and ruthlessness by the lease holders of stone quarries and the owners of the crushers was an inherent part of the very structure of this particular industry. So far as the degree of implementation of the 21 directives of the Supreme Court was concerned, the commissioner found a total failure of the central and the state government to carry out the Supreme Court order.

The Report stated that the commissioner had found: oppression for cheap labour, particularly of members of Scheduled Castes and

Scheduled Tribes; evasion of responsibility and lack of accountability in the use of contractors (middlemen); lack of safety provisions; environmental pollution and degradation; an unplanned and unscientific industry; an in-built criminality as the industry was the preserve of economic offenders and thugs. The Report stated that nationalization would not bring about any desired structural reform unless certain norms were upheld, for example the protection of human resources by the registration of all the workers employed to enable employment security, and the provision of legal protection. It was suggested that all the quarry workers be given the status of small producers by the allotment of mining permits to each so that they can sell the mined product directly to the government; that wages needed to be determined not on the usual rate for unskilled workers but to compensate for the grave occupational hazards faced; that safety measures would need to be implemented, mechanization facilitated and there should be a total ban on the operation of any contractor or middleman; that the natural environment in the areas of stone quarries and crushers would need to be protected and restored and national control established over "minor mineral" resources.

In an order D/-21/2/91 by Chief Justice Ranganath Misra, Justice M.M. Punchhi and Justice S.C. Agrawal
[reported 1991 (1) SCALE 79 [295]]
The Court ordered that a Committee be set up immediately comprising the Director-General, Labour Welfare, or a very senior officer from his establishment, the Chief Judicial Magistrate, Faridabad, Mrs Ramachandran, SC advocate, an officer from the Haryana Government not below the rank of Additional District Commissioner, Swami Agnivesh (for the petitioners) and Mr Rohtagi, advocate for the brick-kiln owners, or his nominee. The Court asked the committee to identify the persons claimed to have been bonded labourers and collect all relevant material in respect of them, within six weeks, so as to assist the Court in making further directions about the requirements of the scheme for rehabilitation.

In an order D/-13/8/91 by Justice M.M. Punchhi and Justice S.C. Agrawal
[reported AIR 1992 SC 38]
The Court recounted the history of the case and reviewed the report of the commissioner Laxmi Dhar Misra on the implementation of the twenty-one directions. The Court found implementation to be lacking in all areas and after the report was submitted, noted, at 43:

The petitioner-Morçha came before the Court with a petition alleging that the directions were not being implemented. That led to the appointment of Mr Mahavir Jain of the Faculty of the National Labour Institute to inquire into the measures and report on the degrees to which the 21 directives issued by the Court had been implemented and to present to the Court a clear picture of the issues involved for enabling it to make its own assessment and come to a conclusion as to whether the directions had been or were being implemented.

Moreover any rehabilitation that was done had not been successful because most of the released and rehabilitated bonded labourers came back to the mines. After surveying Jain's report, at 48-49:

The Court's judgement to regulate such matters has inherent limitation. These are not schemes which could be conveniently monitored by a Court — far less can the apex Court keep track of the matter. Its Registry has congestion. To get attention for a matter of this type from the Court is bound to take some time. Human problems in their normal way do not wait for a time schedule for attention. In such circumstances, it should be the obligation of the state which on account of running stone quarries within its area must in various ways be getting benefits to look after these aspects. ...

In these circumstances we call upon the state of Haryana to attend to the needs referred to above of the workmen in a well-considered and systematic way. Since those workmen who will be working there have to be protected from the vagaries of employment and the anxiety of the employer to draw work without adequate payments, the authorities of the state of Haryana must take care to protect the workmen from the hands of the employer by ensuring compliance with the laws and if there be any vacuum in the laws, the state of Haryana should rise to play the role of a welfare State and play it well. In fact there could be a special cess raised against the quarry activities to be specifically utilized by way of return to the industry and there could be a special fund out of which all the amenities referred to above could be provided. What is wanting is not power but the mind and alertness regarding one's duty.

So the Court ended this litigation, at 49:

We, therefore, dispose of this petition by directing that the state of Haryana shall now ensure that the people who have been identified numbering about 2000 are continued in work with the improved conditions of service and facilities as referred to above and such of them who want to go back to their native areas be treated as released from bondage and appropriate action must be taken in accordance with government of India's scheme forthwith. There shall be no order as to costs.

We had called upon the state of Haryana to deposit Rs 20,000 to meet the expenses of the committee appointed by us. The Registry will look into that matter and on the basis of the statement furnished by the committee put up a note within two weeks for giving direction regarding the honorarium to be paid to the members of the committee.

☆ ☆ ☆

***W P No 7139 of 1982***

***Bandhua Mukti Morcha, through Chairman, Swami Agnivesh*** **v.** ***State of Haryana and others***

A petition was filed under Article 32 of the Constitution asking for protection to the bonded labourers in the Kapoori and Mandola mines in Faridabad District of the state of Haryana.

In an order D/-9/5/83 by Justice P.N. Bhagwati, Justice R.S. Pathak and Justice A.N. Sen
[reported 1983 (1) SCALE 121 [543]]
In an earlier order the Court had appointed Jose Verghese and Ghanshayam Pardesi as commissioners to visit the Pitchopa and other mines to ascertain whether there were bonded labourers and what their condition was. The Report stated that most of the workers were bonded labourers from Rajasthan.

In the present order the Court directed that the workers be rehabilitated in Rajasthan and a copy of the Court order was directed to be sent to the District Magistrates there. CILAS was asked to give Pardesi Rs 1,000 for his expenses in carrying out further investigations.

☆ ☆ ☆

***W P No 574 with WP no 633 of 1986***
***Bandhua Mukti Morcha* v. *State of Tamil Nadu***

A petition was filed under Article 32 of the Constitution by an organization working for release and rehabilitation of bonded labourers, complaining of bonded labour being used in Tamil Nadu. Another petition was filed by Mehboob Batcha of the SOCCO Trust in Madurai on the same issue.

In an order D/-16/10/86 by Chief Justice P.N. Bhagwati, Justice V. Khalid and Justice G.L. Oza
[reported 1986 (Supp) SCC 541]
The Court referred to its earlier orders, as a result of which the state of Tamil Nadu evolved a scheme for the rehabilitation of 157 families working in the Kodaikanal hills. The Court expressed its hope that this scheme, which had received the approval of the Sub-Collector, would be implemented. The SC had also appointed a commission, which had reported to the Court. The petition was disposed of.

## The Raipur Cases

A number of related petitions have been filed concerning bonded labourers in the Chattisgarh region of MP, in particular those found in Raipur.

***W P No 13300 of 1983***
***Chattisgarh Krishak Mazdoor Sangh* v. *State of MP and others***

A petition was filed under Article 32 of the Constitution by members of an organization, on behalf of Kamiyas in bonded labour in MP, complaining that they had been maltreated by the local authorities.

In an order D/-30/3/84 by Justice P.N. Bhagwati and Justice R.B. Misra
[reported 1984 (3) SCALE 93 [603]]
The Court had directed that an inquiry be carried out by Navin Chandra of the National Labour Institute. He was then prevented from conducting the inquiry by the Dean of the Institute, Shri H. Pais, who said that he was not obliged to follow the orders of the SC. In a letter to the SC the Dean had also said that the alleged excesses committed by the magistracy and the police in MP should not be investigated. The Court wondered why he had asked for this,

considering that the National Labour Institute should be interested in the rehabilitation and release of bonded labourers. Affidavits from both the Dean and Navin Chandra were requested. The Court directed that Ghanshyam Pardesi, a legal correspondent, carry out the inquiry in place of Navin Chandra. The cost of the inquiry, Rs 5,000, was to be paid by the state of MP with the money already deposited in the Court.

☆ ☆ ☆

***W P (Civil/Cri) No 1071 of 1986***
***Upendra and others* v. *State of MP and another***

A petition was filed for the rehabilitation of bonded labourers from Raipur in Madhya Pradesh. The petition under Article 32 of the Constitution stated that it was not enough just to release bonded labourers.

In an order D/-25/9/86 by Chief Justice P.N. Bhagwati and Justice S. Natarajan
[reported 1986 (Supp) SCC 558]
The Court acknowledged receipt of a counter-affidavit which claimed that rehabilitation was already in operation. A commissioner was appointed to investigate the matter and the case was adjourned pending receipt of the report. Rs 1,000 were directed to be given to the commissioner as costs.

☆ ☆ ☆

***W P (C) No 483 of 1987 (for preliminary hearing) with W P Nos 927-28, 1185, 1479-82 of 1987 (for preliminary hearing) (Balram* v. *State of MP) with W P Nos 1337-45 of 1987 (for preliminary hearing) (Girdhari* v. *State of MP) with W P No 796 of 1986 (U. Prasad* v. *State of Bihar) with W P Nos 1679-84 of 1987 (for preliminary hearing) (Gopal* v. *State of MP) with W P Nos 87-88 of 1988 (for preliminary hearing) (Rasika* v. *State of MP)***
***Rajinder K. Sail* v. *State of MP***

A number of petitions had been filed under Article 32 of the Constitution regarding the rehabilitation of bonded labourers from Raipur, MP. The main petition was in the form of a letter from an activist of the PUCL, who was associated with Bandhua Mukti Morcha.

In an order D/-12/4/88 by Chief Justice R.S. Pathak, Justice S. Natarajan and Justice M.N. Venkatachaliah
[reported 1988 (1) SCALE 176]
In an earlier order the Court had appointed a commissioner to look into the case, who had subsequently submitted a report stating that a list of bonded labourers had been prepared by the government. Out of the 4,226 labourers claimed to be in bondage by Rajinder Sail, 3,441 cases were accepted.

In the present order, the Court directed the state authorities to take steps for the rehabilitation of released bonded labourers. The Collector of Raipur was directed to submit a report to the Court setting forth in detail the various steps taken by way of rehabilitation and detailing monetary disbursements made to the labourers. The Commissioner was directed to complete the survey of all the villages with the help of the state authorities. In some of the petitions, the Court asked for counter-affidavits to be filed within two weeks, and directed that the matter be listed after two weeks.

A civil miscellaneous petition was filed in April 1989 in W P No 483 of 1987 by the PUCL, the Bonded Liberation Front and Jan Jagriti Kendra raising the issue of rehabilitation of 4000 released bonded labourers in Raipur.

***W P No 483 of 1987***

In an order D/-3/6/89
The Court provided interim relief for the released labourers by directing the State of MP to pay a sustenance allowance of Rs 200 per month for the months of May and June. The Court also requested that the commissioner of the Court make a local investigation to ascertain as to how many of the freed labourers (in W P No 483 of 1987) had been rehabilitated and provided with Rs 6,250 from central government.[14]

***W P Nos 927-28 of 1987 and 1185 & 1679-82 of 1987 and 483 of 1987 and 1120 of 1987 and 1469 of 1986***
***Balram and others v. State of MP etc.***

In an order D/-26/9/89 by Justice Ranganath Misra and Justice M.N. Venkatachaliah
[reported 1989 (2) SCALE 125 [667]]

14 Sail, K. Rajendra "Letters: Judiciary Proposes- Executive Disposes", *The Lawyers*, July 1989, 3.

In an earlier order D/-13/7/89, the Court had stated, at 667:

> Shri P.V. Rajagopal has been acting as commissioner in this area regarding implementation of the Act and the Rules. He is requested to have a local investigation to ascertain as to how many out of the 3949 free labourers have been provided the benefit of the scheme particularly in relation to payment of Rs 6,250 to each of the rehabilitated persons to this Court within 4 weeks from now. Shri Rajagopal shall give preference to this investigation as the Court intends to dispose of this matter before 15th August, 1989.

More reports were submitted regarding three blocks in Raipur area and details were given to the Court on the number of bonded labourers released and the payments made to them. It was noted, at 668:

> The report clearly indicates that the proper attention has not been bestowed on rehabilitation of the bonded labourers who have been released through Court.

The Additional Collector was directed to ensure that rehabilitation and money reaches the released labourers. He was also directed to open bank accounts for those who desire one and to issue certificates of payment to those who do not, within four weeks.

## The Thane Cases

***W P No 1503 of 1984***
***Vivek Pandit v. State of Maharashtra***

A long, thirty-nine page letter was sent to the Supreme Court by a founder member of two organizations working for the release and rehabilitation of bonded labourers. The letter was registered as a writ petition under Article 32 of the Constitution. The Court was asked to ensure the release of bonded labourers in Thane District as subtle obstacles had been placed by the labour and revenue authorities and the police preventing the voluntary organizations from doing release work. The letter gave a detailed explanation of how the system of bondage worked and how detection work had been started by the

Vidhayak Sansad and Shramjeevi Sangathana. The problems that arose were documented, for example, that goondas of landowners had come to the office of the organizations, threatened and abused the people there and physically assaulted the petitioner. The letter described how the case lodged against these landowners had been adjourned three times and that the proceedings had then been dropped because of doubts about whether the Court would be able to resolve the cases efficiently. The letter claimed that the authorities were ignorant of the existence of the Bonded Labour System (Abolition) Act, 1976. The Vidhayak Sansad and Shramjeevi Sangathana had already released about 300 bonded labourers and details were given of their identification and release. Incidents of resistance to the release of labour in bondage by individual harassment, for example, by local politicians, were cited, as were incidents of oppression by the Police Patil. Other details were given: of the Sarpanch Dahisar's efforts to instigate villagers against the Vidhayak Sansad, of the harassment of the Vidhayak Sansad when carrying out its educational activities, of the defunct Vigilance Committee constituted under the Bonded Labour System (Abolition) Act, 1976, of the delay in the conduct of trials and of the questionable haste in payments of differential amounts made by labour inspectors to released bonded labourers. Details were also given of efforts to bypass the orders issued by the Chief Minister so that the interest of land grabbers would be served, and of the failure to restore the movable property of the released labourers. The attitude of the district administration was described in the letter as apathetic and hostile, and the petition concluded:

> I am personally of the opinion that the district administration most probably is acting on direct or indirect instructions from the state government.

The petitioner stressed the urgent need to release bonded labourers, because:

> I feel sorry to state here that the highly educated, topmost IAS, District Revenue, Police and Labour authorities are not only refusing to give co-operation but have adopted a somewhat hostile attitude.

The petition asked the Court to release the bonded labourers.

### *W P No 1504 of 1984*
### *Vivek Pandit v. State of Maharashtra*

A second letter was sent along with the first detailing the problems in rehabilitation. The letter was also registered as a writ petition under Article 32 of the Constitution, and asked the Court to direct what had not been done, i.e.:

(a) to confer powers and impose duties on the District Magistrate for efficient implementation of the Bonded Labour System (Abolition) Act, 1976.

(b) To implement the scheme for payment of grant of Rs 4,000 to each freed labourer.

(c) To give priority to granting Integrated Rural Development Programme loan and subsidy on top priority basis.

(d) To grant house sites and construct huts thereon for needy freed labourers on top priority basis.

(e) To provide funds for carrying out repairs of the dilapidated huts of freed labourers who are not required to be provided with house sites and construct huts thereon.

(f) To form co-operatives for running brick kilns.

(g) To finalize already furnished land proposals and to furnish fresh proposals wherever possible.

(h) To carry out land improvement work (i.e. clearing, levelling and bunding) on the government allotted plots of freed labourers under the Employment Guarantee Scheme.

(i) To rehabilitate 292 freed labourers of Palghar Taluka.

Annexed to this letter was a detailed list of those 283 bonded labourers who had already been released by the Vidhayak Sansad and the Shramjeevi Sangathana.

### *W P Nos 1503-1504 of 1984*

In an order D/-8/5/84 by Justice P.N. Bhagwati and Justice D.A. Desai

In W P 1503 of 1984

The Court gave more time for the filing of the affidavit by the state, after noting the miserable plight of the labourers. Professor Sathe and Dr Vasudha Dhagamwar were appointed to visit the area and investigate into the various averments in the writ petitions. The Court directed that full co-operation should be given to them. Rs 5,000 was to be deposited by the State Government to meet their costs, charges and expenses.

In W P No 1504 of 1984

The Court asked for a counter-affidavit.

*Report of the Inquiry Commission on W P No 1503-1504 of 1984* was completed on 15/7/84 and signed by Dr S.P. Sathe and Dr Vasudha Dhagamwar. The commission found:

1. The bonded labour system is in existence in Thane District on a large scale.

2. The identification of bonded labour has been done entirely and solely by social activists and that this fact is acknowledged by government servants both of revenue and labour departments.

3. The government of Maharashtra has declined to confer the necessary powers upon the DM [District Magistrate] under section 10 of the Act.

4. The state has done nothing to rehabilitate bonded labourers *qua* bonded labourers.

5. The prosecution of bonded labour keepers under section 21 of the Act has been dilatory and there have been no convictions.

6. The Vigilance Committee constituted under section 13(2) of the Act does not satisfy the norms laid down under section 13(2) in particular. No social worker directly connected with the liberation of bonded labourers has been nominated on the Vigilance Committee.

That the main averments in the two writ petitions are substantially correct.

## The Rest of the Cases

***W P (Crl) No 1263 of 1982***

***Neeraja Chaudhary* v. *State of MP***

A letter D/-20/9/82 was sent to a judge of the Supreme Court referring to an article written by the petitioner, the civil rights correspondent of *The Statesman*, a national newspaper published on 14/9/82. The reporter had visited three of the villages in MP (Kunda, Pandharia and Bhairavpura) where released bonded labourers were returned to after the Court had ordered their release in a case filed by Bandhua Mukti Morcha.[15] All of the seventy-five released

[15] See *Bandhua Mukti Morcha* v. *Union of India and others* [W P No. 2135 of 1982].

bonded labourers from these villages were from tribal communities and the article stated that none had been rehabilitated six months after their return and that the released labourers were still living in conditions of hardship and were starving. The letter stated that this situation was continuing in spite of directions by the Chief Minister of MP that they should be rehabilitated. In addition to the letter, a regular petition was filed under Article 32 of the Constitution by advocate Gobinda Mukhoty, annexing a copy of Neeraja Chaudhary's article. The petition contended that once these freed bonded labourers had been brought back to their villages, the administration of the state government, thinking that they had discharged their duty, conveniently forgot about the labourers' existence.

In an order D/-8/5/84 by > Justice P.N. Bhagwati and Justice A.N. Sen

[reported AIR 1984 SC 1099 / 1984 (1) SCALE 148 [874]]

Noting that most of the 135 bonded labourers released had not been rehabilitated even after being taken back to villages in MP, the Court stated, at 1100:

> What would they prize more: freedom and liberty with hunger and destitution staring them in the face or some food to satisfy their hunger and the hunger of their near and dear ones, even at the cost of freedom and liberty. The answer is obvious. It is therefore imperative that neither the government nor the Court should be content with securing identification and release of bonded labourers but every effort must be made by them to see that the freed bonded labourers are properly and suitably rehabilitated after their identification and release.

nd went on to note, at 1104:

> There are fortunately in our country a large number of such dedicated social action groups — young men and women inspired by idealism and moved by a passionate and burning zeal to help their fellow beings — whose services can be used for identification, release and rehabilitation of bonded labourers. We would strongly urge upon the state government to include the representatives of such social action groups in the vigilance committees and to give them full support and co-operation. These social action groups may appear to be unorthodox and unconventional and their actions may be

marked by a sense of militancy, but they alone will be able to deliver the goods and it is high time that the state government should start taking their assistance instead of looking at them askance and distrusting them. The vested interests would undoubtedly be against such social action groups which are trying to organize the poor and the oppressed and would try to attack and destroy such social action groups with all the resources at their disposal including filing of false cases and even physical assaults but the State administration should not allow itself to be dominated or influenced by the vested interests and under the guise of maintenance of law and order, harass and oppress the disadvantaged sections of the community whom such social action groups are trying to organize with a view to making them strong and self-reliant and capable of fighting for their rights through the process of law.

The Court directed that a Vigilance Committee be constituted under the 1976 Act for Bilaspur District comprising Sita Ram Kashyap, an advocate from "Lahar" in Janajgeer Tehsil, District Bilaspur, Chandran from "Lahar", near Korba, Bhainsa Munda in District Bilaspur, J.R. Sachdev, of the Prayog Samaj Sevi Sanstha, P.O. Tilda, Neora, District Raipur, MP, 493114.

☆ ☆ ☆

***W P No 1232 of 1982***
***Mukesh Advani* v. *State of MP***

A letter D/-23/9/82 was sent to the Court by advocate Mukesh Advani enclosing a cutting from the *Indian Express*, D/-14/9/82. The article maintained that contractors operating stone quarries at Raisen in Madhya Pradesh recruited the labour force from Tamil Nadu. They worked in debt-bondage, with no weekly holidays. The sanitary conditions were described as deplorable, the workers were not even being paid the minimum wage, and provisions of the Bonded Labour System (Abolition) Act, 1976, were being flouted. The letter was registered as a petition under Article 32 of the Constitution.

In an order D/-2/5/85 by > Justice D.A. Desai and Justice A. Varadarajan
[reported AIR 1985 SC 1363]

The Court had ordered the District Judge to investigate the matter and submit a report. The money for conducting the investigation (Rs 1,000) was to be paid by CILAS. The District Judge reported that although there was no bonded labour in this area, there was a total absence of the implementation of labour laws. The Court disposed of the petition, stating, at 1367:

> As a first step, the notification prescribing the minimum wages has been issued. The law which need not be restated is that no employer can pay less than the minimum wages. But this remains a paper promise unless an effective implementation machinery, not overawed by these wealthy and generally unscrupulous contractors who can spread their tentacles over officials, is set up. We conclude with a hope that such a machinery would be set up jointly with the Union of India and the government of the state of Madhya Pradesh.

☆ ☆ ☆

***W P (Cri) No 1574, 1573, 1187 of 1982***
***Hav P.V. Sivaswamy v. State of TN***

A letter was sent to the Court by the Secretary/Spokesman of the Great War Ex-Services Organization at Tirukkoyilur in South Arcot District of Tamil Nadu. The petitioner complained of bonded labour from Tamil Nadu being used in the stone quarries of Andhra Pradesh and asked for them to be released and rehabilitated under section 4 of the Bonded Labour System (Abolition) Act, 1976. The letter invoked Article 21, 23 and 42 of the Constitution and was registered as a writ petition under Article 32 of the Constitution.

In an order D/-19/8/83 by > Justice P.N. Bhagwati and Justice Sabyasachi Mukharji
[reported 1983 (2) SCALE 45 [240]]
In an earlier order the Court had directed that vigilance committees be set up under the 1976 Act. As this had not been done exhaustively, the Court directed representatives of AWARE, a social action group based in Hyderabad, to ensure the effective implementation of the programme of release and rehabilitation of bonded labourers. The District Judge of Krishna District was directed to submit a report to the Court regarding the bonded labourers, contractors and the advances paid. This was to be done with the help of advocate Mr Bhatkavatchalam.

In an order D/-10/8/88 by Justice Ranganath Misra and Justice M.N. Venkatachaliah
[reported (1988) 4 SCC 466]
The Court reviewed its earlier orders

In an order D/-25/1/83 the Court had directed the District Magistrate, Hyderabad and a representative of AWARE to make a report to the Court within two weeks.

In an order D/-19/8/83 the Court had asked for details of rehabilitation.

In an order D/-20/10/83 the Court placed its hope and trust in the realization of the suggestions put forward by the state government regarding the implementation of labour laws and improvement in the living conditions of the workers in the stone quarries at Kailaspuram in Krishna District. The Court hoped this would be done by the state government without waiting for court directions. The Court noted that a stone quarry falls within the definition of a mine under the Mines Act, 1952, other legislations also applicable to the workers, were the Mines Vocational Training Rules, the Mines Creche Rules, the Minimum Wages Act, as well as the Contract Labour (Regulation and Abolition) Act. Shri Lakshmidhar Mishra, Joint Secretary, Ministry of Labour, Government of India was directed to visit the stone quarries at Kailaspuram and hold an inquiry as to whether these enactments were being observed. The Court acknowledged receipt of three reports from the District Judge of Krishna District, AWARE and Laxmidhar Mishra and directed that copies be given to the respondents.

In an order D/-10/1/84 the counsel for the state of Andhra Pradesh had asked for time to implement the suggestions and recommendations made by Mishra. This was given and the Central Government was directed to ensure that the provisions of the Mines Act, 1952, and connected laws were observed in the stone quarries of Kailasgiri and report on this before the next hearing. The Court had also directed the state of Andhra Pradesh to submit a list of bonded labourers who had been freed so that directions could be given for rehabilitation. The state of Andhra Pradesh stated in its reply that 1417 bonded labourers had been freed.

In an order D/-7/3/84, the Court asked for three separate lists of released bonded labourers repatriated in states of Orissa, Karnataka and Tamil Nadu and directed their rehabilitation as prescribed by the 1976 Act. The Court further held, at 471-2:

> We would also suggest to the states of Tamil Nadu, Karnataka and Orissa that in constituting the vigilance committees which are also to be associated in the work of rehabilitation of freed bonded labourers, they would involve the representatives of social action groups and voluntary agencies operating in these areas and whatever rehabilitation is provided in the presence of a representative of such social action groups or voluntary agencies so as to ensure that the provisions actually reach the hands of such labourers. These three state governments will submit a report to this Court on or before April 13, 1984.

In an order D/-6/10/87 the Court had expressed its surprise that even though three years had elapsed since it had made directions, there had been no compliance by any of the concerned states. The state of Orissa then submitted a report stating that out of the 86 freed bonded labourers, 80 had been rehabilitated. Compliance reports from the states of Karnataka and Tamil Nadu were ordered to be sent to the Court within three weeks, in the absence of which the Court stated that they would be held in contempt of court. Each state was directed to pay Rs 5,000 to the Registry as costs and for condonation of the lapses.

More affidavits were then received by the Court.

In an order D/-11/5/88 the matter was adjourned to 18/7/88 when the state of Karnataka had been ordered to identify bonded labourers and rehabilitate them, at 477:

> Even those on whom the statute casts the responsibility of implementing the provisions of the Act do not appear to be in a situation to respond. It is difficult for the Court to entertain repeated complaints of this type and devote attention by way of monitoring the administration of the Act, as has been done in this case. We are surprised that about three years were necessary to persuade the state of Andhra Pradesh (where bonded labour was identified and from where repatriation was necessary) and the states of Karnataka, Orissa and Tamil Nadu where rehabilitation was to be provided to perform their statutory obligations. Here again Karnataka has not yet done its part.

In the present order the Court noted that even after thirty-eight years of the Constitution, the appropriate consciousness had not been generated. The state of Karnataka was given two months to file an affidavit. The Court recorded its appreciation of Lakshmidhar Misra. No directions were made for costs.

☆ ☆ ☆

***W A No 245 of 1985, Karnataka***
***State of Karnataka and others v. Taluk Labour Union (Regd.)***

This appeal was against the order of a single judge of the Karnataka High Court in W P No 1810 of 1984, D/-9/8/84. A petition had been filed by the Taluk Labour Union and the Project Director of DRDS asking for payments to be made for the rehabilitation of bonded labourers.

In an order D/-11/3/85
The Court held that:

> If a class of bonded labourers in Channagiri Taluk have been denied reliefs to which they are entitled to under the Act, an investigation has to be made in regard to the claims of such persons.

The Union was asked to give names and particulars of those bonded labourers who have been denied benefit of the Bonded Labour System (Abolition) Act, 1976, within one month so that the Project Director, DRDS can secure them relief. The Court stressed the need for quick action as this was a case concerning the unfortunate weaker sections of society. No order was made for costs.

An appeal was then filed in the SC because of the failure of the Karnakata government to implement the order. Even the SC orders were then violated by the state government.[16]

☆ ☆ ☆

***W P No 10237 of 1985***
***T. Chakkalackal v. State of Bihar***

A petition was filed under Article 32 of the Constitution invoking the Bonded Labour System (Abolition) Act, 1976, and complaining

[16] Panchaksharappa "Short note on rehabilitation of released Bonded Labourers in Channagiri Taluk, Shimoga District..." unpublished paper, D/-9/1/90.

of use of bonded labour in West Champaran, Bettiah District, Bihar. The petition, filed by a Jesuit priest of the KR Educational Association, listed 997 bonded labourers.

In an order D/-3/9/85 the SC ordered the release of some labourers and the verification of the status of those remaining.

The Deputy Collector of Bagha had then submitted a list of 350 who were ordered to be released and rehabilitated within four weeks. If this were done, many landlords keeping bonded labourers would have had to be arrested. As no bonded labourers were released, a contempt petition was filed.

The SC then issued notice for contempt of court on the District Magistrate and Deputy Collector for non-compliance.

The administration then claimed that there were no bonded labourers in the district.

In an order D/-14/4/87, the Court directed that the District Judge of West Champaran, B.N. Singh, submit a report to determine within three months whether any or all of the 350 names submitted were those of bonded labourers.[17]

In an order D/-9/1/92 by Justice A.M. Ahmadi and Justice K. Ramaswamy
[reported JT 1992 (1) SC 106]
The Court noted that proceedings in this case had commenced in October 1985, when a vigilance committee was appointed by the Court to deal with bonded labour in West Champaran, Bettiah District, Bihar. In previous Court orders, Mr K.D. Dewan was asked to visit the villages mentioned, to identify bonded labourers and submit a report to the Court.

Out of the 997 labourers alleged to be in bondage, the state of Bihar did not raise any objection with regard to 350. A report was to be submitted by the state of Bihar on these labourers, but it had not done so. Moreover, the District Judge had told the Court that there were no labourers under conditions such as those stipulated under order in Bandhua Mukti Morcha.[18] The Court stated, at 108:

> *Prima facie*, we find it difficult to accept this conclusion reached by the learned District and Sessions Judge.

17 *Ibid.*

18 See above: *Bandhua Mukti Morcha* v. *Union of India and others* [reported AIR 1984 SC 802/(1984) 4 SCC 1611].

Moreover, as both sides agreed that further action needed to be taken, Mr K.B. Saxena, Additional Chief Secretary of the state of Bihar, was appointed to ensure implementation. Advocate Jose Verghese, appearing for the petitioner, was directed to give Mr Saxena a set of orders so that he would know what the Court expected of him. The Court directed that the report was to be submitted within six months.

☆ ☆ ☆

Cases have been filed regarding bonded labour in the Madras HC. Labourers from Salem district, an area with a large number of Scheduled Castes and Scheduled Tribes, are apparently taken to the stone quarries of Andhra Pradesh. Some of the few who escape and return to Salem have been directed to the HCLAC by the police. Cases have been filed through a legal aid advocate under the Bonded Labour System (Abolition) Act, 1976. A list of bonded labourers is given with the petition, usually by relatives of labourers who approached the authorities in Salem. In these cases it seems that invariably the HC has ordered the release of the labourers and in some directed that they be provided with alternative employment. It seems that they are released, "rehabilitated" and later returned to the mines for work. And the cycle begins. Some of these cases were in the name of the High Court Legal Aid Committee — both writ petitions and *habeas corpus* petitions have been filed by the HCLAC.[19]

[19] S.S. Vasudevan, advocate, interview, Madras, April, 93.

# CASE CHAPTER 8

# Urban Space

## Framing the Issue

The problems arising in urban spaces have encompassed a wide range of issues and controversies. This chapter sets out the cases relating to hawkers and street vendors, slum, pavement and hutment dwellers (hereafter referred to as slum dwellers), other housing issues, land and its use, recreational land, and construction and municipal services. Those affected by the petitions filed include all who participate in life in the cities and towns. The competing interests of those at different points on the socio-economic scale are exposed as land is a scarce resource and the policy and statutory framework in which problems are resolved is biased against the poorer sections of the population.

As part of the impetus for the greater organization of hawkers and street vendors in recent years, PIL has provided a starting point for using the legal system. The Court has been an ideal forum to begin a process of increased awareness for these identifiable groups with particularized problems. The first documented case by the *Self Employed Women's Association*, was filed because of the perception that the issue could be managed by the Court. The statutory framework and constitutional safeguards, led activist groups to believe that the problems of vendors and hawkers could be dealt with. Although the case filed by the *Bombay Hawkers' Union* is not apparently a PIL, it has been included since the impetus of the case came from an advocate who used creative evidentiary procedures to mobilize the issue and the Union itself.

Slums fall into two categories: authorized and unauthorized. In the former, the Slums Census, carried out by each local municipal authority, is the basis upon which slum dwellers get political rights, ration cards, electricity and water supplies. Inspite of these provisions, a permanent state of illegality exists within the slums, as licences are not obtained for basic utilities and for trade. The colonies themselves are legally distinct from other types of housing, governed by special enactments and granted little protection. The allocation of land is discretionary upon the State, which, while distributing its largesse, can denotify slums when land is required for other purposes. Unauthorized slums are even less desirable for their residents, as the State is absolved of even minimal obligations.

Inhabited by domestic servants, Class IV employees, scavengers, unorganized and organized labour, slums are essential to city life. However, slum dwellers are in a constant state of immiserization, at the mercy of the police and other authorities. Even when notices of eviction have been issued, these mean little to the inhabitants as there is a constant flux within the slums and little knowledge of legal rights and procedure. Framing the issues for a petition has been a difficult task as the rights of slums dwellers in relation to the State are not absolute. Because of this the daily struggle of slum dwellers is not something that the courts have been asked to, or have even attempted to, deal with. The first major PIL case on slums, and one of the landmark cases in PIL, *Olga Tellis*, was filed in reaction to horrific evictions and to the defencelessness of the evictees. Other cases have tried to prevent the increased poverty caused by evictions — the theft of belongings and the lack of alternative accommodation.[1] In this way the petitioners attempted to carve out rights and have forayed into a legal system, often without the necessary information or documentation, only with the hope of getting temporary and fragmentary relief.

[1] In addition to the cases documented petitions have been filed in the SC asking the Court to prevent evictions and/or to provide alternative accommodation to the residents of slums in Delhi, e.g. Gole Market (in which the demolition of the slum was stayed), Seemapuri, Minto Road and Motia Khan. Such petitions were also filed in the HCs. For example in a Madras case, the Court held, in 1990, that the authorities should not evict slum dwellers without providing them with an alternative site, because of the imperative of due process.

The section on other housing issues has to be seen in tandem with cases in the chapter on Prisons and State Institutions and on Children, as housing encompasses not just slums and residential colonies, but protective homes and custodial institutions. Cases on housing also include petitions for those displaced in rural areas, as seen in the chapter on Environment and Resources. In this group of cases the transition to cases of broader public interest, rather than social action for the "have-nots" is apparent, as PIL has been a mechanism to gain easy access to justice by those who could approach the Court using other legal provisions. In the petitions filed through Common Cause, the petitioners have used PIL as a mechanism to gain quick access to the courts.[2]

Numerous petitions on 'Land and its use' have been filed, mostly in the High Courts. Having unsuccessfully approached the municipal authorities, petitioning the Court in a PIL has been an accessible strategy. The restrictions of standing in statutory provisions and the limited response available from lower courts has increased the tendency to use the writ jurisdiction of the HCs. Unlike in the earlier sections on hawkers, vendors and slum dwellers, on-going mobilization and organization is not a feature of cases relating to land and its allocation. Even organizations like the Bombay Environmental Action Group (BEAG) have had little long term involvement in the issues relating to the dozens of cases it has filed,[3] inspite of a long-standing concern for environmental issues.

Given the high stakes involved, urban spaces are the setting for many conflicts for which PIL has been mobilized. Struggles relating to the allocation of land and construction have been brought to the Court using the simpler procedures provided by PIL. However, cases filed by environmental organizations on urban land use and constructions, have emerged from a broader concern for the evolution of the city itelf. The need to ensure that a city has "lungs" (green spaces) and recreational areas, that the cultural heritage is

[2] At the investigation of Common Cause a petition was filed in the Delhi HC by some house-owners' associations complaining of illegal construction, in which the Court has appointed committees and has directed the authorities to redesign the old bye-laws taking the current realities into consideration.

[3] In two such cases, for example, the Court stayed construction activity. One case challenged the proposed construction plans by the defence services in Colaba, and another challenged the constructions along the coastline of Raigad District, across the harbour from Bombay.

preserved and that the corruption endemic in city life is checked, are concerns that have motivated organizations and individuals to frame issues so that they become amenable to resolution in court. Access to relevant information is vital in order to check specific violations, which have to be demonstrated in a defined legal manner. Links have been made between different petitioning groups, such as Parisar in Pune and BEAG in Bombay, enabling the latter to file cases relating to civic concerns in Pune. The evidentiary problems presented by the poor of access to information, endemic in all the petitions in this chapter, have been lessened when information has been sought and shared with the Court. For example, by ensuring that it provides copies of government orders to the Court, the Consumer Action Group in Madras, has ensured that the Court will heed its petitions.

The theme of competing interests between social and economic classes that emerges when examining the cases, is also apparent between the citizen and the municipality, in the section on municipal services. The courts have been asked to check the incompetence of municipal authorites in maintaining cleanliness and providing basic utilities. In 1980, the case of the *Municipal Council, Ratlam*, was decided upon by the Supreme Court. Although the case is not a PIL, having originated in the Magistrate's Court,[4] it has been included, having been integral to the relaxation of procedural mechanisms that initiated PIL. All the cases on municipal services, and indeed in the chapter as a whole, ask the Court to ensure that the municipality carries out its duties, and many have been filed in the relevant HCs.

The detailed statutory framework for issues relating to urban space have meant that many of the petitions have had to be framed with care. However, the prevalent concern for environmental issues has motivated some of the petitioners to invoke constitutional provisions. In *G.K. Salil*, Article 47 of the Constitution, a Directive Principle of State Policy was invoked.

## Access to Justice

The *locus standi* of the petitioners in the first sections of cases on hawkers, vendors and slum dwellers, has not been questioned. The

[4] See Appendix B, 'Alternative Remedies'.

expansion of the procedural rule of standing had already been set out by the SC. In its judgement in *Olga Tellis*, the SC definitively decided the question of estoppel of fundamental rights by stating that they cannot be suspended. This declaration permitted a petition, alleging violation of fundamental rights, to be filed in the SC in spite of an earlier petition filed in the Bombay HC for the slum dwellers, which had not claimed the violation of fundamental rights. In the same SC judgement, it was also decided that there can be no waiver of a fundamental right.

Before the expansion of standing had been accepted in the judiciary, the HCs questioned the motives of the petitioner in approaching the Court in a PIL, e.g. *S.S. Sobti* along with *Bhaghubhai H. Devani*. It is possible that the courts were either reluctant to foster PIL, or that they were reluctant to foster the kinds of PILs that were being filed. As the SC acknowledged in *Forward Construction Company*, there can be a clash between two public interests and someone always has to benefit.

In its search for new remedies, in *Municipal Council, Ratlam*, the Court widened the scope of its concern and the kinds of issues that would be justiciable. The justiciablity of the petitions filed on behalf of the slum dwellers and hawkers has not been questioned, as glaring violations of fundamental rights have taken place. In other petitions the scope of judicial review of executive action has been upheld. In *Madras Citizens Progressive Council*, the Madras HC upheld the standing of the petitioners when filing a petition in the nature of *vox populi*, the voice of the people.

Among the cases on land and its use is *Sachidanand Pandey*, one of the most important cases on access to justice and jusiticiability. In deciding whether the land in question should be used for a zoo or for a hotel, the Court expressed its fear that its decision may be perceived as interference in matters of public policy by usurping executive and legislative functions. The Court suggested that guidelines be framed which would address the need for PIL litigants and the courts to exercise self-restraint in the kind of issues and cases litigated as PILs. Considering the jusiticiability of deciding the legality of a construction, under PIL, in *T.N. Rugmani*, the Court referred to *Sachidanand Pandey* to hold that while a petitioner may have *bona fides*, the issue raised may not be maintainable.

In *Forward Construction Company*, the SC set an important precedent, when it held that *res judicata* would only apply to a PIL if the earlier litigation was also a PIL. The scope of writ jurisdiction in general and PIL in particular was discussed in a number of these cases. However, the picture that emerges from an examination of the cases on land use and construction is unclear.

In addition to *Municipal Council, Ratlam* and *Bombay Hawkers' Union*, there are other cases which have been included, despite not being PILs for the purpose of this book. While dealing with petitions such as those filed by *Footpath Dukandar New Lajpat Rai Market Patri Union* and *Pramod Kumar*, the court has blurred the boundary between class actions and PIL, and described the petitions as PILs. This has enabled the Court to frame its order with less regard to established forms of legal reasoning — schemes have been framed and new legal remedies devised. In addition to these cases, *Scheduled Caste and Weaker Section Welfare Association (Regd.)* has been included because the SC order, overturned the HC order, by stating that a PIL petition would be appropriate in such a situation.

## The Court's Response

An examination of all the documented cases relating to urban space reveals certain trends. The courts have been unable to provide any lasting relief to slum dwellers, but all the petitions filed on municipal services (drainage, sanitation etc) and recreational land have been allowed and directions issued.

Seen within the broader framework of the cases on labour and bonded labour, the Court's response to problems of hawkers and vendors has been sympathetic. The Court has become involved in monitoring the formulation of schemes and urging a recalcitrant Municipal Corporation into action, as in *Footpath Dukandar New Lajpat Rai Market Patri Union*. Recognizing the importance of the issues involved, the case brought by *Pramod Kumar* was referred to a five judge bench. However, because of the need for evidence when passing orders, discussion in the courtroom, in *Self Employed Women's Association*, focused on establishing the identity of those affected. It is in *Bombay Hawkers' Union* that we see the beginnings of a tendency for the Court to place the prevention of public nuisance on public streets higher on its list of priorities than poverty.

That the pavements were primarily for pedestrians was categorically stated in *Olga Tellis*. In key judgement for PIL, Justice Chandrachud discussed fundamental rights in a way that had not previously been done by the Court and held that fundamental rights cannot be waived. In response to the plea of the petitioners regarding fundamental rights, a new precedent for judicial rhetoric was set in a judgement which held that the right to livelihood was included in the right to life under Article 21 of the Constitution. In reality, nothing was provided for the pavement and slum dwellers themselves. When considering the substantive aspects of the case, the Court was less innovative. While acknowledging that the evidence before it was insufficient, the Court did not address the need for it to use reliable data. The arguments put forward by advocate Indira Jaising were not referred to, and after expressing deep concern about the situation of pavement dwellers, the Court did not even allow them the right to be heard before being evicted. It was held that any slum could be moved if the land occupied was needed for a "public purpose". Thus the Court's declaration on fundamental rights was not translated into concrete relief or into the formulation of rights and duties in relation to the pavement dwellers. Even if the Court had ordcred some specific reliefs, by the time the judgement was given they would have been redundant. Four years had lapsed since the evictions were carried out.

Litigating for pavement dwellers after the *Olga Tellis* judgement, a worker of the Society for the Promotion of Area Resources Centres (SPARC) in Bombay, noted when interviewed in 1992:

> Right after Olga Tellis did a census in 1985, we learnt from Olga Tellis not to go straight to the court, of course. The judgement had declared that the right to life included the right to livelihood, but in the judgement the court declared that these pavement dwellers were illegal. There was nothing before saying they are illegal, and this ambivalent situation was better.

The judgement has effectively prevented SPARC from being able to challenge eviction, so the activists focused on the theft of the belongings of the evictees, by employees of the municipality. In an unprecedented move in the case of *Nazamunissa Shaukat Ali*, Justice Manohar took evidence and allowed the petition.

Inspite of her horror at the injustices, Justice Manohar was unable to do anything except provide specific relief — guidelines covering the conduct of future evictions were not framed. The conduct of law enforcement officials and other state agents has not been considered in any of the orders.

Much of the ligitation on slums has centred upon factual disputes, which are difficult to decide definitively. Stay orders have been passed preventing evictions, and the Court has defined the length of residence in a slum as a factor which determines rehousing. The Court has conferred discretion upon the the state governments and municipalities, effectively empowering the same officials described as offenders in the petitions. A few legal developments have occurred, for example the Court modified the stance taken in *Olga Tellis*, when after consideration of the Directive Principles of State Policy it held, in *Scheduled Caste and Weaker Section Welfare Association*, that slum dwellers do have a right to be heard. In the case of the *Slum Dwellers of Slamagar*, the SC held that slum dwellers were to be moved to sites located at reasonable distance from the place of employment of its residents. However, when examined in the context of the eviction of slum dwellers in Bhubaneshwar under the orders of the Orissa HC, these orders tell a different story. The evictions were ordered to ensure that land could be made available to MLAs, MPs, Ministers and High Court judges. Moreover, in another order in 1989, the SC noted:

> It is not possible for this Court to say that whether there would be greater injury to public interest by the removal of the unauthorized hutment dwellers or by preventing the Port Trust from putting its own land to proper use.[5]

The courts have been more sympathetic to environmental considerations than the needs of slum dwellers, as demonstrated by the case brought by the *Parisar Society Ltd.* In *V. Lakshmipathy*, even without having received any affidavits from the respondents, the Court held the State accountable for the existence of pollution. The cases on recreational land were decided upon environemntal considerations. The Court has given detailed judgements on the regulations governing land use. Envisioning promenades in the local park, in *D.D. Vyas*, and ensuring that public land is put to correct use in the context of statutory provisions, the Court has been strident about the need to protect the environment. It was only in the case of *Sachidanand Pandey* that the Court considered the need to encourage tourism to be the primary consideration, overriding concerns for the environment.[6]

In *T. Damodhar Rao*, the scope of the right to life under Article 21 of the Constitution was further expanded to include the right not to be slowly poisoned by a polluted atmosphere. In this case the Court noted that, because of the development of environmental law, Article 21 of the Constitution had been distanced from the preoccupation with the individual, echoing a concept that had been introduced in *Municipal Council, Ratlam*. Even in some of the orders on land use and constructions, which are characterized by

5 See 'Environment and Resources' in volume two.

6 *Ram Prasad Yadav (Deceased) and Bombay Mineral and Allied Industries Employees' Union and Bombay Coal and Coke Workers' Union v. Chairman, Bombay Port Trust and others*; (1989) 2 SCC 378 at 381-382.

detailed discussion of statutory and constitutional provisions, the scope of environmental concerns was evident, for example, in the response to the petitions filed by the Palani Hills Conservation Council.

## The Contribution of PIL

The judgements on hawkers and vendors in PIL have sparked off a series of cases in the Supreme Court. Brought as class actions, these cases have elaborately decided upon the rights and duties of the hawkers/vendors and of the municipalities. The law has advanced beyond PIL as these groups have become more organized and aware of the possibilities of legal action. Whatever the gains, the limitations of legal action for poverty issues is also apparent, for example, in the case of the *Self Employed Women's Association* the repeated harassment of vendors by the police could not be prevented by the Court. This case illustrates the importance of an on-going struggle in which the use of law has only been one element. As the petitions are still pending in the Court, and ensuring implementation of the orders has been difficult, other aspects of SEWA's work have been given greater emphasis. Alternative sites were found for some of the vendors, police brutality was resisted through demonstrations and much work has been done to increase awareness. Details of a petition on behalf of the street vendors in Raipur highlights the sharply polarized interests dealt with in this chapter:

> The Raipur Municipal Corporation has started the eviction of small shop-keepers and vendors for "illegal encroachment". Armed with an order from the M.P. High Court, and misinterpreting the *Olga Tellis* case judgement of the Supreme Court, the Municipal Administrator, Ajay Nath, and the Commissioner R.D. Pandey, have rendered many self-employed people jobless and site-less. In the name of "beautifying the city" the administration has discriminated in favour of the rich and powerful in the city. While on the one hand, small vendors have been shifted to Shastri Bazar, the rich business community's "illegal encroachment" particularly at Sadar Bazar has been spared by the Raipur Municipal Corporation.[7]

[7] PUCL & DR (Raipur), "Letters: Ruthless Demolitions in Raipur", *The Lawyers*, July-August 1987, 4.

The Court has not applied itself to the problems of slums, and has confined itself to piecemeal relief. Having been defined as illegal, the legal position of pavement dwellers has often been worsened by legal intervention on their behalf. Moreover, for those working in slums, like SPARC, litigation has been an intolerable burden. Some educational benefit has been gained from the slum cases, as the severe limitations of legal action have been learnt, and as a method of getting immediate relief, like the stay of evictions, PIL has been a useful strategy. The significant legal statements are to be found in *Olga Tellis*, as the Court's pronouncements on fundamental rights have been widely quoted. However, the endemic poverty that has led to the formation of slums has not been mentioned by the courts, and the continual immiserization and criminalization of slum dwellers has never been addressed:

> Since the main reason why most of the undertrials are in jail is because they have not been able to avail of the bail order, the Lawyers Collective has set up a network of lawyers practising in Metropolitan Magistrates courts all over the city, to appear on behalf of those who are unrepresented. They attempt to release them on personal bond and then to see that they are represented at the trial stage. One problem is that most undertrials are "homeless". They do not have a permanent address and live on pavements, slums or at a railway station. Since 50 per cent of the population of Bombay lives in slums, this should not be surprising, but for the law this means they do not have a permanent place of residence, though they have been born and brought up on the pavements.[8]

Thus, in the clash between interests, PIL has not benefitted those in the greatest need of judicial intervention. It has however encouraged the courts to be responsive to the environmental concerns for urban space. This has been apparent in the case of the Sassoon fish harbour in Bombay — after the Court stayed construction, the project was amended to make a provision for a garden. However, the parameters of concern for PIL have been recognized. For example, the judgement in *Sachidanand Pandey*,

[8] Gopinath, Deepti, "Warrants Attention: Prison Rights Project", *The Lawyers*, Vol. 2, No. 10, October 1987, 16-17 at 16- 17.

has had far reaching effects, and has been referred to on a number of occasions in support of the dismissal of a petition as unsuitable for adjudication by the courts.

PIL has made little difference for those who wish to litigate on land use and construction issues, unless the petition raised an environmental angle. Once access to justice has been gained, these cases have been dealt as regular petitions. In two important judgements, in the cases filed by the Bombay Environmental Action Group against the Pune Cantonment Board, the Court held that access to information must be provided, not just to the group in question but to any social action group or interest group or pressure group. It is now possible for any such group to demand to see any sanction, grant or plan approved by the local authority. Given that the municipality is involved in every aspect of urban life, being able to provide the Court with proof that regulations are being flouted increases the chance of a favourable verdict.

Even in the cases filed by organizations in this chapter, concrete details have not been available on the implementation of Court judgements. However, this is one area of concern in which the petitioner can see if the Court's directions have been carried out, for example, if a slum has been cleared or if a building has been constructed.

## Hawkers and Street Vendors

### *W P No 89 of 1982*

### *Self Employed Women's Association and others v. Municipal Corporation of Ahmedabad and others*

A petition was filed under Article 32 of the Constitution by a trade union based in Ahmedabad regarding the vegetable vendors of Manek Chowk and the hawkers of S.T. Station Market in Ahmedabad. They had been evicted by the Municipal Corporation and heavy fines/removal charges of Rs 12.50 per week had been imposed on them. The petition stated that the vendors and hawkers were harassed and unnecessarily prosecuted under the Bombay Municipal Corporation Act, 1949 and the Bombay Police Act, 1951. They had been selling vegetables in Manek Chowk for generations, but with the expansion of the city of Ahmedabad, new laws and regulations meant that they were deemed to be "encroachers" into traffic space. A struggle ensued lasting a number of years during which time the police attempted to extort bribes. When payment was not made, the vendors became the victims of police harassment. It was then that this petition was filed against the Municipal Commissioner, the Police Commissioner and the state of Gujarat, claiming that by denying the petitioners' licences, the Municipality was violating their fundamental right to trade.

The way in which this issue came to Court is interesting. Ela Bhatt, the founder of SEWA, was invited to a meeting of CILAS by Justice Bhagwati in 1981. Unable to attend, she sent a letter of refusal, in which she questioned the rationale of a legal aid programme, stating that the necessary laws do not exist and those laws which do exist are anti-poor and anti-employment. She cited the struggle of the Manek Chowk hawkers as an example of the way in which laws take away rights. Justice Bhagwati treated this letter as a writ petition. Having already heard of the Bombay Hawker's case in which Indira Jaising was appearing, Ela Bhatt then requested this advocate to appear for SEWA.

In an order D/-17/12/86 by Chief Justice P.N. Bhagwati and Justice G.L. Oza
[reported 1986 (2) SCALE 291 [1254]]
The Court ordered that certificates be issued that would serve as temporary licences until alternative accommodation was given to enable the vendors and hawkers to ply their trade. It was held that members of SEWA were entitled to carry on vending vegetables at the place where they had been doing so. The Court stated that of the 218 families of vegetable vendors covered by an earlier order D/-16/8/84 which provided for the issuance of temporary licences, 186 names had been agreed upon by both the Municipal Council and SEWA, and that the remaining 32 names were to be identified by mutual agreement between the Corporation and SEWA. It was held that if any female vegetable vendor, within this category of 32 persons, were not available either on account of death or any other reason, a member of the family of such person shall be issued a temporary licence within three weeks. The Court made a provision that if the family of the female vendor were also not available then the Municipal Corporation was to allow any other woman to carry on vending vegetables upon agreement between SEWA and the Municipal Corporation. It was pointed out that SEWA had already

collected Rs 200 per person. This was directed to be transferred into a joint account in the names of SEWA and the Municipal Corporation and was to be used to make the necessary arrangements and for the welfare of the vendors. Costs of Rs 1,000 were to be paid by the Municipal Corporation to SEWA.

***Spl Crl A No 1265 of 1987, Gujarat***
***SEWA and another* v. *Commissioner of Police and another***

A petition was filed under Article 226 of the Constitution, invoking sections 482 and 483 of the Criminal Procedure Code, 1973 and the Bombay Police Act, 1951. The petitioners asked that the criminal proceedings initiated against SEWA and certain of its members be dropped and to stay further harassment by the initiation of criminal proceedings. The petition referred to the SC order D/-16/8/84 in W P No 89 of 1982, which said that no prosecutions should be made under the 1951 Act.

An application filed by SEWA complained of the repeated harassment by the police of vegetable vendors in Ahmedabad, inspite of 281 vendors being granted relief by the SC in W P No 89 of 1982. The petitioners asked for particular warrants of arrest to be dropped.

☆ ☆ ☆

***W P Nos 5602-5605 of 1983***
***Bombay Hawkers' Union and others* v. *Bombay Municipal Corporation and others***

A petition was filed by a trade union, its President and three hawkers from Bombay. The petition invoked Article 19(1)(g) and 19(6) of the Constitution and sections 313, 314A, 314(3) and 497 of the Bombay Municipal Corporation Act, 1888. The petition described how out of 1,50,000 hawkers in the city of Bombay, there were three distinguishable types: those with four-wheeled carts, those who squat on the streets and those who have stalls. The petitioner claimed that hawkers have a fundamental right to carry on their business and therefore the provisions of the 1888 Act are unlawful, arbitrary and void, since they confer powers to refuse to grant/renew licences and to remove goods.

The case for the Union was defended by advocate Indira Jaising, who used a unique strategy before the Court. The Bombay Municipality had put half-page advertisements in newspapers

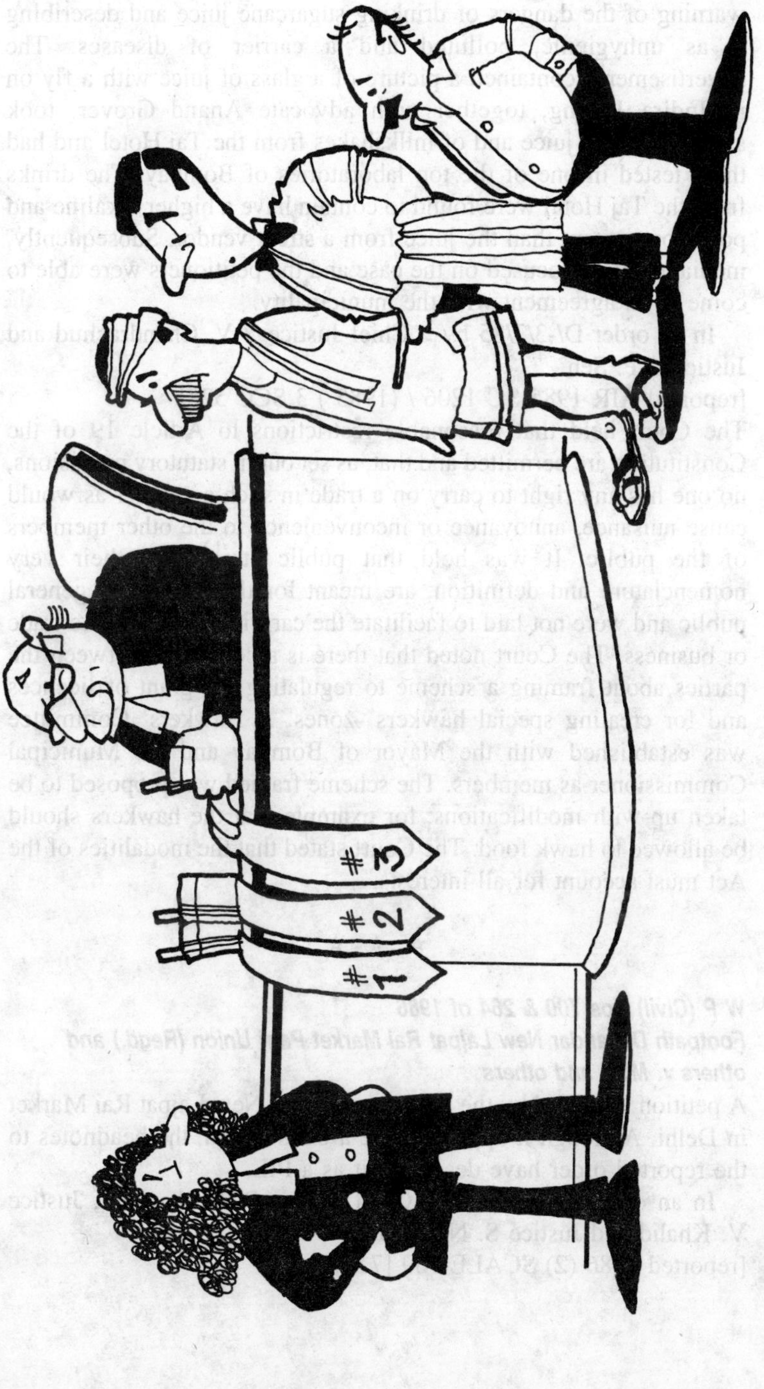
#1
#2
#3

warning of the dangers of drinking sugarcane juice and describing it as unhygienic, polluted and a carrier of diseases. The advertisements contained a picture of a glass of juice with a fly on it. Indira Jaising, together with advocate Anand Grover, took samples of this juice and of milkshakes from the Taj Hotel and had them tested in one of the top laboratories of Bombay. The drinks from the Taj Hotel were found to contain have a higher alkaline and pollution content than the juice from a street vendor. Subsequently, media attention focused on the case and the petitioners were able to come to an agreement with the municipality.

In an order D/-3/7/85 by > Chief Justice Y.V. Chandrachud and Justice A.P. Sen
[reported AIR 1985 SC 1206 / (1985 ) 3 SCC 528]
The Court held that reasonable restrictions to Article 19 of the Constitution are permitted and that, as set out in statutory provisions, no one has any right to carry on a trade in such a manner as would cause nuisance, annoyance or inconvenience to the other members of the public. It was held that public streets, by their very nomenclature and definition, are meant for the use of the general public and were not laid to facilitate the carrying on of private trade or business. The Court noted that there is a consensus between the parties about framing a scheme to regulating the grant of licences and for creating special hawkers' zones. A Hawkers' Committee was established with the Mayor of Bombay and the Municipal Commissioner as members. The scheme framed was proposed to be taken up with modifications, for example that the hawkers should be allowed to hawk food. The Court stated that the modalities of the Act must account for all interests.

☆ ☆ ☆

***W P (Civil) Nos 700 & 264 of 1986***
***Footpath Dukandar New Lajpat Rai Market Patri Union (Regd.) and others v. MCD and others***

A petition was filed by the street hawkers of New Lajpat Rai Market in Delhi. Although it appears to be a class action, the headnotes to the reported order have described it as a PIL.

In an order D/-29/9/86 by Chief Justice P.N. Bhagwati, Justice V. Khalid and Justice S. Natarajan
[reported 1986 (2) SCALE 169 [711]]

The Court held that petitioners were not to carry on their business in front of schools in the area one hour before school began and one hour after closing. Inspite of several opportunities, the Court noted that the Municipal Council of Delhi had still not presented a scheme. Describing this as the last adjournment, the Court held that if no scheme was framed then it would grant an interim injunction against the MCD so as to enable the petitioners to carry on their business, stating, at 711:

> We fail to understand why they have taken so much time to formulate the scheme under which the petitioners will not be deprived of their livelihood while at the same time there will be no obstruction to pedestrians and traffic at the points at which there is usually a lot of congestion.

The matter was to be heard on 21/10/86.

☆ ☆ ☆

***Many petitions of 1986 and 1987***
***Pramod Kumar v. NDMC and others***

A petition was filed by the street hawkers in New Delhi. Although it appears to be a class action, the headnotes to the reported order have described it as a PIL.

In an order D/-30/4/87 by Justice E.S. Venkataramiah and Justice V. Khalid
[reported 1987 (1) SCALE 305 [1300]]
The Court held that no hawker shall carry on business within thirty yards from the main gates of Safdarjung or Ram Manohar Lohia Hospital. Other orders of this nature were given and earlier interim orders were modified. The case was referred to a bench of five judges with liberty to request the Chief Justice for an expeditious hearing.

## Slum, Pavement and Hutment Dwellers

***W P Nos 4610-4612 and 5068-5079 of 1981***
***Olga Tellis and others v. Bombay Municipal Corporation and others***

Petitions were filed under Article 32 of the Constitution. In W P Nos 4610-4612 the petitioners were a journalist, Olga Tellis and two pavement dwellers. In W P Nos 5068-79 there were twelve petitioners, five of whom were residents of Kamraj Nagar basti, four were pavement dwellers, one was a member of the People's Union for Civil Liberties (PUCL), one was from a member of the People's Union for Democratic Rights (PUDR) and one was a journalist. On 13/7/81 the Chief Minister, A.R. Antulay, announced that all pavement dwellers in the city of Bombay would be evicted forcibly and deported to their respective places of origin or removed to places outside the city of Bombay. Some dwellings were demolished, including that of one of the petitioners, so the petitions asked that pavement dwellers and basti/slum dwellers should not be evicted without being provided alternative accommodation. The petitions invoked section 115 of the Evidence Act, 1872, the Bombay Municipal Corporation Act 1888 and Articles 19, 21, 37, 39(a) and 41 of the Constitution.

Before the filing of the SC petitions, a petition had been filed under Article 226 of the Constitution in the Bombay HC by the PUCL on 23/7/81 asking for an injunction to stop the deportation of slum dwellers. Reports had appeared in newspapers about Chief Minister Shri Antulay's intention to launch a massive "Pavement Clearance" programme to deport about one lakh pavement dwellers outside city limits:

> Praful Bidwai and Ivan Ferra, two journalists who were in touch with the PUCL contacted Ashok Desai and Darshana Bhogilal, Advocates, late at night on 22nd July, 1981 and informed them that deportation was likely to commence that very night as there was massive police "bandobast". Various police stations were promptly contacted to ascertain what was happening, but the PUCL lawyers were informed that the reason for the police "bandobast" was so far not known. Between 6.00 a.m. and 9.00 a.m. on 23rd July, 1981 on one of the worst days of the monsoon, deportation commenced in pouring rain. Not only the pavement dwellers of Tulsi Pipe Road (Matunga-Mahim), but also the slum dwellers of Kamraj Nagar (Ville Parle, off the Western Express highway) were forcibly herded into State Transport buses which had been lined up 4 deep to prevent escape. Their huts were demolished and their belongings confiscated and dumped into rubbish vans of the Municipal Corporation of Greater Bombay (BMC).

Families were separated, young children and old people died and a woman even delivered a child in one of the buses. On arrival at various distant places such as Bhusaval, Sholapur, etc., the bewildered people were met again with massive police "bandobast" as the GOM [Government of Maharashtra] feared riots. Non-Maharashtrians were given railway tickets to railway junctions in Gujarat, Tamil Nadu, etc.[9]

In response to the eviction methods used, and the defencelessness of the people whose constitutional rights were infringed, the petition was filed. The PUCL did not support the individual's right to construct shelter in disregard of the city's planning regulations, but advocated the adoption and implementation of policies which would ensure an adequate supply of basic shelter in a planned manner and would preclude the possibility of vast numbers of people having to devise solutions to their shelter problem. In its petition the PUCL stated that the removal of existing unauthorized structures should be done in a phased manner, without infringing human rights and the dignity of human beings.

The petition had been admitted and a stay order against the mass deportations was passed immediately, which was to last until the end of the monsoon, i.e. 15/10/81. In the course of the hearing the Government of Maharashtra conceded that deportation was illegal and unconstitutional and gave an undertaking not to deport any pavement or slum dwellers. The advocate for the PUCL made a statement, on behalf of the slum and pavement dwellers, that he was not claiming any fundamental right to live on the pavement. He gave an undertaking to the Court on behalf of the pavement dwellers that they would not resist eviction and demolition of their homes after 15/10/81. The Government of Maharashtra also gave an undertaking to the Court in which it promised not to evict those hutment dwellers who were covered by the 1976 "slum census" unless they were given alternative pitches. An order was also passed permitting the residents of Kamraj Nagar to reconstruct their huts. The petition was disposed of on 14/8/81.

The PUCL then decided to file a comprehensive petition in the Supreme Court as it was felt that the SC was the only forum which could decide the wide-ranging and important issues raised.

9 "Pavement Dwellers: The Shunned and Shunted — Why has the Bombay PUCL gone to the Supreme Court?", *PUCL Bulletin*, Vol. 4, No. 1, January 1984, 5-16.

Meanwhile, journalist Olga Tellis, listening to the PUCL case being argued in the Bombay HC, felt that the rights of the pavement dwellers were being bartered away by the declaration that they had no right to residence, just because they could not afford to buy or rent one. She then wrote a letter to Justice Bhagwati at CILAS pointing out that these people were refugees from rural areas and it is strange that the Indian Constitution, which is one of the lengthiest in the world, has not a word to say about their status. The letter asked the judge if pavement dwellers were stateless or if they had any rights as Indian citizens. This letter was registered as a petition under Article 32 of the Constitution in the SC, after which a proper petition was filed through advocate Indira Jaising.

The petition claimed constitutional rights for the pavement dwellers, stating that fundamental rights should be a reality for 90 per cent of the people — those who have been deprived of adequate buying power. The petition did not ask for alternative accommodation but claimed a right, for the pavement dwellers, to squat on the pavements. The Court was told that if the pavement dwellers were evicted, their transport costs and rent costs would push them below the poverty line and this would be denying them the right to life. Thus, poverty would prevent them from hiring accommodation near their workplaces and that rehousing pavement dwellers in a slum some distance away cannot be a solution. The petitioners contended that the right to life is the right to squat on pavements, otherwise the pavement dwellers would not be able to live.

During the course of arguments in the Court, it was stressed that these people did not move to Bombay because of the "lure of the city" but because of economic compulsion, to eke out a living, of which they were deprived in rural areas, and that therefore their right to live with dignity gives them the right to live on the pavements. With 40 per cent of industry in Maharashtra located in Bombay, Thane and Pune, it was pointed out that migrant workers move to these areas to get work only because of the concentration of industrialization. Documentation by social workers which stated that these workers live on the poverty line, only taking 2400 calories per day, was referred to. In response to the argument by the Government of Maharashtra that pavement dwellers obstruct traffic, the advocate for the petitioner stated that there is a difference between roads and pavements and that during her 40-year stay in Bombay no one had obstructed her walk to work. After a long discussion on the distinction between pavements and roads, the Government of Maharashtra then pointed out that these people are a nuisance, they are filthy, they do their washing on the street, and they are anti-social elements, indulging in activities like distilling of illicit liquor, and prostitution. It was then that the advocate for the petitioner reminded the Court of the duty of the Municipal Corporation to keep the city clean and the way in which this duty was carried out selectively.[10]

In an interview Indira Jaising, the advocate for Olga Tellis, stated:

> Pavement dwellers are the most deprived, the poorest of the poor, with almost nothing they can call their own. They were totally unprepared and defenceless against the police onslaught. If the corporation had carried out its further plans, this would have been one of the largest forced evictions in world history....
>
> This case is significant because it poses very sharply the question of the fundamental rights of the under-privileged. By claiming a right to squat on pavements, we went against all accepted notions of law and legal argument. Though we were making what appeared to be an outrageous claim, we showed that if this claim was refused, the Constitution would be a meaningless document for all those who cannot buy the fundamental rights to reside in the country and to carry on their occupations freely.[11]

After the petition was filed by Olga Tellis, the PUCL suggested that a common strategy be worked out for the case. However, as Olga Tellis intended to argue for a fundamental right to live on the pavement and the PUCL felt that no such right could be claimed, separate petitions were filed

Thus, another petition was filed under Article 32 of the Constitution in August 1981 by the PUCL. The petition identified the lack of a long-term strategy by the Government of Maharashtra and the Bombay Municipal Council as the cause of the problems. Inspite of the existing provisions of the Land Acquisition Act, 1894, the Maharashtra Slum Areas (Improvement, Clearance and Redevelopment) Act, 1971, the Maharashtra Housing and Area

10 Ruth, Madhu, "Two Women Fight A Historic Case", *Manushi*, No. 9, 1981, 8-11.

11 *Ibid.*

Development Act, 1976, and the Urban Land (Ceiling and Regulation) Act, 1976, the petition contended that these statutes had not been effectively utilized for pavement dwellers. The petition used official govenment figures to demostrate that there was sufficient vacant land in Greater Bombay to meet the housing needs of the hutment dweller population.[12]

Both the petitions were admitted in the SC on 19/10/81. From time to time various interim orders were passed to protect the hutments already in existence on the date the petitions were admitted, and a procedure was laid down to determine which huts had come up after that date as these were not protected.[13]

In an order D/-12/1/83 by Chief Justice Y.V. Chandrachud, Justice V.D. Tulzapurkar, Justice S. Murtaza Fazal Ali, Justice O. Chinnappa Reddy and Justice A. Varadarajan

The PUCL petition came up for hearing and the Court unsuccessfully tried to persuade the Government of Maharashtra and the Bombay Municipal Corporation, to look for a solution to the problem. The Court directed the authorities to submit a list of vacant sites under their control which could be conveniently used to house the hutment dwellers and also to produce the survey of hutment dwellers conducted by the Government of Maharashtra, within a period of four weeks.

According to the PUCL, these directions were only implemented in a piece-meal fashion.[14]

In an order D/-10/7/85 by > Chief Justice Y.V. Chandrachud, Justice S. Murtaza Fazal Ali, Justice V.D. Tulzapurkar, Justice O. Chinnappa Reddy and Justice A. Varadarajan
[reported AIR 1986 SC 180]

Referring to the arguments of the respondent that the petition could not lie because of the earlier petition in the Bombay High Court, it was held, at 192-3:

> There can be no estoppel against the Constitution.... No individual can barter away the freedoms conferred upon him by the Constitution. A concession made by him in a proceeding, whether under a mistake of law or otherwise, that

[12] *Ibid.*

[13] *Ibid.*

[14] *Ibid.*

he does not possess or will not enforce any particular fundamental right, cannot create an estoppel against him in that or any other proceeding. Such a concession, if enforced, would defeat the purpose of the Constitution. Therefore, nonwithstanding the fact that the petitioners had conceded in the Bombay High Court that they have no fundamental right to construct hutments on pavements and they will not object to their demolition after October 15, 1981, they are entitled to assert that any such action on the part of public authorities will be in violation of their fundamental rights.

The Court noted the petitioners' claims under Articles 19(1)(e), 19(1)(g) and 21 of the Constitution that, at 190-191:

> it is constitutionally impermissible to characterize the pavement dwellers as "trespassers" because their occupation of pavements arises from economic compulsions....
>
> The pavement and slum dwellers who constitute 50 per cent of the population of Bombay, occupy only 25 per cent of the city's residual land. It is in these circumstances that out of sheer necessity for a bare existence, the petitioners are driven to occupy the pavements and slums. They live in Bombay because they are employed in Bombay and there is no other place where they can live.

The Court held that the right to life includes the right to livelihood and that the procedure established by law under Article 21 of the Constitution must be fair and just, at 193-4:

> If the right to livelihood is not treated as a part of the constitutional right to life, the easiest way of depriving a person of his right to life would be to deprive him of his means of livelihood to the point of abrogation.

The evidentiary problems were noted by the Court, as it was unable to verify the claim that if the slum-dwellers were evicted, they would be deprived of their means of livelihood, at 195:

> It is impossible, in the very nature of things, to gather reliable data on this subject in regard to each individual petition and, none has been furnished to us in that form. That the eviction of a person from a pavement or slum will inevitably lead to the deprivation of his means of livelihood, is a proposition

> which does not have to be established in each individual case. ... It would be unrealistic on our part to reject the petitions on the ground that the petitioners have not adduced evidence.

The Court held, at 197:

> the procedure prescribed by section 314 of the Bombay Municipal Corporation Act for the removal of encroachments on the footpaths or pavements over which the public has right of passage or access, cannot be regarded as unreasonable, unfair or unjust.

The Court noted that section 314 excludes the principles of natural justice, because it does not specify that notice be issued to the encroachers before an encroachment is removed, and stressed that this situation had to be an exception, not a general rule. The Court stated that normally a hearing is required for all procedures and that justice must not only be done but must also be seen to be done. The respondents questioned the petitioners' assertion that the slum/pavement dwellers should be given a hearing when, by living on the pavements, they had committed an offence. On this point the Court noted that though they may be guilty of trespass, they did not intend to "commit an offence or intimidate, insult or annoy any person", as under section 441 of the IPC, 1860. Describing trespass as a tort, the Court demonstrated that even in the Law of Torts though a trespasser may be evicted forcibly, the force used must be no greater than that which is reasonable and appropriate to the occasion. In the facts of the case, however, the Court held, at 202:

> Normally, we would have directed the Municipal Commissioner to afford an opportunity to the petitioners to show why the encroachments committed by them on pavements or footpaths should not be removed. But, the opportunity which was denied by the Commissioner was granted by us in ample measure, both sides having made their contentions elaborately on facts as well as law. Having considered these contentions, we are of the opinion that the Commissioner was justified in directing the removal of the encroachments committed by the petitioners on pavements, footpaths or accessory roads.

The Court directed that no evictions were to take place until one month after the conclusion of the current monsoon season, i.e. 31/10/85, and in the meanwhile, at 202:

> steps may be taken to offer alternative pitches to the pavement dwellers who were or who happened to be censused in 1976. The offer of alternative pitches to such pavement dwellers should be made good in the spirit in which it was made, though we do not propose to make it a condition precedent to the removal of the encroachments committed by them.

The Court also directed that slums in existence for more than twenty years were to be left intact, unless the land is required for a public purpose. For such slums alternative accommodation was to be provided under the "Low Income Scheme Shelter Programme". Meanwhile, the Slum Upgradation Programme was to be implemented without delay. On the broader question of trespass and encroachment, the Court stated that no one has the right to use public property for private purposes, that pavement dwellers cannot encroach by constructing dwellings thereon and that even pedestrians have limited right of passing. It was held, at 197:

> footpaths or pavements are public properties which are intended to serve the convenience of the general public. They are not laid for private use and indeed, their use for a private purpose frustrates the very object for which they are carved out from portions of public streets.

and stated, at 198:

> There is no substance in the argument advanced on behalf of the petitioners that the claim of the pavement dwellers to put up constructions on pavements and that of the pedestrians to make use of the pavements for passing and repassing, are competing claims and that, the former should be preferred to the latter.

Realizing that there could be no short-term solution to the existence of such squatter colonies, the Court concluded that new opportunities for employment needed to be made in the rural sector.

There was no order for costs.

☆ ☆ ☆

***W P No 8927 of 1981 and W P No 9380 of 1981 (G. Kannan v. Tamil Nadu)***

***K. Chandru v. State of Tamil Nadu and others***

A petition was filed under Article 226 of the Constitution invoking Articles 19 and 21 of the Constitution, along with the Tamil Nadu Slum Areas (Improvement and Clearance) Act, 1971 and the Tamil Nadu Land Encroachment Act, 1905. The petition asked for a direction preventing the eviction of pavement dwellers in the City of Madras.

In an order D/-10/7/85 by > Justice Y.V. Chandrachud and Justice S. Murtaza Fazal Ali, Justice V.D. Tulzapurkar, Justice O. Chinnappa Reddy and Justice A. Varadarajan
[reported 1985 (2) SCALE 3 [31]]
The Court stated, at 34:

> We are satisfied, on a careful consideration of the statements contained in the counter-affidavits filed on behalf of the respondents, that the Government of Tamil Nadu has adopted a benevolent and sympathetic policy in regard to the slum dwellers. Steps are being taken for the purpose of improving the slums and wherever they cannot be improved, alternate accommodation is provided to the slum dwellers, before they are evicted. In view of this position, we do not consider it necessary to issue any writ or direction to the Government of Tamil Nadu. We will only express our confidence that the Government will continue to evince the same dynamic interest in the welfare of the pavement dwellers and slum dwellers.

Alternative accommodation was directed to be provided and, because of the late monsoon in Madras, the Court stated that no evictions were to take place before 31/12/85, provided the dwellers could show that they had been living in the slums from before 30/6/77. The Court held that the other slum dwellers, who had been living there for lesser periods, should not to be evicted before 31/12/85 unless the land was required by the state government for an urgent public purpose. There was no order for costs.

☆ ☆ ☆

**Review P No 836 of 1985 in W P No 12771 of 1985 with S L P (Civil) No 16154 of 1985**

**Slum Dwellers of Slamagar and others, Pennurimai Iyakkam v. State of Tamil Nadu**

An appeal was filed in the SC by residents of a slum in Madras who were to be evicted.

In an order D/-6/12/88

The Court referred to the government's assertion that provision was being made for further amenities and facilities for the slum dwellers. It was held that these provisions should provide adequate satisfaction to the petitioners:

> but we may add the further condition that in resettling the slum dwellers in the areas set apart for that purpose the allocation of individual slum dwellers be made with a view to ensuring so far as is practically possible, that the place of resettlement of the slum dwellers is within a reasonable distance from the related places of employment.

☆ ☆ ☆

**W P (C) Nos 11175-77 of 1985**

**Karnataka Kolageri N.S. Sanghatana and others v. State of Karnataka and others**

A petition was filed under Article 32 of the Constitution by an organization working in slums in Bangalore. The petition challenged the slum demolitions carried out in the city of Bangalore, as no alternative was provided. It was contended that the slum-dwellers had been made homeless because the authorities had not discharged their constitutional and statutory obligations to:

(i) evolve a fair, reasonable State plan for organized industrial allocation and growth around urban areas which would eliminate or minimise congestion in urban areas,

(ii) evolve appropriate rural employment guarantees and measures, based on land distribution and on the maximum utilization of the potential of the land, which would ensure maximum employment throughout the year,

(iii) evolve plans for the even and equal distribution of land in urban areas to house different classes and sections of the population, which would mean evolving a need-based and not a wealth-based housing policy.

The petition challenged the constitutional validity of sections 11, 12 and 13 of the Karnataka Slum Areas (Improvement and Clearance) Act, 1973 on the grounds that they violate Articles 14 and 21 of the Constitution. The petition claimed that the demolition and clearance in question had been triggered off by an evening padyatra of the Chief Minister. It was also contended that this decision was an example of State arbitrariness, along with the Chief Minister's announcement that 15 year old slums were going to be cleared without any further State action. The right of residence of the slum dwellers was upheld, and the petition affirmed the constitutional obligations of the State with regard to housing and public health. The SC orders in the cases filed by Olga Tellis, K. Chandru and R. Venkataramani were referred to, along with a petition filed in the Karnataka HC by "Women's Voice" (a parallel organization of KKNSS) together with another organization of construction workers.

Along with other reliefs, the petitioners asked for the records of the case, that no slums be cleared or abolished without a fair and reasonable housing policy, that the city plan be redefined to include effective land redistribution measures, that compensation be given to those who have suffered loss/damage by the clearance, that immediate shelter be provided for those removed from the cleared areas and that no more evictions should take place till there have been orders from the Court.

Annexed to the petition were letters and representations sent by the petitioners to politicians and administrators, which were used to explain the need to file a petition:

> The petitioners have come to this Hon'ble Court having exhausted access to all administrative remedies and having failed to restrain the respondents from continuing to carry on the said unconstitutional and illegal demolition operations.

An application was filed along with the main petition asking for orders against the phased demolition operations in slums that had been taking place since May 1985.

In an order D/-18/7/85

The Court stayed the eviction and demolition activities in the city of Bangalore.

A counter affidavit was filed responding to the petition in detail and disagreeing with a number of the averments made, regarding dates, housing schemes initiated, housing built and the development plan for the city. The respondents claimed that alternative accommodation had been provided to the evictees and asked the Court to vacate the stay order so that they could carry out their statutory duty.

In an order D/-6/9/90
The Court directed the counsel for the petitioners to file a list, within eight weeks, of all the persons who had been thrown out of their homes and forced to leave their possessions in the process of slum clearance and who have remained unrehabilitated. The list was to contain their names, area of occupation, date of displacement, and any other particulars that the counsel may consider relevant.

In an order D/-11/2/91
The court granted a four week extension to the counsel for the petitioners for filing the report.

In mid-1992 a detailed fifty-one page report was submitted to the Court by Mr R. Venkataramani, the counsel for the petitioners.

In an order D/-25/7/92 by Chief Justice Ranganath Misra, Justice M.H. Kania and Justice Kuldip Singh
The full text of the Court order stated:

> A list of the persons who are supposed to be the beneficiaries of a favourable order, if made, in this proceeding has been supplied by Mr Venkataramani. There is a suggestion that instead of our examining the factual aspects involved in the matter if the Karnataka State Legal Aid and Advice Board is required to intervene to dispose of the dispute after adequate enquiry and hearing of parties, the cause of justice would be better served. We find that apart from a legal issue which has been raised, the main dispute is essentially factual. Holding of an enquiry by us in this petition under Article 32 would indeed be difficult. We, therefore, accede to the request of Mr Venkataramani and Mr Veerappa for the state of Karnataka has no serious objection to our doing so. The Karnataka State Legal Aid and Advice Board is directed to look into the grievances of the petitioners after issuing notice to both the parties and giving them adequate opportunity of negotiating in a conciliatory manner the claim of the petitioners be

scrutinized. We take note of the fact that the State Board is presided over by the Law Secretary of the State who is ex-officio Chairman and, therefore, he would be a responsible officer belonging to the judicial side and the one belonging to the State Government. All the factual aspects of the matter may be examined. The legal question is left open, if necessary to be raised again and on that occasion not before this Court but under Article 226 of the Constitution.

All the three respondent institutions were entitled to join in the conciliation proceedings.

Mr Veerappa has assured us that there would be no dislocation excepting rehabilitation, in the meantime.

The writ petitions are disposed of accordingly.

☆ ☆ ☆

***S L P (C) No 7883 of 1985***
***Ram Prasad Yadav (Deceased) and Bombay Mineral and Allied Industries Employees' Union and Bombay Coal and Coke Workers' Union v. Chairman, Bombay Port Trust and others***

An appeal was filed under Article 136 of the Constitution, invoking Article 21 of the Constitution for those who were resident in the hutments of the Bombay Port Trust lands. These lands were cleared in early May 1985 and the huts were demolished.

In an order D/-29/3/89 by Chief Justice R.S. Pathak and Justice M.H. Kania
[reported (1989) 2 SCC 378]

The Court referred to an earlier order in which Justice P.N. Bhagwati and Justice G.L. Oza had appointed a Commission. The report of the Commission stated that 406 families were involved, so the State Government was directed to rehouse only those families who had been in residence for at least two years as on 1/1/81. A total of fifty families qualified and the Court noted, at 380:

> The commissioner, however, stated that it was possible that some of these persons, who had been unable to establish their residence for the aforesaid period, might have been unable to do so because of their poverty, lack of literacy and want of documentary proof.

As the State Policy on rehousing was not applicable to the Port Trust (its land cannot be regarded as public land in the occupation of the government), the Court urged, at 381-2:

> We realize that the problem of hutment dwellers is a human problem and the removal of hutments is bound to cause untold hardship and misery to the occupants. However, on that consideration, we cannot prevent the Bombay Port Trust from putting its land to its own use. It is not possible for this Court to say whether there would be greater injury to public interest by the removal of the unauthorized hutment dwellers or by preventing the Port Trust from putting its own land to proper use. In order to obviate the hardship referred to earlier, although to a limited extent, we direct that even the hutments on the said lands which are not entitled to protection will not be demolished for a period of six months from the date of signing this order. We only hope and trust that it will be possible for the state government or the central government or even the Bombay Port Trust to make some provisions for providing alternative sites at least to some of these hutment dwellers, if not at all.

☆ ☆ ☆

***W P No 2963 of 1986***

A petition was filed under Article 226 of the Constitution in the Bombay HC by SPARC (Society for the Promotion of Area Resources Centres) workers and hutments dwellers whose belongings had been removed in a demolition D/-23/10/86 by the Municipal Corporation of Greater Bombay.

In an order D/-30/10/86 by Justice Sawant

The Court directed the Municipal Corporation to return the belongings.

Similar petitions were filed by SPARC, including:

***W P No 3381 of 1988, Bombay***

***Nazamunissa Shaukat Ali and another v. Municipal Corporation of Greater Bombay and others***

A petition was filed under Article 226 of the Constitution by two hutment dwellers on behalf of themselves and nineteen other pavement dwellers of Sophia Zuber Road through SPARC. On 3/11/88 their huts were demolished and belongings taken away by the Municipal Corporation of Greater Bombay. The petition asked that their belongings be returned to them or that compensation be paid for the loss of their belongings. The petition was filed on 4/11/88.

In an order D/-7/11/88 by Justice Ashok Agarwal
The Court directed:

> Whatever articles belonging to the petitioners are in possession of the municipal officers shall be returned to the petitioners forthwith.

As the respondents refused to comply with the Court order, stating that the belongings could only be returned on 12/11/88 because of the intervening Diwali holidays, the petitioners filed an application in the Court.

In an order D/-8/11/88 by Justice Ashok Agarwal
The Court issued a fresh directive that the Municipal Corporation and its officers should be directed to return the belongings forthwith.

***Notice of Motion No 3098 of 1988 in W P No 3381 of 1988, Bombay***

The respondents denied having taken any belongings, so the petitioners filed this notice of motion on 16/11/88 against the respondents for contempt of court. The petitioners also asked the Court to direct the respondents to return the possessions.

***Notice of Motion No 3098 of 1988 in W P No 3381 of 1988, Bombay***

In a judgement D/-28/4/89 by Justice Sujata Manohar
Referring to the earlier petitions and orders, the Court noted:

> It is the case of SPARC workers who have given evidence in this Motion that on both occasions all the belongings which were taken away were not returned.... The petitioners and SPARC workers apprehended that unless they moved the court immediately, it was likely that the belongings which were taken away in the demolition of 3/11/88 would be similarly sold by the Municipal workers and officers for private gain and the hutment dwellers would be deprived of their belongings.

The Court held that the respondents had wilfully disobeyed the Court's orders on 7/11/88 and 8/11/88 and directed that they pay the petitioners the money equivalent of the belongings which they lost, which amounted to Rs 10,090. It was noted that the hearing of the motion had taken the Court 59 hours and 20 minutes, as evidence had been called for. The Court felt that the evidence of the respondents did not inspire confidence and stated, at 52-3:

> The petitioners have pointed out that fighting this kind of litigation to vindicate their right is an intolerable burden for the hutment dwellers and that I should lay down guidelines under which such hutment dwellers can be protected in future. The invitation, though tempting, must be declined by me. After all the action to be taken by the first respondents in the case of a given demolition will depend very much upon the circumstances of that case, the attitude of the hutment dwellers concerned, assessment of the resistance which they may offer and so on. It does, however, seem that the present case did not require the harsh treatment meted out by the respondents. The 'E' Ward Officers knew that there was a responsible agency working amongst these hutment dwellers. An offer was made that the huts could be voluntarily demolished by the hutment dwellers and material handed over to the Municipal Corporation. The respondents should have availed of this offer. Secondly, adequate opportunity was obviously not given to the hutment dwellers to remove their belongings.... Surely the hutment dwellers could have been treated more humanely and sympathetically. In fact in the present case the conduct of the Municipal officers and workers has been far from satisfactory.

and, at 54:

> the Corporation ought to lay down proper procedure to ensure that when belongings are taken at the time of any demolitiion, a proper record of such belongings is maintained.

The first respondent was directed to pay Rs 15,000 costs together with the Rs 10,090 on or before 15/6/89.

☆ ☆ ☆

***C A No 1401 of 1991***
***Scheduled Caste and Weaker Sections Welfare Association (Regd.) and another v. State of Karnataka and others***

An appeal was filed under Article 136 of the Constitution invoking

Article 21 of the Constitution, the sections 3 and 11 of the Karnataka Slum Areas (Improvement and Clearance) Act, 1973, section 21 of the General Clauses Act, 1897 and section 10 of the Karnataka General Clauses Act. The petition stated that when an area was declared a "slum clearance area", the slum dwellers who were affected by the government's action were not given an opportunity to be heard. Equality and basic human needs were denied as a major part of the slum area was excluded from the operation of the scheme. A single judge of the HC had denied standing to the petitioner, and a division bench of the HC upheld this order.

In an order D/-2/4/91 by Justice A.M. Ahmadi and > Justice M. Fathima Beevi
[reported (1991) 2 SCC 604]
Stating that although the appellants could not be granted statutory standing under section 3 of the 1973 Act, the Court held, at 608:

> This question need not detain us when the law is now settled that in such a situation even a public interest litigation would lie. Appellant 1 — Association—represents the interests of the slum dwellers and appellant 2 himself is one of the residents in the area. The action of the government on the averments made affects a class of persons and if that group of persons is represented by the Association, they have a right to be heard in the matter.

and stated, at 610:

> The object of the statute and the relief that was sought to be conferred are matters to be taken into consideration in such an action.

The Court also noted, at 611:

> It is one of the fundamental rules of our constitutional set-up that every citizen is protected against arbitrary authority by the State or its officers. If there is power to decide and determine to the prejudice of a person, duty to act judicially is implicit in the exercise of such power and the rule of natural justice operates in areas not covered by any law validly made.

Holding that the object of the 1973 Act was harmonious with the Directive Principles of State Policy, the Court stated that the rights of thc slum dwellers would be prejudicially affected if they were not given the right to be heard, at 611:

> The right to be heard in the matter has been acquired by the earlier action of the authority in considering the area for the purpose of the scheme.

The appeal was allowed with no order for costs.

☆ ☆ ☆

A petition was filed under Article 226 of the Constitution in the Madras High Court by the Annai Sathyanagar-part B Hutment Dwellers Welfare Association, represented by its president Mr T. Pannerselvam. The petition sought a direction to the Housing Secretary and Board not to evict the association members without finding an alternative place for them to live in an adjacent area.

In an order in November 1992 by Justice H. Kanakaraj

The HC directed the Government and the Slum Clearance Board to permit the hutment dwellers of Annai Sathyanagar (Part B) near the War Memorial to put up temporary sheds in the same area from where they were evicted on 13/11/92, until further orders. The Court also directed the respondents to provide food and drink to members of the petitioner-association of about 450 families on the day of the order the next day. The Court noted that the State had not responded to the questions raised in the courtroom, nor had it acted according to law.[15]

☆ ☆ ☆

A letter was sent to the Chief Justice of the Supreme Court by Mr Biswapriya Kanungo, President of the Rajdhani Bastibasinda Kalyan Sangha. The SC directed the Orissa HC to treat the letter as a writ petition under Article 226 of the Constitution. The letter detailed the forcible eviction of slum dwellers in Bhubaneshwar.

In an order D/-20/3/90 by Chief Justice Hansaria and Justice R.C. Patnaik

The Court appointed a judicial inquiry into forcible eviction, to be conducted by Mr Sarojkanta Mishra, presiding officer of the Orissa Industrial Tribunal. The report revealed that hundreds of slum

15 "Court pulls up Board for evicting hut-dwellers", *The Hindu*, 17/11/92, quoted in Legal Perspectives No. 25, 73-74.

dwellers were evicted by the state government so that land could be made available to MLAs, MPs, Ministers and High Court judges.

In an order D/-13/4/91

At the instance of G.P. Mohandy, Secretary of the PUCL State Unit, the HC forwarded a similar matter to the same one-man commission for inquiry. This petition had also been filed by a member of the PUCL branch in Cuttack, Mr Biswapriya Kanungo.[16]

## Other Housing Issues

***W P (C) No 557 of 1987***

***Desh Raj Khurana and others v. Delhi Administration***

A petition was filed under Article 32 of the Constitution asking the Court to issue directions to provide shelter for migrants from Punjab. They were living in DDA flats in Jahangirpuri and were in need of a Transit Camp. The petition seems to be a class action, but was described as a PIL in the reported order.

In an order D/-8/5/87 by Chief Justice R.S. Pathak and Justice M.H. Kania

[reported 1987 (1) SCALE 321 [1313]]

Both the lawyers for the petitioner and for the respondent had visited the transit camp at Jahangirpuri and agreed that for the present it was not possible to contemplate the operation of the transit camp as a shelter for these migrants. The Court stated that it was necessary to ensure that the transit camp was in proper condition before the migrants could be shifted from the flats in Jahangirpuri. A.N. Oberoi, Registrar of the SC, was appointed to act as Commissioner to determine whether the camp was ready for use. If ready, the migrants were directed to vacate the DDA flats and shift to the Camp. The Court stated, at 1313:

> In case any resistance is offered by them, it will be open to the Delhi Administration to evict them forcibly.

In this case the needs of migrants who had left the Piragarhi Relief Camp and occupied the DDA flats was also brought to the notice of the Court. The Commissioner was directed to look into the Piragarhi camp, at 1313:

16 "PUCL Efforts Bear Fruits in Slum-Dwellers Case", *PUCL Bulletin*, Vol. 12, No. 3, March 1992, 22-23.

> We further direct the Delhi Administration to make payment as it has done hithertofore to the migrants from the Transit Camp as well as those from the Piragarhi Relief Camp who have occupied the flats, with effect from the date on which they were compelled to vacate the respective camps and take possession of those flats. Those payments will be continued as before.

The Delhi Administration was directed to pay the Commissioner, and the writ petition was disposed of.

☆ ☆ ☆

A petition was filed under Article 226 of the Constitution in the Delhi HC by an organization called Common Cause. The Delhi Apartment Ownership Act, 1987 states that ownership rights of existing Delhi Development Authority flats (both commercial and residential) would be transferred within three months and Deeds of Apartments would be issued in the prescribed form. However, four years after the legislation was enacted, no transfers had been made.

The petition was admitted and a counter affidavit filed by the Union of India and the Delhi Administration contending that the owners should have filed civil suits to get their Deeds of Apartments, while admitting that there were shortcomings in the Act for which an amendment was proposed. The case is pending and the members of Common Cause have discussed the proposal of a new legislation with the Government.[17]

☆ ☆ ☆

A SPL was filed under Article 136 of the Constitution against the orders of the Delhi HC in a petition filed by Common Cause. The petition in the HC had challenged the notices, issued by the Delhi Municipal Corporation to the owners of vacant housing plots in Delhi, changing the rateable value of the plots. These changes were described as violative of statutory provisions governing the Municipal Corporation of Delhi. Another SLP was also filed under

17 Shourie, H.D., "Common Cause: A Romance with Public Causes", New Delhi, 1993.

Article 136 of the Constitution against the orders of the Delhi HC in a petition filed by Common Cause which had challenged the validity of a statutory provision. This provision states that no appeal can be entertained against any order of an officer of the Corporation unless the entire amount in dispute is first paid by the appellant.

Both the petitions were dismissed by the HC in a two-line order which stated:

> Judicial and quasi-judicial matters cannot be challenged by way of public interest litigation in a writ petition.[18]

☆ ☆ ☆

A petition was filed under Article 226 of the Constitution in the HC of Punjab and Haryana by Common Cause. Additional development charges had been levied by the Haryana State Government on purchasers of housing plots and the developers in the housing colonies of Gurgaon. The legality of these charges was questioned.[19]

## Land and Its Use

***W P No 23138 of 1980, Karnataka***

***V. Lakshmipathy and others v. State of Karnataka and others***

A petition was filed under Article 226 of the Constitution by residents of Banashankari, in defence of public interest, invoking sections 9 and 14 of the Karnataka Town Planning and Country Planning Act, 1961, sections 35 and 505 of the Karnataka Municipal Corporations Act, 1976, sections 6 and 10 of the Urban Land (Ceiling and Regulation) Act, 1976 and section 32 of the Bangalore Development Authority Act, 1976, together with Articles 21 and 51A(g) of the Constitution. The petitioners stated that the location and operation of industries and industrial enterprises in their residential area was a gross violation of the provisions of the 1961 Act. They questioned the industrial activity in factories, workshops and factory sheds, manufacturing greases, lubricating oils and inflammable products.

18 *Ibid.*

19 *Ibid.*

In an order D/-9/4/91 by Justice H.G. Balakrishna
[reported AIR 1992 Kant 57]
The Court quoted from the SC order in the cases filed by M.C. Mehta regarding the pollution of the River Ganges and examined the imperatives of a welfare society, Article 21 of the Constitution and the Directive Principles of State Policy, before stating, at 70:

> By allowing the writ petition, if calamitious consequences visit the concerned respondents as a result of non-feasance or malfeasance or misfeasance on the part of public authorities or public officials, the doors of justice are open to them to sue the public authorities for pecuniary relief by enforcing the principle of accountability.

Examining the allegations of air and noise pollution, the Court held, at 68:

> none of the authorities concerned who have been impleaded as respondents in this writ petition have either denied the existence of pollution or have come forward with any explanation as to what measures have been taken in order to control the pollution. In these circumstances, there is sufficient basis to hold that the grievance of the petitioners as to the existence of air pollution and noise pollution affecting the environment to the detriment of the members of the public is sustained.

The petition was allowed and the licences granted to the industries were declared void and illegal. The Court directed the City Corporation of Bangalore and its health officer to stop the pollution, and issued, at 71:

> a directon to the Bangalore Development Authority to stop operation of the industrial units and to carry out the layout work in accordance with law and remove all encroachments in public lands and roads in the area.

☆☆☆

***C W No 1839 of 1981, Delhi***
***S.S. Sobti v. Union of India and others***
A petition was filed under Article 226 of the Constitution by a former member of the Delhi Development Authority who was also

an alderman of the Delhi Municipal Corporation, a social worker and a ratepayer. The petition challenged the licence deed D/-11/3/81 granted by the New Delhi Municipal Committee to M/s Delhi Automobiles (P) Ltd., New Delhi, sanctioning the construction of a five star hotel on a plot on Barakhamba Road, New Delhi. The petitioner claimed his legal right to ensure that public property vested in the Union Government was not wastefully used to serve personal ends. He also invoked Article 299 of the Constitution.

In an order D/-9/9/81 by > Justice D.K. Kapur and Justice J.D. Jain
[reported AIR 1982 Del 51]
The Court discussed the question of admissibility on the grounds of *locus standi* and held at 52:

> No doubt, the legal validity of a transaction can be challenged by a person whose rights are affected thereby, but the person concerned must be one who is discriminated against, or who has been deprived of some valuable right. He must be an "aggrieved person".

Quoting Justice Krishna Iyer from the *Fertilizer Corporation*, the Court held that not everyone can file PILs. In the facts of the case it was held that the question of political considerations did not arise and that it was not necessary to call an open tender in every case, as this would make it difficult for the municipality to cope with its task. The Court upheld the legality of the decision to allot the land, and dismissed the petition *in limine*.

☆ ☆ ☆

***S C A No 1816 of 1982, Bombay***
***Bhaghubhai H. Devani v. Porbander Municipality and others***

A petition was filed under Article 226 of the Constitution by a Municipal Councillor challenging the sale of municipal land on the ground that it was by a private sale and not by public auction. The petition invoked Article 12 of the Constitution and sections 44, 65 and 80 of the Gujarat Municipalities Act, 1964.

In an order D/-21/2/84 by Justice A.P. Ravani
[reported AIR 1984 Guj 134]
The Court stated that it could not be said that the petition was nonmaintainable even though it was not filed as a public interest

litigation and was not for and on behalf of the poor, ignorant or socially and economically backward class of people who may otherwise be unable to approach the Court. While conceding that the motive of the petitioner may be political gain, the Court held that it is also necessary to look at the contention raised and its implications, at 135:

> In the instant case, strictly speaking, the petition cannot be termed as public interest litigation. But it partakes the character of public interest litigation. The question to be resolved will have an effect on the entire society.

On the facts of the case the petition was partly allowed.

☆ ☆ ☆

**W P Nos 19919 to 19954 and 21172 of 1982, Karnataka**
**Bangalore Water Supply and Sewerage Board, Bangalore**
**v. Mrs Kantha Chandra and others**

A petition was filed under Article 226 of the Constitution referring to section 48 and 95 of the Karnataka Land Revenue Act, 1964, section 95 of the Karnataka Land Reforms Act, 1964 and section 148 of the Karnataka Town and Country Planning Act, 1961. The petition claimed that section 95(5) of the Revenue Act was violative of Article 14 of the Constitution. Under this provision, permission for the use of agricultural land by the occupant for purposes other than agriculture was deemed to be granted within four months if not stated otherwise by a Deputy Commissioner. Mrs Chandra had purchased land which had received permission in thhis manner, so the petition asked the Court to quash the permission granted relating to her land and that of the other respondents.

In an order D/-27/4/87 by Justice K.A. Swami
[reported AIR 1989 Kant 1]
The question of *locus standi* was raised and discussed at length, at 11:

> The expression "aggrieved person" denotes an elastic, and to an extent, an elusive concept. It cannot be confined within the bounds of a rigid, exact and comprehensive definition. At best, its features can be described in a broad tentative manner. Its scope and meaning depends on diverse, variable factors such

> as the content and intent of the statute of which contravention is alleged, the specific circumstances of the case, the nature and extent of the petitioner's interest and the nature and extent of the prejudice or injury suffered by him.

The Court conferred the following standing on the Board that of an aggrieved person, affected by the permissions, and also that of a public utility organization, at 9:

> It has sufficient interest in the matter so as to have a standing to challenge the impugned orders. Even otherwise, as far as the exercise of jurisdiction under Article 226 of the Constitution is concerned, the conception of 'locus standi' is being expanded wherever 'public interest' is involved. Ensuring adequate supply of wholesome water to the Bangalore Metropolis is a matter in which undoubtedly every resident of the metropolitan area is interested. Anything which affects adequate supply of wholesome water, definitely affects the public at large. Therefore, in such a case, it becomes the duty of this Court to exercise jurisdiction under Article 226 of the Constitution. ... In the instant case, public interest is involved because the case of the Board is that if the proposed township comes up on the banks of Arkavathy river, the water flowing into T.G. Halli Reservoir will be depleted. In such an event, as it is already pointed out, the residents of Bangalore Metropolitan Area are affected because T.G. Halli is one of the sources of water for the Bangalore Metropolitan Area.

The Court noted that the provision is meant to expedite the disposal of the application, at 6-7:

> It is not possible to appreciate how sub-section (5) of section 95 of the Act can be held to be violative of Article 14 of the Constitution. It is not a class legislation. It is applicable to all those who seek permission for use of agricultural land for purposes other than agriculture.

Section 95 was upheld, but after dealing with many legal issues involving the Acts, the writ petitions were allowed in that the orders for a change in land use were allowed. There was no order for costs.

☆ ☆ ☆

***C A Nos 2310 and 2311 of 1984 with S L P (C) No 7404 of 1984, D/-26/11/85 from A no 644 of 1982 and OSWP no 2412 of 1982, D/-14/11/83 (Bombay)***
***Forward Construction Co and others v. Prahbat Mandal (Regd.), Andheri and others***

Appeals were filed under Article 226 of the Constitution relating to a plot of land which had been reserved for a bus depot of the Bombay Electricity Supply and Transport (BEST) Undertaking, under the Development Plan for Bombay and the verified Andheri Town Planning Scheme, as framed under the Bombay Corporation Act, 1888. The petition filed in the High Court, challenging the use of the plot, was dismissed. A second petition was filed in the HC by Prabhat Mandal on a ground absent in the first petition. The Supreme Court was asked to decide whether the second petition was barred by *res judicata.*

In an order D/-26/11/85 by Justice R.S. Pathak, Justice O. Chinnappa Reddy and > Justice R.B. Misra
[reported AIR 1986 SC 391 / (1986) 1 SCC 100]
Allowing the appeals, the Court held that *res judicata* under section 11, explanation VI of the CPC, 1908 applies to PIL only if the previous litigation was also a PIL. As the first litigation in the HC, initiated by Shri Thakkar, was not a PIL, but was put up by M/s Western Builders, the second petition filed as a PIL was not barred. The Court stated, at 399:

> Public interest law activities at times champion one public interest which clashes with another public interest thus benefitting one segment of the public at another's expense... The purpose for which the plot was earmarked remains intact, that is, for the construction of a bus depot. In our opinion the other public interest sought to be achieved by the construction of the two buildings in addition to the bus depot is equally important.

☆ ☆ ☆

***W P No 1444 of 1986, Karnataka***
***M.B. Sadashivaiah and others v. City Improvement Trust Board, Mysore and others***

A petition was filed under Article 226 of the Constitution by tax-payers of Mysore complaining that the order of the second respondent (Chairman, City Improvement Trust Board, Mysore) in allotting a corner site to the third respondent at the rate of Rs 400 per square yard was illegal. The petition contended that the site in question can only be auctioned in public after due publicity, as the rules do not permit mere allocations.

In an order D/-23/9/88 by Justice H.G. Balakrishna
[reported 1988 (3) KLJ 91]
The Court held that the petitioners are not *bona fide* applicants, that they delayed in their application and that the rule of estoppel was applicable. As the corner site was allotted by special order of the State Government, the Court held that so long as the allotment is in accordance with the rules, the question of whether the money realized leads to a benefit or loss is inconsequential. Because of the lack of *bona fides* and other reasons, the petition was dismissed with no order for costs.

☆ ☆ ☆

***C A No 378 of 1987***
***Sachidanand Pandey and another* v. *State of West Bengal and others***

An appeal was filed against an order of the Calcutta HC in a petition filed under Article 226 of the Constitution. The petition had been filed by two citizens of Calcutta, one of whom was a Secretary of the Union of Workmen, and the other a life member of the zoo. Both described themselves as lovers of wildlife and well-wishers of the zoo. They alleged that the Government of West Bengal had shown a lack of awareness of environmental considerations in allotting land for the construction of a five star hotel by the Taj Group at the expense of the zoo. The petition invoked Articles 14, 31, 48A and 51A(g) of the Constitution, together with the Bengal Public Parks Act, 1904.

In an order D/-11/2/87 by > Justice O. Chinnappa Reddy and > Justice V. Khalid
[reported AIR 1987 SC 1109]
The Court stated, at 1127:

> This is a case where the decision and the reasons for the decision can only be gathered by looking at the entire course of events and circumstances stretching over the period from the initiation of the proposal to the final taking of the decision. ...

> the present is a case where neither a statutory functionary is involved but the transaction bears a commercial though public character which can only be settled after protracted discussion, clarification and consultation with all interested persons.

The Court held that the Government had taken the relevant considerations into account. After a discussion of the relevant case law and technicalities, it was held that the provisions of the 1904 Act were not attracted as claimed by the petitioner. Justice Khalid stated that the judgement of the lower court, from which this appeal had been filed, showed two things, at 1135:

> one, the petitioners did not take any steps to get the matter heard expeditiously, after they obtained an interim order to get all the work stopped; two, that the State Government made available to the Court all the materials to prove that its decision was taken after mature consideration at all levels.

The judge observed, at 1134:

> Today public interest litigants rush to Court to file cases in profusion under this attractive name. They must be above suspicion...

He went on to stress the need for public interest litigants to have self-restraint, at 1136:

> Public interest litigation has now come to stay. But one is led to think that it poses a threat to courts and public alike. Such cases are now filed without any rhyme or reason. It is, therefore, necessary to lay down clear guidelines and to outline correct parameters for the entertainment of such petitions. If courts do not restrict the free flow of such cases in the name of Public Interest Litigations, traditional litigation will suffer and the courts of law, instead of dispensing justice, will have to take upon themselves administrative and executive functions.
>
> I should not be understood to say that traditional litigation should stay put. It has to be tackled by other effective methods, like decentralizing the judicial system and entrusting the majority of traditional litigation to village courts and Lok Adalats without the usual populist stance and by a complete restructuring of the procedural law which is the villain in delaying disposal of cases.

> It is only when courts are apprised of gross violation of fundamental rights by a group or class action or when basic human rights are invaded or when there are complaints of such acts as shock the judicial concience that the courts, especially this Court, should leave aside procedural shackles and hear such petitions and extend its jurisdiction under all available provisions for remedying the hardships and misery of the needy, the underdog and the neglected. I will be second to none in extending help when such help is required. But this does not mean that the doors of this Court are always open for anyone to walk in. It is necessary to have some self-imposed restraint on public interest litigants.

The Court did state that the Directive Principles of State Policy and Fundamental Duties would be the principal consideration in a case of this kind and emphasized the need to take Articles 48A and 51A(g) of the Constitution into account. Moreover, as the principal consideration was to attract tourism and not revenue, the Court referred to Article 14 of the Constitution to hold that public interest is paramount in the allotment of land and that the Government did act with probity. Details of land allocation/use were discussed, as were environmental issues. The appeals were dismissed.

☆ ☆ ☆

***W P No 1274 of 1988, Bombay***
***Parisar Society Ltd and others* v. *State of Maharashtra and others***

A petition was filed under Article 226 of the Constitution by an organization in Pune concerned with the environment. The petition referred to the Maharashtra Regional and Town Planning Act, 1966 which requires development plans to be made and implemented. Modifications were made to the Draft Revised Development Plan for Pune for the period 1981-1991 which had not received sanction from the State Government till 1987. The petition stated that the final Development Plan for Pune was illegal and therefore null and void as the State Government had made various modifications without inviting objections to the plan as required under the 1966 Act, and without publishing a map. The petition contended that some of the 96 plots that were deleted from the plan in the modifications had been reserved for the housing of economically weaker sections and/or slum dwellers, and stated that no consideration had been given to environmental concerns. The petition asked the Court to prevent any building permissions from being sanctioned under the modified plan.

In an order D/-29/4/88

The petition was admitted by a division bench and an interim order was given:

> In respect of the 96 items listed in the statement prepared by the petitioners, the respondents are restrained from permitting development as per the modifications made by the first respondent by the impugned notification dated 5th January 1987.

Applications were made by individuals who had already got sanction for their buildings, and had started construction, asking for the Court to vacate (withdraw) the stay order.

In an order D/-18/7/88 by Justice Sawant and Justice Kantharia

The Court noted that the petitioner-organization had filed a suit (Suit No 738 of 1987) in the local court on the same grounds as the writ petition, but the suit had been dismissed. The Court held:

> while preparing the development plan it is not the function of the Planning Authority to classify residential purpose into that for economically weaker sections, slum dwellers, etc.

and noted that the petition had not adequately dealt with this contention. The Court observed that the arguments of the advocate for the petitioners:

> [he]… tried to urge before us that since these plots were meant for rehabilitating the slum dwellers, and clearance of slums is necessary for improving the ecology the deletion does affect ecology. Had such a grievance been made in the petition the applicants as well as the Municipal Corporation and the State Government who are supporting the applicants, would have certainly placed before us the necessary data to refute the case.

After analysing the contention that the area was reserved for open, recreation and green belt areas, it was held that there was no substance in this grievance. The Court also found no substance in the petitioner's grievance about the dereservation of plots in general, stating:

> In order therefore to see that the economically weaker sections are housed and are not stranded for want of finance with the Municipal Corporation, the State Government has come out with a concept of guided development for urban areas. According to this concept instead of the land being acquired by the Planning Authority, the owners or persons claiming through owners are permitted to develop the area for the purposes for which it is earmarked and they are enabled to construct and hand over specific portions of built up area to the Corporation either free of cost or at a very concessional rate. This leads to the desired development of the area without the Corporation having to spend huge amounts for the same. Prima facie, therefore, we cannot find any fault with the State Government in deleting the plots in question from reservation.

The interim relief provided by the Court in its order D/-29/4/88 was vacated.

☆ ☆ ☆

***W P No 14183 of 1989, Madras***

***Madras Citizens Progressive Council* v. *The Secretary to Govt. of Tamil Nadu and others***

A petition was filed under Article 226 of the Constitution by an organization in Madras, complaining that exemptions were given to the fourth respondent to the petition, enabling it to hold more land than allowed by land ceiling regulations. The petition also claimed that the first, second and third respondents did not test the genuineness of the fourth respondent when awarding the exemptions under sections 11 and 21 of the TN Urban Land (Ceiling and Regulation) Act, 1978.

In an order D/-17/1/91 by Justice Mishra
[reported AIR 1991 Mad 390]

Describing the petition as in the nature of a *vox populi*, the Court conferred standing on the organization, and stated, at 398:

> But there are certain facts brought to my notice which I only indicate without adjudicating into them in the hope that the petitioner shall, in future, not repeat them. Why the petitioner, before it registered as a society, claimed in its communications to several persons which are all brought on record of this case,

it was a registered society when actually it was not registered? Why did it decide to give legal notices to the fourth respondent and persons like the fourth respondent when there are no such legal notices contemplated for in a public interest action? The petitioner's such conduct in matters of *vox populi* like the one in the case of the fourth respondent may cause apprehensions about the intention of the petitioner. The learned counsel for the fourth respondent has rightly stated that in all proceedings in Court it is necessary that utmost caution is taken to be fair and untainted. Any suspicion that the petitioner moves with unclean hands may in some cases result in the petitioner's intentions to be doubted. The learned counsel for the petitioner has assured the Court that in future the petitioner shall not indulge in any such practice. In deference to his words, I accept the statement made on behalf of the petitioner.

After a lengthy discussion of the substantive legal issues involved, the Court noted, at 397:

> in every case of grant of exemption, it is the public interest that is uppermost and it is the public interest alone which has to determine whether the exemption has to be granted or not. Once such a public interest is noticed and exemption is granted, one shall have to abide by it otherwise the public interest shall suffer both on account of acquisition being delayed and not effected as well as the public interest for which the exemption was granted and not served.

The Court referred to an earlier order in which it had held that the exemption order was of an executive and quasi-judicial nature and that it could not be reviewed by the State Government, but only by a court of law. Referring to the Act, it was held, at 398:

> The State Government cannot just at its whim and caprice decide to extend the period of exemption. It will have to assign reasons and the reasons must conform to the purpose of the Act being not to allow any person to hold lands in excess of the ceiling area.... It cannot also entertain any new ground for exemption because any such thing done while deciding whether to withdraw the exemption or not, will amount to varying the order of exemption which I have already indicated is not permissible.

The petition was partly allowed in that the State Government was directed to dispose of the proceeding under section 21(2) of the Act in the light of the directions and observations made. There was no order for costs.

☆ ☆ ☆

A petition was filed under Article 226 of the Constitution in the Bombay High Court in May 1989 by the Bombay Environmental Action Group challenging the dereservation of plots in Bombay. In the Draft Development Plan (Master Plan) for Greater Bombay certain plots had been reserved for public amenities, like schools, gardens, dispensaries and hospitals. In May 1988, the Minister for Urban Development announced that 285 plots had been dereserved and that more were to follow. The petition claimed that the actual number of dereservations was 600 and stated that the existing low level of civic amenities would be further reduced. The petition challenged the legality of the process of dereservation which did not allow any hearing to the public who have a right to know.

In an order D/-15/5/89 by Justice Sam Variava

The Court ordered the State Government to provide the petitioners with a list of dereserved plots and issued a stay on further dereservations.

In an order D/-13/9/89 by Justice Daud

The petition was dismissed.

Appeal No 1162 of 1989 was filed against this dismissal and was admitted by the HC. The stay order of 15/5/89 remained valid.

☆ ☆ ☆

***S L P (C) No 17045 of 1990***

***Foreshore Cooperative Housing Society Limited, Bombay v. Nivara Hakk Suraksha Samiti, Bombay and others***

An appeal was filed against the judgement of the Bombay HC in a petition under Article 226 of the Constitution in the Bombay HC challenging the allotment of land to a cooperative society and the reduction in lease rent. This society, comprising sitting and retired judges of the Supreme Court and Bombay HC, had been allotted land at reduced rates. The HC upheld the allotment but set aside the reduction of lease rent. An appeal was filed by the cooperative society of judges.

In an order D/-1/2/91 by Justice S. Ranganathan, Justice S.C. Agrawal and Justice N.D. Ojha
[reported 1991 (1) SCALE 33 [109]]
The Court noted, at 111:

> the petitioner does not represent any existing or proposed cooperative society. Since only cooperative societies are eligible for allotment its interests are not directly affected. Also, even as a public interest litigation, the petitioner should have come to the Court at a much earlier stage. We do not say that the petitioner has no *locus standi* or that the petition should have been dismissed on the ground of laches but these are matters which a Court may legitimately take note of in deciding the question of relief.

And on the point of appeal, went on to hold, at 111:

> We are unable to find from the record any special circumstance brought to the notice of the Government which could have justified the reduction in rent which had earlier been fixed after due consideration.

It was further held that it would be up to the society to apply to the government for reconsideration. The appeal was dismissed with no order for costs.

☆ ☆ ☆

A petition was filed under Article 226 of the Constitution in the Bombay HC by the Nivara Hakk Suraksha Samiti, the Bombay Environmental Action Group and the Association of Engineering Workers. The petition challenged certain regulations in the "Development Control Regulations for Greater Bombay, 1991" which control the implementation of the new Development Plan for Greater Bombay. One of the challenges was to regulation 33(10) which set out the measures for the rehabilitation of slum dwellers, and allowed an increased FSI (floor space index) of 2.5 to encourage development. The petition contended that this would encourage the development of costly high-rise structures intended for slum dwellers, but would in reality exclude them from this housing. An article discussing this petition noted:

> The most insidious part of the DC rules is the provision to allow co-operative societies of slum dwellers to bid for the development of the plots where their slums are situated. This gives the whole scheme a socialistic flavour though it is very unlikely that any such co-operative will be able to outbid professional developers.[20]

Other allegations were made about the permitted FSIs, the use of land by textile mills and the development rights for plots.

In an order by Justice Sujata Manohar and Justice I.G. Shah

The Court rejected the three petitions.

☆ ☆ ☆

***W P No 2285 of 1992 c/w W Ps Nos 23470 and 24877 of 1991, Karnataka***

***Prof A. Lakshmisagar and others v. State of Karnataka and others***

A petition was filed under Article 226 of the Constitution, invoking provisions of the Karnataka Land Revenue Act, 1964, by residents of Bangalore concerned about the regular supply of clean water. Forty-two individuals had purchased agricultural land on the bank of the Arkavati River, all of whom were members of a co-operative society called Arkavati Farmers Co-operative Society. Permission for a change of land use was granted to these persons, so that it became non-agricultural land and a new township could be created. The petition challenged this change of land use.

In an order D/-24/4/92 by Justice M. Rama Jois and Justice R. Ramakrishna

[reported AIR 1993 Kant 121]

As this was a complex litigation, involving earlier petitions and orders, the Court examined these and other claims on the land. As the land in question is near a water reservoir which is one of the sources of water to Bangalore, the Bangalore Water Supply and Sewerage Board had been involved in the litigation. In an earlier order the change in land use was struck down by the HC, but this was subsequently reinstated by a Government Order. In the present order, the standing of the petitioners was upheld, the petitions were

[20] Singhvi, Sanjay, "Comment: D.C. Regulations Case", *The Lawyers*, Vol. 6, No. 5, May 1991, 11-12.

allowed and the Government Order was struck down. Exemplary costs of Rs 10,000 were awarded to the public spirited individuals who petitioned the Court.

## Recreational Land

***W P No 8261 of 1984, Andhra Pradesh***
***T. Damodhar Rao and others v. Special Officer, Municipal Corporation of Hyderabad, and others***

A petition was filed under Article 226 of the Constitution by residents and tax-payers of the Hyderabad Municipal Corporation who live around the area demarcated by the development plan as a recreational park. The question raised was whether the Hyderabad Municipal Corporation and the Income Tax Department, Hyderabad can legally use the land owned by them in a recreational zone in the city of Hyderabad for residential purposes contrary to the Development Plan. The petition invoked Article 21 of the Constitution and sections 112 and 464(1) of the Hyderabad Municipal Corporation Act, 1956.

In an order D/-20/1/87 by Justice P.A. Choudary
[reported AIR 1987 AP 171]

The Court held, at 181:

> it is clear that protection of the environment is not only the duty of the citizen but it is also the obligation of the State and all other State organs including courts. To that extent, environmental law has succeeded in unshackling man's right to life and personal liberty from the clutches of the common law theory of individual ownership. Examining the matter from the above constitutional point of view, it would be reasonable to hold that the enjoyment of life and its attainment and fulfilment guaranteed by Article 21 of the Constitution embraces the protection and preservation of nature's gifts without which life cannot be enjoyed. There is no reason why the practice of violent extinguishment of life alone should be regarded as violative of Article 21 of the Constitution. Slow poisoning by the polluted atmosphere caused by environmental pollution and spoilage should also be regarded as amounting to violation of Article 21 of the Constitution.

The Court refe red to the African Charter on Human and People's Rights and the Environment (Protection) Act, 1986, and stated that the common law rights of owners must give in to statutory restrictions. Accordingly, it was held that those resident in an area demarcated for another use in the development plan, must vacate the land. The writ petition was allowed with costs — advocate's fee of Rs 500.

☆ ☆ ☆

***C A No 2750 of 1991 (arising out of SLP (C) No 13940 of 1989)***
***Bangalore Medical Trust v. S. Muddappa and others***

An appeal was filed against the order of the Karnataka HC in a petition filed under Article 226 of the Constitution by residents of the area in question. The petition referred to sections 2(b) and 19(4) of the Bangalore Development Act, 1976, and stated that the conversion of a public park into a private nursing home was illegal. The High Court had allowed the petition.

In an order D/-19/7/91 by > Justice T.K. Thommen and > Justice R.M. Sahai

[reported AIR 1991 SC 1902]

After a discussion on the scope of *locus standi*, Justice Sahai stated, at 1915:

> The rise in exercise of power by the executive and comparative decline in proper and effective administrative guidance is forcing citizens to espouse challenges with a public interest flavour. It is too late in the day, therefore, to claim that a petition filed by inhabitants of a locality whose park was converted into a nursing home had no cause to invoke the equity jurisdiction of the High Court.

He noted that in a private challenge to an executive or administrative action, the dividing line between personal injury and loss, and loss of a public nature is fast vanishing. After a lengthy discussion about the duties of the Bangalore Development Authority and the purpose for which the 1976 Act was passed, the Court held that a private nursing home is neither an amenity nor a necessary improvement over a public park. The appeal failed.

☆ ☆ ☆

***C M W No 24408 of 1991, Allahabad***
***D.D. Vyas and others* v. *Ghaziabad Development Authority, Ghaziabad and another***

A petition was filed under Article 226 of the Constitution claiming that an open space called Adu Park should be used only for a public park and not for any other purpose and asked that blue prints for the development of the park be laid out. The petition was filed by residents of the locality who had been urging the development of the park for some time, and invoked sections 9 and 17 of the Uttar Pradesh Urban Planning and Development Act, 1973 and section 2 of the Uttar Pradesh Parks, Playgrounds and Open Spaces (Preservation and Regulation) Act, 1975, together with Articles 12, 51A(g) and 51A(j) of the Constitution.

In an order D/-13/4/92 by > Justice Om Prakash and Justice M. Katju
[reported AIR 1993 All 57]
Upholding the *locus standi* of the petitoner, the Court held, at 62:

> When a petition can be brought under Article 32 for the prevention of pollution by a group of social workers or journalists, a writ petition under Article 226 of the Constitution for the preservation of free air and for the protection of environment can always be filed by the environmental activists either living in the same locality or otherwise.

After discussing the definition of parks and the need for them, the Court directed that a blueprint be laid down for the park, with trees on the periphery and flower beds and promenades etc. Sources of irrigation were to be indicated in the blue print, staff was to be allotted and the park to be fully developed as a priority within one year. The Court directed that no construction be allowed except in relation to the maintenance of the park. The petition was allowed.

☆ ☆ ☆

***O P No 11038 of 1993, Kerala***
***G.K. Salil* v. *State of Kerala and others***

A petition was filed under Article 226 of the Constitution by the Convenor of the Save Collectorate Maidan Committee. There were three Maidans — Fort, Police and Collectorate — of which the first two had been given to the Military and the Police respectively. As the Collectorate Maidan was the only one left for public use and activities, this petition was filed challenging its allotment to the Khadi Board for a new building. The petitioner-committee had made many representations to the Government and the municipality with no result, so a petition was filed as a last resort, invoking Article 47 of the Constitution. The Court was asked to quash the impugned order and to direct the respondent not to allow any construction to take place on the Collectorate Maidan. Annexed to the petition were many documents and newspaper articles.

## Construction

***C A Nos 557-558 of 1986***

***T.N. Rugmani and another* v. *C. Achutha Menon and others***

Two appeals were filed under Article 136 of the Constitution from the order of the Kerala HC in petitions invoking section 463 of the IPC, 1860, and section 15 of the Kerala Town Planning Act, 1908. The petitions had stated that the Trichur Urban Development Authority and the Municipal Council of Trichur had unjustifiably withheld permission to raise a construction on land that was not earmarked for a scheme for planned development under the 1908 Act. One petition had been filed by a former Chief Minister of Kerala and the local editor of a newspaper, Achuta Menon, espousing a social cause, claiming that the vacancies on the Development Authority had not been filled and that there was collusion between the appellant and the Government. It asked the Court for an order preventing any building from being constructed. The other petition had been filed on behalf of the owner of the plots (by his father under a power of attorney) asking that the plan be sanctioned so that construction could commence. The Kerala HC had appointed a commissioner to look into the allegations of violation of the sanctioned plan. The Court found that the petitioner was not the owner of the plot, and stated that the petition had been filed by the wrong person. The appeal by T.N. Rugmani stated that the HC was wrong in its decision on the maintainability of the petition, as it had decided on events which took place later and not on the facts as they were on the date when the petition was filed.

In an order D/-20/12/90 by Justice K.N. Saikia and > Justice R.M. Sahai

[reported AIR 1991 SC 983]

The Court noted, at 984:

> [the] nature of public interest litigation, its *pro bono* content, justification for entertaining it are not proposed to be gone into but it need be observed that the court being seized of a petition dealing with the same subject matter, it would have been more appropriate if, it could have exercised restraint in light of the law laid down by this Court in *Chhetriya Pradushan Mukti Sanghaarsh Vahini* v. *state of UP* (1990) 3 JT 685 : (AIR 1990 SC 2060), *Ramsharan Autyanuprasi* v. *Union of India*, 1989

> Suppl (1) SCR 251 : (AIR 1987 SC 549) and *Sachidanand Pandey* v. *state of West Bengal* (1987) 2 SCC 295 : (AIR 1987 SCC 1109). Merely because authorities constituted under the statute failed in their effort to get the interim order vacated was hardly any occasion for invoking jurisdiction under Article 226 by way of public interest litigation.

and discussed the limits of PIL, at 984-985:

> Taking up the issue of non-maintainability it may be stated that denial of constitutional remedy, for this reason, cannot be equated with bad faith or lack of bona fide. The scope of the two are different. A person may be honest and his grievance genuine yet the Court may not be able to grant him any relief either because the cause of the action or any part of it did not arise within the territorial jurisdiction exercised by the High Court or the petition may be defective as the person approaching may not be entitled to file it. That is something akin to lack of jurisdiction either before or after presentation of the petition. Even an unassailable cause or an illegal and arbitrary order may fail to move the conscience of the Court due to inequitable and unjustifiable behaviour or conduct in equitable jurisdiction. The basic error committed by the High Court was that it did not keep in mind the distinction between non-maintainability and lack of bona fide....
>
> The High Court, therefore, decided the maintainability of the petition, erroneously, not on the facts as they were on the date when the petition was filed but on subsequent events which took place much thereafter. The finding in these circumstances that the appellant was the real owner and should have filed the petition cannot be maintainable.

The appeal in the PIL by Achutha Menon was dismissed, and the other appeal was allowed. The Court ordered that the appellant be allowed to raise a construction, subject to certain stipulations — that permission should be granted by the Development Authority and that compensation be given if the road is widened. The costs were to be borne by the parties except for those already ordered to be paid for the costs of the Commissioner and witnesses.

☆ ☆ ☆

***W P No 2733 of 1986, Bombay***
***Bombay Environmental Action Group and others v. Pune Cantonment Board***

A petition was filed under Article 226 of the Constitution. Five buildings had been erected in the Pune Cantonment which appeared to have been constructed in violation of the relevant bye-laws and schemes of Building Restriction framed by the Pune Cantonment Board and the GOC-in-C Southern Command (military authority). The petitioners, concerned for the environment of Pune city, had sent letters to the Pune Cantonment Board asking either that they be permitted to inspect constructions within the cantonment area or that they be given copies of the applications made for building permissions together with the plans accompanying such applications and all relevant official documents. As the request was refused, this petition was filed stating that it was the duty of the Board to disclose the information under Article 19(1)(a) of the Constitution.

In a judgement D/-7/10/86 by > Justice Dharmadhikari and Justice Sugla

The respondents had invoked the Cantonments Act, 1924 and stated that the Board was only subject to the control of the Central Government, claiming:

> If the request made by the petitioners is granted, then it will practically amount to creating an extra-legal authority to supervise and control the working of the Cantonment Board, which is not permissible.

The respondents further contended that the observations of the Court regarding secrecy, in *S.P. Gupta*, must be seen in the context of Article 74 of the Constitution and sections 123 and 162 of the Indian Evidence Act, 1872. After analysing the arguments, the Court stressed the need for people's participation in the movement for the protection of the environment, and upheld the bona fides of the petitioners in approaching the Court and asking for the documents. It was held that the right to know flows from the right to freedom of speech and expression guaranteed under Article 19(1)(a) of the Constitution, and the Court stated:

> we feel that such a right of inspection should be sparingly used and should be restricted to the Honorary Secretary of the petitioner no.3 Save Pune Citizens Committee or a person

> specifically authorized by him. It is needless to say that if in a given case the Cantonment's Executive Officer finds that such a request is not made for genuine purposes or that it will be against public interest to grant inspection, then by recording reasons in that behalf, he may refuse such a permission. Obviously, inspection will be subject to the convenience of both the parties and at such a time and place as may be fixed by the Board and on payment of requisite fees.

The petition was partly allowed and the respondents were ordered to make the documents available for inspection.

☆ ☆ ☆

***S L P No 11291 of 1986***
***Bombay Environment Action Group and others v. Pune Cantonment Board and another***

An appeal was filed under Article 136 of the Constitution against the order and judgement of the Bombay High Court D/-14/8/86 in W P No 2127 of 1985. The petition had challenged the construction of the Sterling Centre, a building in the Pune Cantonment area, but the HC had refused relief.

In an order D/-13/10/86 by Chief Justice P.N. Bhagwati and Justice K.N. Singh
The full text of the Court's order was:

> Special Leave Petition is rejected on the facts and circumstances of the present case. We may make it clear that it is not in every case where construction has started or rights of third parties have intervened that the courts will necessarily refuse to exercise their discretion to grant relief under Article 226. Every case must depend on its special facts and circumstances and there may be cases where the ends of justice may demand that the High Court should intervene and grant relief despite the rights of third parties having come into existence where the petitioner may not be guilty of laches or of undue delay. We would direct the Pune Cantonment Board to take care while giving sanction for construction to ensure that none of the Bye-Laws is violated. We would particularly draw the attention of the Pune Cantonment Board to Bye-Law 10 of which observance must be strictly secured in the future.

> We would also direct that any person residing within the area of a local authority or any social action group or interest group or pressure group shall be entitled to take inspection of any sanction, grant or plan approved by such local authority in construction of buildings along with the related papers and documents if such individual or social action group or interest group or pressure group wishes to take such inspection, except of course in cases where in the interest of security such inspection cannot be permitted.

☆ ☆ ☆

***W P No 926 of 1988***
***Consumer Action Group and another* v. *State of Tamil Nadu and others***

A petition was filed under Article 32 of the Constitution challenging section 133 of the Tamil Nadu Town and Country Planning Act, 1971, and certain exemptions granted under this Act. The second petitioner in this case was the advocate, and trustee of the Consumer Action Group, Sriram Panchu. The petition stated that it is a representative action under Order 1 Rule 8 of CPC, 1908 and referred to the Development Control Rules set up under the Act, relating to the Floor Space Index (FSI) and other requirements which ensure that buildings are regulated in a proper manner. An article had appeared in the fortnightly journal Aside on 16-30/6/88 detailing the exemptions allowed under section 113 of the Act, in contravention of the Rules. After the publication of this article, the petitioner made inquiries and managed to obtain copies of sixty-three Government Orders passed during the period 1/7/87 to 29/1/88. The petition stated that the time taken to investigate and collect material led to the delay in filing the petition. The Government Orders revealed a pattern of exemptions, without mentioning the reasons for these exemptions or the public interest content. The petition challenged the legality of section 113 which delegates powers without framing guidelines for their use, and overrides all provisions and safeguards within the Act. It was contended that these powers had been exploited and mis-used against the public interest and are deterimental to the interest of residents of the area. The petition noted that the exemption clause was framed to enable excessive and genuine hardship to be removed, not to give people immunity from the application and control of the Act. The petition asked that section

113 be declared ultra-vires and the Government Orders annexed to the petition be declared as void.

The petition has been admitted and the rule has been issued.

☆ ☆ ☆

***C A No 634 of 1989 etc.***

***Rajatha Enterprises v. S.K. Sharma and others***

Appeals were filed against the order of the Karnataka High Court in a petition filed under Article 226 of the Constitution, by a petitioner espousing a public cause in this PIL regarding the construction of a building in violation of statutory provisions. The petition invoked Article 14 of the Constitution, section 342 of the Karnataka Municipal Corporations Act, 1976, and section 14 of the Karnataka Town and Country Planning Act, 1961.

In an order D/-3/2/89 by > Justice M.M. Dutt and > Justice T.K. Thommen
[reported (1989) 1 SCR 457]
The appeal was allowed and the petition dismissed, as the Court, referring to *Ramsharan Autyanuprasi* and *Sachidanand Pandey* (supra), held, at 468:

> In the circumstances, in the light of what the Commissioner says about the practice of the Corporation in regard to the commencement certificate and in the absence of any evidence of public safety being in any manner endangered or the public or a section of the public being in any manner inconvenienced by reason of the construction of the building, whatever may be the personal grievance of the 1st respondent, the High Court was not justified, at the instance of the 1st respondent claiming himself to be a champion of the public cause, in ordering the demolition of any part of the building, particularily when there is no evidence whatsoever of dishonesty or fraud or negligence on the part of the builder.

☆ ☆ ☆

Two petitions were filed under Article 226 of the Constitution in the Bombay High Court by the Bombay Environmental Action Group (BEAG). The Government had exempted the Sassoon fish harbour from certain provisions of the Bombay Metropolitan Region Development Authority Act, 1974 and the Maharashtra Regional and Town Planning Act, 1966. The petitioners claimed that under the guise of an expansion project, the construction planned was tantamount to a new harbour at the southernmost tip of Bombay, which would add to congestion and place an added strain on civic amenities. In this detailed petition, the exemptions were challenged as illegal.

In an order the Court held that the harbour did come within the ambit of the 1966 Act, thus expanding the scope of the Act to include all Government and public sector projects.

An article by a member of the BEAG noted:

> In this case, court orders staying the work were in operation for over a year. There was a further indirect delay of several years since there was a dispute between the contractor and the Bombay Port Trust regarding cost escalation for the delay. During the pendency of the stay orders (and later delays) the Central Government made several major changes in the project and issued written directives (including two directives by the Prime Minister) to that effect. Thus half of the reclaimed land (about 12 acres) is to be converted into a garden; the work of raising the new garden is to be completed in all respects before the new wharf is opened for the use of fishing boats; the number of fishing boats permitted to use this harbour has been restricted etc. The above measures would greatly reduce the environmental damage caused by the project.[21]

☆ ☆ ☆

A petition was filed under Article 226 of the Constitution in the Bombay High Court by three residents of Mazagon against the Bombay Municipal Corporation, government officials and some other persons. The petition challenged the permission granted for a multi-storeyed building to be built on the grounds of St Mary's School. The petition pointed out that according to the development control rules, no residential building could be constructed on a plot

[21] Chainani, Shyam, "Role of Civic Groups in Regional and Municipal Environmentl Policy — An experience of the Bombay Metropolitan Region" unpublished paper D/-21/3/87, 28.

reserved for a school. They alleged that through mis-representation and fraud, permission had been secured from the municipal corporation.

The allegations were denied by the respondents.

The petition was rejected by the HC in 1992 but when in appeal in the Supreme Court, it was held that the HC had erroneously rejected the petition. The case was sent back to Bombay.

In an order by Justice V.A. Mohata and Justice S.M. Jhunjhunwala

The HC admitted the petition.[22]

☆ ☆ ☆

***W P No 13231 of 1992, Madras***

***Palani Hills Conservation Council ... represented by its President Navroz Mody* v. *State of Tamil Nadu and others***

A petition was filed under Article 226 of the Constitution challenging the illegal construction of a hotel, which violated the mandatory limits prescribed under the Tamil Nadu Hilly Areas Special Building Rules, 1981 and the Kodaikanal Master Plan. It was claimed that extra floors were being added to the Pleasant Stay Hotel and that such massive constructions were putting a strain on the water resources of the area and creating problems of sanitation and waste disposal. The petition stated that if the authorities continued to allow such construction, this premier hill station and holiday resort would be ruined. It was only after there had been no response to the complaints made to the concerned authorities, in person and by letter, that this petition was filed asking the Court to direct that no more illegal constructions be put up at this Hotel. It also asked that no water or electricity be supplied until the existing illegal constuction was demolished.

In an order D/-21/10/92 by Justice Kanakraj

The Court directed that no construction beyond the sanctioned plan be erected during the pendency of the petitions.

A contempt application was filed by the petitioners in 1993 claiming that the order of the Court had been violated.

22 "Newsfile: Litigation Briefs", *The Lawyers*, Vol. 8, No. 2, March 1993, 30.

In an order D/-23/9/93 by Justice Kanakraj
The full text of the order stated:

> Adjourned for enquiry on 12/10/93. The respondents are directed not to make any further construction. The Kodaikanal Township Committee is directed to oversee the matter and prevent any attempt at further construction. This order is made notwithstanding my earlier order dated 21/10/92 and it is made clear that the Respondents are prevented from making any construction whatsoever in the premises.

☆ ☆ ☆

***W P No 6947 of 1992, Madras***
***Palani Hills Conservation Council rep. by its Secretary Philippa Mukherjee v. State of Tamil Nadu and others***

A petition was filed under Article 226 of the Constitution challenging the unauthorized construction of a hotel in violation of the Tamil Nadu Hilly Areas Special Building Rules, 1981, the Kodaikanal Master Plan and the Tamil Nadu District Municipalities Amendment Act, 1992. The petition stated that no sanction had been given for the construction, which violated land use regulations. Moreover the hotel was to be situated near the Bear Shola Stream which provides drinking water to Palani Town. It was stated that such a construction would have serious environmental repercussions as it would deplete the ground water table. Further, the temptation of such a location would be to divert sewage into the stream. The petition stated that because of this construction, Government land was being encroached upon, not only depriving the Government of its land but also the community of common property resources. The petition was filed after complaints made, in person and by letter, to the concerned authorites remained unresolved. The Court was asked to give interim directions preventing further construction on the land in question and to prevent the supply of water and electricity to this construction. The Court was also asked to direct that the unauthorized construction be demolished.

In an order D/-13/9/93 by Justice A.R. Lakshmanan
With the consent of the respondents, the court gave an interim direction that no construction be carried out.

## Municipal Services

***S L P (Crl) No 2856 of 1979***

***Municipal Council, Ratlam v. Vardhichand and others***

An appeal was filed under Article 136 of the Constitution against an order of the M.P. High Court. This litigation had started in the Magistrate's Court when some residents in the municipal area of Ratlam had petitioned the Court asking for directions to the Municipal Council to carry out its statutory duty and its duty under the draft plan. Referring to section 133 of the Cr PC for the removal of public nuisance, the petitioners asked for specific directions to improve the drainage system and prevent the drains from being polluted. The Magistrate allowed the petition, the Sessions Court overturned this order, which was later reinstated by the HC. The petition invoked the section 188 of the IPC, 1860, and section 123 of the Madhya Pradesh Municipalities Act, 1961, together with Articles 38 and 47 of the Constitution.

In an order D/-29/7/80 by > Justice V.R. Krishna Iyer and Justice O. Chinnappa Reddy
[reported AIR 1980 SC 1622]
The Court noted, at 1623:

> The key question we have to answer is whether by affirmative action a court can compel a statutory body to carry out its duty to the community by constructing sanitation facilities at great cost and on a time bound basis. At issue is the coming of age of that branch of public law bearing on community actions and the court's power to force public bodies under public duties to implement specific plans in response to public grievances

and, at 1623:

> a few profound issues of processual jurisprudence of great significance to our legal system face us and we must zero in on them as they involve problems of access to justice for the people beyond the blinkered rules of 'standing' of British Indian vintage. If the centre of gravity is to shift, as the Preamble of the Constitution mandates, from the traditional individualism of *locus standi* to the community orientation of public interest litigation, these issues must be considered.

The Court berated the appellants, at 1624:

> Had the municipal council and its executive officers spent half this litigative zeal on cleaning up the street and constructing the drains … the people's needs might have been met long ago.

Discussing the scope of section 133 of the Cr PC and section 188 of the IPC, the Court stated, 1628:

> Although these two Codes are of ancient vintage, the new social justice orientation imparted to them by the Constitution of India makes it a remedial weapon of versatile use. Social justice is due to the people and, therefore, the people must be able to trigger off the jurisdiction vested for their benefit in any public functionary like a Magistrate under S. 133, Cr PC. In the exercise of this power, the judiciary must be informed by Article 38 of the Constitution.

The Supreme Court reaffirmed the Magistrate's order that the nuisance be removed as required by the Cr PC and the 1961 Act. Drains were to be constructed and managed by the Municipality, so that the flow of water did not stagnate, the big pits and earthen drains near the college were to be closed and filth removed, the big drain was to be covered and the Malaria Department was directed to sprinkle DDT and work towards the eradication of mosquitoes. The SC added to the Magistrate's order, stating that the Municipal Council and Town Improvement Trust should do whatever was necessary to prevent dirty water from the alcohol factory flowing into the drain, at 1630:

> we cannot consent to a value judgement where people's health is a low priority. Nevertheless, we are willing to revise the order into a workable formula the implementation of which would be watch-dogged by the court. …

While refusing to acknowledge the appellant's pleas of lack of funds in its order, the Court addressed itself to the administration, at 1631:

> We are sure that the State Government will make available by way of loans or grants sufficient financial aid to the Ratlam Municipality to enable it to fulfil its obligations under this

> order. The State will realize that Article 47 makes it a paramount principle of governance that steps are taken 'for the improvement of public health *as amongst its primary duties*'.

The action of the magistrate was praised, at 1624:

> The Magistrate, whose activist application of section 133, Cr PC for the larger purpose of making the Ratlam municipal body do its duty and abate the nuisance by affirmative action, has our appreciation.

The appeal was dismissed, subject to modifications.

☆ ☆ ☆

A petition was filed under Article 226 of the Constitution in the Karnataka High Court in 1981 by two journalists, Mr E. Raghavan and Ms Pushpa Girimaji. The petition referred to the sudden death of ten people after drinking contaminated water supplied by the Bangalore Water Supply and Sewerage Board. The petitioners had conducted a survey and had the issue raised in the legislature. The Minister for Housing and Urban Development, Mr Dharam Singh, denied that the deaths were due to the contaminated water. As no verdict was given in this case another petition was filed under Article 226 of the Constitution in the Karnataka HC in 1982 by the Rotary Club of Bangalore in 1982.

The petitions were admitted and the State Government made sure that the water pipes had been replaced. The HC directed that water samples be sent, periodically, for analysis.[23]

☆ ☆ ☆

### *W P Nos 1915 and 1916 of 1984, Bombay*
### *Citizens Action Committee, Nagpur v. Civil Surgeon, Mayo (General) Hospital, Nagpur and others*

A petition was filed under Article 226 of the Constitution claiming that, in spite of constant correspondence, repeated requests and press reports, statutory and public authorities continued to allow the roads,

23 Ataulla, Naheed, "Special Report: The Karnataka Scene", *The Sunday Times of India*, 6/9/92.

sanitation and public health to deteriorate in the city of Nagpur. The petition invoked section 57 of the City of Nagpur Corporation Act, 1950.

In an order D/-19/10/84 by > Justice Masodkar and Justice Deshpande

[reported AIR 1986 Bom 136]

While stating that the furtherance of public interest is vital, the Court stressed that it was not trying to run the Government through the Court in its directions. The Court ordered the implementation of statutory provisions and duties. An Investigative and Remedial Measures Suggestion Committee was constituted to look into the upkeep and betterment of city life. It was held that the HC has the jurisdiction to issue appropriate directions and to give reliefs to the citizens in respect of civic amenities, and that other relevant statutes do not stand in the way of the HC while exercising its extraordinary jurisdiction.

☆ ☆ ☆

***SPL C A No 4916 of 1984, Gujarat***
***Janki Nathubhai Chhara and another* v. *Sardarnagar Municipality, Sardar and another***

A letter was sent to the Court from two members of the Chhara community, describing the unhygienic conditions in which they had to live, and the condition of their locality which became submerged during the monsoon. This was described as a health hazard, as epidemics could develop which would affect the whole of Ahmedabad. The letter was registered as a writ petition under Article 226 of the Constitution

In an order D/-18/1/85 by Chief Justice P.S. Poti and Justice I.C. Bhatt

[reported AIR 1986 Guj 49]

In an earlier order D/-19/11/84, temporary schemes had been worked out. In the present order, invoking Article 14 of the Constitution and order XXIII, rule 3 of the CPC, 1908, the Court ordered permanent measures for the provision of an adequate drainage system for the residents of the area. As the Municipality and State Government had agreed to arrange finances for the provision of a permanent sewerage and drainage system, the case was closed. The Court did, however stress the duty of the State and the action it should take.

☆ ☆ ☆

***C W P No 121 of 1986, Rajasthan***
***L.K. Koolwal* v. *State of Rajasthan and others***

A petition was filed under Article 226 of the Constitution by a lawyer regarding the sanitation of Jaipur city. The petition invoked Articles 12, 19, 21 and 51A of the Constitution, section 133 of the Cr PC, 1973, section 124 of the Evidence Act, 1872, and section 98 of the Rajasthan Municipalities Act, 1959.

In an order D/-19/9/86 by Justice D.L. Mehta
[reported AIR 1988 Raj 2]
Noting that Article 51A of the Constitution empowers the citizen, and lawyers in the case were acting *pro bono publico*, the Court held that it is the primary duty of the Municipal Council to remove filth, rubbish, night-soil, odour or any other noxious or offensive matter. The Court stated that primary duties had to be performed by the Board, and held that there could not be any plea regarding the availability of funds or staff, as the municipality had to arrange for the resources necessary for the performance of its primary duties. Referring to Article 12 of the Constitution, it was held that secrecy about the instrumentalities of the State had become less prevalent. The importance of the DPSPs was stressed, and the Court stated, at 6:

> If the Legislature or the State Government feels that the law enacted by them cannot be implemented then the Legislature has the liberty to scrap it, but the law which remains on the statutory books will have to be implemented, particularly when it relates to primary duty.

The petition was allowed and six months were given to the Municipal Council to clean the entire city of Jaipur.

☆ ☆ ☆

***Aparna Kashyap* v. *State of HP and other***

A petition was filed under Article 226 of the Constitution in the Simla High Court in 1988 by a resident of village Totu, a suburb of

Simla. The petition complained of the non-implementation of the Himachal Pradesh Panchayati Raj Act, 1968 as civic amenities were not being extended to the village. It asked that the Court direct the Municipal Corporation to provide an adequate water supply, to improve sanitary conditions, to provide for a drainage and sewerage system, to improve existing roads and pathways and to construct public latrines and urinals. The petition described the nuisance caused by the deposit of garbage and rubbish by the Municipal Corporation of Simla, which emitted foul gases, affected public health and hygiene, and caused environmental pollution. Apparently, damage had already been done to conifer trees in the area and epidemic diseases had spread. Annexed to the petition was a news report from the *Indian Express* D/-20/8/88 which highlighted the deplorable state of affairs due to the deposit of garbage and waste on the roadside by the Municipal Corporation.

In an order by Chief Justice Balakrishna Menon
[reported 1991 FLT 164 Vol 2 Part 3]
The Court surveyed the SC decisions in relevant cases, e.g. *M.C. Mehta* on the pollution of the River Ganges, *Rural Litigation and Entitlement (RL & E) Kendra, Dehradun* and *Municipal Council, Ratlam* (supra) and held that the rubbish should not be dumped by the respondents. The Court directed that amenities be provided in the Totu area. The petition was allowed and the Municipal Corporation was directed to pay the costs of the petitioner and advocate's fee of Rs 1,000.

☆ ☆ ☆

**Misc P No 302 of 1989, Madhya Pradesh**
***Ram Sahai Varma* v. *State of MP and another***
A petition was filed under Article 226 of the Constitution by an advocate challenging the arbitrary and illegal restriction of movement on a road leading to the courts and educational institutions. This had resulted in serious hardship and inconvenience particularly to students and lawyers and to people from all walks of life. The alternative routes were described as inconvenient and the restrictions as not being in the interest of public safety and convenience. The petition invoked section 74 of the Motor Vehicles Act, 1939, and rule 257 of the MP Motor Vehicles Rules, 1974.

In an order D/-17/4/89 by > Justice T.N. Singh and Justicc K.K. Verma [Gwalior Bench]
[reported AIR 1989 MP 334]
The Court examined the provisions of the Act and Rules, together with Article 19(1)(d) of the Constitution, before stating, at 336:

> There can be no mechanical exercise of power in respect of traffic restriction relying merely on recommendations of a non-statutory body when indeed, in the minutes it is not reflected that in the interest of the general public such restrictions were required for the "safety or inconvenience" of the public generally.

The Court specified the meaning of the provisions in section 74 and rule 257 and stated that some restrictions could be permitted. The petition was allowed.

☆ ☆ ☆

***O J C No 115 of 1990, Orissa***
***M.C. Mehta v. State of Orissa and others***

A petition was filed under Article 226 of the Constitution by a Supreme Court advocate and General Secretary of the Indian Council for Enviro-Legal Action, a registered voluntary organization. The petition alleged that untreated waste water from the Municipal Committee, Cuttack and SCB Medical College Hospital, Cuttack, was being discharged into the Old Canal, making it polluted. Water-borne diseases were being spread as there were many *bastis* near the canal, whose inhabitants used the water for bathing and drinking. The petition invoked Articles 21, 48 and 51A(g) of the Constitution, section 17 of the Water (Prevention and Control of Pollution) Act, 1974, the National Health Policy and the Environment (Protection) Act, 1986. The issue of tourism was raised by the petitioner who stated that when he visited Cuttack hoping to see the rich cultural heritage there, he found instead horrible water pollution.

In an order D/-6/3/92 by Justice A. Pasayat and Justice S.K. Mohanty
[reported AIR 1992 Ori 225]
The Court had directed that the Orissa SLAAB engage a senior

counsel for the petitioner. Referring to the arguments, the Court noted, at 228:

> The assertions in the counter-affidavit are in general terms and are full of contradictions. On the one hand it has been accepted that the Government has taken steps to protect the water of Taladanda canal from pollution and arrangements are being made to prevent discharge of water from the medical campus to the canal. On the other it has been stated that there was no pollution of water, and/or that no specific instance of suffering from such pollution has been indicated.

The findings of the Board constituted under section 17 of the Water Act were used. The Court directed the State Government to act on reports regarding the pollution load in Taladanda Canal and water pollution from mass bathing in Mahanadi during Kartik Purnima (a time of religous observance), and, at 232:

> immediately to consider the reports, and take necessary steps to prevent and control water pollution and to maintain the wholesomeness of water which is supplied for human consumption. Ways and means to prevent entry of sewage water and effluents to the rivers Mahanadi and Kathajodi and Taladanda canal to be worked out. If there is a necessity and desirability of having a Sewage Treatment Plant or Plants, the same to be set up without further delay.

Detailed steps were directed to be taken within one year of the order.

☆ ☆ ☆

### W P No 6728 of 1991, Madras
### Consumer Action Group v. Commissioner, Corporation of Madras and another

A petition was filed under Article 226 of the Constitution by an organization based in Madras complaining that the arches and cutouts erected on the pavements of the city of Madras obstructed the road and impeded the smooth flow of traffic. It was contended that they were flimsy and unsafe, and prevented pedestrians from using the pavements. The petition claimed that, by permitting these arches and cutouts, the respondents were violating provisions of the Madras City Municipal Corporation Act and of the IPC, 1860. The

Court was asked to direct the respondents not to permit such constructions.

In an order D/-25/4/91

Issuing notice on the petition, the court stated that the resondents were prevented from permitting or allowing the construction and erection of arches and cutouts across roads, during the pendency of the petition.